CARI LYNN is a journalist and the author of four books of nonfiction, including *The Whistleblower: Sex Trafficking, Military Contractors, and One Woman's Fight for Justice* with Kathryn Bolkovac, and *Leg the Spread: A Woman's Adventures Inside the Trillion-Dollar Boys' Club of Commodities Trading*. She has written for numerous publications, including *O, The Oprah Magazine*, *Health*, the *Chicago Tribune*, and *Deadline Hollywood*.

Shawn Barber Photography

She has taught at Loyola University and received a master's in writing from Johns Hopkins University. She currently lives in Los Angeles. This is her first novel.

Anthony Masters

KELLIE MARTIN was nominated for an Emmy for her work as Becca Thatcher on *Life Goes On*, appeared for two seasons as Lucy Knight on *ER*, and played the title roles in *Christy* and *Mystery Woman*. She also has written, produced, and directed for television. She serves as national spokesperson for the American Autoimmune Related Diseases Association and owns the online children's boutique ROMP store.com. She graduated with distinction in art history from Yale University. She lives in Los Angeles and Montana with her family. This is her first novel.

Praise for *Madam*

"If you are enthralled with New Orleans and the history of its fabled red-light district, this is the book for you. The evocative characters lovingly created by Cari Lynn and Kellie Martin made me wish Storyville was resurrected and rollicking with harlots and madams today."   —Patti LuPone, actress, singer, and author

"*Madam* is a fascinating re-creation of New Orleans at the end of the nineteenth century, when the churchgoing politicians and power brokers of sin created Storyville. An absorbing peek into the hidden history of the city and her most famous madam."

—Loraine Despres, bestselling author of
The Scandalous Summer of Sissy LeBlanc

"Lynn and Martin tell the story of their protagonist's rise to fame and fortune without piousness, sentimentality, or apology. Thorough research, convincing detail, and true-to-life characters make this a spellbinder of a novel. The reader can almost smell the sweat of the johns and the fragrance of rose attar and shrimp gumbo. The characters' words roll off their tongues like molasses in August."
—Roberta Rich, author of *The Midwife of Venice* and *The Harem Midwife*

"Love the history they wouldn't teach you in school? Then open up Cari Lynn and Kellie Martin's *Madam*. It's a gritty, well-researched story of how Storyville, the largest legal red-light district in the United States, came into being."

—Lois Battle, bestselling author of *Storyville* and *War Brides*

"I encourage you to accept this invitation to escape into the boudoirs and back alleys of nineteenth-century New Orleans and leave behind our modern world for a spell. Kellie and Cari have vividly resurrected a world that most of us have never seen up close, and it's quite a ride!"

—Danica McKellar, actress and *New York Times* bestselling author

"*Madam* delivers a world rich with details and visuals of a time and place long forgotten in our history. If you liked *Memoirs of a Geisha*, you will love following Mary on her harrowing journey to become an infamous madam in a New Orleans red-light district."

—Melissa Joan Hart, actress and author of
Melissa Explains It All: Tales from My Abnormally Normal Life

"With brilliant, immediate language and fascinating detail, *Madam* jelly-rolls us through a gritty 1897 New Orleans underworld, and allows us to cheer as a sweet young prostitute fights all odds to become one of its great madams."

—Jennie Fields, author of *The Age of Desire*

"*Madam* is an utterly enjoyable and fascinating read! It's a story of a true underdog, Mary Deubler, who overcomes adversity while making history in New Orleans during the turn of the century. I found myself rooting for our protagonist from the very first page. Kudos to Mary and to Cari Lynn and Kellie Martin!"

—Ricki Lake, actress, host, and producer

"An odyssey through the underworld and the spirit world of New Orleans, *Madam* is layered in rags and silks and voodoo visitations. This is a story of desperation turned inside out. Power holds court in back rooms and bedrooms but reaches its full potential in the heart and mind of a young prostitute whose prize possession is a pair of striped stockings she plucked from a rich woman's trash. This book manages to wrap transformation in sensuality and historical detail, and set the whole thing to the sound of ragtime. *Bien joué!*" —Rita Leganski, author of *The Silence of Bonaventure Arrow*

"As rich and evocative as New Orleans jazz, Cari Lynn and Kellie Martin evoke a time and place with tantalizing detail, transporting the reader to a world hidden not only by the past, but also by the very society that created it. *Madam* is a wonderful portrait of an indelible figure." —DeLauné Michel, author of *The Safety of Secrets*

"Set in the vivid, visceral world of New Orleans in the late 1800s, *Madam* follows a young prostitute's desperate struggle to survive, thrive, and ultimately achieve self-empowerment in the face of hugely challenging circumstances. With plenty of sex and liquor to go around, Kellie and Cari's debut novel does a stellar job of capturing the essence of what it really means to face our fears and overcome extreme adversity. Cheers to the first real madam!"
—Hillary Fogelson, *Los Angeles Times* bestselling author of *Pale Girl Speaks: A Year Uncovered*

Madam

❧

A Novel of New Orleans

Cari Lynn and Kellie Martin

A PLUME BOOK

PLUME
Published by the Penguin Group
Penguin Group (USA) LLC
375 Hudson Street
New York, New York 10014

USA I Canada I UK I Ireland I Australia I New Zealand I India I South Africa I China
penguin.com
A Penguin Random House Company

First published by Plume, a member of Penguin Group (USA) LLC, 2014

LIBRARY OF CONGRESS CATALOGING-IN-PUBLICATION DATA

Lynn, Cari.
Madam : a novel of New Orleans / Cari Lynn, Kellie Martin.
pages cm
ISBN 978-0-14-218062-4 (pbk.)
1. Deubler, Mary, 1864-1914—Fiction.   2. Procuresses—Louisiana—New Orleans—
Fiction.   3. Prostitutes—Louisiana—New Orleans—Fiction.   4. Brothels—
Louisiana—New Orleans—Fiction.   5. Red-light districts—Louisiana—New
Orleans—Fiction.   6. Storyville (New Orleans, La.)—Fiction.   7. New Orleans
(La.)—Fiction.   I. Martin, Kellie, 1975-   II. Title.
PS3612.Y5445M33 2014
813'.6—dc23   2013022372

Printed in the United States of America
10 9 8 7 6 5 4 3 2 1

Set in Granjon
Designed by Eve L. Kirch

Authors' Note

The characters and circumstances within these pages are based on real people and real events. We have incorporated actual dialogue where it was available and tried to maintain as accurate a sense of history as possible in crafting this narrative. Given that most records of Storyville were purposefully destroyed, we have utilized dramatic license to fill in the gaps.

I come from a long line of whores.

In my nine decades on this earth I have never uttered these words, let alone seen them written, in my own hand, indelibly staring back at me. But now, as a summer storm rages strong enough to send the Pontchartrain right through my front door, I sit with a curious sense of peace and clarity. My past is more than just my own history. Although this story shames me in so many ways, it is the legacy I leave. I must embrace the very truth I spent my life denying.

I come from a long line of whores.

Call them prostitutes, call them women of ill repute, call them madams. It's of little consequence now to try to soften how they earned their way. But they did earn their way, and in a time when even women of means and good breeding held little hope of achieving anything professionally.

Oh Saint Teresa, what an ingrate I've been. Everything I have, everything I am, I owe to them—to her. She'd started life as a bastard girl, not a silver dime to her name. Her family tree was but a stump. And yet, the riches she bestowed upon me: my education, my inheritance . . . this fierce, old Victorian. How the walls moan in the grip of these winds! This house, in all its faded elegance, is all I have left. How I hated that it once lived as a bordello—hot jazz, Voodoo magic, and unspeakable sin oozing from every crevice.

My aunt built this house, but I saved this house. The ghosts would come to me at night, whispering that I couldn't let it go. While New Orleans raced to obliterate any evidence of the red-light district's existence, I guarded this door. Overnight, City Hall purged all records of the women who lived and worked here. Even the names of the streets were changed. It took the highest judge's signature to spare this house from the torch-wielding mob that pillaged and set aflame other bordellos. But how can I blame my beloved city? For I, too, wanted to erase this blight, this scourge on our history.

But it did exist. Storyville was real. And so were the mad-ams. Larger than life, indeed, but flesh and blood through and through, with feelings and smarts even—they were more savvy in business than most businessmen in this town. And yet, they were still just women, devoid of equal rights and treated as vulnerable, useless creatures. These women may have laughed and drunk and frolicked more than most women, but they still ached and loved, cried and prayed, and in their darkest hours, repented.

Now, this house, my house, is all that remains as a testament to an era. If it is this storm that brings down my house, I will go with it. I only hope that this letter and these photographs will survive.

My dearest Aunt Josie, by the grace of God, please forgive me.

Anna Deubler Brady
225 Basin Street,
New Orleans
August 14, 1997

New Orleans, 1907

❧

"Miss Arlington!"

Josie heard the eager call from a man across the parlor. But she didn't feel inspired to turn her head.

"Miss Arlington," the man persisted. "It is *Miss*, isn't it?"

Ignoring him still, Josie sucked in her breath and leaned farther over the new grand piano—a Bösendorfer shipped all the way from Vienna, not that that meant anything to her, but it was supposedly the best, and she was sure that meant something to somebody here. If she had stopped to consider things, she would have presented it as a gift to the house professor of the piano, Ferdinand, but she'd long ago forgotten how to do selfless, meaningful gestures—even for a person who was meaningful to her. These days, it was only about business. And besides, Ferdinand didn't like new pianos; he liked the one that had been weathered from his own fingers, which, to his dismay, had been promptly carted off to who knew where.

"Everybody wants you, Miss Arlington," Ferdinand said, giving her a knowing half smile.

Josie sighed, pursing her painted lips. Her gaze locked with his. "No, Ferdinand, not everybody."

He rolled his long fingers over the keys—the cakewalk, he called it. "As I recall, you were equally lemon-faced this very same day of last year."

She couldn't believe he'd remembered. It was a small act of kindness that made her heart ache, the way only Ferd seemed able. It had been some time since she'd had a twinge like this, but she knew she mustn't go thinking about that now. This day was always punishing, and there was no need to make it worse by getting overly sentimental or—God forbid!—weepy. She shifted her stance, crossing her arms tightly over her chest, lace ribbons (shipped from Belgium, of course) dangling from her wrists and elbows.

The sudden change of her demeanor was not lost on Ferdinand. He knew how she was—the type his *grandmère* would have described as a pomegranate, all ruddy and tough on the outside, but on the inside, a sweetness that couldn't help but bleed.

Another call trailed from across the room, this time a gruff voice slurred with drink. "We request the honor of your presence, Miss Arlington!"

"You best tend to your patrons, ma'am," Ferdinand said softly, giving a little nod as if coaxing a child. Josie took to it, looking at him with heavy eyes. Yes, the patrons. All those men with wandering, grabby hands and sweaty palms. All those demanding eyes and stale cigar breath. And all those billfolds full of cash.

She straightened herself up, smoothing the front of her pouter pigeon gown.

"Not a thread out of place," Ferdinand reassured.

"Of course not," Josie replied, her voice already growing distant. "It's the finest from Paris."

By the time she turned from Ferdinand to face the crowded parlor, her full transformation—one she'd spent years perfecting—had occurred. Her impishness was gone. Her posture was Victorian straight, bosom thrust forward, shoulders pinned back, nose lifted, her expression both hard and sultry at the same time. She was no longer the down-on-her-luck girl Ferdinand had met way back when; she was now the legendary Madam Josie Arlington. A legend of her own making.

Josie glided across the Persian rugs, past Rococo furnishings, crystal chandeliers, sconces, and artwork chosen by the finest art dealers in New Orleans. Yet she didn't notice any of it anymore, not that these objects had ever given her much pleasure. The acquiring of them did, in a sense, for she enjoyed the notion that she could own such fancy, expensive things. But she knew nothing of design or art, and never did she find much beauty or meaning in the pieces she was told were the best anyway. She hardly recognized what was redeeming in these pricey objects people fluttered and gasped over—other than the prestige. Prestige. That was, indeed, something that used to matter very much to her.

The crowd parted as Josie continued the length of the room. The men respectfully bowed their heads and tipped their hats. Her girls curtsied, or, if they'd been inexcusably talking amongst themselves, they scattered like roaches in daylight, knowing full well they were not allowed to converse—attention was to be showered upon the men. Besides, Josie distrusted girls whispering to each other, Lord knows they might be conspiring against her.

She approached the bar, where rows of Champagne bottles stood like soldiers; one by one, they would be plucked up, and, at midnight, the bubbly would be poured over a pyramid of crystal glasses. No one would worry about the overflow onto the rugs or splashes onto the wallpaper or the drunken spills on the velvet settees. The mess was simply the cost of doing business. Anyhow, the maids would come in the morning and scrub, and by the time the rest of the house would awaken in the midafternoon, the entire mansion would be gleaming, ready to start afresh night after night after night.

"At last, Miss Arlington!" a man in a dark tailcoat shouted as Josie reached the bar. The room swarmed about her, every man eager to be in close proximity to the madam whom some deemed famous, others infamous.

Josie launched into her little routine, batting her eyes, walking her fingers up a row of gemstone shirt studs, pinching a cheek. Placing her manicured hand atop a man's, she coyly slid a wedding ring from a hairy finger and tucked it inside his waistcoat pocket. "Just for tonight," she cooed in her soft, sultry drawl. With hoots and whoops, most others followed suit, twisting off their wedding bands.

By design, Josie spoke sparingly to her patrons. Words could only complicate matters, especially from a woman. Words could take away from whatever daydream a man had come in with. And that was the last thing Madam Josie Arlington wanted to do. She was, after all, selling dreams. The few minutes of coitus, that was just the mechanics—it was the dream that a man would take with him, a dream that needed to be strong enough to continue smoldering for days after, weeks even, compelling him to steal away from his family, make a good lie, create some reason to visit Basin Street.

Josie made efficient small talk, asking where someone was from, asking what his favorite pastime was, asking if he'd visited the Arlington before. She did her best to remember faces and names and little trivia, as in, "Well, hello again to my handsome mistah from Mississippi, whose favorite color is redheads." She could make men fawn like schoolboys.

She also knew to do this little parade of hers early in the evening, before the alcohol had taken hold and loosened their tongues and their inhibitions. Even still, there'd always be the ones who couldn't resist the urge to touch her, to rub or pinch her bustled behind, or daringly grab at her breasts. There was a time early on when she'd welcomed these advances, welcomed any sign of being wanted. But those hungry days were long gone and now, upon being touched, she had to stifle the inclination to flinch or, worse, to smack the perpetrator. Instead, she'd patiently remove his hand from where it had unfortunately landed and chide, "Uh, uh, uh, you mustn't spoil your appetite for the delicacy that awaits."

Josie had trained her girls to keep a sharp eye out for this type of misbehavior toward her. The girls knew precisely when to swoop in and cause a distraction that would allow Josie to glide out of the parlor and, once out of sight, scurry up the back servants' staircase, and up, up, up to the solitude of the fourth floor, forbidden to everyone else.

But now, as she scanned the parlor, wanting to catch the eye of one of her girls and give the look indicating it was time to relieve her, she saw no one, only a sea of black worsted wool. No lace, no bustles, no feathered hats or hair bows. This was odd—the girls had been prancing around moments earlier. Josie strained to look to the foyer to see if perhaps the girls had been delayed with welcoming duties. But the foyer was empty, and Josie was suddenly struck with a sinking feeling that something was quite wrong. Maybe one of the girls was ill upstairs and the others were assisting? But why wouldn't someone have informed her if that were the case? She could think of no other explanation, and, with no one near to rescue her, the circle of men hovering about her seemed to be closing in. As they leaned in, their bodies grazed hers. As they laughed, she could feel their hot breath.

Her thoughts darted to Ferdinand—he would undoubtedly help her. But the idea of calling out to him was quickly dismissed, for she knew that if the colored piano player tried to break through this ivory circle, he was likely to get a beating. It was already considered

generous that some of these aristocrats tolerated Ferdinand's presence in the room, even though it was known throughout Storyville
that Madam Arlington's place was loose about these things. Josie
strained to look beyond what felt like wolves circling. She narrowed
her eyes in hope of glimpsing a single one of her girls.

Just then, the lamps sputtered and, all at once, fizzled out. A jolt
of panic shot through Josie, and she felt as if her knees might buckle.
And then she saw glowing lights dancing on the ceiling.

In paraded Josie's girls, tossing streamers and confetti. The
crowd parted to four girls precariously balancing an enormous layer
cake covered in sugar roses. They tried to step in unison as everyone
began to crow, "For she's a jolly good fellow!"

Josie's jaw tightened, her fists clenched. She pushed aside the
men in her way.

"Stop!" she commanded. But she was drowned out as the entire
room joined in singing. She gave a defiant stomp of her foot and
bellowed louder, "Stop! Stop! Stop!"

At this, the singing trailed off. The girls exchanged fretful looks
as the boisterous room was struck uncomfortably silent. Josie's eyes
darted to the piano. Under other circumstances, Ferdinand would
have been quick on the pickup, joining right in with a clever little
riff or even a snarky "ba-dum, dum" when someone told a particularly loud or groan-worthy joke. But this time he knew better, and
he rose from his bench in hope of catching Josie's attention.

He was far from the only one trained on Josie. The entire room
felt like nothing but dropped jaws and wide eyeballs, and it suddenly occurred to Josie they must all be wondering if they'd get to
witness firsthand a notorious Madam Arlington tantrum, the last of
which had made newspaper headlines.

Her eyes found Ferdinand's, and he gave a little shake of his
head as if to gently remind her to hold it all in. She could hear his

voice in her head, *Aw, pretty Mary, don't get all up in your shoulders and make a scene. It's easier to stop now than it will be to take it back later.*

She took a deep breath, allowing her fists to unclench. With a nervous little laugh, she said, "There's been such a mistake." She forced a cool smile. "It's certainly not my birthday." She looked around the room. "Might it be anyone's birthday tonight?"

From the crowd, a man volunteered, pointing to his friend. "It's his tomorrow."

"Perfect!" Josie shouted. "Then this is *your* celebration. And at midnight, I'm sure a lucky lady can figure out a way to make the celebration quite official."

At this, Ferdinand quickly started up "For He's a Jolly Good Fellow" again, and the room confusedly resumed singing. In a shuffle of kid-leather boots, the girls awkwardly rotated the cake to face the patron, who was turning a deep red.

Josie made her escape.

Pulling a key ring from her boot, Josie unlocked a padlock, then turned another key in the doorknob. Hoisting open the heavy door, she quickly disappeared into her chambers, where she immediately bolted the locks behind her. Looking around, she moved through her nightly ritual: check the closet, part the heavy satin drapes to inspect the balcony, sweep up the lace bedskirts to peek underneath. There were people in this town who wanted revenge on her—or so she wholeheartedly believed—and she would take no chances. She was never sure what exactly she was looking for, but this had been her way since the birth of the Arlington on Basin Street, and she'd grown even more cautious and more rigorous now that she'd created what was arguably the most successful bordello. Her neighbors—

those who should have been her sisters within the boundaries of Storyville—did not appreciate her success.

Once satisfied that all realms were clear, Josie began undressing, attacking buttons and ribbons as if she couldn't get out of her clothing fast enough. Off with that suffocating corset, shimmy out of those thick stockings, just leave the bloomers in a heap on the floor. She wrapped herself in a Japanese silk robe that was a long-ago gift from a well-traveled patron—during the time when she still entertained her favorites—and drew her bath.

As the claw-foot tub filled, she dispassionately picked up a gold box wrapped with a bright blue bow that had been sitting all day atop her bureau. She knew whom the gift was from and lazily unwrapped it to find a silver picture frame, engraved in fancy script on the back side: *To the woman who has everything, on her thirtieth birthday. Always Yours, Tom.* She pushed the gift aside, letting the wrapping fall to the floor for the maid to pick up tomorrow.

Except for when she was a very young child and Mama was there to dote on her, she'd always detested her birthday. By the time she was ten years old, she'd stopped reminding anyone of the day and simply let it slip by without a word. But in her own head, her own heart, she could never let it be just a day like any other. At first it held the near unbearable pain of how much she missed Mama. And when that pain eventually dulled with time, thoughts of her birthday became more like an itching under her skin, an annual reminder of how generally lonely the world could be.

Surveying the medicine cabinet full of tinctures, drops, and glass apothecary bottles, she settled on a swig of coca wine. She felt herself begin to relax with just the anticipation of the cocaine that, true as touted, relieved fatigue of mind and body. She shed her robe and stepped into the tub, sinking under until the water was at her chin.

She'd known no immediate blood relative who had made thirty

years old. Ever since she could remember, she'd felt encumbered, as if she were decades older. But now, at thirty, the feeling seemed to overtake her, as if her life must be hastened because she, too, would succumb to a tragic end, just as everyone she'd dared to love. This birthday, one which should have been her prime, felt too heavy to bear. Leaning her head back, she closed her eyes.

"No, Tom," she said aloud, "I have nothing." She held her breath and let the water immerse her.

Ten Years Earlier
New Orleans, 1897

CHAPTER ONE

"Tell him."

The man's face was pained and sweaty as he stared intensely at Mary. She noticed his eyes were a deep emerald. She didn't usually notice such things. There was no point, she believed, in paying attention to any of their attributes, or lack thereof. No reason to bother over the broad swell of a john's shoulders, or the cut of a jawline, or the color of his eyes. A john was a john—handsome or ugly, they were all just customers, blending together by the end of the day anyway, when the only important thing was the weight of Mary's burlap purse.

But this man's gaze, his green eyes looking directly into hers, caught her. Most of the men, most of the time, their gaze looked right past her. They weren't much interested in her face—they couldn't care how full her lips were or how young and smooth her skin was. Or that, under the smudges of dirt and beneath the hard edge she wore, this alley whore was, arguably, pretty. Sure, pretty helped, but a pretty face wasn't what these men came craving.

This was Mary's fifth john today. On the whole, he wasn't much of a looker, his chin was too big for his face and his head too big for his body. But those eyes were warm pools that kept drawing her in. He smelled strong of tobacco—most of them did—but she could tell at least he'd had a recent bath. He gulped some air as he arched his back against the wall of Mary's crib.

Just a little shack, her crib was no different from the rows of other cribs that lined Venus Alley like chicken coops. There was room enough for a thin, saggy kip, and Mary also had squeezed in a tiny bedside table where johns could set their jewelry to keep in sight. She knew this was a nice touch. Likewise, she took pride in keeping her crib clean. She scrubbed it down regularly, and every night she brought home her kip and beat out any fleas that clung to its dried Spanish moss stuffing. The last thing she wanted was for a john to leave her crib itching; that was a sure way to kill any chance of a next visit. Mary liked to think of the crib as her own, and called it such, even though it wasn't really. But soon enough, she hoped, it would come to be.

"Tell him," the john murmured again. He was a first-timer, and Mary suspected he wasn't from New Orleans—she'd watched him take his billfold from his trouser pocket, setting it on the bedside table, and surmised that only a traveling man would walk around with that many bills. His origins were only important in that Mary could assess the chance that she'd ever see him again—with one-timers, she knew not to put herself out too much. Why wring yourself on someone who wasn't likely to give you regular business? And yet, for some reason, she had a yearning to please this man beyond just supplying her body. Unlike all the others, this man hadn't looked away, hadn't looked beyond her, or through her. His eyes stayed locked on hers, searching, yearning to connect.

"Tell him," he said again. "Tell him he's a good boy."

Mary leaned in, nuzzling his ear, then whispered, "You're a good boy."

Suddenly, he pushed her. "Not me, ya dim whore!" he hollered. "Him!"

He pointed to his crotch.

The warmth instantly drained from Mary's body. Right, she thought . . . *him*. Slumping a bit, she sighed to herself. She should know better by now than to let a man fool her. No matter how deeply he stared into her eyes.

"Well?" the john demanded.

Mary silently chided herself for having thought this john may not be trapped like all the others. That was how she saw them all: trapped, secretly coming to her for escape from their wives, their families, their lives. But just because they looked like men didn't mean they weren't still little boys. How many of them weren't still fascinated with the toy between their legs? And how many of them weren't still searching for Mama's acceptance? For a quarter of an hour, she'd play with that toy, entertain it, satisfy it. For a quarter of an hour, she would also be Mama. She would smile as if she fancied him just the way he was. She would make him the center of her world no matter if he had tattered clothes, dirty fingernails, or a lifetime of failures; no matter if he had a face only his real mother could love but perhaps didn't.

Mary sucked in her breath. She sat back on her calves and mustered up her most sultry voice. Then she purred to his loins, "You're a good boy."

His eyes urgently reconnected with hers.

"A good boy," he breathed. He let out a quivering sigh, then murmured reassuringly to himself, "A very good boy."

Mary watched him, feeling the vulnerability of the moment. On both sides. Maybe, she supposed, it wasn't so bad to trip up every once in a while, to be able to hold hope for another person and expect them to be the best way. Yes, she thought, allowing her face to soften, perhaps it was nice to know that Venus Alley hadn't completely hardened her.

Grabbing Mary's hair, the john finished with a yelp that sounded like someone stepped on a dog's tail. And then, lightning-fast, he jumped up. The intensity was so abruptly broken, it was as if it had never happened. With a quick swoop, he pulled up his pants and snapped his suspenders. Then he reached for his billfold. For a moment, he paused, fingering the bills.

Mary tightened the drawstrings of her chippie, its fraying, thinned cotton just barely serving the purpose of covering her. Eagerly, she watched the man touch each bill, his lips silently moving as he counted. If he could just give me an extra dollar, she thought, please, just one extra dollar—we could eat well this whole week and put some coins aside for the baby.

Refusing to look at her now, he asked, "How old're you?"

Mary brushed wisps of her long, dark hair behind her ear. "Nineteen," she said.

The man's jaw tightened. Without removing any bills, he pocketed his billfold and turned to the door.

"Mistah . . . ?" Mary started, taking a barefoot step toward him.

He unfolded his hand, and some change tumbled from his palm onto the floor. The crib door smacked shut behind him.

The coins spun on the floorboards before falling. Mary scanned where they landed—a quarter, two dimes, and a muddy coin she barely recognized. She crouched down and picked it up, inspecting both sides. A picayune? She traced her finger along its weathered surface. 1853.

"Dastard!" she announced to the emptiness of her crib. Although she was too young to remember when picayunes were penny currency, she knew of the coin from her mama's stories. Mama would tell of earning a picayune per trick, only that was back in the days of the Swamp, which was as close as any place could come to Devil's territory.

The Swamp was filled with outlaws and outcasts and, as Mama would say, folks so poor they didn't even own a last name. It was only right that these most undesirable folks of New Orleans staked their claim on the most undesirable part of the bayou.

But her mama wasn't undesirable at all, not with her auburn hair and dimpled grin—no, her mama just had the unfortunate luck to be born to a penniless drunkard who drove his wife to madness. And so, with nowhere else to go, Mama landed herself in the Swamp, where she lived in a brothel in the mud, among clouds of gnats and mosquitoes and wandering gators and copperheads. Murders would tally nearly a dozen a week in the Swamp, and it was common knowledge that even the police were afraid to enter. No wonder Mama had quickly learned to take care of herself—she kept a knife in one boot and a pistol in the other, and she could grab one or both faster than any blue nose on the police force anyway.

It was this scrappiness she'd wanted to impart to Mary, and she would tell her little girl tales of life with the Swamp folk the way other children were told Mother Goose. She barely spared any details, knowing full well her daughter, with no father present, had little chance for a life much different.

But, oh, did Mary love to hear Mama's stories! Stories of how the ladies would jig the night away to Fiddlin' Henry and Banjo Jim, and how they'd dive stark naked into the Mississippi under a full moon, and bet on cock fights, and suck on berled crawfish heads. The people Mama spoke of were larger than life, and Mary wanted to be just like them.

She'd curl up on Mama's lap in a rocker on the porch of the brothel, back when whores could live a dozen to a house without fear of being cleared out by the police. "Did I tell you about America Williams, the World's Strongest Whore?" Mama would ask. She certainly had, but Mary wanted to hear it again and again.

"Men would pay a whole dollar just to try and beat her at arm wrestlin'," Mama began. "And you should see how red those men's faces got when they'd come to find America Williams's arm bent over their own! Those men, they'd be so affronted that they'd pay up even more for a trick with America, wanting to see for themselves if she might be a fraudulent woman. Hard to say, though, what a man preferred to find when America pulled up her dress. A man's pride is a strong and strange thing, Mary."

Then there was Red-Light Liz, the one-eyed harlot. As Mama told it, "If Liz took kindly to a john, she would let him peek under her eye patch. Those johns were sworn never to tell what they saw, but it was known that a glimpse of whatever was hiding there would bring all sorts of good luck." Little Mary imagined a sunbeam of light shining from behind Liz's eye patch.

"And then there was the dimmest whore in the entire Swamp," Mama would continue. "We called her Molly Ding-Ding. She once blinded a john when he stiffed her ten cents. But she hadn't counted the coins right—the poor john had actually tipped her an extra nickel."

Only when Mary grew older did she come to realize that according to most people's standards these women were nothing more than lowly whores. Still, they would never be that to her. These were women who had made their way in the world, all on their own, and

Mary had decided long ago that was the kind of woman she wanted to be.

Mama was able to get out of the Swamp when a great thing happened: the banks of the Mississippi became filled with sailors. At last, a swell of business on dry land! Mama and her friends packed up their few mud-caked possessions and overtook an abandoned building on Gallatin Street. They nailed a sign out front: HOUSE OF REST FOR WEARY BOATMEN. Truth was, the place was hardly habitable enough to be called a house, and the last thing going on there was rest. But Mama and the others were the best welcome a homesick sailor could hope for, and that stretch of the river soon became known as the Port of Missing Men. Mama regaled how, as a ship would dock, she'd lean out the window, flaunting her cleavage. "Hey, sailor!" she'd call. "A picayune will get ya a bed for the night, a drink o' whiskey . . . and some company!"

Mary rolled the picayune over in her palm, Mama's voice echoing in her head. She caught her reflection in a little cracked mirror she'd hung with twine, the only decoration on the crumbling walls of the crib. Her own eyes stared back at her. Mama and MawMaw before her had these slate gray eyes too, a trait passed down through the generations. But only the women. Gray eyes that didn't often cry, but also didn't sparkle. Rarely would they give away what was going on behind them. Eyes of mystery, Mama would say. Use them, Mary. Use them.

A husky voice from outside the crib startled Mary from her thoughts. "Gettin' on in time, Mary!"

Yes, yes, Mary thought, quickly reminded that Venus Alley may well be on dry ground, but it wasn't like the Swamp, where the whores looked out for one another. Here, it was everyone for herself. It didn't matter a darn if a john were mid-action on top of Mary, not if her cribmate's shift were due to begin. Someday, Mary told herself, she'd never have to hear Beulah Ripley's voice at her door again.

But for now, she didn't let Beulah's whining rush her. She brushed off her dirty feet and reached for her boots. In the right toe bed she'd hidden her burlap purse, and from that, she pulled out a little amber bottle of rose oil she'd purchased for a nickel at the apothecary. Removing its tiny cork, she tilted it upside down, using her finger as a stopper. With a dab on one side of her neck, then the other, she inhaled the brightness of the rosy scent. How nice to smell something fresh in this dank, close crib. For good measure, she dabbed some oil on her armpits before corking the bottle. She pressed her feet into her boots and was careful not to tug too hard as she hooked the threadbare laces. Then she hoisted her kip over her back.

As expected, Beulah was hovering on the stoop, fists dug into her hips. Her dark hair, which was usually in dozens of tight braids, had been sheared close to her head ever since the lice had spread around her family. All Mary knew of Beulah's people was that they were Negroes from the cotton plantations. Truth be told she barely knew much more about her own people, just that Mama's father had been a young stowaway on a boat from Germany—as Mama would say, a fitting beginning to a low life.

"Well, la de do!" Beulah said, giving Mary a smirk. "Pretty girl keepin' time today."

Mary gave her a weary glance.

"Why you keepin' time today? Ain't there no johns 'round?" Beulah taunted. "No ship come in?"

"You want I can go find another trick and be a while," Mary barked back.

"Just that you been late three times already this week," Beulah said with a wag of her finger. "Always actin' like you're above your raising."

Mary let out a sigh. "We're all just tryin' to earn a living."

Beulah snorted. "So the bossman can pour your livin' down his throat?"

Mary couldn't have agreed more, but she didn't let on. It was Philip Lobrano who held the crib in his name, and he liked to think he pimped Mary and Beulah even though business tended to come in with no help from him.

"Bossman come collect your pay today?" Beulah asked.

Mary shook her head.

"Oh, he'll be finding you," Beulah warned, her eyes growing wide. "Saw him stumblin' around, and he's crazy with drink. Crazy Devil Man today. Lookin' like something the dog's been hidin' under the porch."

The last thing Mary wanted to do was stick around knowing Lobrano had spent hours sidled up to a bottle of absinthe. She gave a nod to Beulah, for as much as each resented the other, they both shared the millstone of Lobrano. Beulah lifted her own kip onto her back and Mary moved past, stepping from the warped stoop of the crib onto Venus Alley.

Venus Alley was really a street, though it was so narrow and cramped with row-to-row cribs that it had come to be called an alley—also seemed easier for johns to hide their illegal indiscretions on an *alley* as opposed to a wide-open *street*.

Mary had long ago dulled her senses to Venus Alley. There was no way someone could work a place like this day after day without overlooking most of it. She no longer saw how potholes became film-covered pools of muck that sat and stank until the next rain. Or how rats scuttered about like they ruled the place, not even flinching when you stomped at them, their droppings, along with horse dung, a fixed layer on the bottoms of your shoes.

Snotty-nosed children scampered about the Alley too—the unintended consequences of a whore's thriving business. Barefoot, unwashed, unschooled, skinny things, all of them, their stomachs always rumbling, their faces pinched. They ran around with no one bothering to mind them. The stray children barely outnumbered the dogs and cats roaming about, whining for attention. Although the animals often looked better fed than the children since they were wise to all the back doors of saloons and restaurants that threw out scraps. Even the whores seemed more inclined to toss crumbs to the animals than to the kids—animals were a nuisance, but a baby could halt your career and suck up your earnings.

The cribs were the only buildings on the Alley, moldy shanties sinking into the soft ground and threatening to crumble with every summer storm. Even still, it was a fortunate whore who had use of one, as there were just a few dozen.

Up and down the street, whores lounged in the crib doorways. Wearing chippies—which, if you wrapped it right, could come off with one tug—they posed seductively, allowing a shoulder to be exposed or showing leg up to the thigh. They called their pitches like the sellers in the French Market.

"Come looka what I got, Papa!"

"Ya come to the right door fo' a good time!"

"I'll make ya happy as a pig in slop!"

"C'mere, handsome, wanna tell ya sumpthin'. . . ."

Other more desperate whores who didn't have use of a crib prowled the street, going right up to johns and trying to convince them to just lean up against the side of a building. Mary had never stooped to that, not even in her early days, back when she had to skip supper just to save up and buy herself a kip. She could have saved up more quickly had she not been so high-minded, but the way she saw it, she may be an Alley whore, but at least she practiced her trade behind a closed door and on a bedroll.

Also, unlike many of the other girls on the Alley, Mary wasn't hanging on to the notion that some john would fall in love and want to save her. She gave up those daydreams long ago. She'd heard of it happening once or twice and always the man took the girl far from here, where she could start anew as a legitimate woman and wife. But Mary would never leave here without her family, so even if some starry-eyed john were willing to look past her lot in life, he certainly wouldn't want to claim responsibility for her kin, too.

Mary's thoughts traveled to the man with the green eyes and the fluttering sense of what it might be like to really connect with another person. Even though it had only been a fleeting moment or two, it had felt . . . well, nice. And there wasn't too much in Mary's day that felt that way. She tried to imagine a world where her days would only be about catching the genuine affection of a man. But she shook off the notions, too farfetched to even daydream about, and besides, she shouldn't go soft over a john, even for just a moment. Shouldn't ever get caught up in a man beyond what he could do for business.

She continued making her way down the Alley, passing a group of teenaged boys. Barefoot and in knickers and suspenders, they huddled under the gas streetlamp, a small pile of pennies as their wager in a rowdy game of agates. A boy shot crooked, and a bright red marble smacked Mary's boot.

"There goes your masher," one of the boys huffed to the shooter.

Mary picked up the marble, holding it to the light to see that the red sphere was sliced with a bright yellow orb.

"Called a Devil's Eye," the shooter said.

Mary twisted the marble, watching it glisten like the stars and wondering how the yellow eye had gotten into the middle of the smooth globe.

"You can keep it, pretty lady," the shooter offered. "For a trick."

His friend shook his head under a too-big straw hat. "My pop says if you're gonna touch a whore, make sure it ain't no Alley skank."

Another boy joined in the raking—no matter that his clothes were just as frayed and his feet just as dirty as Mary's. "I wouldn't bang her with your dick," he said, pointing to one of his friends. Then he pointed to another. "And with him pushing." At this, they all roared with laughter.

Mary glared at them, tempted to just pocket their curious agate and be on her way. But instead, she gave the Devil's Eye a good throw back into the circle, knocking the other marbles and ruining their play.

"Bona fide lavenders!" she shouted and headed off. They hissed and booed after her. Although she wasn't exactly sure why it was this way, Mary knew it never hurt business to imply that a man had some lavender in him, maybe had certain tendencies, or was a little light on his toes. Chances were, that man would sneak off and come to see her, paying her just to prove her accusations weren't true. Sometimes he was trying to prove it to himself; but mostly it seemed about the opinion of a stranger, even if it was just proof of his manliness to a lowly whore.

Mary moved on, passing a young redheaded boy she often saw sitting on a stoop. He took a puff on a cigarette, exhaling through a freckly, button nose. Lazily, he bellowed, "Maw!"

There was no response, and, from the aimless look on his face, he hadn't really expected one. He hollered again, this time as if he were being stolen by gypsies. "Ma-a-a-a-w!" But none of the whores even turned—no kid of theirs was no problem of theirs. At last, a woman's out-of-breath voice screeched from a nearby crib, "Boy, I says a minute!" The child scowled and took another puff of his cigarette. He reminded Mary of how her younger brother, Peter, had looked as a child, with purplish puddles under his eyes and a slight frame that wasn't frail enough to be called sickly but not solid enough to quit worrying over. Only, Mama would've whipped Peter good for smoking. Not that they had any money to spend on a smoke anyway.

Mary never said a word to any of the children around here— why should she, when every year many wouldn't make it to spring? Heck, she didn't pay much mind to the other whores, either, but for a different reason. Sure, plagues hit hard on the Alley, but any whore who'd come of age here was a hearty breed. That wasn't to say that plenty of women didn't turn dark and shadowy and then disappear altogether, but you'd not be met kindly if you asked after anyone's health—might lead them to think you were gunning for their crib or trying to steal johns. Besides, no one had money for a funeral service, let alone a proper burial, anyway. Mary had long ago realized it was best to just let people fade away, to just keep to yourself and know you were the better for not knowing. Nod at familiar faces, but don't step too close; don't ask questions or effort over small talk; don't bother learning anybody's name.

It was only a hardened person who could live like this, but it was the way of the Alley, where most people barely had a pot to piss in let alone a window to dump it out of. Here, you couldn't expect anything from anyone—not when just one trick could be the difference between a square meal or your stomach begging all night. Not when this kind of struggle, this vying with every other soul here, was your daily toil. Not when people could become fierce with desperation, and that was the worst kind of fierceness.

So it was for the good of all that they followed the unwritten rule of going about your own business and not blinking at anyone else's. Especially when a whore had a big mess on her hands—like the old bat at the end of the row, calling to Mary.

"Help a friend?" she pleaded, her brows raising hopefully as Mary approached.

Looking down, Mary saw the woman's troubles: out cold in her crib doorway was a round, bald man, spread flat on his back, his face salt white. Mary gave a nervous shake of her head. She didn't need to be anywhere near a dead john.

The whore's expression turned ugly as Mary passed. "Egg-sucking dawg," she snapped before resuming a wide-legged stance, wrapping her hands around the man's armpits, and giving a tug as hard as she could. Shaking and heaving under the weight, she slowly dragged the man out the door, his shirt hiking up, his rolls of flesh joggling. She cursed him under her breath. "Devil's spawn, what nerve to just keel over. Coulda crushed me, ya son of a bitch."

As she dragged him, her chippie loosened and eventually slipped around her shoulders, granting the Alley a full view of her saggy breasts. With a breathless grunt, she dropped the body smack in the middle of the dusty, dung-littered banquette. He fell limp and lifeless.

No sooner did the dust cloud clear than Snitch, a twelve-year-old black boy, inched over to watch. He fancied himself the official eyes and ears of Venus Alley, and unlike the rest of the folks here, he always made it a point to know everyone's business.

"Well, ain't this bold," Snitch said with an amused shake of his head. He called out, "Times like this ya wish your crib had a back door." Snitch was flitty as a skeetahawk, darting out of nowhere to circle around everyone's heads. Mary suspected that Snitch's antics were going to be the death of him one day.

A small crowd began to gather, and even Mary couldn't help but linger. They craned to see if they knew the unfortunate fella splayed in the road, but no one's eyes flickered with recognition. The old whore tightened her chippie as she inched away from the body, but just as she was about to full-out ditch him, she noticed a gold wedding band. Her agitated face suddenly registered a spark of luck. With a quick motion she squatted down and laid claim to his left hand, trying to inconspicuously wiggle, then twist, then pull the stubborn ring off his chubby finger.

"Go on now, ain't nobody watchin' but us chickens," Snitch said.

The whore looked up. "Poor scamp's ticker just gave out," she said with a defensive shrug. The ring suddenly released, causing the whore to fall back on her ass with her chippie dropping open again, this time fully. She first slipped the ring into her boot before bothering to cover herself. As she glanced up, she suddenly became aware of all the onlookers. Immediately knowing her predicament wasn't good, she rolled back onto her knees and solemnly dropped her head over the body. She crossed herself and clasped her hands in prayer. "May he rest in peace," she muttered.

Snitch eyed the whore like a wildcat, circling before running off. She nervously called after him, "Snitch, ya keep this to yourself, now!" But he didn't look back. She grimaced, then gave a swift, frustrated kick to the dead man's rib cage, her twiggy foot helplessly bouncing off his numb flesh. As she moved away, she carefully swept the ground with her boot, trying to scuff up the lines in the dirt that linked the body to her crib. "Nothin' happened. Ain't nothin' to see," she called out. "Just a bad ticker."

Mary headed on her way, as did the others, their curiosity sated. They all knew that whore would be walking scared for a time. Not that whores and their peet daddies weren't used to walking scared; after all, no one here was working lawfully. Any one of them could be put under by a steep fine, and there was nothing to keep a whore from getting tossed in jail, especially when the city got its seasonal hankering to demonstrate efforts at combating vice.

Although Mary didn't have much, she counted honesty as one thing she could call her own. While it seemed insincere for a person of the Underworld to be spouting off about honest living, she was quick to justify her profession. It was of a man's own free will if he wanted to use her services. Besides, what else was there for someone like her? She wasn't learned enough to be a teacher, and she didn't have any land to live off, so what was she supposed to do with the other two mouths she had to feed and a baby on the way?

She knew there were some whores who never feared God their whole lives—these were the ones who'd saunter right up to a man on the Alley, spit tobacco juice in his eyes to stun him, and then rob him down to his watch fob. That wasn't her. Yes, she made her living as she did, but she conducted herself fairly and honestly. A person had to find some way to live peaceably with herself, and that was what she abided by.

As she walked, she avoided the corner of Franklin and Customhouse. If Lobrano was drinking, he was sure to be there, at the Pig Ankle, deepening the groove he'd already worn into the corner barstool. It wasn't unlike him to spend most of the daylight there, slumped over glass after cloudy glass of absinthe and washing it down with Lithia water until he saw the Green Fairy herself step from the picture on the bottle and come sit right next to him.

Instead, Mary turned onto Marais Street, on the edge of Venus Alley. The Waffle Wagon was parked up the block, and the sweet aroma tickled her nose. But she had no money to spare for a delight just now, even though her stomach was rumbling. Rather, she focused on the sound of lively piano music, and since it was free to listen, she allowed herself the indulgence. She followed the music to the open window of Pete Lala's Café, an eating place for black folks. It was a jaunty tune that leapt from inside—the kind that made you unable to keep your feet from tapping. Only, the music suddenly stopped, then started up again, then stopped. Curious, Mary peeked in to see what the racket was about.

The café was as tidy as it was empty. She scanned past half a dozen tables with red-checked cloths, the chairs perfectly pushed in, awaiting the next morning's customers. At the very back of the room, a young, light-skinned black man sat at an old, upright piano, banging on the keys with a fever. Banging away—until, abruptly, his fingers paused in midair. He urgently turned to scribble on a piece of paper. Then he tapped his pencil, thinking . . . thinking. . . . He took a crimson silk handkerchief from his pocket and wiped his brow. Then, just like that, he dropped the handkerchief, dropped the pencil, and his fingers flew back to the piano, running up and down the keys.

Mary had never seen a person so full of concentration like that, and his playing, it was some kind of powerful! She closed her eyes and tried swaying to the music, but the kip on her back wasn't exactly a good dance partner.

When she opened her eyes, the piano player was staring right at her, looking straight into her face as if he knew her. Feeling like a little snoop, Mary's cheeks reddened. At this, the piano player gave her a wink. She quickly looked away, blushing even more. She knew she should turn and hurry right off, but for some reason her boots felt like lead.

"Come on in and have a listen," the piano player called.

Mary was immediately struck by how perfect his talk was, as if he were from the North or educated, or maybe both. All she could do was stammer. "I was just dawdlin'. . . . Should be mindin' my own business."

But he called to her again. "My name's Ferdinand."

Not used to friendly salutations, Mary froze. "I . . . gotta get home," was all she could spit out.

"You can come by and hear me another time if you'd like," he offered.

She feebly nodded and forced herself to hurry off. It wasn't until she was down the block that her sense kicked back in. Clearly, she had no manners. Here was someone being nothing but friendly to her, and she . . . well, maybe she *would* go by one day to hear him play again. But she quickly stopped herself. That was a Negro establishment, and she had no place there. And she probably shouldn't be listening to their music, either, although she wasn't exactly sure why. Silly girl, she scolded herself. She had troubles enough without being friendly with a colored fellow.

It was late now and growing dark, so she hurried her pace, not wanting anyone to worry after her. Still, her thoughts kept drifting back to the piano player. He was handsome, with a milkiness to him, a Creole, she bet. She could hear the music in her head, and she timed it with the rhythm of her boots on the dusty ground, and then with the slapping of the kip against her backside, and then with the coins jingling in her pocket. Ah, that damn picayune.

She wondered what Lobrano would say if she told him she'd earned a worthless picayune? Her stomach churned at the thought, and she picked up her stride, not wanting to encounter her number one trouble when he was lit and vulgar.

"Please, Saint Teresa," she said aloud, "see me home tonight without a sign of him."

CHAPTER TWO

JOSIE, THE RAILROAD MAN.

Mary's walk spanned clear across town, to low ground, where houses didn't have plank floors, just the trodden earth. As she walked, the clouds thickened and a fog began to roll in, and it was fortunate she knew the paths well, for when the moon hid like that you could hardly see past your own feet. As her eyes became less and less useful in the growing darkness, her other senses heightened. She noticed, with each step, how sore her thighs were, achy and tight from a long day. And she noticed she smelled ripe, even with the rose oil. Thoughts of a soak in a hot bath and washing off the sweat of johns already began to soothe her.

The ground was soggy, and her boots made a sucking sound as

she brought up each heel. The land was no longer the swamp of her mama's time, but it could get soaked around here when the storms came. After a hard rain, you'd wake up some mornings to find among the street litter rotted caskets and even human bones, washed up from the nearby paupers' cemetery. Everyone in New Orleans knew that nothing stayed buried for long in such moist ground, but what were poor folk who couldn't afford an aboveground tomb to do? Groundwater or not, they still wanted to respect their dead. So they tried weighting the casket with stones or even burying the body with pebbles, but it didn't much matter. Sooner or later, it would float right back to the surface, as if the ground had absorbed the soul but rejected the shell and spit it right back where it came from.

Unless it was storming Mary didn't mind this long walk, for it gave her time alone, just herself and her thoughts. Little Mary, mind wanderin', Mama would always say. It was true, when left to herself she allowed her head to travel beyond her small world. Of course, she had never set foot outside New Orleans, so all she knew of the world beyond was from the newspapers and the few books she'd managed to read. But she had come across enough to compel her to keep a running list in her head of all the things she wanted to do someday. She frequently recited it to herself but never spoke of it to another person:

I want to ride on a train someday.

I want to get all dressed up with a corset and velvet gloves and have my picture taken and put in a fancy frame.

I want to sit in the balcony at the French Opera House and feel shivers from the beautiful voices.

She decided that she could add a new entry right now: *I want to have a man look at me as deeply as the green-eyed john did today. Only, a man with a genuine heart and with nothing messed in his head.* She sighed. That one was a daydream, really . . . maybe even more of a wish. If there were such a man, he wouldn't be in her world, wouldn't want to have anything to do with someone of her ilk. *Little Mary, mind wanderin'.* If wishes were birds, Mama would say, then beggars would fly.

A light up ahead flickered through the fog: at last, her little home. It wasn't much, just one room and an outhouse. Some folks in other parts of town would call it squalor, but Mary knew nothing else. To her, this was what home felt like. Her younger brother, Peter, made sure to keep the bin stocked with firewood, and his wife, Charlotte, had taken care to sew pretty lace curtains, and they all took turns scrubbing the place so it was always spick-and-span.

When Mary thought of those two her heart yearned for all the things she'd like to give them someday. They were so eager and well meant, just starting out together. Peter was seventeen and had always been sickly until love brought color to his sallow cheeks. An honest, unassuming sort, he was reliable as the sunrise. Charlotte, only sixteen, was the kind of girl Mary secretly wished she were like, all maple-sugar sweetness, so much so that even Charlotte's eyes smiled. Poor thing had never uttered an unkind word, and yet, the world was unkind to her when she lost all her relations a couple of years ago to the grippe. She and Peter clung to each other, trying to find their way together. Mary knew they deserved better, and, more important, the baby deserved better.

A rustling in the leaves startled her, sending goose pimples crawling over her skin. She peered around her kip but couldn't see more than a foot away, let alone check if anyone was following her. She felt about for a rock she could wrap her fist around, just in case, when suddenly, a dark figure rushed at her. Hands clutched her waist, pushing her hard against a tree. The rock fell from her grip.

"Scared ya, sissy!" a man hissed.

Immediately, Mary recognized the voice—and the sour stench.

"Damn you, Lobrano!" she shouted, swiping her fists through the air.

Lobrano's hands grabbed at her hungrily. "Where's my day's earnin's?" he demanded.

Mary gave him a shove. "Will you let me put my kip down? And come near the light so I don't go dropping money we'll ain't never find."

They moved closer to the lamplit house, and Mary unloaded her kip, then pulled a wad of cash from her cleavage. Lobrano watched with hawk's eyes as she counted off half and handed it over.

"You sure that be the full of it?" he sneered.

With a shift of the clouds, the moonlight illuminated them. Mary stared straight at his sunken, greasy face, her gray eyes unflinching. "'Course it is," she said firmly. "I'd never skim on you."

Lobrano studied her with a wary squint. He knew those mysterious eyes well, knew how there was chatter going on behind them, a woman's brain click, click, clicking away. This was what unhinged him most, and Lord knew he'd rather be all sorts of things than intimidated by a woman. It made his chest feel tight and uneasy, and the only way to dull that was to remind himself of his power.

He took a step closer to Mary. She stood as tall as his collarbone, and he liked feeling that his frame, no matter how scrawny, towered over her. He ran his hand down her leg, not caring that she flinched.

"I'm sore, and it's late," she said quietly. "And they're expecting me."

"Forget them vultures," he snapped. "Leechin' off every cent. Your brother's a man now. Don't look like a man, that weak sissy, but he can fend for himself." Lobrano leaned into her, pinning her against the tree with one hand as he clumsily tried to undo his belt with the other. Mary closed her eyes, knowing that when he was like this, it was no use to protest. It would be over soon.

"So how come that Negra doin' better'n you?" he asked, still fumbling with his belt.

"'Cause Beulah's got better shifts. How am I supposed to make good money sharing space?"

"You know damn well the coloreds come at night," he said, his spit catching Mary's face. "You gettin' sad enough that you'd serve a colored? That what you're saying?"

It occurred to Mary that this could be her moment. A hundred times to herself she'd rehearsed what to say. Oh Saint Teresa, Mary silently prayed, let him still be high on absinthe! She gulped air, then as steadily as she could muster, she said it: "I need my own crib."

Her words hung in the air, and she could feel the muscles in her face tighten as she waited for him to answer.

He dropped his trousers. "Can't," he said flatly.

"You know I can make money," she pleaded.

"Anderson's got us all by the balls."

"But I'm not old and sagged. I got all my teeth. I can make good money!"

"I says no."

Mary's jaw clenched. She hated how he talked to her like she was still a child, how he talked like he controlled her. She knew she should just stop there and that to push more would be asking for Lobrano to erupt. But she always gave in, always stopped and cowered from him. Her thoughts darted to Charlotte, to Peter, to the baby coming into this world. And she decided here and now to test Lobrano.

"What if," she said coyly, sidling up to him, "what if some other pimp wants to get me my own crib?"

He let go of her waist and grabbed her by the wrists, pushing her hard against the tree. He put his face right up next to hers. "You're so full o' shit, your eyes be turnin' brown," he hissed. "You and your brother'd be in the ground years ago if not for me. You'd be nothin'. Who the fuck's Mary Deubler? Nobody, that's who." Disgusted, he stepped back and let her arms drop.

Mary rubbed her wrists, sure to be bruised tomorrow. There was no denying that a part of what he said was true—maybe she and Peter would have starved, and somebody would be stepping over her bones when the earth spit them out. But she'd been paying Lobrano for years; was she expected to owe him for the rest of her life? She stepped toward the door of her house.

"And go take a bath," he yelled after her. "All that perfume don't cover the cunt underneath."

Mary wanted to scream at him that she had an excuse for the way she smelled—that it was her job to lie under men, even if they were odorous, and it was her job to make them heated. What was Lobrano's excuse for his putrid stink? But she forced herself to say nothing, and instead slipped quietly into her house, where, with a stifled sigh, she bolted the door.

The house was toasty from a crackling fire, and Mary was heartened to see Peter still awake, leaning over the hearth, shifting the embers.

"Hiya, Josie," he said quietly, calling Mary by the nickname he'd used since he was a little boy. He turned to face her, but the smile that usually came so easily to brighten his face now seemed strained.

"She okay?" Mary whispered, nervously looking to the corner of the room, where Charlotte, flushed and sweaty, was asleep on the cot. Mary hadn't realized she was holding her breath until, at Peter's nod, her chest sank with relief.

"Don't know how she's still sleepin', though," he whispered. "That baby be kickin' so hard, nearly knocked me outta bed."

Mary smiled at their sweet girl, her dark hair clinging in damp clumps to her heart-shaped face. She looked still a child herself, with thick lashes and a dainty, upturned nose. Her dry, delicate lips moved faintly and silently from the midst of whatever she was dreaming.

"Hard to believe that tiny thing can have a belly so swollen," Mary said as she leaned her kip against the wall. She then went to the only piece of furniture under their roof that held any meaning for her: a cherrywood bureau that had been Mama's. It wasn't much to look at, especially not for anyone used to fine furnishings, but it did have pretty carvings on its four corners of small bouquets strung together with ribbons. Mary gave the bureau a little shove, then squatted down behind it.

From a hole in the floorboards, she removed a cigar box, its wood smooth and worn. A picture was revealed as she tipped the lid. A scene of a yellow streetcar, the A-B-C line, which, so the box told her, traveled to places she'd never heard of—Akron, Bedford, and Cleveland. She wasn't sure what a streetcar had to do with a five-cent cigar, but she'd decided it was a cheery picture. From her cleavage, she took what was left of her money and placed it in the box. She liked stowing her earnings under the streetcar. It reminded her that there was a whole world out there, that Venus Alley was just a pinprick on a map of the country and that with enough money, someday, she could go see places, she could go to Akron, Bedford, or Cleveland.

The box was weighty in her hands, and she felt awash in reassurance as if the contents of that cigar box were the sole judge of her worth—and her worth was growing. Placing the box back in the floor, she slid the bureau to cover it.

"I have grits warming," Peter whispered. Mary nodded heartily, then bent down to remove a wad of cash she'd hidden in her boot. She handed Peter the cash. But instead of reaching for it, he just stared as if it were tainted. "Don't you ever worry that Lobrano will find out?" he asked.

For several months now, ever since Charlotte became sure she was with child, Mary had been skimming. Why now, she wondered, was Peter suddenly wary of the extra money?

"He doesn't count how many tricks I turn, and he's no way of knowing what tips I get," Mary said, urging the money toward him.

Reluctantly, Peter pocketed the cash. Mary noticed he was fidgeting with his watch, clicking the lid open and snapping it shut the way he did when worries were turning over in his head. But she knew to just let him be, that he'd tell her soon enough what was getting at him.

He set a simmering tin of grits before Mary, and she inhaled the steam. As she ate, she tried to ignore the watch cover's rhythmic snap-click, snap-click. Mama had rescued the watch from discard by a john, and Peter had carried it ever since he was a little boy and it had been as big as his hand. It remained the nicest thing Peter had ever owned, even though it was permanently frozen at half past two.

Finally, Peter offered up his thoughts. "Lobrano was makin' a racket out there," he said, then quickly busied himself again with the hearth, so as not to face Mary. "I could hear how he was talking at you."

Shame landed like a stone in Mary's stomach. Out of respect, they usually avoided such talk. They all knew her work was crude, and there was no reason to go and speak outrightly about it. They talked of her work the same as they did of his selling potatoes in the market or of Charlotte's seamstress work. Just jobs that put food in their bellies and shoes on their feet and kept them in clothes that weren't too tattered, which was more than a lot of folks could claim.

But Peter continued on, troubled in a way Mary couldn't remember seeing him. "What's gonna happen when there's a child around?"

"Why are you harpin' like this, Peter? Things'll be different soon enough."

"Different how?" he demanded.

Mary brought the cup of grits to her lips and let a warm, buttery mouthful slide down the back of her throat. She could feel Peter's eyes on her and had noticed the deepening purplish shadows, just like when he was a child.

"Lobrano's gonna get me my own crib," she said staunchly, and as the words hovered in the air, she wanted so badly for them to be true.

Peter's shoulders drooped, and he stared blankly into the flames. "You keep tellin' that to yourself," he mumbled. "Might as well tell it to a fence post."

Mary ignored him. All she wanted was to savor the last mouthfuls of grits and enjoy the peace of the night with no one grabbing at her, no one wanting anything from her.

But, uncharacteristically, Peter wasn't going to let their talk taper off. He turned to face Mary. "You keep tellin' that to yourself," he said again, only this time his voice rose above their respectful hush. It also wasn't like Peter to raise his voice, especially not to his older sister. But he was staring at her squarely, his jaw quivering. "You gonna tell that to the baby when it comes?"

Caught off guard, Mary recoiled. She could feel her own temper rising at his insolence. It was she who'd been caring for him since he was born, and she who brought in most of the money; he did honest work, but a whore earned more any day of the week than a potato seller. She'd already held her tongue enough times today, and, even more, what was Peter wanting from her anyway? She was doing everything she could to save money for his baby.

Just as she was about to spit back a sharp word or two, a groan arose from Charlotte, who shifted uncomfortably in her sleep. Mary swallowed back the scolding, not wanting to wake her. She gave a smoldering look in Peter's direction. He deserved some reprimand for what he'd said. And then it occurred to her—her little brother was a worried father, that's what this was about. It could be any day now, and the panic of bringing a baby into this world, especially when their own mother . . . No, no, she stopped herself, she mustn't go there. No need to rile up her own tensions any more tonight.

"You must be tired, Peter," she said. "Stop worrying and let me be."

Chewing on his lip, he moved to Charlotte, tightening the blanket around her and softly sweeping the hair from her face. He was a gentle soul toward his wife, and it made Mary's heart ache to watch his tenderness.

He settled himself into the rocking chair and closed his eyes. "You've always been so smart, Mary. Much smarter than me. But when it comes to Lobrano, you hide your smarts. Did you forget? You're Josie." He gave a little smile, but his face still seemed bereft. "You're the conductor."

Mary knew the passage by heart from their growing-up years. It was a story in a magazine called *The Nursery*, which a man friend of Mama's from a place called Boston had pulled from his satchel and given to little Mary. Having just learned to read—Mama made sure her children spent some time in the schoolhouse—Mary read to her brother every night. While Mama was gone working, Mary and Peter would huddle together on the cot they shared and try to cover with giggles each scary creak and crack of their dark, empty shack. Out of all the lines of verse and short stories in that magazine, Peter's favorite was about Josie the conductor. He'd ask for the story over and over again. He'd call out, "All a-boarrrd" when it came to the part where the train left the station with the passengers in two blue cars, the US mail in the green car and Josie commanding the big red engine.

"I ain't smarter than you, Peter," Mary said, knowing full well that wasn't the point he was after.

"Oh, Mary. Lobrano's scared of you, can't you see that? He always has been. I ain't saying this to be nice. I had a long day, and I'd rather be sleeping than sitting here flattering my sister. I'm saying it 'cause it's true. He's scared of your smarts."

Mary had no response. She'd never thought of herself as smart. She thought a person had to be fully schooled to be smart, and she hadn't even completed primary school. Although, she could read and write just fine, which was more than most whores could do.

"Get some rest," Peter whispered to Mary, and she watched as he gingerly crawled into bed, careful not to bother his wife. Mary pulled the curtain that divided the one room, offering a pretense of privacy, and prepared her bath.

CHAPTER THREE

Snitch, eyes wide as saucers, stared at rows upon rows of money. He'd never seen so much money—fives, tens, twenties even, and dozens of stacks. Still out of breath from having raced through Venus Alley to Anderson's Saloon, his chest heaved as he watched Tom Anderson order the cash. He seemed almost hypnotized as Anderson methodically counted and stacked the bills, his chunky gold and jeweled rings sparkling as he carried the piles of money across the room to a walk-in safe.

A dashing, mustachioed dandy, Tom Anderson was the unofficial mayor of the Underworld, and here, in a mahogany-paneled room in the back of his eponymous saloon, he shrewdly and lucratively—very lucratively—ran Venus Alley.

Snitch wondered what a stack of those bills would feel like to hold, and he had to bite his tongue to keep from asking Mr. Anderson if he could touch one. Wouldn't it be something, he thought, just to walk down the street with one of those bundles of cash tucked into his shirt pocket! No, he decided, not in his shirt pocket, that would be too obvious. What's that lump there, Snitch, ya growin' a teat? That's what all those nosy whores would say. No, he'd have to divide the stack and line the inside of each of his shoes—he'd be inches taller walking around on that cash. It's true, y'all, he'd report, money does wonders for a man's stature!

Anderson's baritone voice snapped Snitch from his reverie. "You sure there isn't some small trifle of a detail that you're forgettin' to mention, Snitch?"

Glassy-eyed, Snitch looked up. "Oh no, Mistah Anderson, ain't nothin' to forget. I'm just reportin' what all I saw. He was just lyin' there, fat-assed and dead as a dodo."

Anderson made a dubious face. "A dodo? You even know what that is?"

Snitch shrugged. "Somethin' awfully dead."

Anderson chuckled to himself. Didn't this child know fear? he wondered. He was used to people feeling uneasy around him, but Snitch seemed unaffected. To most everyone else, Anderson cast an intimidating presence. Six feet tall with a solid, robust frame, he always appeared impeccable, from his exquisitely tailored suits to his sable-colored mustache groomed into perfect curlicues. His dark, penetrating eyes were attuned to every detail—they could charm you or shame you. But most notable was his reputation: he was a man who always got what he wanted, no matter what it took.

Tonight's unfortunate incident of a dead body on Venus Alley wasn't sitting well with Anderson. The others in the room, his two henchmen, Tater and Sheep-Eye, were too dim to surmise the possible impact—but not Snitch. Anderson knew how cagey Snitch was, and he watched the boy with a precise eye. Watched him staring down the table of cash like a lizard at a fly, figuring the boy might even be snaky enough to have a projectile tongue, or at least figure how to use his own to nab a bill if he thought no one was looking.

"Someone refresh my memory," Anderson said, "as to how we disposed of the last heart attack."

Tater and Sheep-Eye groggily looked at each other. They were as gruesome as Anderson was handsome. Both bulky with muscle, they also had the swollen, crooked features and jagged, raised scars of men whose faces had been on the receiving end of too many fists. They'd flanked Anderson for years, dealing with the unsavory issues that tended to arise when one ruled the Underworld.

"I recollect we's dumped him in the Pontchartrain," Tater said.

Sheep-Eye nodded. "I recollect that too."

Snitch piped up, "Nothin' was in his pockets, Mistah Anderson. Ain't found no money for my troubles."

Anderson cast a weary sideways glance. "Ain't subtle, are ya, Snitch?"

Snitch twisted up his face, another word out of his reach. "Don't rightly know, Mistah Ander—"

"Well, you ain't," Anderson said. Deciding he might as well have a little fun with the boy, he took a dollar from a pile, watching Snitch's eyes narrow in. "Now, Snitch, you gonna tell me which of my properties this dead trick came out of?" He dangled the dollar, and Snitch, nearly cross-eyed, followed its every move.

"Somewheres on Venus Alley," Snitch insisted. "I promise I didn't see nothin'."

"So the body just appeared in the middle of the road?" Anderson snarled, lifting the dollar higher—maybe the more Snitch tilted his head, the more of a chance something might leak out of it. But Snitch held defiant, the best little liar on Venus Alley. Like taunting a dog with a steak, Anderson teased him a few seconds more, until he finally relented, tossing the boy the dollar and waving him off.

"Thank ya, Mistah Anderson!" Snitch gushed. "You know I do my best for ya!" He gleefully scampered out.

Anderson shook his head, then turned back to his henchmen. "Boys, this ain't good. The City Council's got a stick so far up its ass they can taste wood. One misstep like this may be all it takes for them to release their holy fury." He leveled his gaze. "You ever seen holy fury, boys?"

Tater and Sheep-Eye vigorously shook their heads like children hearing a ghost story.

Anderson's eyes grew large with warning. "Holy fury is the worst kind."

He counted off several bills, handing a few to Tater and a few to Sheep-Eye. "Go to Venus Alley and get that body outta there and into the icehouse quick and quiet. By half past I want no sign that sorry bastard ever stepped a fat foot on the Alley. Then I want you to find out who he was. Someone from the bayou? Was he a son of a bitch from money? Is a posse gonna turn up lookin' for him? Does the whore he was riding need to end up floatin' down the Pontchartrain? Only pay for solid information, and for fuck's sake, if Snitch is the only one you can find who's seen something, hang him by those skinny ankles till he talks."

Tater and Sheep-Eye obediently piled out. Glad to see them go, Anderson closed the door behind them, then shut the safe and spun the lock. Damn whores—this wasn't what he wanted to spend the evening thinking about. He reclined into a buttery leather armchair and stretched his neck from side to side.

This mahogany back room was his haven, more meaningful to him than any room in his own house. To look around was to know Tom Anderson: on the wall hung a framed eighteenth-century map of the Louisiana Territory, entitled "La Louisiane." Several bottles of fine, aged Scotch waited on a hutch. A shelf of books announced interests of capitalism, politics, and persuasion: *The Wealth of Nations*, *Personal Memoirs of Ulysses S. Grant*, *The Federalist Papers*, Plato's *Republic*, and *A Treatise of Human Nature*.

Reaching for his velvet-lined cigar box, Anderson removed a fat J.C. Newman Diamond Crown and dragged it under his nose, inhaling heavily; for a moment, he rested there, savoring the ritual. Then he cut the tip and hovered a silver lighter engraved with his initials, puffing until the cigar was lit. He leaned his head back as he exhaled.

He'd smoked his first cigar when he was twelve. That cigar was the only thing he'd ever stolen from his father, even though he'd detested the old man. He was born and raised in Atlanta, where, as far as he knew, the Andersons still resided on a sprawling cotton plantation originally cultivated by his great-grandpop. If there were such a thing as Atlanta aristocrats, the Andersons were them.

Tom was an only child, for his mother had taken ill during his birth and never fully recovered. Spending most days in her sickbed, she secretly blamed her son for stealing her health; it was Tom's father who blamed him outrightly. The household tended to be painfully quiet, and Tom spent his childhood hushed and shooed, away from Mother, who was always resting, and away from Father, who was creased with worry over his ailing wife. Try as he might to be obedient and helpful, and never wanting to cause more strain than he apparently already had, Tom was nonetheless treated as a bother, a nuisance, and—perhaps worst of all—he was overlooked.

It was the mammies of the plantation, their kind hearts swelling for this lonely, neglected child, who treated him as one of their own. They cooked for him: grits, barbecue brisket, and hoecakes with honey. They brought him along to their spirituals, where Tom ardently clapped and sang and took such an interest that he taught himself how to play gospel on the church organ. They sent him outdoors with their own children, where, in the fields, they'd play for hours. Tom's favorite game was Chickamy Chickamy Fox, where a "fox" tried to outrun the gatekeeper and capture the "chickens." Tom—then as now—made an excellent fox.

It was in those fields that Tom and the plantation kids smoked their first cigar—hand-rolled from a local buckeye dealer—which Tom had slid from his father's desk drawer early that morning. Coughing, they passed around the cigar until they finally got the hang of how to smoke properly.

But all the while, Tom silently ached. He yearned for what he would never have: his mother's affection and his father's acceptance.

He knew he was invisible to his parents and vowed not to be that way to anyone else. No, he decided, to all others he would be essential, charming even, the center of the room, the talk of the schoolgirls, the first team pick of the schoolboys. He would be no one's enemy and everyone's friend—or at least they all would think so. Only he would know the truth: he would need no one. He would be disappointed by no one ever again.

He went about inventing a person who, in a world far from Atlanta, would gain immeasurable acceptance and affection—acceptance of the highest powers that be, and affection from the most beautiful women in the land. He made himself believe he would one day have an empire of his own.

And he would succeed. The irony—perhaps so profound that Anderson himself couldn't grasp it—was that his empire was made up of the sort he knew all too well: the castoffs, the unwanteds, the nobodies. Within this world, Anderson would earn much power. He would enjoy his reputation in the city of New Orleans as a savvy businessman and a charming Southern gentleman—but he would take pride in his Venus Alley reputation as a notorious playboy and a feared leader.

It was at sixteen years old that Tom disappeared from Atlanta. His parents awoke to find their only child gone, no note, no indication as to his destination, no good-bye. For all those years since, Tom held fast to the belief that they never missed him.

Four distinct staccato raps on the door jarred Anderson from his musings. He lazily rolled his head. "Come on in, Mayor."

The door swung open and portly, red-faced Mayor Walter Chew Flower waddled in, carrying a bottle of Raleigh Rye.

"Have I become that much of a jackass that you gotta bring your own whiskey?" Anderson said.

Mayor Flower laughed, his cheeks turning even more splotchy. "It was a gift from the Public Order Committee," he announced. "In full disclosure, they also sent over a box of Dominican cigars, which I opted to keep for myself."

Anderson shook his head with amusement. "They're trying to get to you in all the right places."

"Figured I'd enjoy the irony of sharing their bottle with the infamous Tom Anderson."

"Nothing wrong with taking a gift with one hand . . . and pouring it with the other."

"I like that, Tom. You do have a way with words."

Anderson opened a hutch to reveal rows of glasses for every occasion—stemware, shot glasses, absinthe glasses, highballs, snifters. He reached for two tumblers.

"I never thought I'd say this about a Puritan," Anderson began, "but the new head of the Public Order Committee has some interesting ideas about vice in our city. And I mean interesting as in, I wholeheartedly agree with the man. Imagine that!"

"Ah yes, Alderman Sidney Story," the mayor mused as he stuffed himself into a chair. "He might as well nail a soapbox to the soles of his shoes. Every corner I pass he's in the middle of a Bible-wavin' tirade."

Anderson sniffed the whiskey, gave it a pleasant nod of approval. "Oh, I'm sure Alderman Story wouldn't so much as shake my hand. But his notion of setting up a legal district to contain, as he calls them, the 'lewd and abandoned women,' well, that's a notion I get behind one hundred percent. I'd get up on a soapbox of my own and stand right next to him to show my support."

"Ha!" the mayor said, batting the air with his arm. "You'd sooner become a monk than get the entire City Council to support a legal district of prostitution. The alderman is as good as talking nonsense. Oh, but I do love picturing you planting a soapbox right next to his. He'd be mortified!" Flower broke into little-girl giggles.

Anderson reclined back into his chair, savoring a gulp of whiskey as he watched the already-strained buttons on the mayor's vest struggle against his fit of laughter. He didn't mind Flower, and he'd certainly benefited from how close they'd become, but he couldn't help but often wonder: How did this roly-poly get elected into office? If bullshit were music, he should have his own brass band. It occurred to Anderson that he, himself, should run for office. But not local government—Lord no, the Cabildo was so full of hypocrites. Those local politicians, they were nothing more than reeds in the wind, over here one minute, over there the next—and pocketing kickbacks all around. Bigger sights were in view for Tom Anderson: the Louisiana State Legislature, perhaps. And there was always Washington, DC, still so pearly white—he could go in there and actually have a chance at tarnishing things up.

"It doesn't quite make sense, Mayor, why the City Council's so opposed to Alderman Story's proposition," Anderson said as Flower caught his breath. "After all, creating a legal prostitution district would limit whores to certain boundaries. Folks could stop arguing that whores were corrupting family neighborhoods and that they lived in fear of a whorehouse popping up next door. As we both know, whores'll do many things, but they don't do the real estate market any favors."

It took the mayor a second before the pun sank in. "Oh, *favors*, Tom," he said, dissolving again into giggles. "The City Council could certainly benefit from a *favor* or two, believe you me! So uptight, all of them. But trust me, they won't ever legalize a prostitution district, even if it mandated whores to be chained to the lampposts."

"Now that's an interesting picture," Anderson said, swirling his drink.

"Hell's bells." The mayor snorted. "The City Council's been plotting the demise of Venus Alley for as long as I've been in office. One alderman's voice, and a pretty darn mousy one if you ask me, ain't gonna make a damn of difference. People 'round here don't take kindly to change, you know that. Pour me some more drink, will ya?"

Setting down his own still nearly full glass, Anderson refilled the mayor's drained one, marveling at how the sot could really suck it down.

Reaching for his refill, Flower wedged himself out of the chair to pace the room—for effect, of course. It was an important point Anderson had brought up, and, as the mayor, he wanted to do his best to expound. "See, Tom, the only thing Alderman Sidney Story's accomplishing is to make the City Council riled up. And now they're looking for a way to lash back at Story's unorthodox ideas, show that new alderman he doesn't call the shots, that he can't just traipse in here—oh, and he does traipse! Have you seen him, Tom?" The mayor's cheeks bulged with more giggles.

Tom gave a disinterested shrug.

"Well, it tickles me that such a, how should I put this, such an unmanly man is the one carrying on about legalizing prostitution. I bet Sidney Story has never even been with a woman. I bet this is all some twisted way of covering up something that ain't quite right in his head, if you know what I mean. I bet this new alderman still lives with his mother. Anyway, as I was saying before I interrupted myself, the City Council wants to show him that he can't just traipse in here threatening to change things, spouting off all sorts of unconventional, improbable ideas. Impossible ideas, really. How dare someone come and rock the good ship New Orleans!" He waved his arms in big circles, simulating a rocking boat. "This ain't my view, Tom, but it sure is how the City Council feels about it."

Anderson watched the mayor's little show, thinking the tubby man looked more as if he were losing his balance than rocking a boat. "So, Mayor, do I need to be worried that Venus Alley will be the target of some retaliation from the City Council? Perhaps their way of sending a message to the neophyte alderman and his Public Order Committee that it's still the Council who has at least a modicum of control over vice in this town?"

The mayor gave an offhanded shrug. "Not sure the City Council will bother much. It's not like they can just up and run your gals outta here, Tom."

"Those preacher-leechers can certainly try. Though they might as well let the whores take all the booze and tobacco with them, and they can pack up Mardi Gras, too, while they're at it."

"I don't think you've any worry, my friend. Alderman Story may have convinced the Public Order Committee, and their talk is temporarily loud, but the City Council knows those government committees hardly ever *do* anything. When was the last time a committee accomplished something of note? As I said, no one likes change. You know how long it takes to get the smallest thing done around here." He leaned over as if letting Anderson in on a secret, dribbling his drink down his shirtfront in the process. "Besides," he said, dropping his voice, "too many of the City Council are secret visitors to the Alley."

"Too many of them are secret *profiters* from the Alley," Anderson added. "Doesn't the City Council realize that a legalized district would make it a hell of a lot easier to get laid in this town?"

"You're overthinking all this," Flower said. "The Public Order Committee will soon tire of their own yammering, and everyone'll opt to stick with things just the way they are. That's what always happens, and it's really much easier that way. Certainly makes *my* job easier."

Anderson took a long sip of whiskey. His thoughts traveled to the nameless corpse that had been lying smack in the middle of Venus Alley earlier that night. No matter how lethargic the City Council, if word of this incident got out, they'd surely bolt up and take notice. A dead body would be perfect evidence for the Council to use to squash this new, loudmouth alderman and his crazy ideas about prostitution.

"I can stage a raid if you think it'll quiet the unrest some," Anderson said.

Flower twisted his face. "I don't see the need to go to any trouble, Tom. No one who matters is paying much mind to Alderman Story. Truly, he's nothing more than a flea. A flitting flea." Flower fluttered his stubby arms as he moved to the hutch. "Just make sure there aren't any major incidents involving a whore. You know, nothing that would upset the flow." He topped off his glass. "No repeats, like last year . . . with the congressman." He rolled his head back, sucking in air. "Now, something like that, well, that would really get the water boiling again."

Calmly, with no expression other than deep thought, Anderson swirled his whiskey—could be a congressman getting hauled into the icehouse at this very moment. "I'll just order a raid for good measure," Anderson said definitively. "Never hurts to beat the Bible thumpers at their own game."

Mayor Flower was, indeed, correct: Alderman Sidney Story lived with his mother. They resided on the cypress-lined street of Prytania in the Garden District, in a cozy raised cottage with two rocking chairs out front, hearty ferns hanging from the porch, and a flickering gas lamp at the door. It was quite likely that this thirty-seven-year-old gentleman was unmarried for the precise reason that he still lived with his mother; then again, there may have been other reasons—none of which he had given an ounce of thought to.

He did have thoughts about sex, though. All day long. But not in *that* way—not in any way that involved himself, or any lustful emotion, or body parts. He thought about sex in terms of revenue and property values, boundaries and crime reports. He also thought about sex in terms of God, and this made his pallid face crinkle as he damned to Hell those women of ill repute and the men who utilized them.

What he refused to think about was how many of those men, those partakers of sin, were acquaintances of his. Because this was too despicable to fathom, he blocked it out, like a child plugging his ears. If it were his choice, he would avoid associating with anyone whom he remotely suspected of sinning in this way. But given his higher calling, this wasn't possible. His was righteous work, although it did require that he associate with all types, from Council members to judges to voters. If dealing with sinners and heretics would further his mission to create neighborhoods free from vice, to create an upstanding New Orleans, a pious New Orleans, then so be it.

Just as he preached others should do, Story abided by a strict Jesuit code in his own life. The Storys had been devout members of the Immaculate Conception Parish for generations, and the church held great significance in the city, for the land upon which it stood was a gift to the Jesuits by none other than the founder of New Orleans, Jean Pierre Lemoine Sieur de Bienville. Story was well versed in Jesuit history and knew of the tumult his people had faced—how the priests in New Orleans had lost favor and were stripped of their property and then forced from the city, only to prevail half a decade later by returning to New Orleans, repurchasing the same land (which, in neglect, had become swampland inhabited by alligators), and constructing an awesome, Moor-inspired church with the adjacent all-male College of Immaculate Conception, where Story received his education. Taking heart in the Jesuits' struggles and redemption, Story viewed his own struggle for improving New Orleans as an extension of his forefathers' journey— knowing he, too, would triumph.

The church had always provided him guidance and solace, especially when his father passed. Sidney was but a teenager when Story Sr. did the unspeakable, and it was the church that assisted Sidney and his mother in obliterating all evidence and squashing all rumors so as preserve the family's dignity. For this, Story was eternally grateful, and driven all the more to spread the church's teachings.

Even though it was nearing midnight, a warm light emanated from the front window of the Story house. Ever since Sidney was born, the family inhabited this house in the Garden District, a pristine neighborhood of upper-class white folks, considerable greenery, and distinctly American architecture. Also, and importantly, it was a good distance away from the ethnic areas of the city, like the white Creole quarters and the Vieux Carré, where, in Story's opinion, there existed an overabundance of Spanish and French influence.

Balding, bespectacled Sidney was still perched at his desk, a tabby cat curled in his lap. Johann Strauss played from the phonograph, although a towel was draped over the barrel so as to mute the volume, dare he wake sleeping Mother.

Spread before him on his desk was this month's issue of the *Mascot*. On its cover: a cartoon parody of a City Council meeting, where, in the midst of discussing legislature, the council members downed whiskey as women danced about, skirts raised and dresses plunging.

The alderman, with impeccable penmanship, was composing a letter to his favorite *Mascot* senior reporter—favorite for the primary reason that this particular reporter, Kermit McCracken, espoused the exact same beliefs as Story on every debatable subject.

Dear Mr. McCracken,

Once again, I must commend you for truly fine reporting in this latest issue of the Mascot. *When I read your line: "Young men can no more be made continent by legislation than gamblers can be forced to cease gambling, yet the evil results of their intercourse with fallen women can be minimized by state regulation," I nearly leapt from my chair with applause. It is voices like yours, joined with my own, that will set this city onto the path of change, the path of righteousness, and the path of truth.*

I was, however, dismayed with this month's cover art, entitled "Secret Session of the City Council," which I know is not within your editorial jurisdiction, but nonetheless, I wish to express to you my opinion, as I trust my words will not fall on deaf ears. It is highly offensive to portray, even in caricature form, the valuable and dedicated work of the City Council as if important and confidential meetings take place in Babylon, where women of ill repute lift their skirts inappropriately high as they dance seductively amidst an inebriated spree. Please note that depictions of this kind only serve to undermine the passionate mission shared by you and I, as well as the Public Order Committee, which I head, and which is a most crucial arm of the City Council.

Yours in Christ's Truth,
Alderman Sidney Story

Story held up the completed letter, blowing on it to dry the ink, then gave his work a nod of satisfaction. From a desk drawer that neatly held all his letter-writing paraphernalia, he removed a gold bar of sealing wax, then heated it over the oil lamp. Dribbling the wax onto an envelope, he pressed into the warm pool his favorite seal, that of a crucifix.

CHAPTER FOUR

BROWN MIXTURE, U. S. P.
WITH AMMONIUM CHLORIDE

Each fl. oz. contains Opium .219 gr.   WARNING: May be habit forming. Alcohol 9 to 11%. Ethyl Nitrite .105 to .135% DOSE: Adults a teaspoonful every 4 hrs. or as needed, children 3 to 7 yrs. ¼ teaspoonful; 7 to 12 yrs. ½ teaspoonful.

NOTE: Persistent coughs may indicate the presence of a serious condition. Do not use this preparation when the cough has persisted for 10 days without securing competent advice.

MAINEGRA'S PHARMACY
C. M. MAINEGRA
Cor. Washington Ave. and Annunciation
Jac. 3841-9451   **New Orleans, La**

"Leave it to Beulah to send me to this part of town," Mary grumbled to herself. She'd never been to Rampart Street before, and never would've had reason to go except for the wildfire spread of the gleet on the Alley. From the talk of other whores, it seemed the john with the dark birthmark on his cheek was the culprit, and he'd lain in Mary's crib same as he'd detrousered at several others throughout the week. The itching had only just begun, but Mary wasn't keen on taking chances. More than once, she'd seen Beulah fly out of the crib, fiery-eyed, howling of the burning. And each time, Mary got on her hands and knees and scrubbed that crib top to bottom so as not to worry that the gleet would jump on her.

Whores would talk of their remedies for the gleet, and many swore by the Tan Tonic, which druggists and even cafés around the Alley sold. Others would visit the Gonzales Brothers cart and pay a whole dollar for a bottle of 7.7.7. But Beulah was the only whore Mary knew who had a remedy that saw her back in the crib in but two days and able to make her full shift without even a hint of agony.

So when Mary had come upon Beulah waiting at the door today, she had lowered her voice and asked who was the doctor her people went to see.

Beulah jumped. "No Needle Man comin' near my folk!"

Mary pursed her lips. Why did Beulah have to go making a scene? Leaning in, Mary whispered, "I need a remedy."

But Beulah just stared blankly. Mary leaned in closer and through clenched teeth muttered, "For the burning."

Beulah raised an eyebrow, then gave Mary an up-and-down look, as if it hadn't occurred to her that particular and scrubbed little Mary could be susceptible.

"Ain't no doctor," Beulah said, shaking her head. "She's a Voodoo queen."

Mary flinched. She didn't want anything to do with Voodoo. But then again, she wasn't in any position to lose a week's earnings. She took a deep breath and, hoping to God she wouldn't regret it, asked if she could go see her.

Beulah leaned back and let out a cackle. "Pretty girl gonna show her pale face o'er there on Rampart Street?" She laughed as if that were the funniest thing she'd heard in a long time.

Mary looked at her pleadingly.

Beulah crossed her arms over her chest then screwed up the corner of her mouth. "Awright, girl," she said reluctantly. "Go by the corner of Piety and Rampart. Ask for Miss Eulalie Echo."

Mary nodded her thanks and hurried off, knowing that Beulah was shaking her head, if not guffawing after her.

As Mary walked the unfamiliar cobblestone street, Haitian women strolled by with baskets balancing atop their *tignon*-wrapped heads. Barefoot children crowded around, calling back and forth to each other in song. Up ahead, a round woman in blue gingham stood over a small burner, frying the most delicious smelling rice fritters. She sang partly in French, "*Belles* calas! Clementine has lovely calas! *Tou cho*, quite hot!"

Mary arrived to the corner of Rampart and Piety, where Beulah had directed her, but the only building there was a cigar shop. Her fists clenched as she schemed that if she'd been lured all this way just for a laugh, she'd go find that gleet-infested john and pay him to infect Beulah.

Stepping into the cigar shop, she nearly swooned from the pungent tobacco odor. The place was dimly lit and cigar boxes filled rows of cramped shelves lined ceiling high. Behind a counter sat a brown, wrinkled woman counting short, fat cigars.

Softly, Mary said, "I, uh, was sent here for a remedy." The woman didn't look up. Mary piped up a little louder. "'Scuse me, ma'am . . . was sent here for a remedy. Would this be the right place?" Still, the woman didn't look up, just continued tallying the cigars, moving them from one pile to another, mouthing the numbers and bobbing her head to the count. Was she deaf? Mary wondered. Oh, horse's ass, Beulah!

Mary gave it one last try. "Ma'am, I'm lookin' for a Miss Eulalie Echo."

At this, the woman's head rose. Neatly resting the handful of cigars, she motioned for Mary to step behind the counter. There, she lifted a thick velvet curtain to reveal a doorway and, with a sweep of her arm, bade her through. Silently, Mary followed her down a dark hall, where she was left to wait alone on a stool outside a closed door. The cigar smell was now mixed with a spicy clove scent, and

Mary could hear a strange, crackly chanting coming from the other side of the door.

"*Eh, eh. Bomba hen hen. Canga bafie te. Canga ki, canga li.*"

Voodoo spells, Mary thought, and this sent shivers through her. *Oh Saint Teresa, please forgive me, I'm not wanting to tempt no demon spirits!*

Just then, the door opened and the crackly voice beckoned. "Come."

On command, Mary rose and shakily stepped through the door. The flickering light from dozens of candles cast long, eerie shadows across a tiny room. She glimpsed drooping shelves piled with dusty old books and scattered with bones of all shapes and sizes. Surprisingly, there were also just as many statues of the Virgin— little ones, big ones, wood ones, porcelain ones, on the shelves, on the floor, hanging on the wall. There was even a Negro Virgin, holding her hands out to beckon, while the whites of her eyes against her charcoal skin seemed to bore into Mary, asking, *Don't you know you don't belong here, white girl?* Mary jerked her head away.

Her gaze then fell to a crooked table lined with rows of different-sized jars. In one, a turtle swam furiously, trying to scale the jar and free himself, as if he knew a bad fate was in store. In the next jar, a floating eyeball stared emptily across the room. In another, a fleshy blob, gently bobbing, looked almost like a miniature baby. Mary couldn't help but lean in closer to examine . . . oh my, she could make out little tiny fingers!

A hand touched Mary's shoulder and she jumped. Flipping around, she was suddenly face-to-face with a rail-thin, brown-skinned woman, one piercing amber eye looking fixedly at her, the other wandering off into the distance. The woman had a head of thick, wild hair, pieces of it knotted around small, glass medicine bottles, making the shadow of her leaping onto the back wall look like the Snake Lady herself. Mary held her breath that she wouldn't turn to stone.

"Don't be afraid of Eulalie Echo," the woman said, her voice deep and husky. "Lay." She motioned to a gnarled-wood table lined with a featherbed.

Quivering, Mary willed herself to move forward and climb onto the table, even though her legs wanted to run as fast as they could out of there before she accidentally got cursed—or before some part of her wound up floating in a jar. She managed to squeak out, "I come looking after a remedy for—"

She was silenced by a bony finger in the air. "Eulalie knows. Now, show me the promised land."

Mary leaned onto the featherbed and felt Eulalie pull at her bloomers.

"Hold," she ordered, pushing Mary's leg upward. Mary grabbed her own calf and held her leg in the air as Eulalie looked her over.

Even though she spent most days in this position, Mary was uneasy with this strange woman poking around. "I 'spect you can tell I make my business on Venus Alley," Mary said, surprising herself by the tinge of shame in her voice.

"No matter," Eulalie said. "Venus Alley or high-class mistress, they all come to Eulalie. The gleet ain't partial."

"Even a proper mistress gets the gleet?" Mary asked, thinking it was something that only ran its course among people in the filthy places.

"Half New Orleans got the gleet, child," Eulalie said.

Wincing at a stab of pain, Mary could feel her eyes welling up. "This *is* just the gleet, ain't it?" she asked, suddenly concerned.

"Hush, now. Deep breath." Eulalie pinched a bunch of dried sage between her fingers and hovered the leaves over a lit candle. She trailed the smoke over Mary, and the intense scent stung her nostrils. Her head began to spin. The hazy figure of a man appeared in the room. Mary could make out a mop of dark hair and a scrawny frame. Squinting, she tried to discern details of his face, but he was mostly a blur. Just then, he spoke, and his screechy voice was eerily familiar: *Sign says you pay by the inch. She got thirteen inches there.* Mary squeezed shut her eyes and shook her head.

When she opened her eyes, the man was gone. She blinked, refocusing—he was still gone, as if he hadn't been there at all.

"Whew," Mary gasped, trying to catch her breath. "I just had me a moment." Her heart pounded in her ears and she lifted herself to her elbows, needing to make sure she was still present in the same tiny room, on the table. Eulalie met her gaze. Catlike, Eulalie's focused eye watched her carefully.

"You been to Eulalie Echo afore," she said. It wasn't a question.

"N-n-no, ma'am," Mary stammered. "Never even been on Rampart Street before."

Eulalie cocked her head, looking as if she knew better. But Mary was certain she hadn't ever been on Rampart Street before. Why on earth would she have come here?

Eulalie studied her for a moment longer, then her face softened and she helped Mary sit up. "No worry, child. Eulalie's remedy clear the gleet."

Relieved, Mary nodded and swallowed back the lump in her throat. She silently watched as Eulalie concocted a tincture, pouring and pinching different-colored powders and twigs and leaves from various wooden bowls. From her hair, she unwound a small medicine bottle and added a drop to the mixture. She corked the bottle, then rolled it back up in her tresses and tied it against her head.

"Come," she announced. "Let Eulalie look at your destiny."

"Oh . . . I mean no disrespect, Miss Eulalie Echo, but I don't want to be temptin' no Devil spirits."

A smile crept across Eulalie's thin lips. "That bit o' Devil in your belly's gonna serve you well."

Mary suddenly felt queasy again. "I'll just be on my way with the remedy if that's all right," she said feebly.

Eulalie made no argument and handed her a brown glass bottle. "Pour half in tonight's bath. Half in a bath tomorrow morn," she instructed. "Till then, the gleet's fleas'll infest anything that dare comes near, so you prig yourself up."

"Yes, ma'am." Mary moved to take some money from her boot.

"Keep that money to yourself, child," Eulalie said. With a quizzical look, Mary shimmied off the table. "But promise Eulalie you'll return at the waning moon . . . Mary."

Mary opened her mouth, but nothing came out. This room was doing strange things to her head—she certainly didn't remember having ever been to Rampart Street, and she also didn't recall telling Eulalie, or anyone else here, her name. She pocketed the medicine bottle and with weak knees stumbled across the room, past the jars and the flailing turtle and the Virgin statues. She opened the door and nearly smacked full into the round, violet, bustled bottom of a woman waiting in the narrow hallway.

"Quel culot!" the woman cried, startled. She pivoted, and Mary's eyes grew wide at the sight of her. She was the most stunning woman Mary had ever seen, with mocha skin paled by a thick layer of white powder and contrasted by a frame of fiery red hair. She sparkled with diamonds in her ears, at her throat, and on her fingers. From a thin chain around her neck, the woman lifted a monocle and brought it to her right eye to give Mary a quick up and down scan. "Hmm," she announced.

Eulalie's crackly voice interrupted Mary's trance. "Come, Countess."

Countess? The satiny layers of her skirts rustling, the woman swept past. Eulalie's door clicked shut. Dumbfounded, Mary remained in the hall, the musky-sweet scent of jasmine perfume lingering. A countess, Mary continued to marvel. A real, live countess! Miss Eulalie was right, the gleet ain't partial.

The air felt good on Mary's flushed face as she hurried toward home. She found herself looking close at Rampart Street, trying to see if anything struck her as familiar—the children, the side-by-side buildings painted bright colors, the gingham-clothed cala seller. She grew confused as her mind started tricking her into not knowing if she'd passed these sights coming here or if she'd seen them sometime long ago. Damn black magic! Getting to her already! She quickened her steps, but something was eating at her. She traced the sequence of events that just happened, from start to finish, how she'd left Beulah at the crib and headed straight through town. As she went through each moment, she reached the exact same notion: Eulalie knew her name, yet she was sure as her own shadow she never did tell it to her.

As Mary approached her house, she made out the scrawny shape of Lobrano waiting out front. "Wretch," she muttered aloud. Her head was achy and spinning, and just the distant sight of him drained her. What she wouldn't give for this man to leave her be tonight.

"Where ya been?" he called out, squinting into the setting sun.

She didn't have the energy to call back an answer. He leaned himself against the door, biting his dirty fingernails and spitting them at her doorstep.

"Where ya been?" he asked again as she neared.

"To the French Market," she said flatly.

He looked to her empty hands. "You gettin' too high and haughty to turn tricks?"

Mary gritted her teeth. "Ain't feelin' too good is all. Went to get a remedy."

He studied her, a look of disgust creeping over his face. "You ain't gone and got yourself in a bad way, have you?"

"No," she said, insulted. "I always use the French preventative."

"Good, 'cause you my little cash cow." He moved toward her, his wandering hands trying to pick up where he'd left off the other night.

"Can't, Lobrano," she said forcibly and stepped into the house, only he wedged his foot so she couldn't shut the door. He followed her inside, already having scoped the place to know that Charlotte and Peter weren't home. Coming up from behind Mary, he rubbed himself against her like a feral cat. She could smell the drink on him, a constant smell these days. Her fingers traced the outline of the remedy bottle in her pocket, and she could hear Miss Eulalie's voice warning of the gleet's fleas.

"Ain't a good idea, Lobrano."

He grunted and pushed Mary onto the cot, onto the clean white blanket where pregnant Charlotte slept. She had tried to warn him, but since he wasn't willing to listen, Mary stopped resisting and let her body uncoil. She planned how, not a moment after he left, she'd strip the bedclothes and boil them in a kettle of water. Leaning back, she tried to hide the little smile playing on her face—Lobrano deserved exactly what he was about to get.

CHAPTER FIVE

Dauphine Street

The moonlight began to dim over Venus Alley. It was difficult to tell time here—dusk and dawn didn't feel much different. There wasn't the hustle and bustle of early risers carrying out morning chores or hurriedly heading off, freshly scrubbed, to the business district. There was no ritual in the Alley, nothing got closed down and locked up or unlocked and flung open. No signs were taken in and put out. No one washed windows or swept entranceways. Nothing smelled clean here in the morning—nothing smelled clean here anytime. The doors were always open, the noises always the same. The street sweepers didn't much bother to come around the Alley, and neither did the vendors. Only Sam the Buglin' Waffle Man would roll his painted wagon by and occasionally pipe out a bugle

call and a song, knowing it didn't matter the hour—a hot waffle
was good after a romp, day or night.

The Waffle Man is a fine ol' man,
Washes his face in a fryin' pan,
Makes the waffles with his hand,
Ev'one loves the Waffle Man.

An old woman with matted hair and missing teeth dumped a
chamber pot into the gutter, sending a large rat scurrying. Snitch—
eyes and ears ever present—took chase, following the rat. He
splashed through the murky gutter water, and the rat screeched as
Snitch gleefully stomped on its tail. He quickly released, then gave
chase again. The game continued until Snitch heard a pounding
sound, growing louder and louder. He turned to look up, then froze.
There in the distance, becoming clearer by the second, was a horde
of mounted policemen and paddy wagons charging up the street.

"Lawd," Snitch said aloud. He filled his lungs with as much air
as he could suck in, then let out a piercing wail, the Paul Revere of
the Alley: "Po-leeece! Listen up, all yous, the police are a'coming!"
Then he darted out of sight, taking cover beneath a stairway.

His warning was of little use. By the time the whores who were
not otherwise engaged in compromising positions sauntered to their
doorways, the police were already dismounting, pulling batons from
their belts, and storming the Alley. They kicked open crib doors as
high-pitched screams tore through the street. From doorways and
behind corners, partially clothed whores and trouserless johns made
mad, frantic dashes in every which direction.

Secluded in his hiding place, Snitch took it all in. He'd wit-
nessed a lot of strange things on the Alley before, but never had he
seen anything like a full-out raid. But why *now*? Had someone high

and influential contracted the gleet from this place? Or maybe that fat dead body turned out to be some important muckamuck? Or, Snitch thought, excitedly, maybe the president of the United States was coming to New Orleans for a visit and this was an early spring cleaning?

In the midst of the chaos, Snitch spotted Police Inspector O'Connor. He knew the inspector's ruddy face well, since he was a frequenter of Anderson's Saloon, where he'd sit for hours, knocking back whiskeys on the house.

Referencing a list of some sort, the inspector directed his officers to certain cribs, where their first order of business was to empty them of any whores; next, to barricade the doors with splintery boards.

At the sight of their cribs being boarded up, several pimps who'd been watching from the windows of nearby saloons came racing over. The pimps hadn't bothered to dash over as their whores were being dragged out, but the moment their property was being threatened, well, that was an entirely different story.

"This crib is mine!" a pimp yelled, and the two policemen nailing the boards turned to him and smiled. Before the pimp knew what was happening, he was handcuffed and shoved into a paddy wagon. This sight stopped all other pimps in their tracks, and they skidded and flailed as they reversed their direction. The not-so-dumb ones kept running, but the really dumb ones ducked back into a saloon, or took shelter in an outhouse, or dove into a ditch—only to be quickly forced out by police batons.

Beulah was one of the unfortunate whores dragged from her crib. Her husky voice boomed up and down the Alley as two officers wrestled her to the ground.

"The hell if I know where Lobrano's bony ass be!" she shouted in response to the officers' questioning. "He better pray to Jesus y'all find him 'fore I do!"

"Should we take her in?" one officer asked the other. He grimaced at Beulah.

"The ugly stick sure likes you," he said to her, and for once she had the sense to keep her mouth shut. "Let her go," he instructed his partner. "Don't want to be lookin' at that all night."

"Ya heard him, get on now!" the first officer ordered, kicking dust at Beulah. She stumbled away as fast as she could.

From a safe distance, another watchful eye took in the chaos: Kermit McCracken, senior reporter for the *Mascot*. On his head an ever-present bowler hat, and in his hand an ever-present notebook. It was his personal mission to expose corruption in this city, especially on Venus Alley; given his high calling, he barely ever slept. And now he was practically licking his lips—this was the type of story he lived for. Writing furiously, he recorded how many people had been rounded up and how many cribs had been boarded. After only ten minutes, he'd tallied a dozen cribs barricaded and two paddy wagons packed full, filthy fingers clasping the bar windows as pimps' bruised and confused faces peered through.

After the screaming and commotion died down, the Alley seemed oddly still but for the whimpering of a few wandering, snotty-nosed children, their mothers having run off to save themselves. A sweaty Inspector O'Connor stood in the middle of the Alley, surveying the destruction with a series of prideful nods. "This constitutes a public service to the city of New Orleans," he announced, even though the only Alley inhabitants left were tightly packed in the paddy wagons. "Today," he continued, "we're throwing out the trash." With that, he motioned to his men to head onward.

McCracken scrawled a headline in his notebook: "DISGUSTING DEPRAVITY SILENCED ON VENUS ALLEY! BUT FOR HOW LONG? DOZENS OF DEVIL WORKERS IMPRISONED!" before hurrying after them. He couldn't wait to meet them at the police station and begin his onslaught of questions—this was going to be the story of the year!

Snitch, however, waited until the last officer had disappeared before gingerly emerging from his hiding place. He surveyed the damage. The Alley looked like a battle site with broken glass and debris strewn everywhere; even the rats had taken cover. But Snitch wasn't sidelined for long—oh no, he had his own agenda to pursue. He dutifully ran off, straight to Anderson's Saloon.

Snitch found Tom Anderson alone at the bar, calmly sipping a glass of orange juice, reading the front page news of the *Picayune*. Snitch couldn't believe his fate—could it be that Tom Anderson himself, lord of the Underworld, hadn't heard about the raid, and that he, little Snitch of the Alley, was going to have the privilege of telling him? Nearly giddy, Snitch's chest heaved so quickly he could barely get his words out.

"Saw it all, Mistah Anderson! Scared the bejesus from me! Whole bunch of cribs . . . all boarded up . . . peet daddies hauled to jail."

Anderson sipped his juice and nodded with feigned concern. "Is that so? Sounds horrible, just horrible."

Snitch caught his breath. "Oddest thing, though, Mistah Anderson," he said pointedly. "Inspector O'Connor, he had a list of pimps to arrest. Saw him lookin' it over real careful and crossin' off names. And all o' them, they be the most delinquent peet daddies on the Alley. The cribs that was boarded up, they be the ones Tater and Sheep-Eye always waitin' on to collect."

For a moment, Anderson was caught off guard—but just for a moment. Then he chuckled to himself. He'd known the little pest was crafty, but this was rather impressive. He gave the kid a crooked smile. "Snitch," he said, "you just might have enough gumption to be mayor of New Orleans one day."

Snitch nearly burst with excitement. "Ya mean it, Mistah Anderson? Ya really mean it?"

Anderson reached into his pocket and took out a fifty-cent piece. "Now get on outta here," he said, tossing the coin.

CHAPTER SIX

Mary didn't exactly know why, but as she walked to work, she found herself straying from her normal route and turning onto Customhouse, and then onto Marais, and suddenly, she was standing outside of Pete Lala's Café.

She craned to hear piano music, but there was none. Slowly, she walked by the windows of the café, watching the black folks inside eating and laughing. She spotted the piano, asleep in the back, its lid closed over the keys. She had a sinking feeling, but it was immediately followed by a touch of relief. It was just as well that she didn't encounter that piano player again.

She turned back toward Venus Alley, but as she neared, she sensed something wasn't quite right—the streets that were normally

wide-awake were as quiet as that piano. By the time she stepped
onto the Alley, it was clear a terrible thing had gone down, like a
tornado had ripped through this street alone. Mary picked her way
among the broken boards and shards of glass. A few other whores
were doing the same, trying to see if they could make business today, though clearly the answer was no. Only the rats and raccoons
were frolicking as they scavenged among the debris.

As she neared her crib, Mary saw Beulah sitting out front, smoking a corncob pipe. Beulah looked up, and Mary was surprised to
feel a comfort in seeing that familiar face.

"We all doomed," Beulah announced, and Mary's gaze traveled
to the knotty beams that crisscrossed their crib's door.

"Worst raid these eyes ever seen," Beulah said.

A shiver traveled through Mary as she digested what had
happened.

"Lucky you wasn't here, girl. Sho as shit, was it ugly! Johns
gonna be too 'fraid to ever come back."

Mary quickly tried to console Beulah, as much as her own self.
"You know how short their memories are. You'll see. The next boat-
load of sailors ain't gonna be wise to any of this. They'll hightail it
over with no care in the world."

Beulah gave an empty, unconvinced shrug, then took some puffs
from her pipe.

Some moments of silence passed before Mary timidly asked,
"Where's Lobrano?"

"Here," Beulah said, and reached into her pocket. She pulled out
a stuffed doll stitched from a potato sack, a red yarn *X* marking its
heart. She'd pushed a straight pin into the center of the heart. "I put
a *gris-gris* on you," she hissed to the doll, giving the pin another twist
to dig it deeper. "Feel this for ev'ry dollar I ain't gonna earn, for ev'ry
bite of food I ain't gonna put in the bellies of my kin. Feel it, ya mag-
got, while ya rot in jail."

Mary lurched. "Lobrano's in jail?"

"That's what Snitch told me. Said they dragged his bony ass from the Pig Ankle and won't let him out till he makes the rent." She pointed her pipe toward the other boarded-up cribs. "They be in the same awful fate as us'n."

Mary plopped down on the stoop next to her and noticed that Beulah's arm was scratched and bruised. "Did they rough you up?"

Beulah winced, then shot Mary a look that she should mind her own business. They sat silently again. Mary's gaze came to rest on the black magic doll with the pin through its heart. Should be through his crotch, she thought, recalling the night before. She envisioned Lobrano sitting in jail and figured he should just now be starting to itch and burn, with the worst of the firestorm landing late tonight. She giggled at the thought of it.

"Law, you're soppin' mad!" Beulah said, inching her rear away from Mary. "You be laughin' when we be sittin' here like mites in a steamin' pile of horse shit?"

Mites? The words knocked the laughter right out of Mary, and she bolted up. All this time she'd been spouting off how she didn't need Lobrano, and now he was gone—for a bit at least. Here was her chance to fend for herself. Here was the opportunity she'd been waiting for.

"Beulah, we're gonna be all right," she said sternly, needing to hear the assurance in her own voice.

Beulah waved her off. "You's half-cocked, girl. Good that you's a pretty little thing, 'cause your head ain't workin' right."

"I mean it, Beulah," Mary said as she rose. She had an idea, and maybe it was just half-cocked enough to work. Beulah's mumbling quickly faded as Mary ran off, the notion in her mind so strong she didn't hear or see much of anything as she ran all the way home. Once inside her tiny house, she darted straight to the bureau, pushing it aside and reaching for the cigar box. It was only at this moment, with the box in her hands, that she stopped to take a deep breath.

This was the heaviest the box had ever been. She cracked open the lid and lifted the stack of bills. Lining the bottom of the box, a picture postcard stared up at her. She'd forgotten it was there, and the sight of it brought memories washing over her. It depicted a mansion with a towering cupola, the Arlington Hot Springs Hotel, which seemed ready to swing open its fancy doors. *Come, Miss Deubler, we've had your room ready and waiting all this time. Here, take off your shoes for a polish, and let us launder your clothes while you change into your bathing outfit and soak your worries away in the hot springs. You don't own a bathing outfit? We'll just have to take care of that right away, no need to worry. There's no worry here at all.* Mary thought back to all those days she'd stared at this postcard wishing for someday, that magical someday when she'd go there, just like Mama had.

Releasing the wooden lid, the box snapped closed over the postcard. Her hands shook as she slid all the money she had in the world into her cleavage. She put the box back in the floor and repositioned the bureau, then ran out of the house as fast as she could before she had time to reconsider what she was about to do.

With a steady clip, Mary made her way to Tom Anderson's saloon. She'd never before been in his saloon. She only knew it was the place where peet daddies paid their rent and that it had the biggest, fanciest sign in town: ANDERSON—you could see it a block away.

As she stepped inside, she couldn't help but notice that it smelled so . . . so clean, like lemons and washing soda, not at all what she'd expected since she hadn't ever stepped into a saloon without crinkling her nose at the odor of stale booze and rotted cigars. But this saloon went beyond just clean—the deep wood floors weren't warped or scuffed, and Mary could even see her reflection, mis-shapen like in a circus mirror, in the shiny brass bar rail. Row after row of bottles stretched the length of the counter, advertising that any liquor you could want was available here.

Shyly, Mary approached the barkeep—even he was in a pressed white shirt, black vest, and bow tie. "'Scuse me, sir, where do you . . . I . . . pay rent?"

He nodded toward the back of the saloon, where Mary saw two closed doors. With shaky knees, she headed back, dawdling just long enough to marvel at the gleaming copper ceiling, each square sculpted with designs of circles and spades. Seemed such a stretch to reconcile that Mister Anderson earned all this fanciness from the smut on Venus Alley, where the only tin decoration might be an empty can of beans occupied by a rat.

Deep voices, followed by booming laughter seeped from behind the closed door on Mary's right. She looked over her shoulder, back at the barkeep. "Sir?"

He looked up, motioned to the left door. She was relieved, since she certainly didn't want to walk in on something in progress, but as she hovered her hand over the door, she felt her stomach flutter. *Am I really going through with this? Is whoever's behind this door gonna toss me right out of here? And, my oh my, what is Lobrano gonna do to me when he steps into this hornet's nest?*

No, she reprimanded herself, don't think of that, don't think of *him.* Instead, she willed herself to think of Charlotte and Peter. And the baby, most importantly the baby. She heard Peter's voice in her head, *You're so smart, Mary, you're the conductor of the train,* and with this she knew, in a way she'd never known anything before, that the fate of the Deubler clan was up to her. This was a moment that may only come but once, and now it was here. *Mary Deubler, you will do this.*

She knocked.

"Who's 'at?" came a gruff voice.

"Um, uh, my name's Mary," she stammered through the door.

"What ya want?"

"To pay rent."

At that, the door opened, and she was beckoned in by Tater. Even though Mary had seen him before, making rounds on the Alley, his scarred and crooked mug still gave her the jitters.

Timidly, she said, "I've come to pay what's owed on a crib."

"Which crib?" Tater barked.

"Philip Lobrano's, crib nineteen."

Tater let out a snort. "Ain't this a sight? That mug sendin' his whore to cover his debt. I knows without even knowin' ya, lady, you ain't got the cash to pay the whole of it. And he ain't gonna be let from jail till he's all paid up."

Mary felt her stomach knotting. "How much is owed?"

With a grunt to indicate he was only humoring her, Tater opened a ledger to a page full of names and numbers. His stubby finger trailed down the line, pointing to each name as his lips moved like a child who'd just learned to read. He stopped at an entry. "This one, this say Lobrano?"

Mary leaned in to see, and there it was: the entry giving Philip Lobrano control of a crib—and control of her. Holding her breath, Mary's eyes followed Tater's dirty fingernail to the number at the end of the column . . . $25. Her heart sank. *Damn you, Lobrano, drinking away everything!* It was more than double what she would've guessed. A dizzy feeling began to descend upon her.

"Told ya, lady, you ain't gonna cover it."

"That's nearly four months' rent, ain't it?" Mary asked, her voice now quivering.

"No lady, that be five months', see? Says it right here." He pointed to another entry. Confused, Mary looked to where his finger landed. Sure enough, there was the proof: Lobrano had been lying this whole time, telling her and Beulah that the rent had been raised and that he needed to collect an extra dollar a month from each of them on top of what they already paid him. Mary's dizziness was replaced with a sudden fury. She could feel it burning on her face. "Cheatin' sack o' shit," she muttered, unable to help it.

Tater raised an eyebrow. Mary quickly checked herself. This was a respectable establishment, after all. "It's just that Lobrano's been lying to Beulah and me for a long while," she explained.

"That's who you are, the girl who shares a crib with a colored? Don't rightly know why Mistah Anderson keeps lettin' that slide."

Mary was hardly listening. Instead, with each breath, she could feel the cash against her chest. Her heartbeat echoed in her ears.

"I want to pay it off," she blurted out. "But not to get Lobrano out of jail. I want to pay for the crib, and I want my name to be put there instead of Lobrano's." Even she was surprised to hear the words sound so bold. She pointed to the entry. "Here. My name, not his."

Tater gave her an oafish look. "Ain't followin', miss."

"I want my name on that crib. Miss Mary Deubler, and I'll pay off the twenty-five dollars here and now."

"Don't think that be the way it works."

"I'll pay for the next month up front too. Right now, I'll give you thirty dollars total."

Perplexed, Tater stared at her. Mary's heart was thumping so loud she was certain he could hear it. Finally, he cocked his head. "I 'spect you's just a whore, but the way I see it, your thirty dollars be as good as any."

Mary kept very still, so as not to let on her relief. From her cleavage, she removed the roll of cash and counted off the bills. Only two dollars remained. She'd walked in with her life savings and was to leave with two single dollars to put in the cigar box—the box that had been its heaviest just this morning. What good were two dollars to a new baby? But what good was a cigar box of cash when there was no hope of a better life for that child? Shakily, she handed Tater the money.

Craning over the ledger, she watched like a hawk as Tater scratched graphite through Lobrano's name. But as he was about to write a new line, Mary stopped him.

"Will you write it in ink, please?" she said. He again gave her a confused look. "Not in lead," she explained, "but in ink. Please." She didn't want Tater—or anyone—to be able to scratch out her name the way Lobrano's just was. She didn't want there to be any question that Mary Deubler had paid thirty dollars and was entitled to that crib.

"Picky thing, ain't ya?" Tater said. Mary just smiled sweetly. He dipped a pen in ink.

"The name's Mary Deubler," she repeated, and then spelled it out slowly, watching as Tater formed each letter, his tongue sticking out the corner of his mouth. After he was done filling in the columns and had marked PAID and the date, she gave him her biggest smile. "May I trouble you for one more thing?" she asked.

He gave her a weary look.

"Is there some kind of paper I can have, to prove this crib's paid up and is in my name?"

He rolled his eyes at the hassle, but Mary blinked her lashes and looked at him longingly. With a grunt, he riffled around in the desk, eventually turning up a piece of parchment. Again, his tongue poked out the corner of his mouth as he wrote in big, uneven letters in crooked lines:

CRIB 19 BE RENTED PROPERTY OF
MARY DEUBLER. PAID IN FULL.

"Sign it there too," Mary instructed. "Please."

He wrote: SINED BY TATER. He handed the paper to Mary. It looked as if a blind man had scrawled it, but it would do.

"Thank you . . . Sir," she said, not sure how to refer to him. "Will you please send someone to take the boards down from the crib door?"

"I'll get Sheep-Eye on it."

"Thank you, again," she said, and turned to leave. But then she turned back.

"What now, woman?"

"Just so we're all clear, this ain't no bail for Lobrano."

Tater grinned big enough to reveal missing teeth. "Let him sit and dry out. But can't keep him there forever, ya know."

"Don't need forever," Mary said, and with that, she walked confidently through the door, feeling like her back was straighter than it had ever been, and that her body was lighter, as if the pressure of a peet daddy—of nasty Lobrano—was a sack of meal she'd been hauling on her shoulders and had just unloaded.

The other door to the right was now halfway open, and as she passed it, she couldn't help but peek in. There, just inside the doorway, with a cigar in his hand, stood Tom Anderson himself. Although Mary had never come this close to him, she and everyone else on Venus Alley knew who he was. His name sent shivers through peet daddy circles and caused flutters with the whores. Anderson's eyes caught her gaze, and she instantly flushed. Snapping her gawking head back to attention, she scooted herself out of his saloon as fast as she could.

The entire way back to Venus Alley, Mary kept her hand securely over the parchment that contained a crib number and her name. *Her* name.

Beulah was still wallowing on the dusty stoop, drawing circles in the dirt with a stick, when Mary returned.

"We're goin' back to work," Mary announced.

"Girl, what kind of remedy Miss Eulalie give ya? It's makin' you say stupid talk."

"They're comin' to take down these boards. Only thing, it's my name on this crib now."

Beulah's face crinkled as if she were growing scared of Mary. Just then, a man with a deep mark encircling his eye rounded the corner, stopping to check the number on the crib. Taking a chisel that had been dangling from his belt loop, he loosened the boards, and one by one they clattered to the ground. He kicked them out of the way, then, with a nod to Mary, and a half nod to Beulah, he headed off. To Mary's amazement, Beulah was struck dumb.

"I'm droppin' your rent to two dollars a month, Beulah, but we're switchin' shifts. You get daylight and I get all night. Ya ain't gonna pay Lobrano no more. You're gonna pay me, first of every month. And quit lookin' at me like that. Ain't you never seen a peet daddy with a pussy?"

CHAPTER SEVEN

The Razzy Dazzy Spasm Band, which played
throughout the red light district

$\mathcal{F}$erdinand LaMenthe hunched over the old upright piano at Pete
Lala's Café. He was outfitted in his Sunday best, although he'd
removed his jacket and carefully hung it across a chair to ensure he'd
appear pressed for tonight.

Tonight. Ferdinand knew that just a couple of hours from now
he would embark on a momentous first, and he speculated that he'd
still speak of this night many years from now, recounting tales of
how, in his seventeenth year, he played before the highest of New
Orleans society.

He wasn't so much nervous for his debut as he was eager. His excitement had become so heightened it was prickly, and he'd been unable to keep himself still until he finally settled down to Pete Lala's piano. Even just the simple rituals, scooting the bench to the right distance for his lanky legs, positioning his foot on the pedal, and hovering his hands over the keys, instantly soothed the current sparking through him. His shoulders, which had been inching toward his ears, melted back, and his stomach settled the moment his fingers ran through a simple warm-up—a little jaunt around the cakewalk, as he liked to say in his best rag-talk.

Most evenings, when the customers thinned out from the café, Ferdinand was permitted to trail from Southern staples of minstrels and folk songs and work on his own music. Within the scope of a few moments, he would fully transform from lighthearted piano man to serious composer, pounding and twisting and painstakingly piecing together his original compositions. As was the case now: with creased forehead, he pressed the same three keys over and over, humming to himself as he struggled to make the piano perfectly match the music in his head. He leaned his ear closer to the keyboard, as if listening for the tiniest distinctions or as if he might hear something he hadn't noticed when he pressed the same key a second earlier.

It was amidst this relentless concentration that the rest of the world faded away, and, but for his attention to the piano, his other senses dulled into hibernation. Hours felt like minutes; hunger didn't exist. He heard nothing but the music. Within this space of just the instrument and him was where he found his true self: a jumble of pride and disgust. One moment impressed with his abilities, the next infuriated by his limitations, real or imagined.

A faraway voice called his name, and a wrinkle of irritation crossed his face as if he were absentmindedly flitting at the buzz of a fly. Only, the voice wasn't far away at all. "Ferd," it repeated, now gently demanding. After another moment or two: "Ferdinand LaMenthe, you listen up now."

Jarred, Ferdinand looked up, glassy-eyed. Standing in front of him, holding a steaming clay pot of red jambalaya cradled in a towel so as not to burn her hands, was Hattie Lala.

"Don't make me fuss at you to eat," she warned, setting the jambalaya on a nearby table.

Slowly reentering reality, Ferd caught himself twisting in what surely must have been a sour mug. But he quickly covered, not wanting Hattie to sense she'd disturbed him.

"Don't want you getting so thin you have to stand up twice to cast a shadow," she said.

"You betta listen to her, cap," added Pete, popping his head out from the kitchen.

Ferdinand looked from Hattie to the table, where the meal awaited him. Even though he was onto something in his composition, he forced himself to lean back from the keys, push away on the bench, and move to the table to eat. The Lalas had been good to him, and he mustn't be showing disrespect.

After all, it was Pete Lala who'd supplied Ferdinand with his very first musical opportunity—a paying gig. Sure, it was just playing to locals who stopped in for a hot meal between work shifts, but playing for patrons had given Ferdinand confidence. And the clientele seemed to enjoy the music, so much so that a coal seller told his wife about the fine playing, and she told the wealthy lady of the house who employed her as a servant, and the lady—whomever she might be—went on to inform a prominent judge of young Ferdinand's talent, and, lo and behold, an invitation showed up at the café, requesting Ferdinand to entertain at a fancy-dress party at the home of the Honorable J. Alfred Beares, senior judge of the Civil District Court of Orleans Parish. Tonight was the night.

Mindful not to muss himself, Ferdinand carefully spread a cloth napkin over as much of his pressed white shirt as it could cover and tucked a wide corner behind his collar. He then moved his face as close to the steamy bowl as he could get. The smoky aroma of andouille and beans met his nose, and he suddenly realized he was quite hungry after all, as if the composing had depleted him and the jambalaya was now warming him back to normal sensation, to the sights and smells of the little café and the hum of Pete and Hattie's chatter.

"Eat up," said Pete. "There's gonna be trays of food walking all around you at that party, and you aren't gonna be allowed any of it."

"Leave him be, Pete," Hattie scolded. Having no children of her own to flap over, she looked to Ferdinand with parental pride. "He's going tonight with the honor of playing, not eating."

Pete laughed. "They know how to get their money's worth, then."

Ferdinand smiled a mouth full of stew, knowing it was true— no matter that he was thin as a matchstick, he could eat as if there were five of him.

Pete untied his apron and retired it to a hook, then pulled a chair next to Ferdinand and sank onto it. "Ah, don't it feel good to sit for a minute," he sighed. "So, how's your composing coming along?"

Ferdinand forced his smile to remain. "Slowly," he said, hoping the subject wouldn't linger. "Doesn't matter for tonight, though. No one will be angling to hear my original works. I suspect common Dixieland will suit those fancy dans just fine."

"You're studying so hard," Pete said, "you're gonna be a professor of the piano one day soon."

Ferdinand looked up from his jambalaya. "I like that," he mused. "Professor of the piano."

But in return he got Pete's finger wagging in his face. "I said one day. Don't go getting big-headed now."

As Ferd scraped the last of the jambalaya, he began to feel his nerves kick up again. If he couldn't get back to his music to calm him, he could at least talk about it. He nodded to Pete. "You ever heard any of the greats play some rag? Now, those're the real professors of the piano."

"Don't believe I have," said Pete.

"I snuck into Frenchman's but once," Ferd said. "It's the late-night saloon at the corner of Bienville and Villere. You'd never know anything was happening there because by 'late-night,' they mean things don't get started until near four a.m.!" At this, Hattie gave a disapproving smirk from where she sat with a bucket of fresh shrimp, peeling then tossing them on a block of ice.

"So I went there to see Tony Jackson," Ferd continued. "Now, when Mistah Jackson walks through the door, anyone should get up from the piano stool, don't matter if you're Alfred Wilson or Albert Cahill or Kid Ross. Get up from that piano, you're hurting its feelings! Let Tony play. I should tell you, Tony is not a bit good-looking, but he is the single-handed greatest entertainer in the world."

"You'll be right smart too, Ferd," Hattie said dutifully.

Ferdinand smiled softly; he wished his own relations had offered up just an ounce of the Lalas' applause. Ferd's father had known Pete Lala since they were in short pants, and Pete had been at Ferdinand's christening. Pete was there, too, when Ferd's father was kicked out of the house after liquor ruined him.

But throughout the hard times, there was always music in the LaMenthe house, with instruments everywhere. Horns, harmonicas, a piano of course, drums, a steel guitar, a Jew's harp, even a zither, all having been collected by his mama, his grandmère, his godmother, and even Mimi, his great-grandmother. However, the patriarchs of the family held far less musical appreciation. More so, Ferd's stepdaddy didn't take kindly to him playing what he deemed "a lady's instrument" and threatened to throw Ferd out on his ear if he caught him at the piano. Ferd confided to Pete that he could no more stop playing than stop eating, and he did both to the extreme and with aplomb. And then Ferd's dear mama passed on to heaven.

It had been Ferd's hope when he and his little sister went to live with Grandmère that things would change, for Grandmère had been classically trained on the piano. But she was disinterested in Ferd's musical aspirations, unless they were classical or church related. He knew Grandmère meant no harm, but she feared if she encouraged his music, he'd wind up without an honest job, a carousing tramp like his father.

When Ferd, longing for an audience not seated in pews, had asked Pete if he could play that old piano, he happened not to mention that Grandmère wouldn't approve. Bricklayer, that was Grandmère's plan for him. But when patrons began to talk up Ferd, he finally confessed to Pete that he was there without Grandmère's knowledge. Reluctantly, the Lalas agreed not to say anything if they ran into her. Ferd was still surprised that word hadn't made it back to Grandmère through one Creole circle or another, although he was certain he'd know the moment she found out.

Pete, however, was hopeful that Ferd's grandmère would come around, and he couldn't help but ask if she knew of Ferd's honor that night.

Ferdinand sighed. "I'm still carryin' on as if I were employed to wash your dishes every night. She thinks any person showing off a talent in public is *common*."

"Oh, she'll get on over it," Pete reassured. "Your mama and papa, they'd have been mighty proud, that's for certain."

"Mama," said Ferd, "she was proud of me just for opening my eyeballs every morning."

The setting sun momentarily leveled with the front windows

and hit Ferd in a way that made him tear up—or maybe it was just that he missed his mother. She was famous for her colorful stories and was undoubtedly the source of Ferd's inherited gift of *yat*. He blinked away any tears before they could spill over, and resumed his talk as distraction.

"Papa? You knew the man better than that, Mistah Pete Lala! He played a mighty fine trombone, but blowin' on a brass horn's one thing. He was hardly different from my stepdaddy. Any man making piano music was a sissy cream puff to him. Surely I was meant to do more important things. . . ." Ferd trailed off as he suddenly realized the details of his father's face had grown blurry in his mind's eye.

Lala shifted uncomfortably, not having meant to stir up painful reminiscences. "Best get on," he said quickly. "On up to higher ground, where it's gonna be white as if it were snowin' in New Orleans."

Ferdinand wiped his mouth and rose from his seat, smoothing out his shirtsleeves. Hattie scurried over and, careful not to touch him with her shrimp-peel hands, gave an awkward but motherly hug. "I wrapped you a roll with jelly." She motioned to a sack waiting by Ferd's suit jacket.

Ferdinand was suddenly desperate to leave. He cascaded his jacket over his arm, plucked up the sack, and shuffled out the door. They waved after him, and he felt a bitter swell of emotion. He bit his bottom lip to suppress anything from bubbling to the surface. He wanted to feel nothing but the gentle breeze on his face. He crossed over Customhouse Street and headed in a direction he didn't normally go: uptown.

CHAPTER EIGHT

*a*s the setting sun peeked through the canopy of giant Southern live oaks dripping with Spanish moss, a pink sheen fell upon the regal columns and immaculate white brick of the Saint Charles Avenue mansion belonging to Judge J. Alfred Beares.

Ferdinand climbed the steps, then stood at the imposing front door, attempting to work up the nerve to knock. He breathed in the aroma of sticky sap and the lemon perfume of magnolias just starting to bloom—a welcome change from his part of town, where the only good smells came from someone's cooking.

His eyes fell upon a statue perched near the entrance: a female figure in a flowing Grecian robe holding a sword in one hand and dangling the scales of justice in the other. Ferd surmised that the judge must be a very serious fellow.

Reaching for his crimson silk handkerchief, he dabbed the sweat beads on his upper lip and forehead. The jambalaya began to churn in his stomach, and he chided himself for having eaten so ravenously before a big night like this. With a deep breath, he rapped the brass knocker.

As the door opened, Ferdinand snapped to attention. But he was surprised—and relieved—to see the pretty face of a young black maid.

"I'm playing the piano," Ferdinand blurted out.

The maid raised an eyebrow.

"I mean, I'm not playing the piano presently. I'm standing at the door. But tonight, at the party."

"Oh," she said, then dropped her voice. "You're s'posed to go 'round back, ya know."

'Round back was where the help entered, that much he did know. Apparently she didn't view him as the artist he thought he was.

Coyly, she glanced over her shoulders, and, seeing no one, she quickly beckoned him inside. He scooted in. Stepping foot in the foyer, he couldn't help but give an immediate awe-filled look around, his gaze moving from the lofty, scalloped ceilings, to the crystal chandeliers, to a wall-sized tapestry depicting a regal fox hunt.

"There's the piano," the maid said, pointing across the parlor.

Mouth agape, Ferdinand caught himself, realizing he'd forgotten the manners Grandmère spent years hammering into him. He refocused on the pretty maid. "Miss, sorry for my impoliteness. My name's Ferdinand LaMenthe."

She gave him a shy smile and a requisite nod but didn't return the introduction.

He took the opportunity to lean in closer, as if letting her in on a secret. "This is the fanciest gig I ever played," he said. "But don't tell no one, now."

Again she smiled, a coquettishness toying at the corners of her mouth. Unable to help it, Ferd rambled on, letting her know that he was a classically trained pianist. "Efficient on the violin and guitar, too," he added. "Not meaning to brag, but before I was even in short pants, I'd mastered playing the tin pan." He'd now made her giggle.

"Aw, don't worry none, Mistah LaMenthe," she said. "Them all be stupid drunk by half past. Won't care if ya's playing the piano or a kazoo."

Ferdinand was struck dumb. This was not quite the sentiment he was after. She offered a small curtsy, then scurried back to the kitchen. How piteous, Ferd thought. He mumbled to himself, *Even a blind hog can find an acorn.* No matter; he was here to play a piano, not a girl.

Stepping into the parlor, he ran his hand along a smooth marble chess table that sat between two imposing bear-claw chairs fit for monarchs. Above the fireplace, watching him with deep, unmoving eyes, was a gold-framed daguerreotype of the judge, dressed in his black robe, arms folded over his chest, a gavel in his hand. Ferdinand wondered if someday he might be affluent enough to have a likeness of himself presiding over his own house.

He arrived at a shiny, mahogany grand piano that took his breath away. Intricately carved fleur-de-lis decorated the piano's empire-style legs, while delicate Baroque paintings of scenes from operas graced the side panels and bench. He was almost too afraid to touch the piano. Inching forward, he brushed his long fingers across the fallboard before gingerly sliding onto the bench. He lifted the cover and hovered his hands above the keys and just under the gold nameplate that said it all: STEINWAY & SONS.

⚜

Oh, when the trumpet sounds its call
Oh, when the trumpet sounds its call
Lord, how I want to be in that number
When the trumpet sounds its call.

Ferdinand hummed the words to himself as he pounded out a lively "When the Saints Go Marching In" on the impeccable Steinway. It seemed strange to him to be playing "The Saints" when no one had died, but it was requested by an older white lady who seemed to be enjoying it heartily. Then again, it may have been the bottomless glass of Champagne in her hand that was raising her spirits. Either way, she'd made herself a fixture against the piano and was now leaning over Ferdinand to the point that the ribbons on her hat were dipping into her drink, while the tip of Ferd's nose was practically in her cleavage. It was hardly as if Ferd needed to look at the keys while he played, but that's exactly where he made sure to keep his gaze focused. "Oh, when the saints go marching in!"

The house was swollen with anyone who was anyone in New Orleans politics, business, and high-class white society. And at the center of it all was Judge Beares—hardly the austere man of his portrait. He waved a glass of bourbon as he gleefully held court.

"It's the Frogs, I tell ya!" he shouted, casting a shower of saliva on every poor soul within a few-foot radius. "They started this whole thing when they shipped us their heathens."

Fashionable men and women mechanically nodded as they shielded their Champagne glasses from the judge's spittle.

But one man was truly listening, and intently so: Alderman Sidney Story, who unabashedly plucked off his spectacles and wiped the saliva with his handkerchief. He vehemently shook his head. "While I agree, Judge, that was the origination of the problem, this plague of vice in our city is more complex than—"

Judge Beares interrupted him with a loud hiccup. Then he turned to address the others. "It's their offspring of lewd and abandoned women. Always comes back to the Frogs!"

Story was intent on having the judge's ear—and it was the reason he'd shown up tonight, uninvited—but he was becoming deeply concerned that his message was being corrupted by the steady clip at which Beares was ingesting his liquor.

"Indeed, Judge, their offspring are vermin," Story reinforced. "And just like any plague, we must confine the contaminated—"

"You can take the whore outta France," Beares said, mocking a French accent, "but you can't take the French"—he lewdly lifted and lowered his eyebrows—"outta the whore!" He cracked himself up, and his throng of admirers dutifully laughed along.

Alderman Story found none of this funny, and it would never occur to him to feign it. "Judge," he pushed, "may I count on you to join me in proposing containment of these vile Jezebels who entice men to immorality?"

Beares fidgeted as he reluctantly turned to address Story. He leaned in close enough that he could smell the alderman's hair tonic, spread thick across remaining strands that clung to his high, shiny forehead. "Alderman, this is not the time nor place to discuss your proclivity for a district of vice. You sound like an obsessed schoolgirl. Besides, hounding me at my own party isn't the way to change my mind." Beares hovered for a moment, wanting his words to sink in. "Now," he said, stepping back, "another one of these"—he held up his near empty glass—"that may do the trick!"

"But, Your Honor," Story persisted, "I have a duty to fulfill. The people of this city are looking to me to contain the wanton, the degenerate, and the diseased."

The judge turned askance—was it possible the alderman was still talking?

Story continued, "When Mayor Flower appointed me head of the Public Order Committee, I was given a mandate to lead this lost Southern flock. And that is my sole mission."

The judge glared back, serious now. "Get yourself a drink, Mistah Story. You are in dire need of one."

But for a sip of altar wine, Story didn't drink, and he was about to inform the judge of this, only he was interrupted by one Mr. Smithson, the cousin of a wealthy New Orleans plantation owner, who'd traveled from Georgia just for this party.

"Pardon me, Judge, may I take a moment?" Smithson asked.

"Please," Beares pleaded. "Where were you twenty minutes ago?"

"Without meaning to be rude . . ." Smithson began. The judge burped. Already, Beares wasn't liking the sound of this conversation either—why must his guests be so darn uptight? It was a *party*, after all.

Smithson continued, "There is a person present who is inappropriately making eyes at my wife. Under other circumstances, this may serve to flatter me, but . . . this man is a Negro."

Beares confusedly scanned the room, looking out over the sea of powdery white faces.

Leaning in, Smithson said in an enunciated whisper, "The pianist."

Beares slowly turned his round body toward the music. There, at the piano, was Mrs. Smithson, marching bawdily to "The Saints" and spilling herself and her drink all over the piano player.

"Ferd-i-nand," Mrs. Smithson slurred loudly, "I like that name." Other nearby guests cast withering, sideways glances at the spectacle.

Beads of sweat covered Ferdinand's upper lip, and he ached to reach for his handkerchief, but he didn't dare take his fingers or eyes from the piano keys. "Thank you, ma'am," Ferdinand politely responded. "Was chosen by my godmother. Christened me after the king of Spain. But the king was worthless. Everyone knew the power was with the queen."

Mrs. Smithson cooed and fanned herself, dribbling some drink on the piano. Ferdinand flinched—not the Steinway!

Across the room, Beares reluctantly turned back to Mr. Smithson. "Ah yes," Beares said with a deep breath, "I *see*."

"Judge, you must instruct your Negroes on proper decorum. I don't proclaim to know what's acceptable or not in New Orleans, but where I come from, such behavior can put your entire reputation at stake."

"Yes, yes," Beares sighed wearily. "I'll go handle her . . . him."

With a grunt, Beares made his way over to the piano. "Mrs. Smithson," he gushed, taking her hand and kissing it, "so glad to see you're enjoying yourself."

"Isn't it a divine evenin', Judge?" she chittered.

"Yes, well, my dear, your husband's been looking all over for you." He nudged her away from the piano.

"Toodle-loo," she said with a silly wave to Ferdinand.

Ferd looked to the judge, embarrassed for the woman. Beares inflated his cheeks and then slowly blew out the air. "You know, kid, you got real talent on that piano. I mean it, real talent."

"Thank you, sir. I never dreamed I'd play on a Steinway. It takes my breath away."

Beares started to answer, then decided against it and instead pulled a wad of cash from his vest. "Such stellar playing, I think we're all done for the night."

Ferdinand's fingers halted. Perplexed, he looked to the judge.

Beares leaned in. "I'm gonna be honest with ya, kid. Some of our guests—the stuffy, pigheaded ones with no ear for music—well, they got a problem with a Negro man talking to their wife."

"Sir," Ferdinand said, confused, "I'm a Creole—"

"Yes, but they don't know that in Georgia."

He shoved the cash into Ferdinand's jacket and waved over the young black maid. "Show this good man out. And give him a pint for the road."

She dutifully curtsied, her eyes darting to Ferdinand with a touch of sympathy. She watched as he stiffly pushed himself back from the piano, a mere shadow of the eager young man she'd met at the door just hours earlier.

Judge Beares quickly removed himself from the unjust scene. What a shame, he thought, that others saw color so markedly. He, personally, found no harm in colored Creoles mixing with whites—Creoles had European heritage, after all, just the same as he. Just the same as Smithson. Still, there was no point in making issue; in Smithson's world, as in the rest of the South, a man was either white or he wasn't. It was New Orleans that had blurry vision.

The grandfather clock in the foyer chimed ten, just as Beares felt a hand on his back. What *now*? It was his butler, his head bowed.

"Judge, a guest be waitin' in the foyer."

"Well, show him in."

The butler cleared his throat. "Judge, *she* be waitin' in the foyer."

Beares felt a sudden pang of heartburn. He thrust his empty glass at the butler and hurried to the foyer.

There awaited precisely whom he'd feared: Countess Lulu White, cinched into an ivory corseted dress and ablaze in diamonds. Dramatically, she removed her mink stole and flashed the judge a perfectly disingenuous smile.

"Didn't know you were hosting a soiree, *mon cher*," she said, her tone silky yet biting at the same time.

"Oh . . . my . . . uh . . ." Beares stuttered, then lowered his voice. "You're early."

The Countess brought a monocle to her right eye, which intensified her glare. "Then you have plenty of time to introduce me 'round."

Beares halfheartedly chuckled at what must surely have been the Countess's attempt at a joke. But she expectantly stared at him in an unblinking way that only the Countess could pull off, making the judge squirm even more. "Why don't you go on upstairs and wait for me," he offered. She raised an eyebrow in return, and Beares tried to soothe her with a deep, hushed snarl. "I sure can't wait for you."

All this while, Alderman Story had been strategically eyeing the judge. When he'd noticed that Beares had left the parlor, Story swiftly meandered his way through the crowd, plotting that this would be the perfect opportunity to corner the judge and reinforce his mission. But as Story approached the foyer, he froze at the sight of the garishly dressed, flame-haired, white-powdered octoroon. There was no questioning what walk of life the flashy woman inhabited. Story let out a gasp and instinctively averted his gaze. "Christ forgive you," he blurted.

From the corner of his eye, Beares spotted Story, and, as it quickly sunk in that the situation looked as compromising as it actually was, Beares began to flutter like a fly trapped in a jar. He batted Lulu away, not caring that she balked—she, of all people, didn't take kindly to being shooed.

"Alderman, you're not leaving so soon, are you?" Beares pandered, his voice nervously loud. He hurried over and threw his arm around Story's slight shoulders. "Come back to the party!" Story was stiff as a board as Beares tried to chummily usher him toward the parlor. "Oh, it's always something with the *help*," Beares flouted. He gave a snide shake of his head in Lulu's direction. "They should be called the help*less*, don't you agree, Alderman?"

The judge's words pierced Lulu like a hornet's sting. She watched Beares waddle out of sight, staring cold and hard after him before she finally retreated upstairs.

Upon his exit from the parlor, Ferdinand had been led by the pretty young maid through the kitchen, where a dozen other servants bustled about. Word spread fast among the black domestics of the household, and they looked away as Ferd walked through, thinking maybe if they didn't notice him they could pretend his ousting hadn't really happened. The maid opened the back door leading to the stables and the alley, and the joyous sounds from the party silenced as the door closed behind him.

Ferdinand set off in the thick night air. As he walked, he twisted his crimson handkerchief, rolling his fingers across it as if it were a string of rosary beads. But instead of going home, he crossed over the neutral ground and headed to Rampart Street.

Opening the back door of the cigar shop, he carefully stepped over a line of brick dust at the threshold, meant to keep bad spirits from entering. He found Eulalie Echo with her hand dunked in a jar, grasping at the swimming turtle. She didn't look up at the sound of someone entering, but instead, nabbed the turtle and pulled the flailing creature from the water.

"Ferdinand," she greeted him, still not looking his way.

He watched as she positioned the turtle on its shell and, with a slender knife and a steady hand, sliced open its soft belly. She delicately removed the turtle's heart and held it up.

"*Cowein?*" she offered.

Ferdinand grimaced. But Eulalie just shrugged, the boy didn't know what he was missing. She rolled the heart in a yellow powder and tossed it into a kettle warming on a little coal stove.

"You sensing anythin' fixed about me tonight?" Ferdinand pointedly asked.

Eulalie did a quick once-over, then, with a judgmental crinkle of her forehead, she returned to her concoction, crushing dried leaves and sprinkling them in.

"Godmother," he impatiently coaxed, "be serious here. They were all having a real good time. My ragtime was tight."

Eulalie stirred the kettle. "And now," she said, "Eulalie's secret ingredient." She took a bottle of brandy from a warped shelf and generously poured some into the kettle. Then she took a hefty swig herself. Wiping her mouth with the back of her hand, she offered the bottle to Ferdinand, and this, finally, registered a note of approval. He swallowed some down then looked at her intensely.

"Called me a Negro." His jaw tightened at the words.

"Step back," Eulalie ordered as if she hadn't heard a thing he'd said.

He took a step back as Eulalie tossed a match into the kettle, igniting a leaping flame that nearly singed his eyebrows. Ferdinand jumped back. "Sweet baby Jesus! You with all this hoodoo!"

Eulalie swiped her hands through the flames. "It's the Jim Crow jubilee," she hissed.

"I know what happens on a streetcar. But I was there tonight as a professor of the piano."

"You were there as someone used to passin'," Eulalie confuted. She covered the kettle to stifle the fire. "You ain't never felt what it's like to be unfree in the land o' the free."

Ferd rubbed his temples from all this roundabout talk. Eulalie was Haitian, so of course he couldn't expect her to fully appreciate the higher standing of a Creole. He sank onto a chair, and Eulalie glanced at him, lines darting from her thin lips as she pursed them.

"Don't go lookin' like the feathers have been plucked from the peacock's tail. It ain't all over."

"I've been having such dark spells lately," Ferd sighed, resting his head in his hands.

"You're just comin' into your talent is all," Eulalie said as she dunked a ladle into the boiling kettle.

"Then why does it feel like something's not right, like I have too much darkness in my mind?"

Eulalie ladled out two copper cups and handed one to Ferd. He hesitantly took it.

"Ferdinand, everythin's got two parts. You think your talent be solely the grace of God? Naw, my son, there's gotta be a spark o' the Devil to make it smolder like that. I saw to it."

Her words didn't console him. Instead, prickly shivers climbed up his spine. "What does that mean?" he asked. "You and the Devil had a little talk about me?"

"It means to trust in Eulalie Echo, who always does what's best for you."

Eulalie raised her cup. "Say a prayer," she instructed.

Ferdinand's stomach churned at the notion of praying to a Voodoo god; and yet, it was his feet that had brought him here. His mother had believed wholeheartedly in Eulalie's powers; his Papa had detested the crazy-eyed bat. Ferdinand hated that he languished in the middle—detesting yet craving her magic. It was almost as if she had a spell over him, drawing him back each time he swore not to return.

She stared at him with her focused amber eye as her steaming cup hovered in the air, waiting for his to rise so they could join in prayer. Slowly, he lifted his cup.

"*He-ron mande. He-ron mande,*" she chanted. "*Do se dan, do-go.* Stand proud, Ferdinand. Mistah Crow will come and go. *Canga ki, canga li.* Now drink."

She gulped down her cup, while Ferdinand stared at the muddy broth, hoping his own personal darkness would one day pack up and go as well.

"Drink, child!" Eulalie commanded, as if the spell wouldn't seal until he'd ingested the concoction.

Wincing, he forced himself to knock it back. It tasted like twigs and castor oil and burned on the way down.

CHAPTER NINE

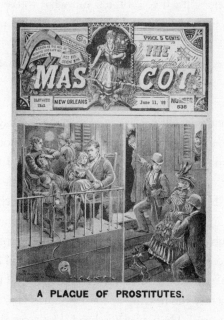

A PLAGUE OF PROSTITUTES.

The last of the party guests had finally trickled out from the judge's mansion—that is, all but for Alderman Sidney Story. The judge had successfully maneuvered Story to the door, but had yet to figure out how to get him through it without a shove.

"Voting for containment is the only realistic answer, Judge—"

"If there's a God in heaven, enough, Alderman. Please, just let a man enjoy the soothing effects of his liquor at this late hour."

Story's eyes were steely. "Surely my plan to control vice in this city is slightly more important than Your Honor's degree of crapulence."

At this, Beares seemed to inflate, his eyes, his cheeks growing wide with fury. He'd been bumbling around like an obsequious idiot, trying to save face with the alderman, but now he'd had it. "You, sir, have long overstayed your welcome! And you know what else you've done? I'll tell you, I'll tell you what you've done. You've strengthened my resolve, thank you very much. You know what that means?"

Story cowered, not even venturing to blink at the spit cascading over his face.

"It means," Beares continued, pushing an index finger into Story's chest, "that you will *not* have my vote on Monday! Now, once and for all, good night!" He slammed the door in Story's face.

Story blinked back his disbelief as he eyeballed the big brass door knocker. Just then, he heard from inside a high-pitched wail: "My lovely! Oh where are you?" Story felt his stomach lurch. With trembling hands, he pulled a worn Bible from his breast pocket. He quickly thumbed through the pages, reaching the passage he desired. He read aloud: "'I know your works, your toil and your patient endurance, and how you cannot bear evil men. I know you are enduring patiently and bearing up for my name's sake, and you have not grown weary.'" He bowed his head. His voice quivered with fierceness. "Lord, my Lord, I have not grown weary!"

It was, indeed, that the door had barely clicked shut before the judge was bolting up the stairs just as fast as his stubby, drunken body could take him, undoing the buttons of his vest along the way.

"Count-tess," he called, singsongy. "Where are you, my sumptuous peach?"

As he rounded the balustrade, he caught sight of Lulu striking a sparkly pose at the end of the hall.

"*Mon cher,*" she cooed. "I was beginning to think you'd forgotten I was banished up here all alone."

"Oh, my peach, out of sight but hardly forgotten." He caught a whiff of her jasmine perfume and grinned devilishly. "It's time!"

"What time is that, Your Honor?" she responded drolly, trying to muster the energy to play along.

"Judgment time!" he shouted and broke chase, running down the hall toward her, the chandeliers on the ceiling below shaking and clinking under his weight.

Lulu dashed into the master suite, ducking behind a Japanese folding screen. The judge, licking his lips, watched her silhouette as she peeled off her gloves then began undoing her dress, swirling her hips to punctuate the pop of each button. Beares hung on every gesture of Lulu's well-rehearsed performance. And he giggled like a schoolgirl when she finally dropped her dress.

"Now I take off all my clothes," he announced, "because I've been baaaaad!" He struggled his way out of his jacket and stomped off his pants. Once naked, he lifted a white barrister's wig from a drawer and fit it onto his balding head. He was now ready for her.

On cue, Lulu stepped from behind the screen. Only, she wasn't naked, but instead wore all her jewels and a long black judicial robe. "Order! Order!" she shouted. The judge quivered at the sight of her.

From a shiny wood box, she ceremoniously removed a gavel, then tapped it against the palm of her hand, as if deliberating.

"Ooh, what's my sentence, Judge?" Beares asked, his grin growing wider.

Lulu stepped close to him, and he could smell the opium on her breath. Only, she wouldn't let him touch her. Instead, she reached out with the gavel, pinning it against his chest. She backed him through the French doors and onto the balcony. "Let the punishment fit the crime," she said. She leaned Beares over the banister and with a swift motion of the gavel, spanked his bare ass.

"Oh, Judge, mercy!" Beares yawped.

"You, the accused and condemned, must do penance as ordered by the Countess, your sensuous lover."

"Yes, my sensuous peach!" he wailed. "My savage!"

She spanked him again. "Your sensuous lover has been devoted to your every wish and whim for many a year now."

Spank.

"Oh yes," he cried, "you've been a mighty fine fuck."

At this, Lulu stopped. Her face hardened. "Have I pleased you, *Master*?" she asked icily, straying from their well-worn script. "That's what my mama would have been forced to ask."

"Mercy, Judge!" Beares cried, oblivious to the change in Lulu.

Her eyes narrowed. "Mercy, Master," she said. She felt her fingers tighten around the gavel. "Only, my mama wasn't wearing diamonds." She spanked him again, this time, quite hard.

Beares craned to look at her. "Now, that hurt, whore."

Good, thought Lulu, glaring back. But Beares simply gave her a wink then turned back into position, shaking his pale, dimpled ass to indicate he was ready to receive his next spanking.

Lulu glowered at his hideous backside—not that his gluttonous front side was any more appealing. For years they'd played this stupid game, and every time he was as thrilled as a child on Christmas morning. She smirked. What an idiot. He'd laid his blubbery body next to hers how many times now? Hundreds? But, she wondered, did he even know a single thing about her? Did he know she was fluent in four languages? Did he know she owned a library of books, all of which she'd read? Did he know she was an avid art collector who'd traveled the world in search of the finest paintings? Did he know that despite her roots she'd made all this of herself? Of course not. It had been years, and he knew her not at all. He'd never asked about her. He'd only asked for spankings, and that she, the so-called *help*, seclude herself upstairs so that none of the society folks at his party would see his dirty little secret—when, Lord knew, half the men at the party were themselves patrons of Lulu's bordello.

"Ohh, Juh-uhdge," Beares impatiently sang out. "What's my next se-e-en-tence?"

A look of repulsion fell like a veil over Lulu. She steadied him with her foot, grasping the gavel now with both hands. She wound back her arms, then let go a mighty swat that lurched the judge straight through the railing of the balcony.

He snorted a part laugh, part gasp. And then, a heavy thud.

For a second, all was silent, as if the night were holding its breath. Then came a puny voice from below. "A little harsh."

Lulu peered over the balcony at the prostrate judge.

"Help me up," he called.

She smoothed her hair and adjusted her jewels. "I thought you knew," she replied. "Good help is hard to find."

The crickets' chirring wound down as a faint orange glow crept over the white bricks of the Saint Charles Avenue mansion. For a long moment it was quiet and peaceful, just as it was on any given dawn. And then, shattering the tranquility, came a pop followed by a spectacular white flare.

A photographer reapplied a line of flash powder and positioned his 4 x 5 camera over the body of Judge Beares, lying ass-up in the grass, still wearing the barrister wig, his head cocked around and a smile lingering on his pale lips.

Just as the photographer was about to shoot again, a hand snatched the cable release from his grasp. Startled, he spun around to find Police Inspector O'Connor.

"I'll be damned if this tragedy turns into a three-ring circus. Now get the photographic camera out of here!"

The photographer sullenly backed away, just as a team of uniformed officers moved in to form a blockade around the body. No sooner did a swarm of newspapermen descend, suddenly buzzing about like bees from an overturned hive.

"For feck's sake," O'Connor muttered to himself, "is there ever such a thing as hush-hush in this town?" He was relieved to see the ambulance, drawn by a brown mare, pull up. Out piled four crew with a stretcher and a white sheet. In but a few minutes, Beares, barrister wig and all, disappeared into the back of the ambulance wagon and was carted away.

"Inspector, can you declare what has taken place here?" a reporter called out. Then another: "Was it murder?" And another: "Suicide?"

O'Connor grimaced, knowing he wasn't getting out of here without a statement. Fine, then, he'd say something so they'd shut their yaps. He cleared his throat and the crowd immediately quieted, looking to him with pencils poised. "I can verify that the body was indeed that of Judge J. Alfred Beares. An upstandin' citizen, yes he was. Our Judge Beares, for all his righteous work on behalf of the city of New Orleans, will be missed." At this, he turned on his heel, but the reporters jumped at him.

"Inspector O'Connor!" One reporter's voice cut above the clamor. It was McCracken of the *Mascot*, in his ever-present bowler hat. "Is it true the Judge held a party last night that was attended by disreputable denizens?"

The crowd hushed. Again, O'Connor cleared his throat. "'Twas a fancy-dress party was all. High society."

"How about one particular *lady of the evening*?" McCracken pushed. "Refers to herself, ironical as it may seem, as 'The Countess'?"

"Nothing at all of that sort has been verified at this time, presently," the inspector said, adding his most convincing nod.

Another reporter piped up. "Inspector, any evidence of foul play?"

"This is last and final, and what I know for sure," O'Connor declared. The crowd collectively leaned in. "Criminality isn't a factor in this case." He stretched out his arm to point overhead. All eyes followed the direction of his hand, landing on the splintered rails of the second-floor balcony. "See?" he said, shaking his head at the unfortunate circumstances. "It was just a rotten railin'."

CHAPTER TEN

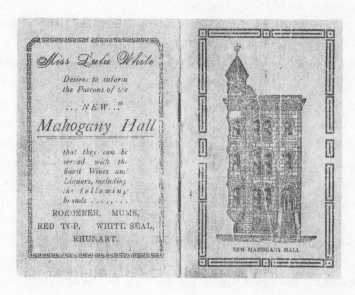

From the front, Countess Lulu White's bordello looked fast asleep, but around back the kitchen was aglow and full of hustle-bustle as Addie, the head servant, her hair wrapped in a kerchief and an apron crossed over her plump figure, shuffled about.

A few hours earlier, Addie had heard rumblings outside and roused herself enough to peek from the window of her attic bedroom. In the back courtyard, where the carriages were parked, she saw a veiled Lulu step from a paddy wagon. Oh, what's Miss Lulu up to now? she'd wondered. It wasn't every day that the Countess got a ride in a paddy wagon. She watched as Lulu handed the policeman a roll of cash and gave his cheek a little pat.

Not more than a couple minutes later did Addie hear the tinkling of the bell summoning her. She made a beeline down the servants' stairs to the kitchen, slapping her face all the way in an effort to appear awake for her employer.

She was instructed that guests were expected. At this hour? But her place wasn't to question. She roused her teenaged daughter, Boo, who stumbled about like a drunken sailor as she changed from her nightclothes. Addie got the kitchen warm and humming, with coffee brewing and three snifters buffed and arranged on a silver tray. In the wine cellar, she pulled out the step stool and selected from the top shelf the Countess's favorite: aged *framboise eau-de-vie*. She knew the top-shelf liquor was only to be used for visits from esteemed guests or for very good or very bad occasions. She thought it safe to bet that tonight—ah, this morning, already—met at least two of these prerequisites, though she hadn't yet a sense of which two. With a knife, she slit the bottle's sealing wax, and a strong aroma tinged with raspberry tickled her nose. She made sure to pour equally among the three glasses, and then turned to Boo to deliver the tray.

Poor Boo, she'd fallen asleep at the kitchen table, her bent arm barely able to support the weight of her drooping head.

"Wake up now," Addie said gently. "Ain't no time for makin' sleep."

The girl barely stirred. "Boo!" Addie said with a stomp of her foot, and her daughter jumped, then looked around, confused.

"Go bring this brandy over by the Countess."

"Ain't it too early for drink?" Boo asked groggily.

"Oh no, not too early a'tall. Not when somethin' big's goin' on. Big an' bad, I think. The Countess, she come in the back door, trying to be quiet as a mouse, and now she's up there with Mistah Anderson and the mayor. I saw them come through the back door too."

Boo's eyes widened; she was awake now.

Addie carefully handed off the tray. "Remember, be quiet as you can," she instructed. "Don't go lookin' any of them in the eye, and then make haste." Before releasing her daughter, she straightened the girl's collar and smoothed back her hair. "Awright, go on."

Boo delicately carried the tray up the narrow servants' staircase, down a long carpeted hall, and arrived to the drawing room. The door was closed, but it neglected to stifle the sound of voices that seemed loud and angry.

"This is exactly what they've been waiting for," a man said, "and you just up and hand it to them on a silver tray."

Boo looked to her own silver tray. Definitely not the right moment to enter. She stepped back, propping herself against the wall. She counted to a hundred, then carefully balanced the tray as she opened the door and, as light on her feet as she could be, slipped in.

The drawing room was smoky and dark, the thick velvet drapes tightly drawn. There was a chill, despite the crackling hearth, and the fire cast strange, flickering shadows across the walls that were lined with shelves of books.

Lulu—still in her ivory dress—reclined on a chaise longue. She took a deep inhale from a gold, foot-long cigarette holder.

Tom Anderson, a cigar in hand, paced the room. Gonna wear a groove in that beautiful rug the Countess brought from the Orient, Boo thought.

"Here I was, shaking like a dog shittin' razors," Anderson said. "So I order the raid, and turns out, that heart attack, he was no one. A nobody. After all that! So I'm in the clear and sleeping soundly every night, and now . . . this? Dear Countess, did you have to throw his ass over? Couldn't you just have . . . bitten his ass?"

If Lulu was straining to remain calm, no one would have ever noticed, for her voice came out as controlled as if she were talking about the weather. "Tom, I don't bite people's derrieres. I may be many things, but I am not a savage."

"My dear Countess," Anderson replied, "you say that as if there's something wrong with a woman possessing a little savage."

The mayor reddened as he noticed young Boo. "Whoo, a bit hot in here," he said, abashedly fanning himself. He was stuffed into a leather ball-and-claw armchair, his stubby legs barely touching the floor.

But Boo was used to bawdy talk. Undaunted, she set down the tray then swiftly backed out of the room, quietly turning the doorknob until she heard it click into place.

Lulu reached for a glass, swirled it under her nose. She smiled at Addie's fine, and calculated, choice—*premiere qualité*.

Anderson continued, "Surely, a woman of your intelligence is aware of the consequences of manslaughter—that is, when it's a man of such esteem."

Lulu, never one for being clumsy, nearly spilled her drink. *Manslaughter?* She quickly busied herself with her cigarette as her mind raced. Dramatically, she took a long inhale—Beares had expired? How could that be? She exhaled slowly, slowly—she'd seen him, talked to him. Bruised, maybe. A broken limb at worst. Wouldn't all that flesh have cushioned the fall? Or perhaps the bastard had been too drunk to realize he was injured? Certainly her intent had never been manslaughter; she would have opted for a balcony higher than the second floor if that had been her desired outcome.

She quickly halted her thoughts. Anderson and the mayor mustn't know she'd blundered this horrendously. "*Mon pigeon,*" she said with steely calm. "You were saying?"

"I was saying," Anderson continued, "that all actions do have consequences, and the most notable consequences in this case will be the *unintended* ones."

Lulu funneled all her strength into showing no sign of weakness—no sweat, no quiver, no flinch. Although she knew that if anyone could see through her it was Tom Anderson. She eyed him from over her snifter as she slowly sipped, anything to distract her, and him. She'd known Tom for nearly fifteen years now, and they'd always had a harmonious and respectful working relationship. Never had he berated her like this before, and in front of the mayor no less. After all, they were on the same side, their interests aligned, so what was the point of this preaching? Sure, she'd heard the infamous stories of Anderson's wrath when crossed—everyone in the Underworld had—and most of the stories were advertised by Anderson himself. But she hadn't crossed him. She had done nothing to him but be a loyal business partner.

"Just so I'm clear, Tom," she piped up, "how many consequences shall I be anticipating? Intended or otherwise."

The mayor relished this contest of words between two of the slickest tongues in New Orleans.

It was Anderson's turn. He paused to suck on his cigar, releasing the smoke into the air in one . . . two . . . three perfect rings. He replied, "There is but one consequence that's especially noteworthy."

At this, Lulu pushed her hand to the sky. "*Zut alors!*" The unflappable Countess was beginning to ruffle.

To Anderson, this was a minor triumph, and the joy danced in his eyes. "Oh yes," he continued, "the unintended consequence will have serious effects on the *demimonde*."

The mayor's head bobbed to Lulu, it was her turn to fire. But she'd be damned if she was going to play this game any further. She would not speak another word. Anderson seemed not to notice and amused himself by blowing more smoke rings. The ticking clock echoed.

Finally, Flower could take it no longer. "What, Tom, for Chrissake, what the flyin' fig are these consequences?"

A grin percolated on Anderson's face. "You see, after tomorrow, the Underworld isn't gonna be the Underworld anymore." Lulu's eyes narrowed on him. "Alderman Sidney Story is going to take full advantage of the death of his adversary. With the judge gone, Story's going to push through the ordinance for a legal district of vice. And he's gonna do it quick. Real quick! Get it passed before a new judge is appointed."

Flower gasped. "Tom, you're right!"

"The alderman's mission in life is to relegate all lewd and abandoned women to the back o' town. Well, Countess, Mayor, I do believe we're sitting in the back o' town."

Flower slapped his plump thigh. "Jambalaya and a side of pecan pie, I never thought this would happen!"

Lulu silently fumed at Anderson for playing her as he had. Dear Lord, for a moment there he had her worried that maybe her standing with the police wasn't as solid as she'd thought. Here she was expecting him to inform her that she was to be charged or carted off to jail, when all this time he was practically bursting with *good* news. She downed the rest of her drink as he blathered on.

"We've got the country's most sensual city, and it's time we make outsiders privy to all this decadence. Let them come with their bulging wallets and indulge."

"Oh yes, I like the sound of that," the mayor squealed.

"All types of folks will promenade to New Orleans, be them military folks, gambling folks, hell, even churchgoing folks."

"Churchgoing folks?" Flower asked.

"My dear Mayor, folks will drop to their knees and pray at the altar of good times."

"The altar of good times!" Flower giggled. "I'll swan!"

"We're gonna turn red lights into bright lights!" Anderson said, then turned to Lulu with a quizzical look. "Do you find any of this interesting, Countess? It's rather life-changing for you, don't you think?"

"It is a very interesting twist of fate, indeed," she said. "Although, I must inform you, the back o' town isn't going to be the back o' town for much longer." She watched as a groove formed in the middle of Anderson's brow. "Wouldn't you know," she chuckled. "Now it is I who has a secret."

A wry grin played on Anderson's lips. He gave her a bow to proceed.

"There's no need in making you go around your elbow to get to your thumb," she said with a barbed smile, "and I'm far above asking you gentlemen to play a child's guessing game, so I'll get right to the point."

Flower craned forward, his belly bulging.

"I know for a fact," Lulu continued, "the Southern Railway's coming."

"Not anytime soon," the mayor bemoaned. "Oh, the red tape! And trust me, I've incentivized. For two years I've been bending over backward, even spoke with Mistah J.P. Morgan himself."

Lulu flicked her cigarette ash. "Perhaps you've just been bending the wrong way."

"Do tell, Countess," Anderson said.

"Oh," she replied offhandedly. "A lovely gentleman I know. He visits town occasionally. It's his signature you need. And you're getting it."

At that, Flower slipped from his chair and plopped onto the floor. "It's happening!" He salivated. "This railroad will be my legacy!"

Lulu added, "He also happened to inquire about a suitable location for the new depot."

Anderson couldn't help but laugh to himself, what a spitfire she was. "Shall I venture to guess you suggested smack fucking dab on Basin Street?"

Lulu lifted her chin with satisfaction. "Whores will be waving hello every time that train whistle blows." She looked at Flower, red-faced and still on the floor. "Puts some hot pepper in your jambalaya, don't it, Mayor?"

Lulu watched as the fire's last embers flaked away. Alone now, she'd banished the servants and hadn't moved from her perch on the chaise longue since Anderson and Flower had left some hours earlier. Her makeup was smudged and the silk of her dress had grown stretched and misshapen. The bottle of *eau-de-vie* had long since been drained. Dragging herself up, she trudged upstairs and locked the door with a large iron key. The morning sunlight streamed in through the tall cathedral windows. She squinted as she pulled the heavy damask draperies, plunging the bedroom into darkness but for a flickering sconce, its flame nestled within dribbled layers of wax. She didn't deserve the warm sun right now, she thought.

She melted onto the velvet chair at her dressing table. Her movements were lethargic as she unclasped her diamond earrings, setting them aside. She wiped away what was left of her caked lip rouge and her white face powder. She pulled off her thick eyelashes and they fluttered to the ground like dead butterflies. She unpinned her fire-colored wig to reveal her own dark, matted hair underneath.

By the faint light, she stared into the mirror. The Countess had disappeared. What was left stared back, unrecognizable. *Who am I? Madam or murderer?* She had made sure that everyone who mattered had been paid off and that all the proper channels had been taken care of. Now she should pray for Beares's soul. She, the illegitimate child of a slave. Her father, the rich, white master—himself educated in law—had killed many of her people. Maybe this was an odd sort of retribution. Or worse, she feared, she had inherited his cold blood.

CHAPTER ELEVEN

Young newsboys in New Orleans

"Extra, extra! Hot off the press!"

At the fountain of the Saint Louis Cathedral, its regal steeples glowing in the sun, a newsboy waved the *Mascot* as scores of riled-up townspeople threw him pennies and nickels even, not caring about the change. Hungrily, they grabbed the paper, which boasted a half-page headline:

WAS PILLAR OF SOCIETY SLAIN BY SHAMEFUL LOVER-WHORE?

Next door, within the Spanish arches of the Cabildo—where, ninety-four years earlier, the Louisiana Purchase had been signed—a meeting was about to be called to order. Alderman Story could have requested no better location in the city for the monumental announcement he was about to make. Pacing with anticipation, he watched as men crowded in until the Cabildo was packed shoulder to shoulder.

When the church bells sounded the nine o'clock hour, Story proudly stepped to the podium. He surveyed the boisterous crowd, waiting for them to quiet, and noted among them: numerous businessmen who'd contributed to his fundraising efforts, each of the six men serving under him on the Public Order Committee, a red-faced Mayor Flower, and his priest, Father Montague.

"Gentlemen, gentlemen, please," Story said, trying to call the room to order. But his mousy voice hardly rose above the din.

A shout came from the crowd. "These whores are polluting our fine neighborhoods!"

"Yes, and I appreciate y'all gathering—" Story began, but he was quickly overtaken by another shout.

"They're corrupting our children's pure minds!" Calls of agreement filled the room. Story feebly stomped his foot and rapped his palm against the podium, but the crowd ignored him. Finally, one of the men of the Public Order Committee came to his aid, stepping up onto a chair and booming, "Let the room come to order!"

A prominent vein on Story's high forehead pulsed with frustration as the room at last quieted. "Gentlemen," Story began again, "I appreciate you attending this emergency meeting on such short notice, and I promise we'll all get to church on time." He paused, making certain he reveled in the moment. "We've been talking and talking about this, and in light of last night's events, we're now going to do something about it. But first, please join me in commending the fine investigation of Mister McCracken, who exposed this abhorrence." Story dramatically held up the *Mascot* and motioned to the front row, where Kermit McCracken, bowler hat in hand, nodded to the erupting applause.

"Thank you, Alderman," McCracken said. He turned to face the room. "Gentlemen, my story is my truth. A source who had attended the good judge's party suggested to me that a certain woman of ill repute arrived to the judge's house around the hour of ten last night. Curious as I was, I made it my business to be stationed at this woman's residence and place of business in the wee hours of the subsequent morning. What I saw was astounding." McCracken felt the weight of the men's anticipation. "One Miss Lulu White was escorted to her den of sin by none other than our New Orleans police department. She stepped from a paddy wagon as if it were her personal carriage and handed an officer a roll of cash, even touched his cheek with affection."

Hisses and groans arose from the crowd. Story and McCracken exchanged a meaningful glance as McCracken retreated back into the crowd.

"When our city's protectors side with derelicts and diseased whores," Story declared, "this, my friends, is corruption in its most evil and despicable form." He cast a wary look at the mayor. "Don't you agree, Mayor Flower?"

All heads turned to focus on the mayor. Noticeably sweaty and uncomfortable, Flower gave a forced nod.

"First it's the judge. Which one of us God-fearing men is next?" an onlooker shouted.

Story quickly continued, fearful he'd lose control of the room again. "Now, I can institute fines," he said as powerfully as he could muster, "but those whores will just pay them. And I can institute jail time, but those whores will bribe their way through. I can stand here and proclaim prostitution more illegal than it already is, but I can't make it unpopular. And that, gentlemen, is the blasphemous reality!"

Father Montague stepped forward, a picture of calm reason, and the room respectfully quieted. "We must set boundaries to keep our neighborhoods safe from vice," he instructed.

"Thank you, Father," Story said, but the priest held up an index finger—he wasn't finished. "And," he continued, his voice more forceful, "these boundaries will protect our property from devaluing."

Story pursed his thin lips. Even his priest had an agenda. "Thank you, Father," he dutifully repeated.

"Alderman," a man bellowed from the crowd. "Send them whores to the back o' town!" Yips of agreement followed.

Another called out, "Put 'em in the back o' town, not next door to us, and not on high ground!"

From this, a chant arose, embracing the room: "Back o' town! Back o' town!"

Story gritted his teeth. The back o' town was his plan, his mission—and his thunder would *not* be stolen. He commandeered a chair and stepped up onto it, only, his fear of heights prevented him from letting go of the chair back, and he crouched awkwardly, one arm waving in the air, while the other securely gripped the rungs. "Hear me out! Hear my plan!" he attempted to shout above the melee. He looked as if he were afraid of a mouse scurrying about on the ground, and the sight was pitiful enough that the crowd piped down—let the sorry little man have his moment.

Ever so gingerly, he climbed down from the chair and resumed his stance at the podium. As the crowd stirred, Story collected his notes, finding where he left off. "I propose laying boundaries for a district of vice. I believe the answer is to section off the back o' town." He spoke with deliberate clarity, as if he were oblivious to the scene that had just occurred. But he'd labored over his speech, and this was one for the history books—he would *not* be overlooked because an impatient crowd had parroted his words and his ideas! "We shall designate thirty inconsequential blocks where we can sequester inconsequential denizens. Within this district and under law, whores can engage in the Devil's business, so long as they pay proper license fees and remain contained within the borders for work *and* as their permanent residence."

"What're the boundaries, Story?" someone shouted. Murmurs of restless agreement rippled among the crowd.

"I'm getting to it," Story snapped. Behind him, rolled and mounted on the wall, was a map of the city, and he reached for the string to open it—only he was too short to nab it. Swatting away a tall man who stepped up, Story instead slid over the trusty chair and climbed upon it, but he still couldn't bring himself to let go and reach up to grab the string. The room shuffled, quickly moving past feeling embarrassed for the Alderman and now growing downright irritated. Finally, the tall man grabbed the string, unfurling the map.

Story climbed down and repositioned his askew glasses. He then turned to the map and landed a delicate finger on the back of town. "Thirty blocks," he began. He landed a pin through a piece of red yarn. "Bound by Canal Street . . ." He trailed the yarn across the desolate stretch of Canal that boasted nothing more than a streetcar line. "Basin Street . . ." He looped the yarn around a second pin where Lulu's gorgeous bordello resided among aged Victorians in various states of disrepair. "Saint Louis Cemetery Number One . . ." He rounded the yarn around New Orleans's oldest cemetery, where crumbling tombs housed such notables as the city's first mayor, the French inventor of the game craps, and the most notorious Voodoo queen, Marie Laveau. "And finally," Story concluded, "Claiborne Avenue, with great apology to the inconveniently located Saint James Methodist Church. And, of course, colored whores will be relegated to the back of the back o' town."

He turned to beam at the red-lined square on the map then pointedly stepped back to the podium to deliver his final words, his voice rising with the fervor of a preacher. "This ordinance will go into full effect in one month's time. By the first of January 1898, no longer will decent folk be burdened with the eyesore or proximity of vice. If whores prosper in the District or rot there, it's of no good man's concern!"

Applause broke out. Story scanned the inspired faces, all the while resisting the temptation to take a bow. It was his finest moment indeed.

Just outside the Cabildo, his face pressed to the half-open window, waited Snitch. He'd seen and heard the entire event, and, hopping down from the windowsill, he made a mad dash through the tall iron gates and back to Venus Alley.

Every Sunday morning, Mary could be found in her crib, on her hands and knees.

Scrubbing.

There was barely any traffic on Sundays, given that it was difficult for most johns to reconcile coming to a whore on the day of the Lord, especially when he had to pass several churches en route to the Alley no matter what direction he was coming from. So Sunday morning was a good time for Mary to clean.

It was hardly a chore today to wash the floorboards and walls knowing that it all belonged in her name. Charlotte had come along, and she stood at the doorway, sweeping with a broom made of palmetto leaves. They were going to make this crib shine more than any other on the Alley.

Lo and behold, a john approached, but with one look at Charlotte's swollen belly, he quickly made a sharp turn in the opposite direction.

"It's kind of you to come help, Lottie," Mary said, "but you're just awful for business."

Charlotte giggled, then stopped, concern flashing across her face.

"What is it?" Mary asked.

"This baby's having too fine a time, pressin' here and pressin' there. Remind me not to laugh again till it's born, otherwise I might really embarrass myself."

Mary smiled to herself and plunged her rag into the bucket of water.

"What d'ya think we should name the baby?" Charlotte asked dreamily.

"I've been prayin' the baby's a girl," Mary said. "Hope you don't mind. Wouldn't hurt you none to do some prayin' too. But only pray to women saints. We don't need to be asking men for nothing." She rose to her feet, surveying the floorboards. "Don't need to be getting on our knees for one single more man."

Timidly, Charlotte asked, "You hear anything from him?" as if she shouldn't speak Lobrano's name. "Feels like a different world without him over us."

"Sittin' in jail, far as I know. But can't get too used to him not being around. They can't keep him forever."

Charlotte shifted uncomfortably. "I just . . . oh, Mary, I'm scared of what he's gonna do when he finds out. He'll want vengeance like we ain't never before seen, and Lord knows we've seen plenty of his wrath. Oh, Mary, I just—"

But Mary cut her off. "Of all things, Charlotte, that ain't something you need to worry over." She tried to keep a strong face but knew in her bones that Charlotte was right. She'd been running so high from the turn of events that she hadn't allowed herself to really consider what Lobrano would do, could do. Besides, thoughts like that would have quickly squelched her ambition, would have had her turning right around at Anderson's, tail between her legs. Yes, she suspected, it would be the wrath of Lobrano like they'd never before seen, but how could she carry on hour after hour, day after day, anticipating such hellfire and brimstone?

"How'd you get that brave to do this, Mary? I don't know any girl as brave as you."

Mary gave Charlotte an obligatory smile. Only time would tell if she'd been brave, or stupid.

Just then, they were startled by a loud clanging from the Alley. "Listen up, y'all!" someone shouted, and they looked down the street to see Snitch with a tin cup in one hand and a frying pan in the other, banging them together as he ran around in a circle.

"Has he gone mad?" Mary said, and she and Charlotte stepped onto the Alley to get a better look.

"Listen, all yous whores!" Snitch shouted, gasping for breath.

"Shut your goddamn yap, Snitch!" a whore called from a crib. But Snitch was undeterred and commandeered a crate to stand on. Whores lazily came to their doorways to see what was eating him.

"Got a important announcement—"

"You the mayor o' Venus Alley, Snitch?" another whore piped up. Laughter rumbled through the street.

"Y'all won't be laughin' when ya hear what I gotta say."

"Spit it out, then, Snitch!" Mary shouted.

"I just come from the Cabildo—"

At the mere mention of the Cabildo, a shirtless man with a bow tie still around his neck darted from a crib, holding up his pants.

"All them muckamucks," Snitch shouted, "they be layin' boundaries for a new district of vice. And I'm gonna be the first to tell y'all, Venus Alley ain't in them boundaries."

A crowd had gathered now, and everyone turned to each other, murmuring with confusion.

"What does that mean, Mary?" Charlotte asked.

Mary called out to Snitch, "You sayin' they gonna up and move Venus Alley?"

Snitch shook his head. "Don't 'spect this shit hole's part of their plan."

Commotion erupted from the crowd. Charlotte searched Mary's face for an answer, but Mary couldn't even look at her, her mind was spinning so fast. If this was true, then what, oh Lord, had she done? She felt dizzy. The crib was supposed to be their future, not a piss pot. Oh Lord, oh Lord, this couldn't be true, couldn't really be happening—it was probably just Snitch telling tales, he and his blather.

"Where the fuck's Tom Anderson?" a whore shouted. "Did he send you to tell us?"

Snitch's eyes grew wide. "I swear I ain't seen Mistah Anderson—"

"Yeah, where the fuck is Anderson?" another whore yelled. "That bastard be makin' all that money off us. Why ain't he standin' up for us?"

"Oh Lawd," Snitch moaned. He hopped down from the crate just as an apple went flying across the street, smashing a window. The whore who threw it marveled at her aim. "Fuck you, Tom Anderson," she added. Others in the crowd loudly agreed.

Mary quickly realized the scene on the Alley could get bad. She watched as Snitch raced off, knowing full well where the little prattler was headed. Go tell the boss man that his Alley whores were fixing to riot. Mary took Charlotte's arm. "C'mon, it's back to scrubbing," she said, doing her best to sound unaffected. "No use worryin' till we know for sure we got troubles to worry about."

A strange hush fell over the Alley as they all waited. It was as if they were collectively holding their breath, waiting for someone to tell them if they could go on working, or if they were going to starve to death. Folks milled around, picking their teeth, kicking the dirt. Mary had cleaned so hard, she'd worn a hole straight through the rag. Never had the crib been so spotless.

And then, a hullabaloo rose up from down the street. Mary and Charlotte rushed to the door.

Emerging from a cloud of dust, Tom Anderson, surrounded by

his burly men, strode like a posse into town. All of Venus Alley moved into the street.

"Ah, a crowd of women scorned," Anderson said to his men. Coolly, he made his way to the center of the Alley, and the whores and pimps formed a dense circle around him. Charlotte and Mary lingered in the crib doorway, not wanting to be too close in case things took an ugly turn.

"Ladies and gentlemen," Anderson boomed, flashing a wide grin, "my friends, my colleagues—"

"Ya sold us down the river, Anderson!" a whore shouted. Hissing swept through the crowd and fists rose into the air.

"Want me to corral 'em, Mistah Anderson?" Tater asked.

Anderson surveyed the rabble and, for the first time, considered the weight of the whores' desperation. Compassion wasn't a feeling he was comfortable with, but even he couldn't disregard their dire circumstances—this was their livelihood. Without whoring, they would starve to death. He motioned Tater back. "Let's try talking to them first," he said.

His smile disappeared as he shifted tactics and earnestly looked out over the ragged crowd. "Y'all have every right to be angry," he announced. "I'm angry too. I fought this ordinance tooth and nail. You may see me as someone with a modicum of power. Well, I've been wielding everything I can against them supposedly God-fearing men running around on a witch hunt. There's one particular rat, Alderman Sidney Story—"

"Story's got a weeny wick!" a whore shouted.

Anderson snickered. "Anyone here vouch for that personally?" The crowd laughed in spite of themselves. Anderson took it in, knowing he was getting them to come around. "Not a one?" he asked. "Well, at least Story practices what he preaches!" He watched the faces in the crowd soften, chuckle even, and he immediately knew he had them back where he wanted them.

"So it seems, my friends, that today, Alderman Story finally got his tiny cock rubbed. I was as shocked as y'all at the news of this Story District . . . this . . . *Storyville*." He paused, impressed by his own cleverness; that did have a nice ring to it. "See, I'm here to personally tell you, that no one's abandoning you. We're gonna get through this, and we're gonna do it together. Look around you. Do you like how you're living now? This, my friends is an opportunity for change. For rising up. For making a better life. I even heard talk of black whores having their very own street to conduct business. Imagine that! When this ordinance takes effect in one month's time, you can rest assured that Storyville will make things better. This is liberty and justice, even for whores. God bless New Orleans!"

The crowd broke into applause. Anderson tried to meet people's eyes as he humbly nodded with appreciation—stifling any hint that inside he was gloating.

A pimp shouted, "Ya runnin' for office?"

Anderson chuckled modestly. One of these days, he thought. One of these days.

Charlotte started clapping, then looked to Mary and abruptly stopped. Mary was stone-faced as she wondered why everyone was applauding—weren't they listening to what Anderson *wasn't* saying? The rules were changing, but what were the new rules? Just where would they go if Venus Alley was to be shuttered? And then what would that cost? And would there be room for them all? She hadn't heard him speak of these things. But one thing was clear, and crushingly so: what was the point of having your own crib if you didn't have the Alley?

CHAPTER TWELVE

City Hall, New Orleans

Hunched over his desk at City Hall, the city treasurer absent-mindedly glanced up from his ledger, only to have the numbers he was tabulating blown clear from his head by the sight before him. Stepping into the rotunda were the most garish gaggle of women: Countess Lulu White, surrounded by seven of her young ladies. The treasurer suddenly found himself in the midst of more plumes, diamonds, taffeta, and perfume than had ever been present at one time in City Hall. He promptly sneezed.

"Why, bless your heart," Lulu cooed, "and a very good morning, Monsieur. I have traversed all the way to City Hall today, in this unseasonably warm weather I might add." She fanned herself dramatically. "Accompanied by my lovely nieces . . ." The ladies curtsied.

The treasurer took a gulp of air.

Lulu continued, "I'd like to receive my license to operate an official and legalized house of amusement in the new district."

"Well, ma'am," the treasurer stammered, "you are the first—"

"Of course I am!" Lulu interjected. "Before you stands the premiere proprietress of Basin Street." Her girls gloated and fawned, clapping their hands and playfully bowing.

It had only been a couple of days since the incident with Judge Beares, and only in this city would the lead suspect freely waltz into City Hall without so much as a care. But never would Lulu let anyone know that the unjustness was not lost on her. Her belly hadn't stopped churning since, although she knew she had to carry on—approaching the advent of Storyville with her head held high, as a countess would.

The treasurer's voice was squeaky. "No one's quite prepared yet, this all just happened."

But Lulu just looked at him expectantly.

He nervously shuffled through papers. "Ah, here, the notice." He scanned the paper. "As written, the fee for said license is one hundred dollars—"

But before he could finish, Lulu ceremoniously presented a crisp one-hundred-dollar bill.

"With the addition of," the treasurer continued, "a one-dollar tax."

"Oh, silly me," Lulu exclaimed. "I have your dollar bill. Right here . . ." She leaned over to spill her cleavage in the treasurer's face, a sliver of green buried in her ample bosom. The ladies snickered.

Aghast, the treasurer averted his eyes. "Ma'am, that is not appropriate."

"No? Oh, but your dollar's right here. . . ." Lulu gave her chest a wiggle. The treasurer was having none of it and refused to look at her.

"Monsieur Treasurer isn't being much fun." Lulu pouted. "Poodle, darling, would you mind helping me fulfill this ever-so-ridiculous tax?"

Poodle stepped forward from the group of ladies. She was all of twenty years old and had a head of pouffy, white-blond hair, the inspiration for her name. She leaned her face into Lulu's bosom and pulled out the dollar with her teeth. The others gave her a round of applause.

Lulu took the dollar from Poodle's jaws and handed it to the treasurer. "Monsieur . . ."

With disgust, he took a handkerchief from his pocket in order to swaddle the dollar. Accompanied by a perturbed grunt, he slid over the license certificate. "Sign."

As if on cue, a pink-cheeked girl, Fannie, her lips painted to look like a baby-doll's, presented Lulu with a tortoiseshell pen. Ceremoniously, Lulu announced each word as she wrote with flourish: "Countess. Lulu. White." Complete, she displayed the certificate for her girls to see, and they marveled as if it were the Constitution of the United States.

"Ladies," Lulu announced, "we are official . . . legal . . . harlots!"

The Pig Ankle saloon was as dingy as it was empty, but for the few regulars who seemed to blend into the warped wood, worn barstools, and clouds of smoke. Lobrano, only six minutes out of jail, was already sidled up to the bar.

"Absinthe," he barked.

He'd been released from the jail cell after he'd started going into fits and spurts, violently shaking and sweating as if he was with a high fever—this, after he'd been screaming for days that his crotch was on fire. The jailkeep and other inmates didn't know what to make of these spells, but they weren't keen on taking any chances of catching the sickness, or the demon, whichever was possessing Philip Lobrano. On instinct, however, Lobrano knew he wasn't ill with influenza or Devil spirits. It was the drink. He needed his liquor, and his body was screaming and writhing in every which way trying to tell him.

The bartender filled a tall glass halfway with green liquid. Over the glass he placed a slotted spoon, setting a sugar cube atop it. As he dribbled water over the spoon, the sugar dissolved, and the drink swirled to a murky white.

Lobrano paid no mind to the ritual. His legs were jittering and his teeth chattering, and he grabbed for the glass, draining it in two swallows. He let out a soothed sigh as the liquor coursed through his body. *Hot damn, that's some good tonic.*

"Another," he barked.

As the bartender repeated the process, Lobrano's eyes landed on a copy of the *Picayune*, left atop the bar. A front-page picture of debonair Tom Anderson, his mustache perfectly trimmed and coiffed to curl upward at the tips, gazed back. "What's this say about goddamn Anderson?" Lobrano asked the bartender.

"Says Anderson's saloon in the new district's gonna have electric lightbulbs." He placed the second drink in front of Lobrano. "Supposed to be bright enough to see when civilized folk leave a tip."

"What's the new district?" Lobrano grunted.

"Read for yourself," said the bartender, pushing the paper toward Lobrano. But Lobrano waved it off, then took his drink and headed to the back of the bar, unabashedly grabbing at his still-itchy groin.

Madam

143

A cotch game was in progress, being played by brothers Cooper and Clint, as much Pig Ankle fixtures as Lobrano. Both burly and unwashed, their ruddy looks made it difficult to tell one from the other. Not that it mattered. Lobrano plunked himself down at their table.

"He ain't dead after all," Clint said dryly.

Cooper made a face. "Smells like he's half-dead."

Lobrano ignored their banter. "What's this about a new district?" he asked.

Cooper laid down a card. "Leave it to Anderson to soak up the gravy."

"Seems a lot of talk just for him openin' a new bar," Lobrano grumbled.

"Have you been hiding under your mama's skirt? It's the tenderloin they're talkin' 'bout," Cooper said.

Lobrano gave him a confused look.

"Ain't you heard any of this? A legal district? In the back o' town?"

"Oh, that ain't never gonna happen," Lobrano smirked. "Folks're happy right the way things are."

"Oh, it's happenin'," Clint said. "Sure as eggs is eggs, it's happening."

"Gonna make an honest man outta ya, Lobrano," Cooper added. "You in the game or what?"

Lobrano dug in his pocket. He had a few bills that had been returned to him upon his release, and he threw a dollar on the table. "Business been good lately," he declared.

"Sop it up, then, 'fore the well dries," Clint replied.

"They can't just come in and take what's mine," Lobrano said. "I got two gals and a crib—"

"Not for long, you don't," Cooper insisted.

Lobrano waved him off, reassuring himself that nothing ever really changed in New Orleans. Venus Alley was as old and essential to life in this city as . . . well, as his glass of absinthe.

"Don't crawl cryin' to me when the day comes," Cooper said. "I been stockpiling. Added two more flocks of geese. Where there's whores, there's a place to lay. And these classy gals ain't gonna want no kips full of moss. They're gonna want featherbeds."

"Classy gals?" Lobrano said. "They was nothin' but filthy whores last I checked. Don't come cryin' to me when you're sitting on a pile o' goose shit."

"I got Chinamen scoring poppies as we speak," Clint said.

Lobrano gave a condescending shake of his head. "Yellow Peril? Listen, somethin' as harebrained as that district would put out all us hardworking folk. It ain't gonna happen."

"That absinthe make you addlepated, or were you just born that way?" Clint asked. "Put some of that hard-earned money on the table or quit wastin' our time."

With a bill going to pay for more drink, Lobrano knew he was cleaned out. "I . . . uh," he fumbled. "I put in a trick with my best girl."

The brothers exchanged looks. Cocking his head, Cooper pondered the offer.

That night, Venus Alley was alive with a chorus of copulation. A finale of loud grunts came from Mary's crib. And then her crib door smacked open and out sauntered Cooper, buttoning his pants. Mary quickly trailed after him, clutching her chippie to her naked body. Her lip was bloodied.

"Hey, ya ain't paid!"

"Been taken care of."

"No, it ain't."

Cooper let out a laugh. "Your old man pawned you away quicker 'an a lame horse."

She stopped cold. "From the jailhouse?"

"From the Pig Ankle."

Mary's hand fluttered to her mouth, and only then did she realize she was bleeding. So Lobrano was free.

"Pawned you away quicker 'an a lame, *blind* horse."

Mary smoldered as she looked at Cooper. Something primal raged up in her, a deep, wild surge that had always been kept at bay.

Cooper laughed loud and long, in a way meant to humiliate her—just as Lobrano would do.

And then Mary's dam burst. She flew at him, pouncing like a cat with its claws out.

All Cooper could see was a ball of fury with sharp nails launching toward his eyeballs. He instinctively lunged, shoving her with the force he'd use on a man his own size. Thrown back, Mary's head slammed hard against the wall. She slumped to the ground.

For a second, Cooper flinched with panic—he'd underestimated his own strength against the slight girl. But he was relieved to see Mary groggily look up, and with the knowledge that he hadn't killed her, he hurried off fast enough to kick up a cloud of dust under his boots.

It was near a half hour later that Beulah trudged toward the crib, kip on her back. As she caught sight of Mary collapsed on the stoop, she dropped her kip and rushed toward her, kneeling down to lift her limp head. "Mary, y'all right?"

Mary mumbled gibberish as her eyes rolled back.

"Come to, Mary!" Beulah shouted, but to no avail.

❧

Unsure where she was, let alone what day it was, Mary tried to focus on a hazy figure hovering over her.

"Hush now, dear child," a crackly voice said.

As if walking through smoke, Mary came to find herself, of all places, in Eulalie Echo's room in the back of the cigar shop. Only, Mary was six years old, dressed in a smock with saggy tights, her hair in a long braid.

"You pay by the inch?" a man's voice said. "She got thirteen inches there."

Mary was given a shove toward Eulalie, and she sputtered forward, her knees shaky.

"Show the Negra your long hair," the man's voice ordered.

Gently, Eulalie fingered Mary's long, dark braid, oddly entranced by it. "This your child?" Eulalie asked the man.

"She's my sister's girl. Her ma's ailing, and we need money for remedies."

Mary's eyes darted questioningly in the direction of the man. "Ain't that right, Mary?" he said.

Eulalie awaited the little girl's answer. Mary wished it were real and that she could say yes, her mama was just ailing and not a dreamy memory. It ached the way he lied about her mother, his own sister. But Mary knew what she was supposed to answer, and she could only imagine what might happen if she didn't. Her little face hardened as she masked her fear. She gave a small, mechanical nod.

Eulalie met Mary's eyes, and, despite the strangeness of this dark-skinned woman with one eyeball wandering off into the distance, Mary felt a sense of comfort emanate from her.

"All right, then," Eulalie said gently as she took a pocketknife from her apron. Mary couldn't help but notice the knife wasn't a common, tarnished one, but a fancy sort, with a rosewood handle and a glinting blade. As Eulalie brought the knife to the long braid, she whispered in Mary's ear, "Don't worry, child, this is so you can learn who you are without pretty to confuse you." Then she leaned in even closer, her breath warm against Mary's face. "A queen knows who she is."

She gnawed at the braid while silent tears rolled down Mary's cheeks. The knife worked its way through, and the braid landed in Eulalie's grip. Mary was left with jaw-length, jagged hair.

"You're the ugliest boy I ever seen," the man taunted.

Mary stifled a sob.

"Oh, little boy's cryin' now," he said, and there was a jab at her shoulder. "C'mon, little boys are tough. Look at ya, sissy." Another jab. "C'mon, ain't little boys s'posed to fight back—"

He went at her again, but Eulalie stopped him. She aimed the knife directly at the hazy figure of a man. "One day," Eulalie warned, "you'll be on your knees to this girl, asking for forgiveness."

Mary suddenly jolted awake. She was in her crib, alone, drenched in sweat. Catching her breath, she gingerly touched her hand to her sore head, then winced from the pain. She slowly looked around, as if to get her bearings. Everything was in place. She tried to do the same with her thoughts, paging through her mind and recalling what she could—she remembered coming to work, and then, she shuddered at the sudden recollection of Cooper, but after that her memory trailed off.

Sunlight streamed in from the tiny window, catching the glare of something shiny on the bedside table. Slowly, Mary turned to see a pocketknife. She took it in her hand, running her finger along its smooth rosewood inlay.

CHAPTER THIRTEEN

Mary stood at the entrance of the Pig Ankle, silhouetted by the sunlight filtering into the dark saloon from the open door.

"Can I help ya?" the barkeep asked.

Mary scanned the bar, which was empty but for an old, doddering sailor in breeches and a threadbare seaman's frock, mumbling to himself.

"Ya seen Lobrano?" Mary asked the barkeep.

He gave her a withered look. "He went out to take a piss . . . 'bout an hour ago."

Mary nodded—typical Lobrano—and turned to go.

"Ain't paid his tab neither," the barkeep added.

"'Course not," she muttered, the door slamming behind her. She angled round to the side of the Pig Ankle, figuring it was the closest piss spot, and peered down the alley. There, slumped up against the side of the building, was Lobrano, passed out cold next to some beer barrels, his pants undone.

For a long moment, Mary stared at him. The knot on her head throbbed, and each pulsation made her detest him more. Her fingers traced the outline of the knife in her little burlap purse. Without so much as a conscious decision, she found herself hovering the open knife over his limp arm. It occurred to her how easily she could slit his wrists. She then moved the blade to his throat, drawing an invisible line straight across. One motion like this and she could be done with him, done with him forever. It excited her and terrified her to even think that way. What if she did it—who would miss him? She and Peter were his only kin, and she doubted any other person in this world would care, let alone notice, if Philip Lobrano disappeared here in this alley—found crushed under one of the barrels, maybe, or some other supposed accident a notorious drunk had seemingly brought upon himself. Any officer of the law would just as soon dismiss this sorry case.

The knife quivered she was clutching it so hard, leaning in so close she could see the pulse in his neck, could see exactly how easy it could be to snuff him out. With each rhythmic beat of the vein it was as if Lobrano's own body was tempting her. *Do it. Do it. Do it.* Pleading with her even—take him from his miserable lot.

Quickly, Mary stepped back, as if forcing herself from transfixion. She folded the knife and hurried off despite herself.

Shaken, Mary weaved her way through the crowded marketplace in the French Quarter, gazing emptily as the vendors tried to sell her their wares. Their callouts, normally catchy and singsongy, seemed to accost her from every direction:

Bring out your pitcher,
Bring out your can.
Get nice fresh oysters from the Oyster Man! Oyster, Sally?

My horse is white, My face is black,
I sell my coal two bits a sack.

"I am *Signor Cornmeali!*" cried the cornmeal man. "*Buongiorno,* cornmeal?"

The bottle man pushed a handcart by. "Any bottles, any bones, any rags today?"

"Mop-n-broom!" called the blind broom man, stomping his cane with each syllable. "Mop-n-broom!"

"Pole-y. Pretty, pretty pole-y," sang the pole seller.

Mary had never been bothered by the chicken seller before, but today she shivered as he swung his chickens, limp but still live, banded together like a bunch of turnips. "Get your big fat spring cheek-in!"

Even the silent Choctaw squaw who knelt at the curb selling powdered sassafras seemed to question Mary with her unblinking black eyes.

Mary continued onward, in her own hazy world, until something up ahead caught her eye: a crew of fancily dressed ladies, decked out in plumes and jewels. They confidently approached male passersby, looking them straight in the eye and handing them calling cards.

"The inaugural party is at Countess Lulu White's mansion," one of the girls recited to a dapper dan who'd veered over.

Mary spotted a wayward calling card on the ground, and she scurried to pick it up. She wiped a footprint from the card, which depicted a line drawing of a young woman's profile, along with fancy script:

Miss Poodle
"She'll pant and lick you all over!"
Countess Lulu White's Mahogany Hall,
235 Basin Street

From among the girls, Mary picked out the pouffy-haired one who resembled the drawing.

"Well, aren't you the tomcat's kitten," Poodle cooed to a suited man. "Will I see you this Saturday? It's going to be a bigger celebration than Mardi Gras even. You will not be disappointed, I promise."

"And I'm sure to see you there?" the man asked.

"Of course! I am privileged to live at the Countess's house, you silly goose!"

Momentarily forgetting about her throbbing head, Mary watched in awe. The Countess's girls looked fresh and gleeful, with round, pink cheeks—they all must eat three squares a day, Mary thought. She twisted a strand of her own brittle, dirty hair and felt herself shrink in comparison to these girls with their curled up-dos, their tufted bustles, their pale, unfreckled faces shielded from the sun by fancy, stylish hats.

Poodle playfully tugged at the dan's coat. "Tell them at the door that Poodle sent you." She then leaned in closer to him. "You're my number one, but why don't you bring some gentlemen friends too? This is a momentous event, after all." She pointedly handed him a calling card, and in return he suavely kissed her hand.

"Until Saturday eve," he said.

They were interrupted by a brown-haired girl, who butted herself in. "And it's all legal!" she shouted. At that, all the girls rallied to the battle cry, whooping and cheering.

A blond pixie lifted her skirt to flash two very prim and proper ladies who happened to be walking by. "Legal!" she shouted, baring her bloomers. The ladies darted out of the way as if she were a rodent. "Heavens!" one trilled, her nose upturned. "I pray President McKinley will bring an injunction against this awful district of vice!"

Mary couldn't help but giggle at the prim women, batting themselves as if they'd walked into a swarm of gnats. Just then, one of Lulu's girls looked her way, and Mary instinctively cowered. She knew the reality: they were stunning, and she ought to be embarrassed by her dirty face and soiled clothes. She melted back into the crowd of the bustling market, where she'd be lost among the low class, the invisibles.

As she made her way through the marketplace, she was surprised that each snippet of conversation she caught was about the new district. A little boy asked, "Mama, what's the tenderloin?"

"A cut of meat," the mother snapped, "and don't ask such things again."

A suited man strolling aside a minister inquired how Saint James Methodist Church could coexist with such unholy practices occurring right next door? The minister sighed. "It's a sad, sad day that our beloved church is caught in the boundaries of Satan's new district."

Mary even went by Café Du Monde to sit and rest a moment among the folks eating beignets and drinking chicory and coffee au laits from china teacups. "They're calling it Storyville," a suited man told another. "Bet that just tickles the Alderman." They both laughed.

Mary's head pounded, and talk of the new district only made it hurt more. She hastened her way toward Peter's potato stand, feeling relief wash over her as she heard his call from down the aisle.

"One potato, two potato, three potato, four! Nice Irish potatoes!"

Catching sight of Mary, he gave a big smile, only his face went flat as he got a look at her swollen, blood-caked lip. "That a gift from Lobrano?"

She ignored the question. "Can I just set here a bit?" she asked as she slowly sank onto a crate.

Peter began to mindlessly fidget with his watch, clicking and snapping the cover. "Did Lobrano do that?" he persisted, but Mary just looked away, vacant. "Answer me, Mary!"

"Don't duty me," Mary snapped. "I put food on the table and a roof over your head. You ain't got no right to ask for one thing more, Peter."

She recoiled, instantly hating herself for lashing out. Her heart was racing, and although she'd thought it was a good idea to come here, that it might help to just sit with her brother, she decided she better leave before she blurted out something else she'd regret.

"I'll see you back at home," she said. "And I'm fine, don't worry after me."

She wandered off, but found her feet taking her to the only place that seemed to make sense. She passed women carrying baskets atop their heads, passed Clementine selling rice fritters, and walked straight into the cigar shop.

The front room was empty, and Mary made the rash decision to boldly step, uninvited, behind the velvet curtain. Moving cautiously down the hallway, she saw Eulalie's door was open. She peeked in.

Her back to the door, Eulalie was meticulously stitching a taxidermy cat, poised as if hissing. Mary cowered at the sight of it.

"Too late to turn back now," Eulalie murmured as if she had eyes in the back of her head of thick, wild hair. "So you returned to Eulalie at the waning moon after all? It's a peculiar moon month. That milk moon will be up to her majestic tricks soon. Playin' her little hiding game. Just you wait and see."

Eulalie's talk sounded like gibberish to Mary. She hadn't come here because of the moon. With a deep breath, she took a step into the cramped room. It smelled strong of musk and grass. "Miss Echo, did you come to my bedside last night?"

Eulalie held a magnifying glass to inspect a stitch on the cat's belly. "We must make a sacrifice in Congo Square," she replied. "Tonight at dusk." Still, she didn't turn to face Mary.

"Miss Echo, I need to know," Mary insisted. "I saw some wild sights in my dreams and I need to know if any are true."

"See me there tonight, at the scarred oak. Bring three silver dimes to put in the tree's hollow."

"I didn't come here looking to make a sacrifice—"

"Fine, then," Eulalie said, dismissive. She returned to her stitching on the cat. Mary waited uncomfortably, and as the seconds of silence ticked away she couldn't exactly figure out why she wasn't turning to leave.

Finally, Eulalie piped up. "If your mind sees fit to change, remember to bring a little offerin' to the queen Marie Laveau. She guides Eulalie from the spirit world."

Feeling empty and drained, Mary turned to go but was startled by the screeching of a chair as Eulalie flipped around to face her. She held up a bony finger.

"The underworld is rising. The time o' queens be comin', and you, child, must be ready."

Ready for what? Mary wondered. But she let Eulalie's words resonate. Here she was, about to be stripped of her crib, her life savings, and her means of making a living, and if Eulalie thought an offering to her spirit guide would help, what more did Mary have to lose? She flinched at how to-the-letter the answer suddenly was: nothing. She was as low as anyone could be, so why should she fear anything anymore?

She mustered up a voice. "What do you think Miss Laveau might want for an offering?"

Eulalie gave her a tiny smile. "Oh, Marie? She like a tin pail o' crayfish bisque . . . but not too red hot, too red give the queen some nasty bout of indigestion."

Across Rampart Street was the notorious Congo Square, a clearing bordered by thick woods, and the place where, during slave times, Africans could gather legally. In the old days, it was every Sunday afternoon that black folks would congregate to sell or trade the handful of goods they were permitted to make on their own—or those they made in secret. But it was during the nighttime when Congo Square really came alive with chanting, drumming, stomping, and pulsating bodies and ritualistic ceremonies that made the place sacred.

Mary had heard Beulah talk of going to Congo Square, and how she and her kin would raise a ruckus there until all hours of the night. Beulah called the square holy ground, and Mary always reckoned she'd meant *holy* as in church. But now, after her dealings with Eulalie Echo, Mary suspected Beulah meant *holy* as in black magic.

With one leaded step after the other, carefully steadying the offering of a pail of soup, Mary wondered if the bump on her head had caused her good sense to get jumbled. She approached the clearing and sloughed off a chill as she scanned the square. Her eyes quickly found the unmistakable gnarled oak Eulalie had described.

Slowly, she walked toward the tree and set the pail at its twisted roots. From her pocket, she took three dimes. Three precious dimes. Even more precious now that her cigar box of savings was nearly empty. She envisioned the picture of the train on the box but instead of traveling to interesting, unknown places, she imagined it to have no steam, barely inching along until it could inch no farther and came to a whining standstill.

"Am I crazy, Saint Teresa?" Mary said aloud. Three dimes. That was a pound of butter. A steak, maybe two small steaks even. And here she was about to trade sustenance for what could likely be the work of the Devil? But Eulalie's words echoed in her head: *The time o' queens be comin', and you, child, must be ready.*

Mary knew the truth, that a steak or a pound of butter wasn't going to make a damn bit of difference in the long run if something big didn't change. Angel or devil, if Mary couldn't keep working, that baby would come into the world hopeless.

Ceremoniously, she placed a dime in the hollow and announced her wish. "Good fortune for Peter." She wished upon the next dime. "Good health for Charlotte." And then she studied the third, lingering over it, lingering over the wish for herself.

"Flames!"

Mary jumped. There was Eulalie, sitting just inches away, as if she'd been there the whole time.

"Flames, for you," Eulalie said. "That fire in your belly. Ask it for yourself. Go on, ask Marie Laveau."

"I . . . I don't know."

"Come now, don't want Miss Laveau's supper goin' cold." Eulalie reached toward the bisque and dipped a finger in to taste. "Just the way she likes it."

"I don't know what to ask for," Mary said timidly.

"Ask for what you want. Ask Marie, the high Voodoo priestess who guides Eulalie from the spirit world. Marie is power. When she did rituals on Saint John's Eve, thousands of folks traversed for days just to take sight of her."

"This ain't temptin' the underworld, is it?"

Eulalie let out a cackle. "The underworld? Child, you *are* the underworld."

Mary realized her knees were trembling. "You're scaring me some, Miss Eulalie."

"Fear makes change. Isn't it change you're after?"

Mary desperately nodded. She screwed up her courage and wrapped her fist around the dime. "I gotta find my own way," she said, her voice tiny, and she moved to throw the dime in the hollow, but Eulalie stopped her.

"You're talkin' to the queen! Ask big, ask for real."

Mary bit her lip. Closing her eyes, she thought of the Countess's girls at the market, pink-cheeked and clean and happy and making business with no shame. Making business by throwing a fancy-dress party, for Lord's sake! From somewhere deep within her chest, Mary found her voice. She declared, "I want to work in a proper house, on a proper mattress, making a fair living." She watched the dime disappear into the dark hollow.

"Queen Marie Laveau, please hear this child!" Eulalie called, pressing her palm to Mary's forehead, forcing her to kneel. "*Danga moune de te! Canga do ki li!* Mother Haiti, Mother Congo, receive her!" Reaching both hands to the sky, Eulalie began to tremble as if a current were traveling through her. "Oh holy day! Rise up, child!"

Mary looked to her awkwardly, not sure what she was supposed to do.

"Rise!"

Shakily, Mary stood.

"The time o' queens is comin'!" Eulalie writhed as she stretched her arms higher and higher toward the sky. Her body quivered, writhing more and more as if she were having a spell. And then she dropped, wilting as if the current had been suddenly cut off.

"Leave the dimes in the hollow," she said flatly. She picked up the bisque and sauntered off.

Mary stared after her, wondering what was supposed to happen now. She didn't feel any different. The three dimes didn't magically turn into three hundred. Was she supposed to go home and wait for the lightning? The lightning that was going to burn down the Alley but spare just her crib?

A few paces away, Eulalie paused. She looked back offhandedly. "And Saturday night," she said, "at the Countess's party, just go 'round to the back door. The colored folks'll let you in."

CHAPTER FOURTEEN

The Countess's party? There was no way, black magic or not, that the likes of an Alley whore would be welcomed at the Countess's party. Mary might as well show up knocking at the front door of the president of the United States's house for all it mattered. And yet, she found herself compelled by Eulalie's orders, even though she was certain she'd become a laughingstock, booted out onto the street where she belonged.

Her worn boots picked their way along the cobblestones. They seemed to have a mind of their own, these boots, desperately coaxing her along Basin Street, past ornate, looming Victorian mansions that must have been grand in their day but were now left to crumble and rot in the unfashionable back of town. Her heel stuck between a gap in the stones and she stumbled, catching the hem of her pale blue dress. She heard the sound of fabric ripping and she felt herself well up—this dress couldn't stand to be any more tattered.

She'd bought the dress from a whore on the Alley called Birdleg Nora for the special occasion of Peter and Charlotte's marriage. Birdleg Nora had probably stolen the dress, or at best was gifted it by a john, but it was relatively high style, with leg-of-mutton sleeves and a sashed waist, and she'd needed money fast. Mary got it for a steal. She'd matched the dress with striped silk stockings, which were all the latest rave from Paris—Mary knew this because she always heard the vendors telling the high-society ladies, who would pay an unbelievable two dollars a pair! Of course, Mary hadn't bought the stockings; rather, one day she overheard an angry lady yelling at a shopkeeper that her stockings hadn't even lasted through one washing. Come closing time, Mary lingered around the rubbish and, sure enough, there was the returned pair, with just a small run that could easily be stitched up.

The tiny wedding had been held at Holy Trinity Cathedral, with a young priest agreeing to bless the union only because, when Charlotte's parents were alive, her family had attended regular mass there. Since the priest had never seen Peter's face in his pews, he'd sped through an abridged version of the marriage ceremony, all the while tossing disapproving glances at the only other attendant, Mary. Unless God really did speak to him, Mary wasn't sure how a man of the cloth would know she made her way on the Alley, especially since she was dressed in the fashion of a society girl.

Still, his stare had sent a prickly rash down Mary's chest, and the dress's lace collar suddenly felt like a choke hold. Mary hated the notion that her lot in life was already tarnishing the new life her brother and Charlotte were about to begin. And she resented the thought that if ever there was a man who would want to marry her, he wouldn't be able to do so under the eyes of God. The moment she returned home from the church, she tore off the dress, convincing herself it was a relief there'd never be an occasion to wear it again.

She'd found the dress in her bureau drawer, wadded up, just as she'd left it. After a good ironing, it was wearable. But as soon as she shimmied the dress over her head and buttoned herself up, she could once again feel prickly heat flush her chest and belly. It was as if the dress had kept her shame within its lace and seams all this time.

Waiting until Peter and Charlotte were out, she changed and then hurried from the house, not wanting them to glimpse her as they'd most surely inquire about the dress, the silk stockings, and that she'd braided a ribbon into her hair and dabbed on her rose oil more generously than usual. The last thing Mary wanted was to reveal her farfetched longing to become one of the Countess's girls, and she couldn't bear the thought of Peter and Charlotte asking all sorts of hopeful questions she couldn't answer.

Now she tucked the dragging seam into her boot and continued on, but with each step closer, doubts pelted her, reminding her that bastard girls who made their way in a crib should know their place. And her place had been set the day Lobrano sent her, with a push, into the middle of the Alley. She didn't want to think back to that day, but the memory was suddenly with her, spilling out like a cracked egg. How she'd stood there trembling as Lobrano shouted, "Virgin! That's right, bona fide virgin! Pure as rain!" She'd wanted to disappear right then and there, and if not for little Peter, eyes hollow and sunken, grasping on to her leg, she would have run, would have run away from there and away from Lobrano. But instead she remained frozen as men jeered while passing by. A barkeep she recognized from a nearby saloon presented Lobrano with two dollar bills. He had always leered at Mary through the saloon window when Lobrano left her and Peter waiting outside while he sidled up for a drink. Now the barkeep's hand was on her shoulder, leading her away. She didn't dare look back at little Peter as she and the man disappeared behind the saloon. He forced himself on her and covered her mouth in case she tried to scream. But she wouldn't scream; she knew better. Screaming would only add on a beating. She was twelve years old.

The sound of reckless merriment grew closer as Mary saw Lulu's glowing bordello ahead. The opulence took her breath away, most especially the lit stained-glass archway of LULU WHITE that fanned the door. She'd never seen anything so dramatic. Stifling back all the voices in her head telling her she wasn't worthy of even standing on this plot of land, she allowed herself to become momentarily hypnotized by the allure of what possibilities lay beyond that door. If only she could catch the Countess's favor . . . then her life could change in an instant.

After a deep breath, she headed around back, just as Eulalie had instructed.

The kitchen was in chaotic swing. Addie tilted a bottle of sherry into a cast-iron pot that nearly bubbled over with turtle stew. Then she moved over to a large pile of oysters on the half shell and, as delicately as her haste would allow, placed them onto china plates. Boo frantically poured Champagne into flutes that were quickly whisked away by the waitstaff. All the while, a young black boy scurried underfoot, collecting scraps that had fallen to the floor.

"You take those droppin's out by the alley, Little Louie," Addie said to the boy. He opened the back door to reveal Mary, her hand hovering in the air, ready to knock.

"Miss Addie, there's a lady there," Little Louie said.

Addie turned her head to glimpse a white girl. "Ma'am, the front door's 'round front."

Sheepishly, Mary said, "I was told to come 'round back."

"Confused, girl? Ya look like you're here for the party. . . ."

"I am." Mary nodded eagerly.

Addie gave a shrug; she didn't have time for this. "Well, you got empty hands. Take this tray on your way in." She whisked Mary inside, handed her a tray with Champagne glasses, and gave her a push toward the party.

The lavish parlor was packed and swinging. Mary gripped the tray of clinking glasses as she shuffled forward into the crowd. A line of topless can-can girls weaved around the room, singing, "I kick up one leg, then the other. Between the two I earn my living!"

From Mary's tray, the Champagne glasses were plucked up, with the last glass in the hand of none other than Countess Lulu White. Face-to-face, Lulu stared at Mary, raising a perfectly drawn eyebrow. Mary opened her mouth to explain, but nothing came out.

"Countess!" a voice called from across the crowd. "Countess! We're toasting!" Forced to turn her gaze, Lulu looked to see an already tipsy Mayor Flower sloppily pouring a bottle of Champagne over a pyramid of glasses. "Come, Countess, let's toast!" he bellowed.

Lulu gave Mary a steely, final glance, then, with a dismissive pivot, she glided off to the center of the room, where she struck a stunning pose in her elaborate crimson gown and diamond-and-feather tiara. Joining her was none other than Tom Anderson, handsome and debonair as could be in a top hat and tails. The mayor handed Tom a glass, then grabbed one for himself, licking the dribbles of Champagne from the rim. "Monsieur Fleur!" Lulu reprimanded.

"Cut the music!" Flower shouted, and the piano went quiet. At the thought of a piano player, Mary craned to look across the room, her eyes finding a shiny grand piano. She sucked in her breath with the hope that it might be the player from Lala's café. But instead, an expressionless white man with gray hair sat at the bench, looking stiff and out of place. Mary drooped a little with disappointment—how nice it would've been to have a familiar, welcoming face.

"My dear friends," Anderson boomed, commanding everyone's attention. "This is a great honor. As you know, I don't believe in sumptuary laws. I think it degrades a citizen to take away the privilege of choosing for himself between right and wrong."

Flower piped up, "It's indeed every man's God-given right to choose wrong!"

At this, Lulu nudged Flower out of the way, repositioning herself front and center, lest she allow him to embarrass himself—or, more important, her—any further.

"We New Orleanians are making history tonight," Lulu said, dramatically enunciating each word. "Mademoiselles, come, gather 'round me." Twenty of Lulu's girls stepped forward with the swishing of satin, taffeta, bustles, and lace, the twinkling of jewels, and the swelling of cleavage. Lots of cleavage.

Lulu continued, "We, the *demimonde*, are at long last coming into power. Embrace your sisters and recognize this remarkable achievement." The girls linked arms, some leaned their heads against one another's shoulders. "Generations from now, women with money to their name, with rights on their side, and with esteemed societal standing will speak of this precise moment, with immense gratitude . . . to us."

Mary found herself moved by the Countess's words and noted the same reaction in her girls as they clasped hands and tapped their hearts.

Lulu raised her glass. "Gentlemen and ladies . . ."

As if that were their cue, her girls—sentimentality quickly forgotten—catcalled, shimmied, and hoisted up their breasts as if offering them to the crowd.

"To Storyville!" Lulu shouted.

"To Storyville!" The crowd answered.

More corks popped, and soon a bevy of whores were chasing Mayor Flower through the parlor, drenching him with Champagne. He squealed and giggled uncontrollably.

"*Attention, mes amis!*" Lulu called, and directed all eyes to the balustrade. Heads turned to look up to the second-floor landing, which was to serve as a makeshift stage. A line of Lulu's girls costumed in Victorian dress and powdered white faces solemnly marched out.

"We, the respectable women of New Orleans, transcend our sexuality," one of the Victorians announced in a high, very proper trill. "Look how we achieve a state of pure passionlessness and frigidity." They all froze like corpses, with expressions of smelling something foul.

"Oh, look, it's President McKinley," another shouted, "coming to bestow his personal gratitude for our pious devotion to the crusade against vice in all forms, be it liquid or naked."

A girl dressed as President McKinley, with fake bushy eyebrows, her hair greased into a side part, and a cleft drawn with kohl on her chin, took the stage and ran through the line of Victorian women, rubbing "his" nose in their breasts. One by one, the women fainted, and the crowd, including Mary, burst into laughter.

"But I didn't even get my wick dipped yet!" protested President McKinley, surveying the passed-out women.

On cue, Tom Anderson, dressed as Alderman Story in wire spectacles, slicked-back hair, and a conservative bow tie, rode in on a costumed horse. From the piano came a "William Tell Overture" gallop. "I'm Alderman Sidney Story, here to save the day!" he announced.

"Thank God!" moaned President McKinley. "I'm turnin' blue!" McKinley sidled up to the horse as if to have intercourse.

Anderson/Story cleared his throat. "Ahem! AHEM!"

"Oh, oh. Pardon me," McKinley said, turning to Anderson so the two of them could go at it doggie fashion. The audience roared.

Suddenly, there was a loud crashing sound from offstage, and Anderson/Story clutched his chest as he slid to the ground. "It's true!" he moaned. "The almighty has struck me down for this gruesome fornication!" He died an exaggerated death. After a dramatically still moment, he popped up and took a bow to thunderous applause.

President McKinley stepped forward and handed Anderson a golden medallion. "I'd like to take this opportunity, as president, to officially bestow Mistah Tom Anderson with the honorary title, Mayor of Storyville."

Anderson accepted the medal, wiping fake tears.

From the audience, Mayor Flower perked up. "Somebody call for the mayor?" he asked, confusedly drunk. "I's the mayor!"

As the party resumed, Mary looked around aimlessly, then, locating the servants' back staircase, she furtively wandered to the second floor. She knew she needed to work up the courage to approach the Countess, and that if she left tonight without doing so, she'd never forgive herself. But for now, she felt awkward remaining in the parlor with no one to talk to and thought she'd have a look around, if nothing else, to at least dream about what life could be like.

She marveled at the statues, the sconces, and the ornate furnishings that seemed to have been assembled from all over the world. She stopped to touch her fingertips to the velvet wallpaper. She'd never seen a wall this fancy. And she couldn't help but grin as she stumbled upon an indoor flush toilet—of course the Countess had such luxuries! She closed herself in the water closet just for the experience of it. But when she moved to the faucet her eyes lit up as, lo and behold, there was hot water that gurgled from the spigot.

As she emerged, she heard women's voices and laughter from down the hall and followed the sounds to a cracked-open door. She tried to hold herself very still as she peered in.

There were the girls from the skit, changing back into their party dresses. Mary also recognized many of them from the marketplace, especially the pouffy-haired Poodle, who seemed to be holding court.

"He just put his head in my lap and started crying like a baby," Poodle said, then she took a long, dramatic drag from an opium pipe and passed it on.

"What did you do then?" another girl asked.

"Well, Fannie, I took him to my breast and rocked him like a baby."

"That's beautiful," Fannie sighed.

"Girls," Poodle instructed, "if it's love they want, then it's love you give. If they want to get a switching, go find the sturdiest branch—" Poodle's eyes happened upon Mary. "Oh! Seems we have a peeper."

The others turned to follow her gaze. Caught, Mary cowered behind the door.

"You can't run off without telling us who you are," Poodle called.

"Got a name, peeper?" Fannie said.

Mary wanted to run, but instead she forced herself to take a baby step into the room. She squeaked out her first name.

Another girl piped up, "Mary, Mary, quite contrary. How does *your* garden grow?"

"Who are you, anyway?" Poodle asked.

The question hung in the air. What was Mary supposed to say? *Oh, just an Alley whore* didn't seem like it would go over too well.

"Hmm, if you don't know who you are, maybe this'll help you find out," Fannie said, offering the opium pipe to Mary.

Mary stared at it, confused. She'd never smoked anything, let alone opium.

"I can think of some other things you can do with it, but for now, why don't you just smoke it," Poodle said.

Hesitantly, Mary brought the tip to her mouth and sucked in her breath. The smoke burned the back of her throat, and she began to cough. But then a tingly warmth started in her fingertips and quickly washed over her. "Y'all the Countess's girls?" she asked.

"You silly goat," one of the girls said. "Of course we—"

But Poodle interrupted. "Are *we* the Countess's girls?" she said haughtily. "See this fleshpot?" She rose and sensuously ran her hands along her body. "This is the most refined, cultured, educated cunny you can get anywhere in Dixieland. The Countess takes only the best."

Mary could now feel effects from the opium, and her body grew relaxed and heavy. "What's she like, the Countess?" Mary asked. The girls burst into laughter, and Mary flushed as she giggled along with them.

"What's all this ya-ya about the Countess?" Poodle asked.

"What she said tonight about women earning their own way," Mary began, her inhibitions waning. "Well, do y'all think she'd ever take me as one of her girls?"

Poodle looked down her nose, scrutinizing Mary. Just who did this wayward girl think she was, and how'd she even get invited to the Countess's party? "Gypsy, what do you think?" Poodle asked. The girls gathered in a circle around Mary.

"Well, the attire aside," said the dark-haired Gypsy, "she does have a decent complexion."

"She's got tits," Fannie added, and reached over to cup Mary's chest with both hands. "And firm ones."

Poodle trounced in the middle of the circle, pouty that she was no longer the focus of attention. "Well, Mary, there is 'the test.' You remember, girls, the test." The others quickly caught on and gave exaggerated nods. "Come."

Smoothing her shimmery silk purple dress, Poodle led the group out of the room. Mary followed, trailing the back of the line like the runt of the litter.

They traveled back downstairs and over to the piano, where the player was pumping out standard-fare ragtime tunes. The girls joined right in, kicking up their heels and flouncing their skirts. Mary awkwardly tried to join in, too, but not since she'd been a little girl playing "Ring Around the Rosie" had she danced in public.

"Mistah Piano Player, can you play faster?" Poodle said, and the tempo picked up. "Mary, Mary, quite contrary, you get on up there for a ride!"

Fannie joined in. "Ride!"

Mary wasn't sure what they meant, but it certainly didn't sound good. All she could do was give a befuddled shake of her head.

"Oh, but it's part of the test," Gypsy said.

"Get on up! Ride!" the entire gang taunted.

A look of terror flashed on Mary's face as she found herself being hoisted onto the piano. Poodle barked an order: "Kick up your legs!"

Helplessly, Mary obeyed and did a leg kick.

"Shimmy!"

Mary twisted her hips.

"Show your bloomers!"

Reddening now, Mary bit her lip.

"Ain't like a whore to blush," Poodle admonished.

Her heart racing, Mary saw no other option but to play along. She lifted her skirts, flashing her bloomers to the room of fancy folks. And then something unexpected happened—the crowd applauded. She couldn't believe it. Were people clapping for *her?*

"That's it, honey!" a man called out.

"Give us more sugar!" another shouted.

Reveling in the newfound attention, Mary turned around to flash her bloomers to the other side of the room. With a flirty smile, she shook her rear. The crowd ate it up.

Across the parlor, even Tom Anderson was watching, clinking the ice cubes in his glass of gin and tonic.

Lulu glided up next to him.

"Who's your new Sarah Bernhardt?" he asked, pointing toward the piano.

"If you're referring to the little tart on my Steinway, I haven't a clue," Lulu clipped.

"She's quite stunning," Anderson replied.

Lulu was taken aback. "You can't be serious. How can you compare *that* to all I have to offer?"

"Countess, I thought you to be above envy."

"Tom, you, of all people, deserve the highest caliber. That is *not* one of my girls. Her clothes are rags, for God's sake."

"My dear," said Anderson, "it's not her clothes I'm interested in."

Not more than a quarter hour later, Poodle led Mary up the regal front staircase.

"Don't dawdle," she ordered. "I, personally, wouldn't have thought you were quite ready."

"Ready?" Mary asked.

"Well, I'm assuming . . . I mean, we are one gal short, for several months at least," Poodle shook her head. "She didn't listen when I warned her to always use the French Preventative."

Mary stopped cold—was she about to become one of the Countess's girls? Her stomach flip-flopped.

"I suppose I should tell you the rules," Poodle said begrudgingly. "No swearing, no drinking more than a sip or two, and no talking to a man if another girl is talking to him. It's a dollar fine for each cuss word and five dollars for getting tipsy. And try to use proper diction. Now come on, why are you just standing there?"

Poodle opened a heavy mahogany door and scooted Mary inside, then disappeared as the door clicked shut. Mary suddenly felt lost without Poodle ordering her about, and as she stood by herself her knees grew weak and the room seemed to engulf her. It was the most glorious room she had ever seen, with plush carpet, peach striped wallpaper, crystal chandeliers, and a massive four-poster bed, draped with sheer curtains and piled high with fringed pillows. She scanned to a dressing area at the far end of the room, where, at a full-length mirror, stood the Countess. Lady's maids buzzed around her, cinching her corset and billowing the skirts of her latest gown change, this one a deep violet.

Mary waited, her heart pounding in her ears. But after a few moments she began to wonder if anyone had noticed her enter. As it occurred to her that no one seemed aware she'd been standing there, she decided to speak up. She squeaked, "Um, ma'am—"

Without turning to acknowledge her, Lulu sharply corrected, "I am Countess, not ma'am."

Mary nodded dutifully, although no one so much as looked in her direction.

A maid delicately took Lulu's hand and powdered it with white talc. Another maid began to powder Lulu's cleavage. "See what I must endure?" Lulu announced. "One can never be shy of perfection when one is the premiere madam of the Delta. This toilette powder is from Paris, the finest money can buy. Amazing how it coats my skin in flawless alabaster, *n'est-ce pas?*"

Mary remained silent.

A maid carefully slid a glimmering diamond ring onto Lulu's finger. "Ah, isn't this too dear? It was given to me by a Belgian duke, or was he a prince? No matter, he was quite impressed by my mastery of Dutch. I'm a master of many tongues . . . and I also speak five languages." Lulu laughed at her own joke, but Mary wasn't sure if she should laugh too. She wasn't even sure that the Countess was speaking to her. Lulu continued, "Too bad German isn't one of them. When in Vienna, I couldn't negotiate with ease for this." She motioned to a gold-leaf Klimt painting. "Isn't it sublime? I'm sure I overpaid, but I just had to have it."

The maids finished and Lulu shooed them away. At last, she turned to face Mary. She lifted her monocle to her eye and discerningly scanned her from her hair down to her shoes. Mary didn't know where to rest her eyes and tried not to fidget as the Countess looked her over. At last, Lulu removed her monocle, but her pallid face gave nothing away.

"My dear," the Countess instructed, "a woman doesn't just lift her skirt and expect to be regaled with such riches."

Mary eagerly nodded. "I understand, Countess, and I'll work so very hard for you."

Lulu paused, putting together the girl's misconception. She gave Mary a condescending tilt of her head. "Just because you have pretty in your favor doesn't mean it hides what you really are. I am a businesswoman. And you, my dear, are bad for my business."

Mary was taken aback. "But I thought—"

"You have no place here," Lulu said with a dismissive wave of her hand.

"Please," Mary begged. "There were men downstairs eyeing me. Let me show you what I've got. Please, don't I deserve a chance?"

"*Deserve?*" Lulu said with a biting laugh. "I chose my path very carefully. You choose to debauch yourself to anyone who'll throw a picayune your way."

Mary cast her eyes down. In a tiny voice she said, "It was never my choice."

For a second, this resonated with Lulu. After all, what little girl dreamed of growing up to be a whore? But when your mother was a slave and the man who fathered you a wealthy plantation owner, you take the money to keep your vow of silence and you use it to recreate yourself. Lulu felt an unexpected surge of emotion, old wounds that, since Beares's death, had been threatening her like a crack in a levee. Lulu shook the thoughts from her mind—they all were dead and buried, and damn this nobody of a girl for unearthing even a speck of memory.

"Leave!" Lulu ordered spitefully. "And if you know what's good for you, you won't step foot on Basin Street again."

Trembling, Mary knew she must obey, but something fierce was burning in her. Maybe it was the opium, maybe it was the fire in her belly Eulalie spoke of, but whatever it was, it made her not want to take her eyes from the Countess. She would leave, would back her way out of this room and would be gone from this house, but not without Lulu knowing that no matter how ratty, how skint, how unlearned, Mary Deubler wasn't going to look away in shame.

Lulu's face was full of acid. The brazenness of this Alley whore was shocking. How dare she try to stare down the Countess? And yet here were these penetrating eyes, gray eyes, Lulu had noticed—who in the world had ever heard of gray eyes? She was usually quite adept at overshadowing people, yet this gray stare smothered her. Lulu flinched.

And Mary saw it. A crack in the Countess's flawless veneer.

CHAPTER FIFTEEN

Buddy Bolden (standing, second from left) and his band

$\mathcal{F}$erdinand had heard of the fancy-dress party on Basin Street and was disheartened that he'd not been asked to play—especially since he'd learned that it had been through a servant of Countess Lulu White's that he'd been recommended to play at the judge's party. He knew of the Countess, herself an octoroon—her skin as passable as his own. But he was coming to realize that sometimes folks hated in others what they most hated in themselves.

In an effort to take his mind off all he was missing, he decided to go hear some of the real masters. Only, he was stuck watching his little sister while Grandmère was with relatives for the night. After restlessly sulking about the house, he decided he couldn't be held back by a seven-year-old. He needed to hear the music and wouldn't be sated any other way. "Get your coat, Améde," he declared. "We're going out."

"Where are you taking me?" Améde demanded as they ventured down Rampart Street into the all-black part of town.

"You ought to be thanking me," Ferd said. "Where I'm taking you is a treat."

"Grandmère's gonna tan your backside for taking me 'round here," she scolded.

"Oh hush, Améde. If you were old enough to tell me what to do you'd be old enough to mind yourself."

Améde's eyes widened as she noticed a pair of women with low-cut bodices lounging about the street corner. "You're taking me 'round the ratty people?"

"Ratty? Little girl, this here's flavor. There's a whole big world you haven't seen."

She made a prissy face. "Ain't my world."

"Isn't," Ferdinand corrected. He shook his finger at her. "Hard head bird don't make good soup."

Améde pouted until she spotted Clementine, a colorful *tignon* wrapped atop her head, singing, "*Belles* calas!" in her operatic voice.

Améde and Ferd inhaled the aroma of hot fried dough.

"Please, Ferd, can I have one? Please?" Améde begged.

"Now, listen, Améde, we're gonna make a deal. This evening's gonna be our little secret. Grandmère doesn't need to be wise to no calas and no nothin' else about tonight."

Améde eyed him suspiciously. "Only the Devil Man make a body lie."

"I'm not asking you to lie. This is business."

"Isn't your business washing dishes?"

Evading the question, Ferdinand stepped up to the cala stand. "Miss Mouth will take one, please," he said, handing over a nickel.

The woman passed a piping-hot fritter to Améde. "Clementine says be careful, *tou cho*! Quite hot!"

Ferd nudged Améde. "Act like you got some raising."

"Thank you, ma'am," Améde said obediently. Clementine started up her song again as the siblings continued on, Améde's face immediately decorated with powdered sugar.

They turned onto Perdido Street, where the saloons and honka-tonks were ramping up for the night. Ferdinand came to a stop in front of Union Sons Hall, built some twenty years ago by a group of free black men. During the week the hall held association meetings and charity programs, and on Sundays it was used for worship by the First Lincoln Baptist Church, but on Saturday nights it was where legends were born.

"Here we are," he said to Améde. Only, he hadn't considered that he could hardly bring a little girl in there—at least not while it doubled as what the ragtime folks called "Butt Hall." It wasn't just the music that was rowdy, it was the dancing. Bodies rubbing against each other, steaming, sweating, to the point that "funky butt" became the call line for the time during the night—especially a sizzling, summer night— when one of the musicians would shout, "Open a window, the odor's rising!"

With no other choice, Ferdinand took Améde's hand and led her around to the alley, where he was relieved to find a back door half-open. Music spilled out—the sound of ragtime mixed with blues and played rough and fast, unlike any other band music.

Ferdinand peeked in to see, center stage, a handsome twenty-year-old dressed in a tailored mohair suit and looking as fitted out as a white society man—only, he held a tarnished cornet, a castoff from the Civil War that had landed in the hands of a poor black boy, as did many of the war band instruments. He wiped his mouth with a handkerchief before bringing the horn to his lips.

"There he is," Ferdinand said, shaking his head in amazement.

"Who?" Améde asked, but before her brother could answer, a horn rose above the din. Ferd broke into a wide grin.

"Buddy Bolden . . . King Bolden. Man, can he play loud!" Ferd watched as he played the cornet with the force of his entire body.

"He can't read music, ya know," Ferd told Améde.

"Even *I* can read music!"

"I know you can, and you keep at your violin, but that man isn't like us. He was born to play that horn, he didn't have to learn it."

As the piano joined in, Ferd's gaze shifted to a wrinkled man at the keys. "And look there, it's Tanglefoot Robichaux! Older than sin and still manipulatin' those keys."

"Lemme see for myself," Améde insisted, sidling up next to Ferd to peek in. Reluctantly, he moved aside to let her have a look.

"Mistah Bolden can play the blues on brass," Ferd instructed. "What he can't say in words, it comes out in his music. Ya hear it, don't you?"

Améde listened hard. Then her face lit up. She nodded, smiling big. "I hear it, Ferd! I hear it."

"It's the gnat's ass, ain't it?"

"Isn't," Améde corrected.

Ferd playfully swiped the air, then took his sister's hand and twirled her around. They found some crates to sit on and watched as a crowd of black folks poured into the hall. Whenever Buddy stopped playing to wipe his mouth with his handkerchief, the crowd hollered, "Blow, Buddy, blow!"

He responded with his horn, which he called Baby. Ferd noticed—but kept to himself—what a ladies' man Buddy was. He always had a throng of women admirers and would pick two lucky ones to stand by the stage: one woman to hold his hat, and the other to hold his liquor. Of course, it was also part of the honor for the women to carry his belongings back to his bedroom after the show.

As the night went on and the temperature began to rise, Buddy called out, "I can tell my children's here, 'cause I can smell 'em!" And at this, the crowd went wild.

Ferd decided it was time to get Améde home. The music trailed them down the block, and Ferd knew that the band would play and the whiskey would flow and the people would bawdily dance until the wee hours of the morning.

And then, when the last die-hards were shooed away at sunrise, the windows and doors would be thrown open to air the place out, the spills would be sopped up, and carbolic soap and scrub brushes would be taken to the floor. The empty bottles would be carted away and the cigar smoke beaten out of the rugs. All just in time for the preacher and parishioners to arrive ready to pray at 9:30 A.M., none the wiser to the clouds of sin that still lingered. Except, of course, for those folks who silently nodded to each other, having had just enough time to catch a few hours of sleep, bathe off the stink, and put on their church clothes.

Chapter Sixteen

No 90 Spanish House, 150 Years old.

Mary trudged home from Basin Street, face smeared, hair fallen. She felt like a penned-up racehorse who'd been so raging to get loose that she ended up washing out in the stall before the race had even begun.

To add to her troubles, as she approached home, she could see Lobrano pacing out front. No doubt he'd found out about the crib by now—and Lord knows he was drunk as a skunk, too. Her first instinct was to turn and run the other way, but she was too exhausted to go wait him out somewhere else. She just wanted to go home, to be in the same room with the only people on earth she cared about and who cared about her. One of these days she was going to have to confront Lobrano anyway. Might as well be tonight, when she was already so beaten there wasn't much more he could do to her that would hurt.

She walked up to the house, and Lobrano locked his stare on her, taking in her fancy dress.

"You got some sweet daddy you're fuckin'?" She tried to walk past him, but he blocked her way. "I heard some talk of what you done, but can't be more than just ya-ya . . . ?" He paused expectantly, waiting for her to explain, but she said nothing. Cocking his head, he continued to wait, his beady eyes attempting to bore into her. Normally, she broke out in a sweat when Lobrano sized her up like that. But now she felt nothing.

And then from inside the house came a pained moan. Mary instantly snapped from her numbness. "Charlotte?" she cried out.

"Oh, she's been havin' it tough," Lobrano said flatly. "Best for all of us that no baby see the light of day."

Mary had no time for repulsion. She drew up all her strength and shoved past Lobrano, bursting into the house.

Peter jumped up. "Thank God, Mary," he said, looking pale and drained. "She's been laborin' some hours now."

With a reassuring nod to Peter, Mary rushed behind the drawn curtain. A black mammy, who was the closest they could afford to a midwife, mopped Charlotte's flushed, sweaty face.

"Oh, Mary!" Charlotte cried, "I've been so scared."

"Baby's takin' its sweet time is all," the mammy said reassuringly.

An intense contraction hit Charlotte, and she arched her back.

Mary grabbed her hand. "Lottie, you're doin' real well. You're gonna be just fine."

"How can you say that?" Charlotte wailed. "Your own mama—"

But Mary quickly commanded, "Charlotte, now, you listen to me. Your baby's gonna show us her face soon enough."

Tears filled Charlotte's eyes, threatening to overflow. Mary stroked her arm, trying to calm her. "There, now, the baby's gonna be beautiful. I wonder who she'll look like?"

From the other side of the curtain, they heard the front door open. "Get your soaked ass outta here, Lobrano," Peter warned.

Charlotte looked to Mary, panicked.

"I promise," Mary whispered, "he ain't comin' nowhere near you or this baby."

"Mary!" Lobrano shouted. "How could you betray me, your own kin? You fuckin' some dandy? You ridin' some pete man?"

Mary looked apologetically to the mammy.

Another contraction washed over Charlotte. "Oh dear God!"

Back on the other side of the curtain, Peter clenched his fists with each wail from his wife. "Ain't gonna tell you again, Lobrano," he said staunchly.

"I's a right to know why that cow betrayed me," Lobrano demanded.

"My sister ain't your property."

"We's all blood, but she took my crib and left me to starve! How'd you think I was gonna get by? The only reason you're both alive is 'cause of me—"

"She's the one been keepin' you alive," Peter stormed back.

"You ingrates," hissed Lobrano. "I took pity on you pissants. That whore who was my sister couldn't keep herself from gettin' indisposed. Thank the Lord the next little brat didn't make it, but curse the Lord for taking my sister at the same time. And curse Him for leaving me to deal with the both of yous! I should've let you rot. I could've, ya know. You owe me your life, and this is what ya do to me?"

Peter palmed the worn watch he'd been nervously fidgeting with. He knew in his gut that as soon as he'd come of age he should have stepped in to protect Mary, to protect his own family. He stared Lobrano square in the face. Solemnly, he said, "We're both sorry excuses for men."

Mary had risen to watch them from the curtain, her gray eyes unflinching. Her stance as rigid as a barricade. "You're not the man of this house," she said. "Peter is. And he told you to git."

Looking from one to the other, Lobrano only just realized how much Peter towered over him. Even Mary seemed to loom larger. Or maybe it was just the absinthe. Woozy, he inched toward the door.

"Could've left both you sissies for dead. Maybe I should have." He ambled helplessly, and, at last, the door slammed behind him.

Peter's eyes landed on the rosewood knife resting on the bureau. Snatching it, he defiantly headed to the door.

"Let him go, Peter," Mary said.

"Need to make sure he stays away from my family." Peter spoke with an authority Mary had never heard from him before, like a growling dog marking his territory.

She wearily shook her head as she watched Peter disappear. Before heading back to the other side of the curtain, she squeezed her eyes shut. "Dear Saint Anne," she whispered, "please don't let Charlotte bring another cock into this world."

Nestling back aside the bed, Mary cradled Charlotte's hand. They could hear the men carrying on outside, and Mary began chatting, trying to drown them out. The louder the men got, the more Mary jabbered on—what can they knit for the baby? Maybe she'll get these gray eyes. Will she have Peter's nose or Charlotte's? At some point, Mary noticed that the men's voices had stopped. The night was suddenly quiet but for Charlotte's labored breath. Mary waited for the creak of the door, for Peter to come back in. But there was nothing, just silence.

Unnerved, she rose. "Let me get you some more water," she said, taking Charlotte's tin cup. She stepped to the other side of the curtain and pointedly looked out the front window. Time seemed to slow as she saw Lobrano hovering over some sacks of potatoes. Why would Peter have hauled out potatoes? And then, there was a snap in her mind, and the sight came into sharp focus.

She raced outside. "Oh God!" she cried. There, on the ground, was Peter, his shirt turning blood-soaked.

The knife tumbled from Lobrano's hand. He dropped to his knees, trembling. It was Eulalie's voice that rang out in Mary's head, *One day, you'll be on your knees to this girl, asking for forgiveness.* Mary saw, crystal clear, the vision from when she was six years old: there was Eulalie pointing the knife at Lobrano.

"Mary . . . Mary, I didn't mean . . . you gotta believe . . ." Lobrano sputtered, but he was already invisible to her as she knelt at Peter's side.

"You're gonna be all right, Peter, you hear me?" she cried.

Lobrano held out his arms helplessly, then made a crawling, stumbling run for it.

Mary raced back into the house. "Charlotte, Peter and me gotta take care of something," she called out. "You be strong and bring this baby into the world."

"What happened, Mary? What's wrong?"

Mary popped her head behind the curtain, giving Charlotte the warmest smile she could muster. "Everything's all right. We'll all be in tall cotton soon enough, don't you worry." She let the curtain fall closed and moved quickly to the bureau, hoisting it aside and grabbing the cigar box. There was her week's earnings in full, plus the profit from Beulah. It wasn't much, but at least it was something. Spotting her kip against the wall, she hurried outside with it.

"Peter, you stay with me," she said as she pulled him onto the kip. With strength she never knew she had, she dragged the kip down the road.

Mary had no sense of how much time it took to arrive at Hotel Dieu Hospital. It could have been minutes, it could have been an hour. She'd talked to Peter the whole way, telling him the story of Josie the Conductor. She hadn't realized he'd lost consciousness.

"Help! Somebody help me!" she called as she hauled the blood-soaked kip into the hospital.

Nurses turned and gasped, as the sight smacked of a whore and her unfortunate trick.

"You can't bring that in here," a nurse snapped. "This is a sanitary—"

"He's been stabbed. My brother!" Mary pleaded.

"Oh, your brother," another nurse said with a grimace.

"He *is* my brother. Here, I got money to pay!" Mary opened the cigar box, and bills and coins, along with the hotel postcard, cascaded to the floor.

The nurses remained frozen. "We don't want your money. You and your john need to be on your way, girl."

Mary began to cry, angry, frustrated tears that burned her cheeks. "Please . . . my little brother."

Another nurse gingerly stepped forward. With a touch of sympathy, she knelt beside Peter to take his pulse. "Sorry, miss. The only thing I can oblige you with is a death certificate."

Everything went silent to Mary. The figures before her blurred together. Her legs buckled, and she sank to the ground.

CHAPTER SEVENTEEN

Jackson Square; the Cabildo is left of the Saint Louis Cathedral

p and down the signs bounced: THE TRAVELERS AID SOCIETY PROTESTS STORYVILLE! Buttoned-up Jean Gordon and her equally buttoned-up crew weaved through the crowd in Jackson Square, picketing and chanting, "Jesus knows your wretched soul!"

But as the Cabildo doors opened, a hush fell over them. All eyes turned to watch as out sauntered squat Mayor Flower, mousy Alderman Story, and the men of the Public Order Committee.

The mayor waved a scroll. "Signed and sealed!" he called out. Cheers erupted while Jean Gordon rallied her brood with hisses and boos.

A soapbox was set down in the middle of the square, and Flower hoisted himself onto it. "The way I feel about this ordinance for Storyville—" he began, but was quickly interrupted by Alderman Story nearly tripping over himself.

"That is *not* the name of the district!" Story shouted, his voice even higher-pitched than usual. He nervously flailed his arms. "It's called . . . the District!"

"Ain't our good Alderman modest?" Flower said with a chuckle. "Yes, so, as I was saying, the way I feel about this ordinance for *the District* is the way I felt about the prohibition debate in our fine city. People from the countryside were for prohibition at home, but when they came to New Orleans they were wet and wanted New Orleans to be saturated. We recognize that New Orleans represents a destination for people who need balance in their disciplined lives. And now people will have the right to pay a trip to the new district, if it's within their code of ethics. My friends, our sincerest hope is that this ordinance will produce a self-contained, upstanding business district of its own right."

The Travelers Aid Society was drowned out by the cheering.

But one major Storyville proponent—and arguably the individual with the most to gain from the turn of events—was clearly absent: Tom Anderson.

At that very moment, in the back of town, Anderson was overseeing workers as they strung Nobels Extradynamit around the dilapidated houses of Basin Street. After a series of thumbs-ups from on down the line, a lever was pushed and, with a great boom, smoke billowed up as the houses crumbled down. Anderson surveyed his street—what would look like ruins to anyone else was a million-dollar avenue to him. His saloon would be on the corner, and as Storyville business expanded, he'd build one bordello after another.

But for now, he was to start with the two houses left standing on Basin: Countess Lulu White's Mahogany Hall, which Anderson had a hefty stake in and, two doors down, a vacant but exquisite Victorian with a towering cupola. There was something that had attracted him to the Victorian, even though he'd considered tearing it down because of its state of disrepair. But unlike the other houses now in rubble, this one had an attention to detail, an artistry, a personality, with detailed iron lace, decorative masonry, and copper finishings that had aged to a glowing blue-green patina. But his favorite feature was presiding over the front door: an intricate plaster relief of a cherubic woman with flowing hair, her face framed by seashells and flowers and a cornucopia overflowing with fruit. It was as if the house already had a symbolic madam. And now it needed a real one.

Not far from Basin, rats scurried over crumbling tombstones and random bones that had surfaced in the paupers' cemetery. Next to Mary stood Charlotte, gently swaying as she held a tiny swathed bundle. Solemnly, they watched as two gravediggers lowered an unadorned pine box into the ground.

"If anythin' of value's buried with him, best take it back," one of the diggers said. "This swampland don't keep much down."

Mary shook her head.

Trudging by, another gravedigger dragged a coffin on a rope, the body inside shifting loudly from side to side. There was no such thing as respect for the dead here. A haggard woman trailed the coffin, cursing it. "You son of a bitch, gamblin' and drinkin' away everythin'. From your own daughter! Here's where you spend the rest o' your days. The pauper's lot. You happy now?" The teenaged daughter, in a tattered black dress, was stone-faced behind her.

Mary couldn't help but look, and, as they passed, her eyes met the daughter's. The girl attempted to hold her head high, as if to say, *You're no better off.*

It was true. Peter had never done anyone harm, but his fate was the same. No sepulchre, no funeral, just some tears and the hope that his body would stay buried.

The baby started to whimper. Charlotte had named her Mary Anna, explaining that's what Peter had wanted too. The notion of another Mary Deubler in the world felt heavy, and Mary thought back to her own mama, who had wanted her children to take their father's last name—even though there was no father in sight. The Lobrano lineage was tainted with misfortune, she'd said, and she wanted her children to have a chance with a new family line. It seemed clear that the Deubler name too had fallen short; it held nothing to offer to this new generation.

Mary envisioned her namesake growing up and having to come to this forlorn place to pay her respects. The pauper's lot would be all she'd know of her father. At the thought of that, Mary feared she might be sick right there at the gravesite. She took some deep breaths. "Charlotte, why don't you go on, take Anna home." She steadied herself. "Anyway, it looks like rain."

Tears streaming down her face, Charlotte nestled the baby closer. Sweet Charlotte, she looked as if she might break in two from the weight of her heartache, and yet her wet eyes still smiled when she looked at her tiny daughter. Baby Anna was slight, like Peter, but—thank God—not sickly. She had Charlotte's doll-red lips and Peter's sandy hair but had indeed inherited Mary's gray eyes. With slow leaden steps, Charlotte moved away, her head hung low.

Once Charlotte was out of sight, Mary crumpled onto the ground, her body feeling as if it might cave in on itself. Never had she felt this helpless. She'd waited all morning at the parish sheriff's, only to be told that if Lobrano were found, he could be tried, but that with no witnesses and with the murder weapon the property of the Deubler house, it would be near impossible to prove Lobrano hadn't acted in self-defense. In other words, a woman with no money and no husband shouldn't bother with justice.

As she watched the gravediggers shovel stones, she wondered how it would be possible to feel anything other than this pain. Would she ever again be able to smile at a simple pleasure, like picking lilacs or relaxing into a hot bath? How could she want to tap her feet to some rollicking piano music from a handsome player? Her heart couldn't flutter like that anymore, she was sure of it. She lay back and closed her eyes, wanting the ground to swallow her up and spit out her bones.

The stones hit the coffin with an echoing thud. It seemed the worst sound she'd ever heard. But at that, she forced herself up and grabbed a shovel. She needed to do anything other than just let this happen.

CHAPTER EIGHTEEN

Saint Louis Cemetery No. 1

𝒩earby, but seemingly a world away, another kind of funeral was occurring. Ferdinand, along with a crowd of worshipers, moved in a sprawling mass to the gates of Saint Louis Cemetery Number One.

The mourners were dressed to the nines. The women wore wide-brimmed fancy hats or carried colorful parasols, and they all fluttered oriental fans against the stale air. The men donned three-piece suits with bow ties and decorated themselves with sashes promoting the Young Men Olympians. Ferdinand was properly suited, with a bright blue handkerchief he carefully folded then fluffed to display from his jacket pocket.

To black Creoles, there was no such thing as a gloomy funeral, especially when the deceased had lived as long and colorful a life as Tanglefoot Robichaux. It was only fitting that a musician of his stature have the grandest of musical funerals. A large brass band had already escorted the family and close friends from their home to the cemetery and now was playing dirges until after the burial, when the tempo would pick up. Ferd spotted Buddy Bolden paying his respects through his cornet, alongside other characters he knew from hanging around the back doors of honkatonks, like Buddy Zulu on bass trombone and Blind Freddie on the clarinet.

A large woman sidled up to Ferd. "Did you know Mistah Tanglefoot?"

"Not personally, ma'am. But I wanted to be in the second line today to honor him."

"He played that piano right up to the end," the woman said with an impressed shake of her head. "May he rest in peace in the marble orchard."

As they moved closer to the cemetery gates a craggy old man with an Olympians sash nudged Ferdinand. "This will be how we all rejoice for you," he said. "If you're a member."

"Gee, sir," Ferd said with a flinch. "I'm not long out of short pants."

But the man pressed a knotty finger to Ferd's chest and studied him with filmy eyes. "Ain't never too soon to consider such matters."

The man's intenseness sent a shiver through Ferd. "I'll think on it," he replied, inching away. Fortunately, the crowd began parting to allow the huddle of relatives to walk through, and Ferd maneuvered himself to the other side, away from the Olympians man. The band played a slow, mournful version of "The Saints," and Ferd joined in the singing:

Lord, how I want to be in that number,
When the saints go marching in.

As he sang, his eyes fell on a young boy, about six years old, whose face was painted in Voodoo makeup to look like a skull with hollow eye sockets, shadowy cheekbones, and jagged teeth drawn over his lips. The boy had climbed up onto a ledge and was clutching the cemetery gate as he sang with the crowd. And then, as if the boy felt Ferd's gaze, he deliberately turned his head. His blacked-out eyes instantly found Ferd, fixing on him. He sang:

And when the moon, turns red with blood,
And when the moon turns red with blood
Lord, how I want to be in that number. . . .

Ferd suddenly felt queasy. The crowd seemed to be closing in around him. The singing grew muffled and drifted off as his own heartbeat became louder and louder in his ears. Only it wasn't his heartbeat—it was the pounding of an African drum. And Ferd was no longer amidst the funeral crowd but hovering somewhere near Congo Square. Flickering candles lit the square as Eulalie Echo, in a multicolored African caftan, bells dangling from her wrists and ankles, danced around the boy in Voodoo makeup. But the little boy wasn't ardent and steady like the one staring from the cemetery gates. Instead, he was scared and trembling and tried to run, but Eulalie grabbed him and held her hand on his head to keep him still. Her eyes rolled back as she chanted: *"Eh! Eh! Bomba hen hen!* At great cost I ask this of the Gatekeeper of Hades, whose powers are many, that he will bestow to this child a gift of great worth."

From the trees of Congo Square stepped an African man, holding a writhing sack. He pulled from it a live chicken. The boy began to whimper. The drumming grew louder and more intense as Eulalie danced around and around. She chanted, *"Danga moune de te!"* The chicken shrieked, a loud *baKAW* that sent the little boy wincing. He turned his head away just as there was a sharp cracking sound, and the chicken was silenced. Blood splattered across the boy's cheek.

Ferd jumped. An Olympians man next to him put a hand on his shoulder. "You all right, fella?"

Catching his breath, Ferd looked around. The band had stopped playing, and the grand marshal was consoling Tanglefoot's relatives. There was no sign of the Voodoo boy. Ferd desperately searched the crowd, turning himself around in a complete circle, but still nothing, no sign of any child with the face of a skeleton. Silently, Ferd cursed himself for having such ridiculous, dark thoughts at someone's funeral.

In an effort to clear his muddled mind, he trained himself on the grand marshal, who was stepping up to address the crowd.

"Dear family and friends, as the official grand marshal of the New Orleans Young Men Olympians, I ask that y'all join the main line in celebrating the joyous release of Mistah Tanglefoot Robichaux's beloved soul to heaven."

A lively tune of "Didn't He Ramble" started up, and any hint of mournful tone vanished as everyone began to dance. Still dazed, Ferdinand was swept up like a rag doll in the crowd as a line began to form, turning the funeral procession into a full-out parade. Everyone sang as they jubilantly danced on down the street.

Didn't he ramble? He rambled,
Rambled all around, In and out the town.

Ferd forced his feet to shuffle and his lips to move as he joined in, even though his mind was still whirring over such a devilish vision.

The crowd sashayed and stomped, and anything that could be waved was gleefully thrust in the air—handkerchiefs, umbrellas, hats, banners, all bouncing on down the street. They would parade around the neighborhood until arriving at the reception, where table after table would be overflowing with potluck dishes. Ferd had planned on stuffing himself silly on sandwiches and gumbo, corn bread and corn on the cob, sweet-potato cakes, and pralines. That was, if his stomach would quit doing flip-flops. He focused on the music, the rhythm, one foot in front of the other, don't think, just sing.

Didn't he ramble? He rambled,
He rambled till the butchers cut him down.

Suddenly, the music trailed off, and, with people almost toppling one another, the Creole parade slowed to a halt. Everyone craned to see what was going on. At the head of the line, the Olympians' parade had been met by another parade, coming from the opposite direction. As the mourners caught sight of the other side's banners and sashes, a communal groan spread through the crowd. It was the Olympians' nemesis: the Freedmen's Aid Society. The Olympians were Creoles; the Freedmen, Africans.

"Good ole Tanglefoot always did love a boundary war," sighed a man near Ferd. Both parades knew what was in store, and on each side the women and children pushed toward the back, shaking their heads with disappointment. In turn, the men puffed up their chests and closed in the gaps.

Ferdinand felt dizzy enough that he wished he could move back with the women, but he knew the craziness in his head did not justify acting like a crazy and that shirking a boundary war wasn't something a man could live down. So he steadied himself, rooting his feet to the ground.

"Listen here, this be our line today," the Olympians' grand marshal called out. "We're honoring a great musician."

"This ain't your line to cross," the Freedmen's grand marshal replied.

And then, a shout came from the Young Men Olympians' crowd, "Says who?"

A shout back from the Freedmen's crowd, "Y'all a bunch of Johnny *Crapauds*!"

The Freedmen's marshal stepped up close to the Olympians'. "Cross this line, it'll be your Frenchy ass."

Ferdinand felt himself break out in a cold sweat. Didn't anyone else see what was going on here? As if Jim Crow weren't bad enough on its own, here was dark skin against dark skin. Was he the only one who knew that the rest of Dixieland made no such distinction? He wanted to step up and shout: We should be aligning against everyone out to get us all! And for a second, he considered actually doing it, but his head was so muddled with chants and visions that he wasn't sure he was in his complete right mind.

He would be no use in a boundary war, especially not today. Praying no one would notice, he inched his way from the crowd, and when he felt he was as much in the clear as possible, he dashed toward home, repeatedly checking over his shoulder to see if the Voodoo boy was following him.

Mary couldn't bring herself to return home after the burial. Tearstained and muddy, she walked alone, up and down streets, with no destination and hardly any awareness of where she was. A light rain fell, but she didn't care, the coldness felt good on her hot cheeks, reminding her that at least she had some feeling left in her body. She found herself on Basin Street, picking her way through the rubble. She lingered as she passed the Countess's bordello. *Let the fire-haired madam come out here and shout at me, what does it matter? What does anything matter anymore?*

Her eyes fell upon the neighboring Victorian, and she was compelled toward it. Beneath years of abandonment—the peeling paint, rusty hinges, and crumbling stone—was a unique beauty of a house. She marveled at the castle-like cupola, rising five stories high, and wondered what the view of the city must be like from up there. Raindrops dribbled down the cupola's leaded windows, creating tiny prisms of light, and she envisioned herself looking out from the highest window, just as a princess might.

From her pocket, Mary retrieved the postcard of the Arlington Hotel. She'd been carrying it since Peter died. It made her think of Mama, and she'd wanted it close to her. She held up the postcard, framing the picture of the hotel with the house in front of her. They bore an uncanny resemblance, right down to identical cupolas. Inexplicably, she felt a sense of peace.

But it wasn't until she stepped closer, up the walkway and to the boarded front door that she looked up and saw her: the woman of the house, smiling down upon Mary with the gentlest of faces. It was as if this house had been expecting her.

Mary wasn't sure how long she'd been standing across the street from Tom Anderson's saloon. She'd been watching Tater, who was sitting on the stoop, whittling a stub of wood. She knew what she wanted to do—what she needed to do—but just had to convince herself to cross the street.

She watched Tater's face scrunching as he maneuvered his carving knife. Mary was certain that over his years working around the Alley he'd done unspeakable things, and it soothed her to think that her request of him would hardly be the first and certainly not the last.

She waited some more, until Tater rose, and after he'd walked some paces from the saloon, she hurried after him, trailing behind his clomping boots.

"Mistah Tater," she called out, and the beast of a man turned his head.

His eyes narrowed at the sight of her. "Ain't no refunds," he grumbled and continued on.

"No, it's regardin' . . . a different matter. A *paying* matter."

At this, he paused. Mary motioned him around the corner, where they ducked into a shadowy alley.

"You know of my old bossman, Philip Lobrano?" she said.

He scoffed. "What collector don't?"

"Well, he did somethin' . . . somethin' truly awful." Mary gulped back the lump in her throat. "He's a beast . . . a killer. Took the life of my little brother. Thing is, the sheriff needs witnesses, and there weren't none, but me. And guess I don't count for much. He left a newborn baby with no father. So for the sake of the child, I need to take the law into my own hands, ya see." She paused to study Tater's face. He was still listening. "I need to make sure I have your confidence," she said. He nodded.

From her chemise, she pulled the earnings saved up from the week, including Beulah's rent, plus the little cash that had been left in the cigar box. "Mistah Tater, if you could know the things he's done through all my years—"

But Tater was already itching to move on. He didn't need to know, didn't care. "Good as done," he said. As he went to stash the money, his whittling fell from his pocket. Mary picked up the stump; on a smoothed side, Tater had carved a likeness of Jesus.

CHAPTER NINETEEN

Canal Street

At the Public Order Committee's weekly meeting, Alderman Story stood at the head of the room addressing the dozen committee members as if he were still in front of the boisterous crowd from the Cabildo. "We are in our glory today," he said, holding his arms toward the sky. "It is through our dedication and determination that we have achieved high distinction for our beloved New Orleans by putting on the map this country's first and only legalized and regulated red-light district."

His sermon-like rant was interrupted by a woman's high-pitched shout: "You hypocrites!"

All heads turned to see the angular, pale face of Jean Gordon peering in through the open window and taking a spiteful look around the room. "Ye serpents, ye generation of vipers!" she hissed, eyeing each and every man. "How can ye escape the damnation of hell?"

"Mrs. Gordon!" Story gasped, his face flushing crimson.

"I'm talking most of all to you, Alderman Story," she spat. "How can you escape the damnation of hell with your Storyville going on a page of our history?"

"You, ma'am, are impertinent," Story said, hurrying to close the window. But Mrs. Gordon, as the president of the Travelers Aid Society, didn't see it that way, and as Story attempted to shut the window, she flailed her arms.

"The Travelers Aid Society will not be silenced!"

Story was all but pushing her head back out the window, wrangling with her limbs, and somehow, he finally managed to inch the window closed. Muted for the time being, Jean was still in full view, gesticulating wildly. She slapped a picket sign against the glass pane: STORYVILLE IS THE DEVIL.

At this, Story brusquely pulled the drapes. He loped back to the table, attempting to regain composure. "Before resuming business, I'd like to note the usage of a highly inappropriate moniker for the District."

"Tom Anderson's terminology," one of the committee members offered up.

"The point being," Story scoffed, "that the only acceptable references for our district are, simply, 'The District,' or, if you must, 'The Tenderloin.' Consider all other terms slanderous. And rather insulting."

Men's eyes darted to one another; they were all guilty of using *Storyville*.

"Alderman, I mean no dissent," one man piped up, "but I'm seeing the ailment progressing still. Lewd and abandoned women are habitating in the house right next door to mine, as if all our effort has been for naught."

"I know we'd all like to just round up the trollops and dump them in the swamp," Story replied, "but this major upheaval can't possibly be expected to transpire overnight. According to the ordinance, there's still a fortnight's time." He quickly referenced the ordinance document, running a delicate finger down the page. "Ah yes, here is the precise language: 'After the deadline, it will become unlawful for any woman notoriously abandoned to lewdness to inhabit or sleep in a house, room, or closet outside the District boundaries. White and octoroon women of ill repute will reside below Canal Street. Negro whores are relegated to Franklin Street.'"

He looked up from the page. Without the open window, the already warm room was growing close, and men began to dab handkerchiefs at their perspiring foreheads. "I'm sure there will be stragglers," Story continued, "but by and by, the transition's gone tolerably well, and I have reason to believe it will continue as such."

"What's the recourse if whores don't abide by the January first deadline, Alderman?"

"We will start by instituting a significant fine. If they still don't abide, they'll be jailed without question. I'm hopeful there won't be but sparse cases of noncompliance."

"I've already seen sporting women promenading to the back o' town," a member offered up. "Like rats following the Pied Piper!"

Another chimed in that with many brothels already vacated, his street felt as serene as it was back when he was just a boy.

"Have y'all seen the expense going up on Basin Street?" another member asked. "Fine as our Uptown mansions. What strange irony if the whores come to fancy themselves too refined and prideful to let rowdiness muss their elegant new homes." They all chortled in agreement.

"Gentlemen," Story said as if bursting with a secret, "I daresay, I suspect lewd and abandoned women might be fixing to behave themselves in the back o' town. Now, wouldn't that be a dandy?"

❧

Mary slammed her shoe against a tack as she hung a rough hand-written sign on her crib door.

FANCY GIRLS
$1 WHITE GIRL
50¢ NEGRO GIRL

From behind her she heard Beulah's throaty voice. "Ya think I can't read? I ain't half the snatch you are."

Mary sighed as Beulah marched over to her, hand on hip. "It's just the way it is, Beulah."

"Says who? The white man?"

"This here is my crib now." She wished the words evoked the pride they were due, but they fell flat to her ear. Still, for the time being, she was in charge. And the first thing she saw to was that an open can of lye, diluted with water to temper the odor, be concealed under the bedside table—if ever Cooper came by, or if ever another john raised his hand to her or tried to stiff her, she'd throw the lye on him. It was a tactic she knew other whores used—the entire Alley knew because you'd hear a burned john screaming bloody murder. Mary had never looked kindly on scarring a man for life, but her mind had seen fit to change. "Beulah, you gonna take your shift or what?"

Not used to answering to another woman, let alone little Mary Deubler, Beulah arched like a cat. She huffed, "Who died an' made you Lobrano?"

The color drained from Mary. Except for the parish sheriff and Tater, she hadn't told a soul what had happened, so Beulah was blind to the wide-open wound. And Mary wasn't about to explain. Besides, there were no words, no tears, no emotion left. She felt like a hollow shell of a person. She stepped back to the crib door, raised her shoe, and gave the sign another fierce smack.

Snitch ambled along Robertson Street, kicking a stone down the road.

"Hey, Snitch!"

The boy eagerly looked around, glancing at windows, doorways, and balconies, but saw no one. "Who's callin'?" he asked into the air.

"Snitch!" the voice snarled. "For Chrissake, ya dumb mutt. Down here."

Snitch spotted a hand beckoning from under a stoop. "Who there?" he asked as he cautiously inched over.

The hand lurched out and grabbed Snitch's shirt, yanking him under the stoop, where he was suddenly face-to-face with Lobrano.

"Jesus, Snitch! No point in me hidin' if I gotta come knock you in the head."

"Mistah Lobrano, what in the hell ya doin' down here? And you sure look mawmucked. Time for a bath, too, if ya don't mind me sayin'."

"Keep your voice down." Gaunt and hollow-eyed, Lobrano peered over his shoulders in jerky motions. "They been askin' 'bout me?"

Snitch inched away, knowing the man was in a bad state—even worse than usual. "Who been askin'?"

"Everybody."

"Can't says I heard nobody askin' after ya, Mistah Lobrano. How come you ain't runnin' your gal no more?"

"Oh, they be talkin'," Lobrano assured him. "I'm sure they're lookin' for me."

"Like I said," Snitch insisted, "I ain't heard no one lookin'—"

"Whatcha got today?" Lobrano interrupted, his face twitching.

"What's into you? You're skittish as a long-tailed cat in a room full of rockin' chairs."

"I want that fix you sell."

Snitch began to dig into his satchel, when he paused. "Got a dollar for me, Mistah Lobrano?"

Lobrano stared at him as if he could cadge his way through. But Snitch wasn't budging, and stared right back. He knew how desperate Lobrano was, could tell by the dripping sweat on his face and the tremor of his hands.

With a huff, Lobrano dug in his pockets, counting out his change. "Spare me a nickel?" he pleaded.

"Aw, now, if I spare all y'all, I'll be bare-assed," Snitch said.

"Just this once," Lobrano pleaded. Snitch eyed him warily.

"For fuck's sake, it's just a goddamn nickel!" Lobrano snapped.

Knowing Lobrano's volatility, and that he was practically trapped under this stoop with a crazy lout, Snitch gave in and pulled a small paper bag from his satchel. "Ya remember the kindness I'm showin' you now," Snitch said before handing the bag over.

Near salivating, Lobrano made a jittery grab for the bag, ripping into it. He scooped up a dirty fingernail of white powder and snorted it.

Snitch shook his head as he climbed back to the street. He continued on to Venus Alley, where he was met by a whore everyone called Martha Washington, for she was surely the oldest whore around. The trull had to be fifty, maybe even sixty years old, Snitch figured, something ancient, especially for this cesspool. Martha lingered outside a crib, offering her saggy breasts to passersby.

"Get it while it's hot! Hot pussy!" she called through several missing teeth.

Men gave her pitiful looks as they passed, and one mercifully tossed her a coin. But as she scurried to retrieve it from the ground, Snitch swooped in, scooping it up.

"Snitch! I'll whop your ass!" she hollered.

"Gotta catch me first, ratty ole bat!" Snitch taunted and took off running, smacking full-on into another boy carrying an armful of complicated-looking contraptions, all of which came clattering to the ground.

But as Snitch looked up, he realized this wasn't a boy at all, but a little man. A grotesque-looking little man with a bulbous forehead and a hunched-over back. Snitch's eyes widened. "S . . . s . . . sorry, mistah."

Before the man could respond, Snitch took off again, hightailing it down the Alley.

The man was not unused to this kind of reaction, and he quietly began to gather his belongings, first picking up his 8 x 10 camera and inspecting it with concern. He peered at the ground glass, tested the knobs, touched the delicate bellows, and dusted the lens with his shirt sleeve. He breathed a sigh of relief that everything seemed unharmed.

All the while, Mary had been watching from the stoop of her nearby crib. Eager to see the contraption and, more so, to occupy her unsettled mind, she wandered over.

"Whatcha got there?" she asked.

The strange fellow looked askance at the worn shoes in front of him and continued picking up the scattered parts from the ground.

"That a photographic camera?" she pushed.

He couldn't help but glance up at this pest, but his crinkled forehead softened as he took in the dark-haired girl and her gray eyes. He gave her a shy nod before returning to survey his equipment.

"Ain't never seen a photographic camera up close," Mary said. "That's a fancy contraption. Careful, because some folks 'round here might try to swipe that."

The odd little man shifted uncomfortably, not used to this much attention from a female. Awkwardly, he leaned in the opposite direction.

As Mary studied him, her brow furled with sympathy. "You ain't some kind of half-wit, are ya?"

The man took a deep, annoyed breath, then squeaked, "No." The high pitch of his voice wasn't exactly convincing.

"All right, then. Well, I'll just leave you be. But if I were you, I wouldn't stick around here for long." Mary turned back to her crib.

The man collected his equipment in his arms, but before heading down the street he furtively looked over his shoulder, watching Mary as she walked back to her crib and straightened the sign nailed out front.

A john was waiting for her, kicking around dirt at the crib door. "Just about to go elsewhere," he said. She forced a smile and promptly led him inside.

Later that night, after the john and three others since him had come and gone, Mary sat on the step of her crib, staring at the moon. She clutched the Voodoo doll Beulah had left behind, the black yarn X marking the heart of Philip Lobrano. She balled it up in her fist and then watched as it sprang back to shape. She would riddle the effigy with daggers and burn it in flames if she thought it would actually affect Lobrano.

"Excuse me, miss," a voice squeaked.

Mary glanced up to see the odd-looking camera man, all his equipment still in his arms. "Come back for a trick, little man?"

His jaw dropped.

"I hate to disappoint you," Mary continued, "but I ain't on the clock now. Ya see, I'm sitting here doing something a whore ain't supposed to do. I'm thinking. That's what I'm doing. So leave me be, all right?"

"Miss, if I might be so bold," he squeaked. "I have come to request a photographic sitting. Thank you."

Mary chortled. "Oh, I ain't doing no nudie photographs. Let's just get that straight."

The little man squirmed, "Oh no, no, no, no."

Mary eyed him, such a strange fellow, with a head too big and body too little and a voice too high. "Then what do you want me for?" she asked with an empty shrug. "I ain't much use with my clothes on."

"It's a portrait, miss." He bashfully dropped his head, addressing the ground. "You have a kind face."

Mary was caught off guard by how touched she was. Perhaps this was the nicest thing a stranger had said to her in a long, long time, if not ever. Her clenched fist softened and the Voodoo doll fell from her clutch.

It had been one of her secret wishes to one day have her photograph taken and put in a frame. She had envisioned that she'd be dressed in a corset and wearing velvet gloves, and that she'd be in a proper setting—a parlor, a gazebo maybe—but no matter, here was a professional photographer wanting to train the camera on just her.

"Suppose I could put on my striped stockings," she said, a brightness filling her voice for the first time in a while. "My name's Mary, by the way." She held out her hand, but the little man didn't dare take it.

"E. J. Bellocq," he said, casting his eyes away from her.

"Well, come on in, Mistah Bellocq."

As Mary rolled on her stockings, Bellocq purposefully busied himself with preparing and assembling his equipment.

"Shall I sit or stand?" Mary asked. But he didn't answer. She draped a sheet over the little table and brought in a chair from the stoop. Then she removed from a crevice in the floorboard a near-empty bottle of Raleigh Rye. "Would you like a drink? It's the good kind. A john paid me in a half-full bottle. And this is a special occasion, not every day that a girl gets her photograph made."

"I abstain," Bellocq replied softly, and Mary gave him a respectful nod, even though he still hadn't looked her way. Carefully, she poured herself just a splash, holding the bottle to the light to note what was left.

Mary sat and waited, and eventually attempted to fill the awkward silence with small talk. "Worked hard on making this crib something to be proud of," she said.

Bellocq spread flash powder on a metal tray and coated the wet plate.

"Scrubbed these boards till my hands were raw," she continued. "See those curtains? My brother's wife sewed them up." She gulped. "His widow," she corrected, a quiver in her voice. It was as if she needed to practice saying it to a stranger. She watched as Bellocq set the camera on the tripod. The word *widow* meant nothing to him, and why should it? How could anyone know of her pain or that the word also meant a child would never know her father?

As he adjusted the tripod, his eyes fell on a picture postcard tacked to the wall. He lingered.

"It's a pretty photograph, ain't it?" she said. "Better than looking at the johns. It's the Arlington Hotel. Somewhere far away."

Bellocq wondered how this Alley whore knew of places far from here. He'd like to know of those places too. But he was sure he never would. He ducked beneath the cape of the camera.

Mary found herself nervous, having no idea what to expect from getting a photograph taken. The weight of it was sinking in: never had she imagined when she'd woken this morning—of all mornings—that one of her daydreams would come true. Now all she had left to do was to ride on a train, and get all dressed up and go to the French Opera, and then she could die and go to Heaven! She smiled sadly to herself. And there she would tell Peter all about it.

Trying to ease her mind, she yammered on. "You came at a good time, Mistah Bellocq. This is the best my crib's ever looked. And it is mine, you know. But, see, the thing is . . . turns out a crib ain't something you can be proud of." She took a sip of her drink then raised the glass and regarded it wistfully.

Bellocq squeezed the shutter release. There was a sudden flash, then a sizzle.

CHAPTER TWENTY

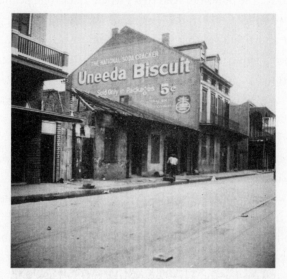

Toulouse Street

*P*eanut shells were littered about Tater's feet, and the ones that didn't make it that far still rested on his belly. He polished off the last of the sack of nuts and belched. It was sunset, with a full moon already bright in the sky.

A couple of hours had passed since Tater had been waiting, and by this point he was itching to just go yank the scallywag out. Except that would have made too much of a scene. So instead, he continued to watch the stoop, hoping that Snitch—who'd angled for a whole silver dollar—knew what he was talking about. Tater figured the dimwit fugitive would have to take a piss at some point—or better yet, a crap. He'd always wanted to off somebody while they were crapping, if for nothing else than the hilarity of it.

At last, he saw what he'd been waiting for. A mud-caked boot dangled out. And then, hunched over as if contortion would help him be less visible, Lobrano crept from his cover. He scuttled around to the side of the building. And that's when Tater rose, peanut shells raining from him. He trailed Lobrano, watching him stagger and stumble and thinking that this would almost be too easy. Where was the challenge in going after someone this addled? Like taking candy from a . . . drunkard.

The sun had set, and Tater inched along in the shadows as Lobrano turned into an alley and started to loosen his belt.

"Go on, make it a good one," Tater announced.

Lobrano's movements seemed delayed as he realized someone was talking to him. Slowly, he turned to give a squinty look over the alley. "Is that you?" he called, outstretching his arm. He felt around in the air, squinting all the harder. As Lobrano glimpsed Tater, a warm smile spread across his face. "There ya are, ya came back. This mean ya forgive me?"

"That'll be for the Lord Jesus to decide," Tater said, inching closer.

Lobrano closed his eyes. "I already set myself right with Jesus." He was barely able to keep his balance. "Jesus says you're the one who needs to forgive me. Okay, sissy girl?"

Tater bristled. "Who ya callin' sissy girl?"

"Come on, sissy, let's do like old times." Lobrano stumbled forward, nearly collapsing into Tater's arms. "Come close to me, tell me you forgive me."

Unnerved, Tater stepped back as Lobrano grabbed for him. "Come here, we're kin, remember? You and me ain't got no one else in the world." He reached out, and his hand brushed Tater's crotch. Tater jumped, and at that very moment, the moon disappeared.

Darkness fell over them like a curtain being pulled across the sky. Tater panicked, wondering if this was the end of the world and everyone was going haywire. Or was it just he being called to Heaven—or Hell?

Oh dear God, he prayed. Was pledging this act of violence summoning evil spirits? Breathless, he turned in circles, growing discombobulated as he tried to find his way from the pitch-black alley. He tripped and fell flat on his face, surrounded by the scratching of rats as they scattered from where he landed. Scrambling up, he broke into a run, not caring which direction he was headed, so long as it was out of that alley.

Some moments later, the black curtain began to lift, and the moon crept back into its place. But Tater kept running, his heart feeling as if it might explode from his chest. "I promise to God," he panted aloud, "my days of no good are over!" He decided to tell Anderson first thing in the morning—that is, if the dear Lord let him live through the night. He swore he'd become as good as an altar boy.

But the next morning, Tater couldn't bring himself to tell Anderson. He couldn't bring himself to do much of anything except blubber like a child. He spent much of the day in the outhouse, trying to toughen himself up, but every time he thought he was okay to go back out and face the boss, his bottom lip began to quiver, and back to the outhouse he'd run.

"Ya got the shits?" Sheep-Eye asked.

Tater's inclination was to nod, but that would be a lie. And he could hardly lie on his very first day as a changed man.

"I ain't doin' so good," he stammered. And then his chin started to tremble, and off he ran, the outhouse door swinging shut behind him.

Lobrano was hurting too. He'd known hangovers, but he'd never known heartache, and now the combination was enough to make him want to down another bottle of absinthe—if only he could move.

He had no recollection of the night before, which was how he'd wanted it. He began to wonder if it were possible to will oneself to death. He should fill his pockets with stones and walk himself into the Mississippi. Oh, if only he could move. But when he tried, his head fell back, heavy and slack, and the world began to flip over itself like a carnival ride.

He decided he'd sleep the rest of the day, and when the stupor had lifted, he'd leave a parting gift for Mary, and then he'd collect the stones.

CHAPTER TWENTY-ONE

$\mathcal{B}$aby Anna bounced along in a wrap attached to Charlotte. To help make ends meet, Charlotte had gone promptly back to her seamstress work, and her arms were full with a mound of dresses she'd carefully mended. Normally she returned the mending to the dress shop on Customhouse Street, but today the shopkeeper had to tend to an ailing relative, so Charlotte was instructed to deliver the dresses to the owner. The address was Basin, and she was surprised when she turned onto the street to find it in the midst of construction.

She carefully picked her way among the debris, and as she stopped at her destination of number 235, her jaw dropped. She stared up at the stained-glass archway: LULU WHITE. The mansion bustled with workers on ladders painting the trim and women in straw hats planting hyacinths all up and down the walkway, while servants swept up after them all.

"'Scuse us, ma'am."

Charlotte looked over her shoulder just in time to career out of the way as a pristine white piano was hoisted up the walkway by three sweaty men.

"Oh goodness me!" Charlotte cried.

The men, red-faced, veins bulging, maneuvered the piano inside. Charlotte, lagging behind, followed them through the open door. Her eyes widened at the gorgeous foyer, with its cathedral ceiling and contrasts of large white marble columns against dark mahogany floors and balustrades so polished and shiny you could see your reflection staring back at you.

There was even more flurry indoors, with wallpaper going up and crates of Champagne being unloaded. In the parlor, two of Lulu's girls, both fashionably dressed in camisoles and culottes, stood on chairs as they struggled to hang heavy damask curtains while a particularly bossy, pouffy-haired girl ordered them about. "Higher now, Birdie!"

"Poodle, it's heavy!" Birdie moaned.

"But it's not straight," Poodle insisted. "Move the left higher, Gypsy. Not that side, the *left*."

In the midst of the hullaballoo the white piano—miraculously—went unnoticed. "Ladies, where you want this?" one of the movers, his voice strained, piped up. But he was ignored, the girls instead focusing wholeheartedly on their task at hand. With quivering arms, the movers lowered the piano to the floor, shaking out their limbs.

Charlotte wondered if these girls were so spoiled that even something as outlandishly gorgeous as the white piano didn't warrant their attention. To her, of course, every last detail was breathtaking. She was grateful for four walls that didn't leak when it rained, and to be standing *here*—just this foyer alone was enchanting, with its huge vessels of fragrant lilies and the way the sun sparkled through the stained glass, casting rainbow prisms throughout the room.

"Sakes alive, higher, ladies," Poodle called. "Y'all got to raise it up!"

Charlotte worked up her courage and said in a tiny voice, "Got your mendin'. . . ." Of course, no one noticed.

A sudden operatic squeal rang out, echoing throughout the vaulted foyer, and there in an archway appeared the Countess, taking sight of her new, white treasure.

"Oh rhapsody!" she cried, gliding into the room. "Just like pearls. Come, Mistah Flabacher, come have a first look!"

Strolling behind her was a well-fed man with a short auburn beard and a brown three-piece suit. After Marshall Field (owner of what was referred to in Chicago as the Marble Palace department store) recommended his services, Sheldon Flabacher was hired by Lulu to oversee the promotion of not just her bordello within Storyville, but of the mystique and allure of her bordello well beyond New Orleans.

"Mistah Flabacher, doesn't this practically publicize itself?" Lulu said, running her hand along the alabaster.

"As creamy as your fair complexion, madam," he replied, to which Lulu raised an eyebrow; she wasn't exactly creamy white. She thought it best to educate the Union man.

"That's coco latte, Mistah Flabacher. An octoroon is a mix of many, shall we say, flavors. A little French, a little Spanish, a sprinkle of African. It's a divine blend of exotica." She glanced into the parlor. "Poodle! Show these boys where the music making will be, and have them discard the old Steinway."

With a pout, Poodle stepped down from her perch. "Good luck without me," she said lowly to her worker bees, and then waved to the movers. "This way." The men and the piano teetered after her down the hall. Gypsy and Birdie finally let their tired arms drop, breathing sighs of relief.

No one, still, had bothered to notice Charlotte, who was quietly hidden in the corner. She stepped forward, trying once again with her plea, "'Scuse me, ma'am—" But she was promptly interrupted by a loud knock on the front door, even though it was still wide open.

Through the doorway popped a bowler hat. "I'm here to see a Mistah Flay-*botcher*," announced Kermit McCracken. He removed his hat as he stepped inside.

Flabacher hurried over with an effusive grin, hand extended. "That's Flay-*bocker*. Sheldon Flabacher. From Chicago."

But rather than shake his hand, McCracken opened his notebook.

"Well, thanks for coming by on such short notice," Flabacher said, flustered. "Let me introduce you to the Countess." He turned toward Lulu and was surprised to glimpse a quizzical look on her face. "This gentleman is writing a newspaper article on the commencement of Storyville," Flabacher explained, "and I thought it the perfect opportunity to show him around. No such article would be complete without due attention to you, madam."

Lulu let out a caustic giggle. "Oh, the *Mascot* always gives me plenty of attention. Isn't that right, Mistah McCracken?"

McCracken cleared his throat.

"Ah, so the two of you are already acquainted?" Flabacher asked, disappointed he wasn't presenting the Countess with a new and important contact.

"Mistah McCracken, if my publicist wants to grant you an official interview, then *bien sûr*," Lulu said with a wave of her hand. "*Entrez-vous!*"

Over by the window, Gypsy and Birdie confusedly looked at each other. "What's a *publist*?" Birdie whispered.

"Someone who *publisisizes*," Gypsy said knowingly.

McCracken looked down his nose at Flabacher. "Mistah Flay-*bocker*, isn't publicity just haughty boosterism?"

Flabacher feigned a polite grin. "I'm afraid you're stuck in old times if you think ill of advertising."

"Oh, haughty . . . naughty," Lulu interjected, not wanting to drag out McCracken's visit any longer. She opened her arms, gesturing to the grandness around her. "This most gorgeous Mahogany Hall, now legal, will be christened *Maison Joie*."

McCracken winced at the use of *christened*.

By this time, Charlotte had completely lost her nerve and shrunk into the corner, realizing she'd just have to wait it all out.

From the still-open front door, two men in white gloves appeared, carefully clasping a large rectangular package, paper and twine covering it for protection. As Poodle sauntered back into the foyer, she caught sight of the new delivery. "The painting?" she cried, rushing over to tear away the wrapping like a little girl on her birthday. But as the paper fell and the framed painting was revealed, Poodle's smile dwindled. She cocked her head, as if needing to view it from another angle. Then, solemnly, she turned to the Countess. "I think it melted."

Lulu smiled gently. "It's called Impressionism," she said, more for McCracken's benefit than Poodle's. "This is Monet's masterpiece *Vétheuil in the Fog*. A very famous Parisian opera singer and art collector once felt as you did, rejecting the painting directly to Monet's face. Several years later, the painting received the honor and acclaim it deserved. It is dubbed 'The White Symphony.' And now it finds its rightful home."

"Ah, with the white piano! I see the theme," Flabacher regaled. "Mr. McCracken, the Countess has exquisite taste. Truly exquisite."

Poodle nuzzled herself up to Lulu, placing her head on Lulu's shoulder. "I didn't mean to insult the painting, Countess."

Lulu gave her a motherly nod, then tickled Poodle under the chin.

True to her name, Poodle began panting like a puppy. Gypsy and Birdie giggled, and even Charlotte couldn't help but stifle laughter.

"You getting all this, Mistah McCracken?" Lulu said. "Here's another tidbit just for you: I specially designed a music box . . . built into my mattress. You ever heard of anything like that before?"

McCracken was stone-faced, his pencil flying across the notebook. And then the room was pierced by a long, high-pitched wail.

Lulu froze, one eyebrow raised. "Did y'all hear a . . . *child*?" She said the word as if a child were akin to the Devil incarnate. All eyes suddenly found Charlotte, pressed into the corner.

Meekly, Charlotte offered the dresses. "Ma'am . . . your mendin'."

Just down Basin Street, a spike drove through a railroad tie. For as far as the eye could see the chain gang swung at one spike after another after another, sparks of steel on steel flying. Everywhere were workers, stacks of bricks, stacks of beams, and lumber wagons emblazoned with L'HOTE LUMBER MANUFACTURING COMPANY.

Surveying the construction was Tom Anderson, a smile stretching from one end of his curled mustache to the other. He still couldn't quite believe his monstrously good fortune that the train depot had happened upon his Basin Street. He'd always fancied himself a pioneer of sorts, but this was trailblazing to a degree even his wildest dreams hadn't touched—in a short time he would go from kingpin of an alley to overlord of an empire, the first ever of its kind in the United States. He'd fallen into bed the night before with such contented disbelief that he couldn't help but laugh out loud as he lay there. So fulfilled was he that he didn't even ring for an evening companion.

He caught sight of a familiar bowler hat sauntering over from

Lulu's bordello. Well aware of the comings and goings around here, Anderson knew that Lulu's new spin doctor had some asinine plan to solicit the *Mascot*, and as much as Anderson despised the so-called newspaper, if there was any mention of Storyville in print, there better darn well be mention of him, too.

"Believe it, Mistah McCracken," Anderson called. "Our little Basin Street's gonna indubitably be world famous. You're a most privileged man getting a sneak peek."

"Yes, the pleasure's all mine, I'm sure," McCracken said, not bothering to mask his sarcasm.

But Anderson kept up his pertness. "I'll personally give you a tour." He began walking down the line at a brisk clip. McCracken struggled to match his pace and take notes at the same time, which gave Anderson a smug bit of satisfaction. "Right here," Anderson said, pointing to a pile of rubble, "we have what will be the talented Miss Emma Johnson's French Studio." He pointed on down the street. "On the corner there I'm building the most dazzling saloon you'll ever lay eyes on. And at the end of the banquette, of course, is the finest and first bordello in all of Storyville, Countess Lulu White's Mahogany Hall."

"Yes, I've already had the privilege of touring that . . . place," McCracken said.

Anderson stopped walking, turned to McCracken, and dramatically pushed the reporter's notebook aside. "There are things the Countess has been keeping secret. Now, just between you and me, Mistah McCracken, the Countess is planning a room covered every inch with mirrors."

McCracken smirked. "How refined."

Anderson started up walking again, glancing back to make sure McCracken furtively noted the "secret." "I'm sure the *Mascot* would be very interested to learn the multitudes of dollars our little District is already pumping into the economy of this fine city," Anderson continued. He spotted George L'Hote, owner of all the lumber trucks scattered across the construction site. "And here's a perfect example of the prosperity to be found as a result of the Story ordinance." Anderson cupped his hands around his mouth and called out, "Mistah L'Hote!"

L'Hote turned, and his face flashed concern. Obligingly, he headed over.

"Good to see you, Tom," L'Hote said, his voice tinged with caution.

"Likewise. I was just telling Mistah McCracken here, of the *Mascot*, how business is booming at an all-time high thanks to Storyville."

"Business is good," L'Hote said stiffly.

"Ah George, no need for modesty," Anderson said, slapping L'Hote on the back. "Isn't this the best year in the history of L'Hote Lumber Manufacturing Company?"

L'Hote's face was slack. "We're fortunate to be having a good year."

Anderson noted L'Hote's resistance. "Well, I couldn't be happier with the lumber, George. Mistah McCracken, if you pardon my manners, I'd like to take advantage of Mistah L'Hote's presence and talk a brief business."

McCracken motioned to go right ahead, and Anderson ushered L'Hote out of earshot.

Leaning in, Anderson spoke quietly through pursed lips. "I heard a nasty, nasty rumor, George. Y'all aren't requesting a petition to the court over the boundaries of Storyville, now, are you?"

L'Hote shifted nervously. "Tom, I'm in quite a pickle. My family home, my eight children and dear wife, we abide only a block from here. Surely you understand not exposing children to immoral conduct."

"I ain't a family man," Anderson said flatly. "But what I do understand is that a wise man doesn't take my money with one hand and then shove it up my ass with the other. Are you a wise man, Mistah L'Hote?"

L'Hote took a hard swallow before Anderson answered for him. "'Course you are, and a wise man knows when to keep his mouth shut." He gave L'Hote another hearty slap on the back. "Glad we had this little talk, George. As I said, your lumber's working out real well."

L'Hote tried to speak but faltered, and instead hung his head as he walked away. Anderson turned back to McCracken and, hardly missing a beat, continued his charged rhetoric, bloviating as only the mayor of Storyville could.

"Mark my word, Mistah McCracken, and by that I mean you can quote me: people will cross the ocean just to set foot in Storyville."

McCracken raised a skeptical eyebrow.

"It's true," Anderson insisted. "Life without pleasure"—he inhaled deep through his nostrils, sucking up the breeze of success—"ain't no life at all."

CHAPTER TWENTY-TWO

Urselines Street

From the look of Venus Alley Mary sensed she was the only one feeling the weight of its impending close. Business bustled on as usual. Whores chirped about nothing except catty goings-on. Pimps collected their rent.

It knit at her that Tom Anderson hadn't returned to the Alley with any sort of update. They were two weeks away from doom and no one even knew what their options were—let alone if there *were* options. It seemed the others just assumed they'd be accounted for, that Anderson had some equivalent to the Alley ready and waiting in the new district. But Mary doubted that was true. She hadn't yet admitted it aloud, but it was becoming clear to her that Snitch was right when he said this shit hole wasn't part of the plan.

She had hoped someone would've stepped up and tried to unite the whores and peet daddies in figuring out what to do next. But no one had taken the lead, and although Mary liked to think she would have risen to the task had Peter still been around, she now felt all her energy channeled into just getting through a day.

Oh, the effort it now took going through what used to be mindless motions. She had to practically force herself to bathe and choke down something to eat. And then there was the task of putting on a strong demeanor before Charlotte—even when Charlotte rushed in with stories of the Countess's mansion and how Mary was pretty enough to be one of her girls. Mary had never lied to Charlotte before, but she'd dug her nails into her fist just to feel something other than the brick in her throat as she forced a tiny smile. "It takes more than pretty," she'd said softly, then scooped up the bucket to head to the well even though she'd already brought in their water.

What she craved was to crumble in a heap and stay curled up for however long it took until the pain eased. But instead, what pounded in her head with each labored step were the words *two weeks*. Two weeks until Lord knew what was going to happen to everyone here. She wanted to shout at the top of her lungs, Why are y'all milling around like it's any other day? What do you think is going to happen come next Friday?

Johns came and went, Mary forcing a coquettish grin. She no longer kept track, no longer counted the money they handed her. She just shoved it into her boot. Why bother? What was a nickel more or less when the days were numbered? She needed steady money, not pocket change.

Late that night, a black john approached as she was sitting on the stoop.

"Lookin' for Beulah?" Mary asked.

"Lookin' for anybody," he said.

"Gotta come back in the morning when Beulah can serve you."

His jaw tightened. "But I got two dollars for here and now."

"Listen, mistah, I don't give a yaller over the color of anybody's skin, but you know as well as I do, it's passable for a white man to take up with a Negra, but it ain't lawful the other way around."

He took two dollar bills from his wallet and held them out to Mary. She stared at the cash, then her eyes cautiously darted right and left. Seeing that no one was looking, she tilted her head, motioning him to go into her crib. "I'll be a minute," she said, her voice low.

She took a little stroll around the Alley, not wanting anyone to see her going in directly after a black man. When she felt all was clear, she went and serviced her john.

Sunup, sunset, the nondescript days blended into one another. Every morning Mary hoped to feel a small bit renewed, but each day was somehow just as painful, if not more so, than the one before. It was now a week before Storyville opened, a week before the demise of Venus Alley. One week before life as Mary knew it would come to a halt. She was prepared to beg on Basin Street if it came to that— not for tricks but for food. And it would, she figured, in the not-so-distant future, come to that.

Another john was on top of her, yet she didn't feel anything. Squeezing her eyes shut, she counted the seconds until it would be over, when something hit her in the face. She bolted her head up to find the Voodoo doll resting next to her cheek. Her heart seemed to stop for a moment as she wondered from where the doll could have fallen. And then she realized it didn't matter. It was the sign Lobrano was gone. She felt her body go cold. She wasn't sure if she should rejoice or mourn. It was an eye for an eye, but now two lives were taken. And now she, too, had blood on her hands.

For the rest of the night, the Voodoo doll lay on her kip, for she was afraid to touch it. She wasn't quite sure if she was afraid that jarring the doll might reverse the deed or that it might burn her skin for being a murderer. In the eyes of the law, she was no better than Lobrano. Even though the law barely acknowledged poor, unmarried girls like her.

She decided to leave her crib early, not wanting to run into Beulah and have to go through the motions for one more person. Besides, she wanted to get home and sit with Charlotte and the baby, the only comfort she had in the world. Charlotte put on a good face, focusing all her attention on the little one. She couldn't fall apart, she was a mother now. And Mary couldn't either; she was mother to them all.

As she opened the crib door she saw a small burlap bag waiting on the stoop. She eyed it warily before picking it up. Something was inside, something small and light. Slowly she pulled open the strings to reveal a bundled scrap of white cloth. As she unfurled the cloth, a locket fell into her palm. She gasped.

Faltering, she caught herself and stumbled back into the crib where she leaned against the wall before slinking down onto the floor. The locket, this locket, it looked exactly like the one her mama had, gold with a fleur-de-lis engraved on the front. But there was no possible way this could be Mama's locket. Mary had last seen that locket the day Mama died, having tearfully taken it from her body shortly after mother and baby were pronounced dead. Mary had slept with it under her pillow that night. But in the morning, it was gone. She'd frantically looked everywhere. After a few days she'd solemnly accepted that the locket her mother had worn, the gold that had been smooth against her chest, was nowhere to be found. She'd reconciled herself by believing it must have been buried with Mama after all—it was the only consoling notion she could surmise.

And now, nearly ten years later, that locket was there still in every hazy memory she had of her mother. But why, why just days before her life came apart, would an identical locket appear at her doorstep?

There was only one way to know if it was authentic, if indeed it was Mama's. With tears streaming down her cheeks, Mary slowly opened the locket. There, nestled inside, was a lock of auburn hair braided together with a lock of black hair. Mary began to shake as the memory flooded back. How she'd snipped a piece of Mama's ginger hair then snipped a piece of her own. How she'd painstakingly braided the two, always wanting to keep Mama with her, and then nestled the braid into the locket—only to find it missing forever. Forever until today.

She neither saw nor heard anything as she flew out of the Alley and over to Rampart Street. She didn't notice if she spoke to the woman at the front of the cigar shop, all she knew was that she collapsed into Eulalie's arms, sobbing.

Eulalie wasn't typically the motherly sort, but there was something so vulnerable about this girl who'd first come to her trying to be tough as old leather. Eulalie tightened her grip around Mary, smoothing her long, dark hair.

Mary couldn't remember the last time she was hugged like this. She felt the locket pressed against her chest and imagined the arms to be Mama's.

When Mary finally had no more tears to cry and she was able to breathe deeply enough to speak, she no longer wanted to tell Eulalie about the locket or to ask for help in saving her crib or finding work. Instead, she talked about Peter.

"Oh, Miss Echo," she sighed, fighting back another crying spell. "When will I get over this pain?"

Eulalie gripped Mary's shoulders. "You'll never get over it, child."

Mary's heart sank. She was hoping there would be some remedy, some concoction Eulalie could make that would ease the torment or at least lessen it enough that she could lay her head down and sleep without fitful, sweaty dreams.

"Never?" Mary asked, her lip trembling.

Eulalie stepped closer then, looking into Mary's face. "But you will get through it. And then it will become part of you. It will make you who you're supposed to be."

CHAPTER TWENTY-THREE

Milkman on Esplanade Avenue

"So, what are you planning to do after Venus Alley is shuttered?" Tom Anderson asked Snitch. Anderson was having his morning coffee and eggs at the bar, the *Times-Democrat* newspaper spread before him. For the past week, Snitch had been hanging around Anderson's Saloon as if he were looking to ingratiate himself.

"Mistah Anderson, you know what they say 'bout New Orleans? 'When you need something all ya gotta do is holla out your back door.' Well, all them ladies in the fancy houses, who d'ya think they're gonna be hollerin' for?"

Anderson couldn't help but chuckle at the boy's inadvertent double entendre.

"See, my plan is I'll get them anything they want, Mistah Anderson. All they gotta do is holla."

Anderson considered Snitch's idea. "I think that dog'll hunt," he said with a nod. "You could make a whole little delivery company of sorts."

Snitch's mouth formed an *O*. "You mean with people workin' for me and all? Just like you, Mistah Anderson?"

"Now, don't go gettin' ahead of yourself." Anderson sopped up egg yolk with a chunk of bread then shoveled it into his mouth the way men do when there are no women present. "You want to know the secret to business?"

Snitch's head frantically bobbed up and down.

Anderson leaned toward him to impart his words of wisdom. "Always remember, pigs get fat and hogs get slaughtered."

Snitch's face scrunched in confusion.

"It means," Anderson explained, "don't get greedy."

"Aaah," Snitch said, letting the lesson sink in. "I'll be a pig. Just you wait and see, Mistah Anderson, I'll be a pig!"

Mary lay underneath a thin-as-a-rail john. He moved like a squirrel, skittish and darting about, and it was fortunate his eyes were squeezed shut so that he couldn't see Mary's twisted face. She quickly realized there was no trying to match his lack of rhythm, so she surrendered to her kip, lying there idle as a rag doll. He didn't seem to notice, or didn't care; either way, he had prepaid, and that's all Mary was concerned about.

A banging on the crib door hardly thwarted the squirrel, and Mary lazily called, "Busy! Come back in five minutes!"

But a man's voice barked back, "Gotta talk now."

The john was still stuttering about as Mary leaned up onto her elbows. "Said I'm busy!" she yelled, louder this time.

"This can't wait," the husky voice insisted.

She fell back onto the kip. "Sakes alive, what can't wait?" she muttered. "Hey, mistah," she said to the john on top of her. "You about ready to finish your business?" He was a mute squirrel, and she realized she'd need to coax him into wrapping up. "Come on, big fella, I know you want to," she cooed.

"Bonnie!" he suddenly shouted.

Mary went with it. "Come on for Bonnie, come on!"

"Oh, Bonnie," he cried. And then that was that. The moment he took a breath, Mary slipped out from under him, pulling her chippie up around her and tightening the wrap. She opened the door enough to stick her head out and was surprised to be face-to-face with Sheep-Eye, the creepy-looking brute always following around Tater.

"Mistah Anderson is requestin' to see you," he announced.

A worried line shot across Mary's forehead. What could Tom Anderson possibly want with her? "'Bout what?" she asked.

Sheep-Eye shrugged. "Whaddaya think he wants with a huzzy?"

Mary dug a fist into her hip. Could Tom Anderson himself want a trick? There was a fluttering in her chest. From *her*? "When?" she asked.

"Tomorrow. Come by Anderson's Saloon at ten."

Mary bit her lip. "Can't he come here? My crib is sparklin' clean. Unless he wants to pay me extra for the time I'm away from my shift. That's the busiest time of night, y'know."

"Ten o'clock in the morning," Sheep-Eye grunted.

Oh, an early bird. She could service that. Especially if that bird ruled the roost. Mary nodded, and Sheep-Eye turned to go.

She resisted the urge to call him back over to ask, Why me? She and Anderson had never exchanged so much as a hello. And there were so many beautiful and classy ladies swarming around him—

how could she possibly compare? But instead, she watched Sheep-Eye trudge off, his thick body swaying like a pendulum.

"I want to see you in three days."

Startled, Mary turned around to face the squirrel, having forgotten he was even there. "Right, mistah. See, tomorrow's the last day—"

"Fine, tomorrow, then," he said.

"I'll be here. . . . That is, Bonnie'll be here. Sundown to sunup."

All night Mary drifted into dreamy thoughts of Tom Anderson. How right fine he had looked in his crisp suit at the Countess's party. She'd never associated with people rich enough to wear dinner jackets and bow ties, and just the outfit alone would have made her stop and look at Anderson. But there also was no denying that he was perhaps the most handsome man she'd ever laid eyes on. As the girls on the Alley would say, he was finer'n frog's hair. But of course, he would hardly be Tom Anderson without his prestige and power, and for Mary to be face-to-face with the lord of the Underworld, well, there wasn't a Spanish fly more potent than that!

In between johns, Mary tried to catch some beauty sleep. It wasn't good for business not to be out on the stoop flaunting herself, but she allowed her mind to wander a dozen steps ahead—if Anderson took a fondness to her, could she become his mistress? On his payroll even, just like Tater?

As the sky began to lighten, she found herself growing giddy with excitement. A sloppy, chubby john's body that threatened to crush her morphed into Anderson's tall, taut physique. An odorous, whiskery man became a powerful chieftain. By sunup, she'd serviced an imaginary Anderson six times over.

She cleared out of the crib earlier than usual, barely feeling the weight of the kip on her back as she hurried home. Charlotte and the baby were asleep, and Mary attempted to squeeze in some shut-eye, but she could only stare at an intricate cobweb dangling in the ceiling beam. When baby Anna began to whimper, Mary tended to her, having herself given up on sleep. By the time Charlotte stirred, Mary had already ironed her best dress and was heating water for a bath.

Charlotte's eyes grew wide as Mary relayed the news, and the two set about a grooming process, the intimate likes of which they hadn't orchestrated since it was Charlotte in the tub, preparing for her wedding night. Mary was scrubbed and filed, her hair washed and combed and the straggly ends trimmed off with shears. She washed her face with lemon and two pinches of sugar until her cheeks shone, and then scrubbed her teeth with a scoop of bicarbonate soda on her index finger. Then she powdered herself all over with talcum.

When her hair was dry, Charlotte counted one hundred strokes with the brush, then tightly braided Mary's hair into sections, wrapping them into a flawless bun atop her head. She then twisted ringlets around her fingers to frame Mary's face, and a little castor oil did the trick to smooth back flyaways. Mary was then corseted, the strings pulled tight—and with shined shoes, holeless stockings, and rose oil dabbed at her ears and wrists, she stepped back for Charlotte to have a final look.

Nearly welling up, Charlotte gave a motherly nod. "You look beautiful," she said softly. As Mary left the house, Charlotte called after her, "Now, don't go mussing your hair. You pretend like you don't even have hair on your head!"

She hadn't told Charlotte about the locket—or that she was wearing it.

Mary wasn't used to the city at this hour. It was a genteel scene as she strolled through the French Quarter, nodding at shopkeepers and restaurant owners as they lingered outside their doors, awaiting the rush of the day's business.

Anderson's Saloon was no different, spit-spot clean and still empty. While the Alley bars tended to have the regular drunkards who didn't care about waiting for a respectable hour to start drinking—or who didn't even know what time it was in the first place—Anderson's was a classy establishment where patrons didn't trickle in until at least after the lunch hour. Mary approached the barkeep, and it wasn't until she heard the quiver in her own voice that she realized how nervous she was. "I'm here to see Mistah Tom Anderson."

The barkeep barely looked at her. He called across the bar, "Girl says she's here for the boss."

In the back, from behind his half-open door, Tater's mug peeked out. Both he and Mary tried to conceal any sort of expression, even though each one—unbeknownst to the other—was inspired to well up. Tater trudged from the room, motioning for Mary to come over. She'd gathered that the closed door next to Tater's was that of Anderson's office—she'd caught a peek in there before—and sure enough, Tater gave the door a rap.

"Mistah Anderson, here's the Venus Alley girl you asked after."

Mary caught herself holding her breath. To hear Tater announce her like that was disquieting. Had he told Anderson about their deal? Is that what this was about? She looked searchingly at Tater, only he wouldn't meet her eyes and, instead, abashedly turned his head.

Mary tried to parse her thoughts—was she here to be the coy

call girl, or was she here to plead her case, plead for mercy? The door opened, and there stood Anderson, freshly shaven and dressed in pressed trousers, a spotless white shirt, and suspenders, looking every bit as handsome and intimidating as Mary had envisioned. He gestured for her to come in, and his professional manner, which would have otherwise seemed refreshingly polite, now appeared suspect. She almost wished he'd eyed her up and down and then led her to a back room with a cot; at least then she'd know her purpose. Instead, he said, "Please have a seat."

She could barely look him in the face and cast her gaze down as she stepped into his office. She caught his clean scent, like a crisp pine tree. She hoped her own rose scent still lingered, but it was just oil she'd dabbed on, not fancy French perfume that had real staying power.

Anderson closed the door and Mary waited for him to turn the lock. *If he locks it, then certainly this is about a trick.* But the click of the bolt didn't come. Anguish clotted in her as she approached two large leather armchairs with bear-claw legs. She slid into the far one, feeling the cool leather against her stockinged thighs. The chair seemed to swallow her, leaving her feet dangling. She imagined what it might be like to curl up in this chair by the fire, holding baby Anna, and the thought momentarily soothed her.

Anderson sat across from her, and she watched his hands cradle the chair's wing arms. She could tell things about a person by their hands. All the pretty boys, with their long, tapered fingers, made more for china teacups than for wielding an ax. All the farmers, with their square, calloused hands, and the miners, with scars that had stories to tell. Anderson's hands were more manly than she would have ventured, more muscular than was typical for someone of his wealth, someone with an office this nice and chairs this cozy. But his nails were those of a rich man, clean and shiny. Mary curled her fingers to hide her own dull nails. Though they were scrubbed and filed, they weren't buffed like Anderson's, and it felt shameful to be a lady sitting with a man with better nails. She also noticed the jeweled ring on Anderson's right hand, and the absence of a wedding ring on his left. It would have been the talk of the Underworld had Anderson taken a wife, and for some reason, Mary was reassured to see his bare ring finger.

"You're probably wondering why I called you here today," he said.

Her eyes darted about, not sure where to rest.

There was an expectant silence, as if he were waiting for her to speak. Did he want her to confess to her vengeance? Or was she supposed to describe something bawdy—not that she was sure she could even speak like that to him, and here of all places.

"Would you like some water?" he offered, and at this, her nerves calmed. If he was going to shame her or turn her in to the authorities, he wouldn't draw this out. She nodded and he quickly rose, pouring from a silver pitcher on the hutch. Their hands grazed as he gave her the glass, and the feel of his skin against hers sent a charge through her. But no sooner was he back on the other side of the room, in his own chair.

She took a sip, and then said the only thing that came to mind. "Can't blame you for wanting your trick aways from the Alley."

He cocked his head as if perplexed, and she immediately felt stupid for speaking.

Leaning in, Anderson rested his forearms on his thighs. "Miss Deubler—it is *Miss* Deubler, right?"

Mary nodded.

"Please don't take offense, but I haven't called you here for a trick."

Her palms started to sweat. If Anderson spoke Lobrano's name, she didn't know what she'd do, didn't know if she could keep the angry tears back. She commanded herself not to cry in front of Tom Anderson. She was not going to crumple and demean herself. She straightened up her spine. Hold your head high.

"This is a bit of a sensitive nature," Anderson began.

Mary took a gulp of air, hashing out what she'd say—*a person can't choose their kin, Mistah Anderson.*

"My God, Miss Deubler, you look as if I'm scaring you out of your wits. There's no reason for you to be frightened of me. I have only your best interests at heart with my proposition for you. I think you'll find it as interesting as I do."

Mary's mouth squeezed into a line. A proposition?

"I've been noticing," Anderson continued, "that you are a woman with an open mind and a high degree of intelligence." He paused as if waiting for Mary to concur, but she was too busy wondering if he hadn't summoned the wrong girl. Sure she could read, a rare ability on the Alley, but why would he care about that?

"One decision I commend you for is your willingness to share your crib with a Negro. Those are my folks too, practically raised me, you see. You should hear me play spirituals on a church organ!" He chuckled, but it fell flat as Mary stared blankly at him, her mind clicking away in confusion. "Anyway," he continued, "you, like a very intelligent person, recognize that people are people, and also that a dollar's a dollar, business is business. You are a true capitalist."

Mary had never heard of a capitalist before, and now she was one?

"But you know, of course, that Storyville's not so open-minded. Colored folk are going to be relegated to Franklin Street, and that just isn't going to be appetizing to those folks from the North who don't possess all sorts of crazy notions about one people being better than the other."

Mary hoped she wasn't letting on how lost she was—why was Beulah Ripley now a part of this? Heck, she'd been sharing space with Beulah for years, something Lobrano had drummed up when he needed extra cash. Lobrano couldn't have cared if Beulah had two heads, so long as she could turn a trick and count well enough to know if a john was paying her right. Then again, she supposed Anderson had a point, that not everyone would have been amenable to taking shifts with Beulah, thinking she'd spread vermin or carried disease. Reluctantly, Mary also thought back to the colored john who'd come by her crib with two whole dollars.

"So you're probably wondering what I'm proposing," Anderson said, "and I recognize you may already have other plans. But if I can entice you, I think we'd have a nice business opportunity if there were a house in Storyville that welcomed whites and blacks . . . quietly, of course." He studied her face, looking for some flicker of agreement, but Mary still wasn't following.

Sure, fine, welcome coloreds, she thought. She wanted to say aloud, *I'll be left out in the cold, starving, thank you very much.* But she kept that to herself. She chewed on her lower lip, hoping all this would suddenly snap into some kind of sense.

"Shame on me," Anderson said, flashing his smile, "I've been doing all the talking. Can I get you something real to drink? Is it too early for a whiskey? Is it ever too early for a whiskey?"

"Oh, thank you, but no." Mary said softly.

He raised himself from his chair and moved to hover near her. She breathed in his clean scent again.

"So, you're keeping me in such suspense," he said. "Do tell me what you think of my idea."

Mary blanched. "Uh, well. To be honest with you, Mistah Anderson, I don't know what your idea has to do with me."

He chuckled. "You are a sharp gal. See, the notion I had is that you can run a house, a regular bordello, and no one around here will be the wiser that the coloreds can come there too. It'll just be our little secret."

Mary felt a rising heat again. She gulped down the water. *Holy Mary Magdalene, are my ears playing tricks on me, or did Mistah Tom Anderson just propose I run a bordello?* Her head grew light. The room began to turn very bright, then very white.

"Miss Deubler, are you all right? Miss . . . ?"

Anderson popped his head out the door. "Tater, we're gonna need some smelling salts in here."

CHAPTER TWENTY-FOUR

"Miss Addie, I smell your cookin' all the way up the banquette!" exclaimed Little Louie as he hauled a bucket of coal into the Countess's kitchen.

Addie paused from the mound of dough she'd been kneading to give the boy a motherly nod. His face was smudged with coal dust, but rarely was he without his wide, bright grin.

"Sit yourself on down," Addie said. "Here's some *cubie yon* and dirty rice for you." She scooped some fish stew from a cast iron pot simmering over the fire and set the bowl on the table. Louie climbed up into the chair and dug into the stew as if it were to be snatched away at any moment. Addie observed the ravenous child, and as soon as he'd filled his mouth a few times she added another ladleful to his helping.

"So how Mayann be?" she asked.

Louie shrugged.

"You tell her I been askin' after her," Addie said.

"Yes, ma'am," Louie answered between mouthfuls. "Will tell her next time she come 'round."

Yep, just as Addie had suspected: Louie's mother had run off again.

"I'll pack some *lagniappe* for you, and for your sister and grand-mama, too."

"You're very kind, Miss Addie," Louie said.

Addie didn't know what came over her, but the boy's words moved her to tears. She didn't show him, of course, just dabbed at her eyes with her apron, then got back to the dough. "Well, land sakes, Little Louie, I ain't never seen anyone eat so fast. Slow yourself down, that bowl ain't goin' nowhere!"

"When I'm done, want me to bring the coal upstairs?" Louie asked.

"Naw, the Countess is up there with some muckety-mucks. Think it's important talk, so don't want them to hear no racket." She sighed. "Things are changin' 'round these parts. City ain't never gonna be the same."

The muckety-mucks upstairs were Anderson, Flabacher, and the Countess, holding court in the library. The topic of conversation: the promotion of Storyville. Lulu was poised on her chaise longue, her long gold cigarette holder dangling from her gloved fingers. Anderson and Flabacher sat on opposite sides of the room from each other, both sucking on fat cigars. Smoke clouds lingered in the room despite the French doors that opened onto a veranda, sheer curtains swaying in the gentle breeze of the evening.

"Mistah Flabacher had the brilliant notion of printing a bulletin describing my elegant château," Lulu said, "and putting it right in men's hands as they get off the train."

Anderson studied Flabacher. What an obsequious blowhard, he thought. How could Lulu be wasting time with this bag of hot air? But he smiled politely. "They raise 'em bright in Chicago," he said, tapping his forefinger to his head.

Flabacher smiled back with feigned modesty.

"Here's another idea," Anderson said, tilting back his head and blowing a perfect smoke ring. "We could do an entire directory. A booklet describing all the new bordellos and their lovely madams."

Flabacher was quick to pipe up. "While an interesting notion, Mr. Anderson, clearly, the Countess's place is too regal to simply be lumped with all the other houses."

"Tom, since when am I so ordinary to you?" Lulu said with a playful pout.

"There's not an ordinary inch on you, my dear," Anderson replied. "Don't be misunderstanding me, your château will have the first and best listing. You can include a professional likeness of this house even. Thing is, we can sell advertisements in our own directory. Local merchants will pay to advertise, knowing their wares will appear right under the nose of every man stepping from that train. We can get our own promotion and turn a profit on our little directory, all at the same time."

Lulu cocked an eyebrow. "I knew there was something I liked about you, Tom Anderson," she said.

Flabacher, however, was slightly confused by the idea. "So, let me get this straight. . . . You're proposing advertisements in our advertisement?"

"*Voilà*, free publicity!" Lulu exclaimed. "And with a little on the side *pour vous*, Tom. And a little on the side *pour moi*."

Flabacher gave a slow nod as comprehension began to settle in.

"Our booklet needs to have the perfect enticing introduction to Storyville," Lulu continued. "Mistah Flabacher, you'll find writing materials in the desk there. Could you notate this, please?"

Flabacher shuffled to the desk as Lulu began composing aloud: "To know the right from the wrong . . . to be sure of yourself . . . go through this little book and read it carefully. And then when you visit Storyville, you will know the best places—"

Anderson cut in, "To spend your time and money, as only the very best homes are advertised." Flabacher's hand was flying as he tried to keep up with the two of them—back in Chicago, he had girls to do this for him.

Lulu thought for a moment. "Tom, if this booklet is so very exclusive, we should charge a fee to each madam. After all, if only the very best homes are advertised, it's a privilege that we're allowing them in our booklet, no?"

"Of course," Anderson agreed. "Privileges never come without a premium. But until we can properly determine which houses are the very best, we should give each the benefit of the doubt and sell them all an advertisement."

"Indeed!" Lulu snickered. "But it must remain a tasteful little booklet. It would seem déclassé to be *too* obvious with our motivation."

"We should have a motto of some sort," Anderson proposed. "All good, profitable organizations do."

Lulu lit up. "We should borrow our motto from true royalty. 'The Order of the Garter'!"

Anderson didn't often admit if he was stumped—and it wasn't often that he was—but he gave Lulu a shrug. "Educate me."

Lulu placed her cigarette in a silver ashtray. "The story goes that King Edward III was dancing at a ball with the Fair Maid of Kent, the most beautiful woman in England, when, God forbid, her garter slid south and made a shocking appearance at her ankle. The court was all a-snicker, but Edward did the unthinkable: he plucked up the garter and placed it around his own leg. Quite chivalrous. Then again, perhaps he liked it. You know those English fops, always prancing about with all their playmates."

"We call them homosexuals in the Midwest," Flabacher offered.

"Yes, well, Edward then declared his famous words: *Honi soit qui mal y pense*, 'Evil be to him who evil thinks.' The court was shamed into silence, and the motto became known as—"

Anderson finished her sentence. "The Order of the Garter."

Over a steak-and-eggs breakfast at his saloon, Anderson presented the booklet copy to Mayor Flower, who read it aloud.

"The names of the residents will be found in this directory, alphabetically arranged, under the headlines 'White' and 'Colored.'" Flower looked to Tom. "Colored? You sure you want to be covering all territory here? Maybe a separate booklet for the colored houses since they're in a separate area?"

"Nonsense," Anderson said. "A man should have free will to choose any house he wants, and we're just listing all the options. Besides, some folks want to be very open-minded."

"We have laws against too much open-mindedness."

Anderson looked at him pointedly. "There are some extremely wealthy men of color, you know."

With a skeptical grimace, Flower continued: "The names in

capitals are the landladies." He chuckled, "*Landladies*, I like that, Tom."

When he finished reading, he set the booklet on the checkered-cloth-covered table, then searched through his jacket pocket. "There's just one final thing," he said, uncapping his Waterman's fountain pen. He wrote on the cover in capital letters: THIS BOOK MUST NOT BE MAILED.

Anderson nodded broadly. "That's why you are the mayor, sir."

Flower puffed up his chest. "Always abiding by the rules and regulations."

Anderson nodded. "As someone once said, an honest politician is one who stays bought." They both chortled.

Flower shoveled down half his plate in two bites. "You think merchants will be open to advertising in the booklet?"

"Yes. Well, eventually. They just need to realize Storyville is the next boomtown. With our own type of gold."

"How many advertisements y'all sold so far?"

"One," Tom replied. "To Anderson's Saloon. Word is the owner's a very generous fellow."

In the midst of a freshly cleared field, E. J. Bellocq adjusted his tripod and 8 x 10 camera. His choice of subject matter: a tree stump. The little man looked to the setting sun, waiting for the perfect moment to click the shutter.

"Mighty hot today," a voice boomed. Leaves crushed under the heft of one Mr. Flabacher, perspiring in the late-day sun.

Bellocq quickly ducked beneath the camera's black cape in hope of avoiding interruption or, for that matter, any conversation.

Undeterred, Flabacher made his approach. "Hello there, friend. The name's Sheldon Flabacher," he announced to the cape. "I inquired at the New Orleans Camera Club and was told I might find you here."

Silence.

Flabacher followed the line of the camera to the tree stump, then gave a perplexed twist of his mouth. "Doing some 'field work,' I see." He chuckled at his own pun. "Well . . . I hear you are one mighty fine photographer."

Under the cape, Bellocq remained as still as he could, like a reptile trying to blend into the surroundings.

"Yearbooks," Flabacher rattled on, "and I understand you even did some stock photographs at the shipyard. That must have been . . . fascinating." He cleared his throat, at a bit of a loss. "Look, fact is you're one of five folks in town with a camera, and I need some photographs. It's for a special promotion, and you seem open to . . ." He glanced to the tree stump. ". . . photographic exploration. So what do you say?"

Bellocq clicked the shutter, and Flabacher took that as a resounding yes. "Grand! I've taken the liberty of transcribing the pertinent details." He removed a card from his shirt pocket. "Sunday afternoon, 235 Basin Street. You'll be photographing some lovely ladies. The compensation is modest but meaningful." Awkwardly, he placed the card on top of Bellocq's cape. Delighted to have you aboard, friend!" He stood there with a dumb grin, waiting for the cape to lift, but there was nothing except stillness, as if the little man had petrified under there. Flabacher's smile quickly dropped, and with a shrug, he trudged off, dabbing his brow with a handkerchief.

As soon as the labored breathing and heavy-footed clomping faded, Bellocq emerged. He pocketed the card.

CHAPTER TWENTY-FIVE

FUN! FUN!! FUN!!

DON'T MISS THE
French Balls
GIVEN BY THE
C. C. C. Club and
Two Well-Known Gentlemen

ODD FELLOWS HALL
SATURDAY NIGHT BE-
FORE MADRI GRAS AND
MADRI GRAS NIGHT

The Balls have
been famous for
years, so if you
are out for a
good time don't
miss them.
Tickets for sale
at TOM ANDER-
SON'S SALOONS,
and LAMOTHE'S
RESTAURANT,
716 Gravier St.

Ferdinand angled his way around the crowd of parishioners milling in the aisle, dodging the old ladies yammering about who'd
passed on recently, and the younger ladies yammering about someone or other's new beau, and the men yammering at all the ladies to
sit down already, the Lord's tired of hearing your *yat*.

As he finally approached the pulpit, Ferd could see Grandmère
scolding him under her breath while her hands deftly played a med-
ley of hymns. He slid in next to her on the piano bench and tried to
relieve her, but she wasn't giving up the keys easily.

"Asking too much to praise the Lord on time?" she said through a forced grin.

"Sorry, Grandmère."

"Where were you this morning when I came to wake you? I couldn't even tell if your bed was slept in. This about a girl?"

Ferd shook his head. If only she knew that he'd been practicing on Lala's piano and hadn't realized night had slipped into morning—she'd have far preferred it be about a girl.

Grandmère finally acquiesced the piano and took her rightful place in the choir. Ferd continued on flawlessly, and as the crowd began to sit they joined the choir in singing "What a Friend We Have in Jesus."

Maybe it was his lack of sleep, or maybe just force of habit from composing for the past several hours, but at the end of the song Ferd surprised the congregation—and himself—by finishing with a jaunty, raggedy riff. As his fingers left the keys, he was met with silence, only a nervous cough or two filling the void. He didn't dare glance to Grandmère, for she was sure to be agape.

And then, from the front pew, a woman called out, "Amen!"

Ferd looked over to see a garishly stunning woman, aglow with diamonds. What, he wondered, was Countess Lulu White doing here?

Throughout the rest of the service, Lulu recited her psalms with the piety of a nun. Whomever coined the phrase "sweating like a whore in church" was certainly not speaking of the Countess.

After the service concluded, Ferd attempted to make his way back down the aisle in the midst of all the reconvened *yat*, when Lulu put a sparkly hand on his shoulder.

"May I speak with you, Mistah LaMenthe?" she asked.

They stepped back into a pew. "Your playing precedes you," she said. "I happen to have one of the most gorgeous pianos you'll ever lay eyes on—and an upcoming party that could use some quality ragtime. I've been searching for the best, as they say, professor of the piano. Consider this to have been your audition."

Ferd began to flinch, feeling Grandmère's eyes on his back. "I'd be honored, ma'am"—he dropped his voice—"but we'll have to speak about it another time."

Lulu gave a knowing nod. She dipped into her pocketbook, then discreetly tucked a calling card into Ferd's jacket pocket. With a wink, she sashayed down the aisle, her teal bustled gown making a swishing sound with each pronounced punch of her hips.

"I'd sooner be buried in a croker sack than be caught dead in that." Ferd turned to see Grandmère beside him.

"That ain't a nice thing to say in church," Ferd quipped.

Grandmère gave him a gentle wallop. "Isn't!" she corrected. "What small talk was she making with you?"

Ferd began walking a couple paces ahead so Grandmère couldn't see his face. "Just complimented the playing."

Grandmère's lips pursed. "She's not a member here, that I'm sure of."

"Maybe she's a visitor in town. She just liked the playing is all."

Grandmère pressed her chin down, creating a couple of rolls at her neck. "Don't go thinking the sun comes up just to hear you crow."

"Don't worry on that, Grandmère," Ferd said, "Not a worry a'tall."

"*Bienvenue*, Mistah Koehl, Mistah Lafon, Mistah Haydell, Mistah Sinclair," Lulu cooed as she glided through her parlor. She struck a stunning pose in an elaborate pink satin gown, feathered tiara, and her monocle. What used to be just a Saturday eve had already become the night to see and be seen at none other than Mahogany Hall.

"Madam, we've come all the way from Birmingham to make your acquaintance."

Lulu pivoted to face two well-dressed men, their hair perfectly oiled and parted. "I'm Pierce LaRue, and this is my brother, Acey." They bowed as if she were a queen.

"A pleasure," Lulu said. "How are you both enjoying the true heart of Dixie?"

"We'd have argued that point before tonight," Pierce said.

With a wink, Lulu sashayed onward, but was startled by a loud smacking sound. She turned around to see that Acey LaRue had just spanked Poodle.

"That hurt," Poodle groused, rubbing her bottom.

"You Yellowhammers behave yourselves, now," Lulu called. With a slight shudder, she continued moving through her adoring crowd.

Flabacher waddled about the room like a mother hen, checking his notebook, his watch, then peeking into the punch bowl and motioning to a servant to fill it. He noticed a little rush at the front door and felt his stomach churn when he saw it was Tom Anderson who'd just arrived. He'd decided Anderson was ridiculously cocksure and, admittedly, intimidating.

"I have a gift for you, Countess," Anderson boomed. Flabacher watched as Lulu's body seemed to react to Anderson's presence. Although she was always sensual, she turned lithe, catlike, practically wrapping herself around him. He wondered if Anderson paid for sexual favors with the Countess, or if she simply gave him freebies when no one was looking.

"A gift?" she said, her voice trailing over a few octaves.

Anderson presented a copy of the *Mascot*. "Page eight."

Lulu flipped to the page and her face lit up. She took her monocle and clinked it on her Champagne glass, summoning all eyes to her. "Excuse the interruption, but if you would please indulge me, it will give me abundant pleasure to share with you what's been proclaimed: 'Miss Lulu White's dazzling dishonor.'" She let out a throaty laugh. "By all means, if one must have dishonor, for God's sake, it should be dazzling!"

The crowd clapped and whooped. "Oh, but wait, there's so much more!" She cleared her throat for affect. "'Sinning for silk, by Kermit McCracken. Young girls sacrifice humble virtue for disgusting depravity. A horrible state of affairs is permitted to go on uninterrupted by authorities'!"

Flabacher could feel his temperature rise from his toes up to his ears. That damn reporter had set a trap—and, as a newcomer, he'd walked right into it. But how could he have known the *Mascot* had such an agenda? *Yellow journalism!* he wanted to shout across the room. *McCracken's a muckraker!*

Lulu continued reading, "'The *demimonde*, or females of questionable character, are not infrequently encountered by half- or totally intoxicated men—'" At this, the men in the room began to cheer. "'A taste of what the entire back o' town will become once Storyville is officially under way the first of the new year.'"

"Tastes damn good to me," a man called from the crowd.

"Well spoken," Lulu replied. She was met with resounding concordance as she dramatically tossed the *Mascot* into the fireplace. "*Laissez les bons temps rouler!*"

The rowdy applause could be heard all the way outside, behind the mansion, in the carriageway, where Ferdinand was anxiously pacing, awaiting his cue.

Another act also waited, a magician dressed in a purple turban and flowing pants, along with his sidekick, a skittish white-headed

Capuchin monkey. The magician addressed the monkey, speaking in a thick indistinguishable accent. "Alma, this is big night for us." The monkey pinched the magician's nose. "Please to stop pacing," he said to Ferdinand. "Making Alma nervous."

"Sorry, Alma," Ferd said. He shifted his stance to lean awkwardly against the side of the bordello with his arm outstretched. The magician gave him an odd look. "Don't wanna wrinkle my suit," Ferd explained. "So what is it that y'all perform?"

"I am Pharos the Mysterious. Alma is my assistant for spectacular magic show."

The back door opened and out popped Flabacher's head. "Magician, you're up."

Pharos gathered Alma and hurried inside, leaving Ferdinand alone with his nerves. At once, Ferd resumed pacing.

The magician was led into the parlor, where a collective squeal of glee erupted at the sight of Alma. "Awww!" the girls cooed. "I declare, aren't you precious!" Alma ate it up, waving and bowing.

Pharos presented a deck of cards and removed the Queen of Diamonds, displaying it for all to see. With some quick twists of his hands the card disappeared. All eyes followed Alma as she took off, bounding across the room. She stopped at an unsuspecting, ruddy-looking man, Sullivan, then startled him and the crowd by scurrying up his leg and pulling the Queen of Diamonds card from his shirtsleeve. The room oohed and aahed.

"Don't think I'm sozzled yet," Sullivan said with a thick Irish accent, "but did a monkey just pull a card from me shirt?"

Lulu sauntered by and handed Sullivan a fresh drink. "What else you got up your sleeve?" she asked, and Sullivan's cheeks quickly splotched. Then she said under her breath, "Come find me later, Sully. I'll escort you out."

Meanwhile, Alma dodged dancing feet to climb up the plump

leg of Mayor Flower, who was waltzing with one of Lulu's girls. Tickled, Flower bubbled over with laughter as Alma perched herself on the mayor's head.

"Lookee!" Flower called out. "Lookee everybody, I'm a monkey stool!"

In barely the blink of an eye, Alma scurried back down and across the room, climbing to her perch on the magician's shoulder and discreetly sliding two wallets she'd pinched under the magician's purple turban.

By this time, Flabacher had summoned Ferdinand and led him through the kitchen, where Addie and other black servants were hustling about. Little Louie piped up, "Hey, mistah, you got a monkey too?"

Ferd chuckled. "No, cap, I'm the one gonna be playing the piano."

Louie puffed up his cheeks in excitement. "Oh, mistah, I wanna make music someday too."

Addie chimed in, "All that hot air you got, little man, you should try blowing on a horn!"

Louie called after Ferd. "Maybe I can sneak out just for a little and watch you play, mistah?"

But Addie was quick to shoo at him. "You will do no such thing, Little Louie Armstrong! You're stayin' right here where I can keep my eye on you, and where your eyes ain't seein' nothin' naughty."

Ferd winked at the boy as he followed Flabacher from the comfort of the cozy kitchen over the threshold into what seemed another world. As Ferd took sight of the parlor, his own eyes popped. He thought the judge's party had been rollicking—*this* was debauchery like he had never seen. Scantily clad girls, free-flowing alcohol, men pinching, grabbing, caressing whatever was in their line of sight. It made Buddy Bolden's Butt Hall seem like a grade-school dance.

Flabacher noticed the gobsmacked piano player. "Get used to it, friend, they're a wild bunch." He ushered Ferdinand to the far corner, where the pearly white piano awaited. That piano was the only thing that could have possibly distracted Ferd from the scene around him.

"Hot damn," he marveled.

"Well, go on, play it," Flabacher said.

Tentatively, Ferdinand slid onto the bench, allowing the glory of the piano to envelop him. He then took sheets of music from his jacket.

Flabacher's brow creased. "I thought you were a professional player. What's with all the music?"

"My own compositions, sir."

He gave a wary look as Ferd arranged the sheets, then grew even more restless as Ferd stretched his fingers. "Any day now, kid."

"Yes, sir," Ferd said, and began to play. The crowd, seemingly one by one, paused to ponder the unfamiliar music. Lulu took note, studying the crowd's reactions. For the moment, Ferd became unconcerned with anything else in the room. He closed his eyes and let his fingers glide along the keys, the perfectly tuned piano reverberating through his every bone. But as he finished the first piece, he opened his eyes to discover the faces in the room staring at him. He took his hands from the piano, and there was a silent pause.

It was Tom Anderson who began to clap; he knew how to appreciate fine music. The rest of the crowd, however, wasn't quite sure what to make of this new sound, yet they joined with polite applause. That was, with the exception of the LaRue brothers. They exchanged steely looks with each other, their thin lips tightening into even thinner lines.

"Can you play 'A Picture of Her Face'?" someone called out.

"And how 'bout 'Maple Leaf Rag'?" another partygoer piped up.

Chagrined, Ferdinand set aside his handwritten music and began to play the requests.

A bit before eleven o'clock, Lulu noticed red-faced Sullivan give her the nod. She disappeared through the kitchen and out the back door, where she met him around the side of the house.

Propping her leg on the porch rail, she removed several bills from her kid-leather boots. "Three dollars per week, plus twenty-five cents per girl," she said, placing the money in his hand.

Sullivan considered the cash. "It's all legal now, aye? You don't really need me."

"The way I see it, you've been good to me over the years, Sully. Besides, there's still the Sunday law, and the liquor law, and whatever other law I might occasionally overlook." She touched his cheek. "And it's always good to have the law on my side."

At that, Sullivan tucked away the money. "Till next week, then." He took his police badge from his pocket and affixed it to his shirt.

As Lulu reentered the party, Flabacher pulled her aside. He whispered to her, and a peeved frown crossed her face. She whispered back, then, with a deep breath, she headed across the room toward the piano.

Ferdinand saw her coming in his direction and grew uneasy. He did not want a repeat of his exit from the judge's house. He picked up the tempo.

"You're the toast of the night, Professor," Lulu said, leaning herself against the piano. "I knew you would be. And I just adore your original work. You're amazingly talented, but you don't need me to tell you that. We must have you perform at Frenchman's."

"Frenchman's?" Ferdinand exclaimed. "You really think they'd let me play?"

"*Mon pigeon*, it should be their pleasure, those folks know good sound when they hear it. Meantime, though, there are, how shall I put it, some imbeciles here who couldn't carry a tune in a bucket."

Ferd bit his lip, recognizing where this was headed. "Don't they respect I'm Creole?" he asked.

"Like I said, they're tone-deaf *and* imbeciles. I'm not exactly pearly white, if you know what I mean."

Ferdinand bowed his head and stopped playing.

"Oh, you're staying," Lulu said firmly. "But we're going to have to do a little compromise. . . ."

Flabacher and a servant shimmied over, carrying a silk threefold screen. They placed it between Ferdinand and the rest of the room.

"Now, this is just for tonight, *mon cher*," Lulu said. "It's inauguration season, and I can't have my patrons ornery." She winked at Ferdinand. "Just *hornery*."

As they all disappeared to the other side of the curtain, Ferdinand sighed and resumed playing, his view of the party completely blocked. Then, as if to add insult, he heard a woman shout: "When there's a popping, lift it above your stockings!" A cork popped, followed by raucous cheering from the men: "Higher! Higher!"

Ferdinand fidgeted—he was definitely missing something good! He tried to play while craning his neck around the screen, but to no avail.

A woman called out: "When it's clinking glasses you hear . . ." And a chorus of ladies' voices responded: "Show your rear!"

The crowd erupted in laughter at what must have surely been the girls baring their behinds to the room.

Another woman's voice rang out, "When the bubbly hits—"

That's it! Ferd thought. He was determined now. He continued on the piano with one hand while burrowing a finger through a seam in the screen's silk lining.

The woman finished her rhyme, calling out, "Show your

tits!" just as Ferdinand craned to squint through a tiny hole he'd created—wide enough for a sneaky eyeball to glimpse a dozen of Lulu's girls happily pop out of their bustiers. He'd never seen a live naked woman before, let alone a dozen!

"The Lord taketh away," he said to himself, "and the Lord giveth." Losing his train of thought, he stumbled over some wrong keys. He quickly bolted upright, his sightline gone, but that was all right, he'd seen something he'd never forget. Regaining his capacities, he played with new vigor, his face frozen in a happy, glazed-over expression. For the rest of the night, he completely forgot the affront of the screen.

As the alcohol took effect, the partygoers began pairing off, the girls taking the men by the hand and leading them upstairs, disappearing behind closed doors.

Lulu and Tom Anderson retreated to the quiet of the drawing room, where they shared some brandy and Lulu warmed her stockinged feet at the fireplace.

"Why don't you take a girl for the night, Tom?" she suggested. "Gypsy's perfected the fine French art of fellatio, or so I've been hearing."

"As tempting as that sounds, I should keep a . . . professional distance."

"Since when?"

"Since Storyville."

Lulu raised an eyebrow. "Since Storyville, or since you may be running for state legislator?"

Anderson turned to marvel at her. "You're good, Countess," he said with a wag of his index finger. "Very, very good."

Although she knew Anderson had a penchant for politics, she

never thought he'd actually thrust himself into the ring. But apparently, it was true, and she felt a twinge of envy—she would never say so, but she didn't want him going off to Baton Rouge. She liked him right here. She rose, moving across the room to stare out the window, lest any indication on her face give her away.

"I've been seeing the vacant house down the street all lit up as of late," she said. "You haven't told me your plans for it."

Anderson took a long, contemplative swallow of his brandy. "It all just came about. I happened upon a sweet little thing who'll do whatever I say and won't mind servicing the Negroes."

"I see," Lulu said, trying to keep a measured tone. "It's an awfully large and grand house for servicing Negroes."

Anderson weighed his words, careful not to sound overly enthusiastic. "It won't be only Negroes. She'll run a proper full-service house."

"Do I know her? Surely I must have heard of her?"

"She calls herself Josie Arlington."

"Hmm . . . Don't believe I've ever come across a Josie Arlington." She repeated the name over in her head, knowing that immediately after Anderson left she would summon everyone in her circle, from Sullivan to her politico clients to the little Alley scamp Anderson paid off every now and then, to find out just who this Josie Arlington was. But for now, she kept a steady demeanor. "Where's Miss Arlington from?" she asked nonchalantly.

Anderson knew Lulu wouldn't take kindly to his planting a neophyte in a bordello as beautiful as Lulu's own. He thought it through. She had to find out eventually, and he'd rather it came from him. But admitting to Lulu that her biggest competitor in Storyville was going to be a lowly girl he'd plucked from the Alley, that was taking it too far. Besides, Lulu needn't know details that no longer mattered.

"Where's she from?" Anderson repeated, then chortled. He leaned his head to rest against the wingback chair. "Where's anybody from? Where're you from, Countess?"

She turned to face him, catching his eyes. A sly smile played on her painted lips. "Same as you," she replied. "Everywhere and nowhere."

Ferdinand stared with disbelief at the thick roll of cash that had made its way into his palm via Mr. Flabacher. He tucked the money inside his jacket and, still wearing his happy-glazed expression, stepped outside. The cool air felt refreshing on his flushed cheeks. By the light of the flickering gas lamp, he strolled across the porch, inhaling the fragrance of hyacinths, the perfume only adding to his delirium. He thought of the Greek tragedy of Hyacinth, which he'd read about in literature class, and how the beautiful, young boy became the victim of a jealous wind god. His thoughts then darted to the Countess's offer to have him play at Frenchman's, and he grew giddy all over again. Just then, he tripped over something on the porch and staggered to catch his balance. He looked down, wondering what in the heck was sprawled out like that. Only it wasn't *what*, it was *who*.

"Sorry, sir," Ferd stammered. "I didn't see you there."

A man drunkenly stirred. "Where ya goin'?"

"Just getting on my way," Ferd said, and he continued forward.

Another voice rang out. "How dare you turn your back to my brother, Negro." Stepping from the shadows was Alabama boy Acey LaRue. "You disrespectin' my brother?"

Ferd felt a chill come over him. "I mean no disrespect, sir," he said.

"Don't *sir* me. You don't even have the right to speak to me."

Pierce LaRue hoisted himself up from the ground. "Where we come from, we owned your kind."

They moved closer to Ferdinand and he could smell the alcohol on them.

"This here's a backward town, Negroes minglin' with the superior race," Acey said.

Ferd's heart pounded. His muscles began twitching.

"I think you need a lesson 'bout how the world really works, boy."

Pierce drunkenly lunged, but Ferd took off running at full speed, his long legs bolting down the walk and across the street. One thing was for certain, the lanky kid could run, and the LaRue brothers, in their dinner suits and inebriated states, were after him like a pack of turtles—only, in Ferd's mind this was hardly the case. To him, the burly men were on him like wolves. He didn't look back the entire way.

When he at last charged up to Grandmère's house, he thrust himself through the back door and hurried to bolt it behind him. Gasping for breath, he collapsed to the floor, his chest heaving. He looked down at his hands. They were shaking.

As if it couldn't get worse, he heard stirring in the house. Now he'd gone and woken Grandmère, and he'd have to explain his whereabouts. If the Devil was trying to scare him away from music-making, the attempt was a darn good one. But Ferd didn't recognize the footsteps as Grandmère's slippered shuffle. Instead, two tiny bare feet approached. A little girl, arms crossed, stood before him.

"You going off to hear the blues on brass without me?" Améde demanded.

Ferd hid his shaking hands behind his back. "Shhh."

"If Grandmère catches you," Améde warned, "she'll slap you to sleep, then slap you for sleeping."

"You go on back to bed, Améde."

"You ill or something? You don't look right."

Slowly raising himself up, Ferd took off his sweat-soaked jacket—his gorgeous tailored jacket, hadn't wanted it to see a single crease earlier in the night, and look at it now. With his legs exhausted, he hobbled toward his room.

"Ferd," Améde whispered after him. "Tomorrow . . . another cala?" She gave a devious but hopeful smile as if to remind her brother of their little secret.

"No more calas," Ferd said wearily. "We're staying put."

"Are you getting dim? What I'm trying to say is—"

"I know, Améde. The music's dead and buried for now."

"You're being scary, Ferd."

"Sometimes things are scary, little girl. Now leave me be." He closed his bedroom door and crawled into bed, cradling himself.

The morning sun shone brightly through the stained-glass windows of the Countess's bordello. Empty Champagne bottles, party masks, wilted flowers, and articles of clothing were strewn about the parlor. House rules mandated that no john was allowed to spend the night, and while the girls had done a good job of shooing the males out, they'd lost the energy to get their own selves upstairs. Instead, sleeping girls still in their party dresses were draped over the sofas and nestled into the bear-claw chairs and curled up on the fur throws.

The only sound in the house other than snoring was a rhythmic scrubbing, then a sloshing of water, then more scrubbing. On their hands and knees, Addie and Boo maneuvered the scrub brush around the sleeping whores, pushing aside a leg or lifting a dangling arm. The girls were out so cold, no one stirred.

"They could make a preacher cuss," Addie mumbled.

No one even flinched when a loud knock sounded at the front door, except for Addie and Boo, who looked questioningly to each other. "Who in their right mind's coming by now?" Addie moaned. She nodded to Boo, who wiped her damp hands on her apron before unbolting the door. As she peered out she nearly gasped at the sight of a large-headed, misshapen little man, his arms full of all sort of contraptions.

"Yes, sir?" she said warily.

E. J. Bellocq's shrill voice was almost as disconcerting as his appearance. "Please inform Mistah Flabacher that the photographer has arrived. Thank you."

Wide-eyed, Boo nodded and shut the door.

"Well, who's there?" Addie asked.

"The photographer? A buggy-lookin' one, Ma."

They both turned to see Flabacher, fresh and dressed in a three-piece suit, entering the foyer, having come in from the guest quarters, a gold pocket watch in his hand. "Well, good morn—" his voice trailed off as he saw the slumber-filled parlor, "My oh my, this isn't very sightly, is it?"

"The photographer be on the porch," Addie informed him.

"Well, at least someone has an appreciation for time," Flabacher muttered.

He led Bellocq around to the back courtyard, where, amidst clotheslines of petticoats and stockings, Bellocq busily set up his tripod, wet plate, and camera. Flabacher shuffled about impatiently, checking his watch. "There was another big opening party last night," he explained. "They're throwing opening parties every Saturday night up until the official opening of Storyville on New Year's Eve. Still, though, it's half past noon, surely one of them should be up by now." He called into the open kitchen window. "How's that pot of coffee coming, Addie?"

"Still brewin'," she called back.

"I need one of those gals," he said.

"Which one?" Addie asked.

"Uhh . . . one who's coherent?"

Addie popped her head out the doorway to give him a look. "This coffee's strong, but ain't gonna float no iron wedge."

"I know, I know," Flabacher said, "but can you just go wake one? The photographer's on the clock."

A few moments later, Addie reappeared, propping up a girl dressed in nothing but her petticoat and garters. "This be Lucinda," Addie announced.

"Lucinda, great!" Flabacher boomed. They helped her into a wicker chair and she promptly nodded off, wilting like a dead, makeup-smeared flower.

Bellocq looked through the ground glass of his camera, then stepped back helplessly.

"Hello? Lucinda?" Flabacher said.

Her head rolled around, and she cracked open an eye . . . but then her neck lolled again.

"Lu-cin-da! We need you to wake up!" Flabacher called in her face. This time, she curled her legs up onto the chair, but to no avail; she was just getting more comfortable. Flabacher threw his arms into the air. "Well, this just dills my pickle," he exclaimed. "Mister Bellocq, can you make the photograph in an artistic way so we can't tell she's . . . out cold?"

Bellocq stared blankly at Flabacher.

"Splendid!" Flabacher said. "Fetch me when you're done." He stomped off into the house, shaking his head and muttering to himself.

Bellocq wasn't keen on being left alone with the sleeping whore. After all, his last photographic job had been doing class pictures for the Catholic primary school. He inched toward her. Keeping distance as if she might suddenly snap to and bite him, he awkwardly stretched out his hand to touch her shoulder. Delicately, he lowered her petticoat strap. It drooped to reveal her breast. Bellocq stared for a moment, then, satisfied, he quietly stepped back, ducking behind his camera.

Chapter Twenty-Six

When Tom Anderson had suggested, strongly, that Mary take a new name, she wasn't sure what to pick, or even how she should feel about it. "This is your chance to reinvent yourself," he'd told her. "You can change your identity completely. Leave behind Mary Deubler. Become the woman you always wanted to be, or never thought you could be, or didn't even dare dream of being. Your fate is in your own hands now."

His words were intoxicating. They were everything Mary could have wanted to hear, and yet, she didn't feel anything near what she would have imagined. Here she had the opportunity to shed her former self and to create a new one from thin air. She could instantly become a Russian princess, or a circus acrobat, heir to an aristocrat, or even an African priestess. She could create any lineage and a jaw-dropping story of how she'd come to be a madam.

But something was tugging at her. Peter had been the only male Deubler, and she suddenly felt a twinge of nostalgia for a self she was only beginning to know.

Anderson, however, was thrilled with the notion of remaking Mary. His eyes grew twinkly as he talked to her of what she could be. It was everything, and more, than even her most secret dreams, and yet she heard very clearly all that he wasn't saying: he never spoke of what she was.

She'd be the first to admit that an Alley whore wasn't something to be proud of, but there must be more to her than just Alley whore, she felt sure of that. But Anderson wanted her made up like a fairy tale.

So she chose the first name Josie to keep Peter's nickname for her close. His words would remind her that no matter what invention she went on to become, it was she who was the conductor of this train.

Arlington would be her surname, after the hotel in the picture postcard. Her mama had been there once. When, or with whom, Mary wasn't sure, but the postcard was one of the only remaining items that had meant enough to Mama that she'd kept it in the top bureau drawer. One day, Mary believed, she'd go to the Arlington too. She'd go with someone special, someone who knew her as Mary, not as a concoction of a person.

After she'd chosen her new name, Tom Anderson arranged for her to meet with what he called a beautician.

As Mary approached Paulina's Boudoir on Canal Street——the

likes of which she would never have dared step foot in, given that she couldn't afford a hairpin, let alone an outfit there—she felt as uneasy as she had when approaching Miss Eulalie's that first time. This was just as much another world to her.

She was met at the door by a perfectly coiffed woman with a flawless alabaster complexion. "You must be Josie," the woman practically sang out. Mary was taken aback. She opened her mouth to say, No, I'm Mary, but then it sank in that, yes, she must be Josie.

"I'm Paulina, come in, we have such beauties waiting for you! Mistah Anderson wants you to be adored and pampered. You won't walk out of here until you're a new person!"

There it was again. Mary gulped.

For the next several hours, Mary was indeed transformed. Her hair was washed, cut, and styled with curling tongs that had been heated in the fireplace, and then swept back and high in a jeweled hair clip to "show off her gorgeous décolleté," or so said Paulina. Mary hadn't been aware she possessed a décolleté. She smiled politely, not sure if it was her ears, chin, or what part exactly that she was supposed to be showing off.

Paulina then moved Mary to a dressing table decorated with a silver vanity set and all sorts of fancy bottles and tins and jeweled boxes.

"First, you'll want to start with blotting powder," Paulina instructed, dipping a puff into a silver tin of rice powder and dabbing it on Mary's forehead, chin, and nose. Mary fluttered, trying to hold back a sneeze. "As for your eyes," Paulina continued, "some high-society ladies use belladonna drops to create a misty look that men supposedly love. You can try it, but if you ask me, I think belladonna brings on a delirium. Personally, I prefer just a little Vaseline on the eyelids. That will give some luster to your gray eyes."

Paulina reached for a matchbox and slid it open. "You're lucky, you already have dark lashes, but you can still add a bit of drama." She struck a match, then held it to a cork wine stopper. When the edge blackened, she waved out the match and blew on the cork to cool it. Mary's lids flitted as Paulina brushed the cork over her lashes. "You'll get used to it," Paulina said. Mary blinked her eyes open.

"Now, this is my favorite!" Paulina held up a little ceramic pot decorated with a pink flower. "Liprose. I travel all the way to Paris, to the House of Guerlain, and I buy dozens to give only to my most prized clients. To think, I used to slice beets to color my lips." She dipped a small brush in the pot then carefully painted Mary's mouth. "Now you must take care to apply this very lightly. You don't want to end up looking like a . . ." Paulina quickly caught herself. "You just don't want to look tawdry is all."

Paulina leaned back to admire her work. With a satisfied grin, she picked up the hand mirror and turned it for Mary to see. Mary had felt a girl walking into the boudoir, but what peered back at her in the mirror was a woman. While Mary studied herself, Paulina yammered on, her voice growing more and more distant as Mary's image of herself as a madam grew more and more certain. For the first time, Mary understood what Tom Anderson saw in her, and she believed she could, indeed, play the role. She wouldn't be a madam like the Countess, who wore her face like a mask. Instead, with the grime gone and the weariness hidden, Mary looked like a shiny penny.

"I want you to treat your face with lemon juice twice a day," Paulina chattered. "You want your complexion to be fair and delicate, my dear. And I suggest you always use a parasol when you're outdoors, even just for an errand or brief stroll. Oh, and you must use Pears soap to wash! You'll smell like the English countryside." Mary's head spun as she half listened to all the things she must and mustn't do.

The mirror was plucked from Mary's hand as an array of clothing was paraded in. "Bonnets have fallen out of fashion," Paulina explained, "but wide-brimmed hats are all the desire!" Mary didn't own a single hat, but no worry, Tom Anderson was set to change that.

"See, here's how I keep up on the very latest." Paulina handed Mary a magazine. The cover showed a drawing of a sailboat, and at the top was a banner with a lounging, barefoot woman on one side peering into a looking glass, and a lounging, barefoot woman on the other side reading a newspaper; a scroll unfurled between them that said in capital letters, VOGUE.

"We'll have you looking like a Gibson girl in no time," Paulina clucked.

Mary was presented with heeled, fine kid boots, the tops decorated with tassels, and then a full-length cloak and a little sable jacket lined with velvet. The only thought keeping Mary smiling was imagining the look on Charlotte's face when she brought home all the riches.

But then it occurred to her: how *would* she get all of this home? She had no carriage, and if Paulina suggested to help, well, Mary would be too ashamed to have her—or anyone of this ilk—by the house. Amidst the coiffing and dolling, little beads of sweat began forming on Mary's forehead and the back of her neck. She took a moment to excuse herself to get some air.

Outside, as she breathed deeply, she noticed how the passersby looked at her. The society women greeted her with friendly smiles, and the men gave her lingering but respectful nods. Never before had she experienced such reactions from strangers—she was used to these women looking down their noses, and these men grimacing or, at best, giving her a sleazy leer. So this was the life of Josie Arlington.

She returned inside to continue with her transformation.

To Mary's great relief, it was Paulina's idea to arrange for the clothing to be left at the shop until Mary, that is, Josie, was ready for it to be delivered to the bordello. Anderson hadn't yet informed Mary where her bordello might be. She imagined it would be a tidy little framehouse, maybe two bedrooms, three if she was lucky. It didn't even occur to her that it may have a bathroom indoors.

When Mary entered her tiny, dirt-floor house that eve, Charlotte was in the rocker, nursing Anna.

"Mercy me!" Charlotte gasped. "How did you come to be all dolled up so fancy?"

Mary hadn't yet breathed a word of Anderson's offer to Charlotte. She'd kept waiting for him to rescind, for someone to come and tell her it was all a cruel joke. But with each day that passed, it began to sink in. And now, as she stood in front of her own little mirror, it became real. She was to be a madam. She was Madam Josie Arlington.

Mary waited until the baby was asleep in her cradle before she explained it all to Charlotte. Hanging on every word, Charlotte barely blinked. "Mary, no!" she kept exclaiming. "You're lyin' like a no-legged dog!"

"Charlotte, I daresay, it's all true."

"It's the stuff of fairy tales and tall tales and things that don't just happen, especially not to people like us."

"We're not 'people like us' anymore, Lottie."

Still, there were some details Mary had to figure out. No matter that she'd be a madam, there was no place for baby Anna in a whorehouse. Mary knew she needed to save up money to put Charlotte and Anna somewhere nearby, but not in the District. She believed that Anna should be kept from any knowledge of how Mary earned a living—and even knowledge of the Underworld in general. Anna would not see this life as a default, the way Mary had and Mama had. No, this way of life would not get passed on to yet another generation. Anna would have an education and opportunities, Mary would make certain of it.

But in the meantime Mary was going to need to provide for them once the Alley closed, and she dreaded the necessary conversation with Anderson regarding her cut of the monies. It would be then that Josie the conductor would make her debut, and Mary decided that her new persona would be an expert in ways of business. Savvy, that's what Josie would be. She'd heard that word used to describe Anderson, although she'd never before heard it used to describe a woman. But as Anderson said, Josie was her creation. So Josie could be the first savvy woman.

The next morning, Mary returned to her crib. She was dressed in her ordinary clothes, makeup washed off, wielding her kip. Until she was officially a madam, she had no other means of supporting herself, so she had no choice but to return to the Alley so long as it still existed.

When she saw Beulah, she told her nothing of the news, but instead handed her a round tin of pomade called Madam C.J. Walker's Wonderful Hair Grower. Paulina had given it to Mary, saying it was the latest from Saint Louis, in case Mary associated with any octoroons who had traits of Negro hair.

Beulah regarded the image of a black woman, hair parted and combed, gracing the package. "Well, butter my biscuit," she said. "Where'd you come by this?"

"One of my gentlemen callers, a salesman," Mary said, a little white lie for now. "Had plenty in his carpetbag."

CHAPTER TWENTY-SEVEN

The Old Absinthe House

Anderson had noticed that something wasn't quite right with Tater. His normal disposition was oafish, bumbling about, and always underfoot. But now, Tater looked nervously askance whenever Anderson approached, and from his window, Anderson often caught sight of Tater leaning against the side of the outhouse staring off vacantly. His henchman might as well be in a monastery for how quiet and pensive he'd become.

Tater sensed Anderson had noticed, and knew he couldn't keep on like this. He couldn't keep avoiding his boss, and if he lost this job, he'd lose his lady as well—although she was practically on her way out anyway, mostly because Tater had taken to sleeping at the office so she wouldn't see his nightly blubbering spells. He tried to convince himself that he'd just been spooked and to let it all go. But that wasn't working. So he came up with another plan.

He trudged to Venus Alley and pounded on the door to crib nineteen. When it opened, he thrust a wad of cash at Mary Deubler.

"It's what you paid me," he said, his words coming out fast. "I need to do right by the Lord, so take it all, just take it all back. Ain't gonna sin no more, okay? No more. Maybe I'll rough people up some, but had me a sign from the heavens, and I'm changin' my ways."

Mary confusedly took the money, and Tater looked pleased to be rid of it, as if the cash were tainted. He quickly turned to leave. Then he glanced back over his shoulder.

"He ain't dead, ya know. Or maybe you didn't, but thought ya should." And with that, he ran off.

Mary stood there, mouth agape. But she'd felt certain Lobrano was gone. She looked at the money, and now it was her turn to see it as tainted. She didn't want her money back; she'd wanted Lobrano to pay for what he'd done.

But then a strange thing happened. She felt a wave of relief. As much as she'd wanted justice, there was a peace in knowing that she hadn't done something evil after all. She'd somehow tricked herself into believing that if Lobrano were dead, it would avenge Peter's death. But Peter was gone and not coming back, and Lobrano's whereabouts wouldn't change that.

She closed her crib door and straightened the pile of cash before slipping it into her cleavage. For the first time since Anderson had bestowed her with such good fortune she felt she was a decent enough person to deserve it.

Never again would she let anyone hurt her or her family the way Lobrano had. Never again would she need a man the way she thought she'd needed him. No, she didn't need a pimp; she didn't need a husband even. She vowed that as soon as she got ahead, she'd pay back her debt to Tom Anderson and become a fully independent woman. She would never again owe anyone anything.

A sugar cube dissolved into a glass of green absinthe, swirling it to a milky white. With a shaky hand, Lobrano brought the glass to his rotted mouth. He quivered as he took a deep swallow.

Too worried of being spotted if he went to the Pig Ankle, he'd wandered over to Bourbon Street and sat alone in a corner of The Absinthe Room, his collar turned up to shield his face. Sweaty and strung-out, he shot paranoid looks at the few patrons. He motioned to a barmaid. "'Nother," he said breathily.

"Ya best dig in those deep pockets, 'cause you was short on your last one," she snapped. He impatiently waved her away. Little did she know that his pockets were full—of stones. One drink more would have been nice, but what did it matter anyway? He'd be at the bottom of the Mississippi after this.

A husky voice rang out in the otherwise quiet bar. "Rough tonight. Rough tonight, batten down!"

Startled, Lobrano turned to see an old sailor in his seamen's frock, shuffling through the bar with a cane. "Hear me now," the sailor called out to the near-empty room. "The sea shows mercy to no man. But the spoils, they be there. Mark this!"

The few other patrons ignored him, but Lobrano's eyes grew large. The old man shuffled closer. "You. A young sailor?" He pointed a knotty finger at Lobrano.

Lobrano shook his head.

"I believe you are," the old man said, his finger inching closer and closer. Lobrano squeezed shut his eyes, attempting to shake off his absinthe haze. But when he opened his eyes, the old sailor was closer still.

"You. Turn turtle. Bayou bound. You."

Lobrano slowly nodded. Yes, he was bound for the bottom, but how could this fogey have known?

"Must be time," the sailor continued. "But only the full moon be revealin' Lafitte's gold."

"Lafitte the pirate?" Lobrano asked.

The sailor gave a bulgy-eyed nod. "The spirit of Lafitte will guide you to forty gum trees. Batten down. Moon ain't full yet. Must be overhead." The sailor leaned closer, his white whiskers almost touching Lobrano. "Cursed, but it be there."

The barmaid came by and gently hooked her hand around the old sailor's elbow. She steered him in the direction of the door. "Sorry, ain't no scraps for ya tonight, Ollie," she said. "Best be gettin' on now, we're 'bout closin' up."

Ollie looked at her meekly, then shuffled out the door.

His vision fuzzy, Lobrano watched the old sailor go. "Lafitte's gold," he marveled to himself. Then, as if trying to soak in the details, he repeated over and over, "Forty gum trees, forty gum trees, forty gum trees. Cursed, but it be there."

Lobrano called over the barmaid. "Ya ever heard of Lafitte the pirate?" he asked.

"Who me?" the barmaid said. Irritated, Lobrano turned to face the rest of the near-empty bar. "Anyone here know of Lafitte?" The few folks barely looked his way, thinking he was either drunk as a doornail or demented in the head—or both.

The barkeep piped up. "Lafitte and Andrew Jackson planned the Battle of New Orleans right upstairs."

Lobrano looked up at the ceiling, astonished. "What about the contraband? Lafitte's gold?"

"Supposed to be buried along the bayou, ain't it?" a grizzled man at the other end of the bar called out. "Never heard of anyone findin' nothin'."

"But do ya know anyone who's gone looking?" Lobrano asked, leaning on the edge of the stool.

"Can't say I do. Supposed to be haunted, that gold." The man took a sip of his absinthe. "Like half the things 'round here."

"Forty gum trees, under a full moon, forty gum trees," Lobrano chanted. Visions appeared before his eyes: a pirate stealing through the night, holding a purse bulging with gold coins that he dropped like breadcrumbs along the swampland. Lobrano could make out every detail of Lafitte's long-nailed fingers reaching into the burlap bag. He could hear the clinking of coins, oh the multitude of coins! How each coin caught the glint of the moonlight before it disappeared into the earth.

"Barmaid!" Lobrano shouted. "I need something to write with!"

"This ain't no schoolhouse, in case ya haven't noticed," she called back.

"It's important. Need to write a note."

The barmaid reluctantly brought over a pencil and square of paper. "You know how to write?" Lobrano asked her.

"My penmanship ain't the best," she said.

"Don't matter. I need you to put, 'To Mary.'"

The barmaid, concentrating now, wrote it in childlike block letters.

Lobrano continued, "Going to find the contraband."

The barmaid cringed. "Don't know how that ought to be spelled."

"Gold. Going to find the gold. Half will be yours. . . ." He gulped. "To make up for what I done."

The barmaid glanced up at Lobrano, and, for a moment, she felt of touch of sympathy—until her thoughts shifted to wondering just what it was the bastard had done.

Despite his spinning head, Lobrano noticed how her eyes had

narrowed into disapproving slits. He wanted to tell her he wasn't completely despicable, and that there were so many times he'd wanted to pawn that gold locket for cash, but he hadn't. Hadn't been able to squelch his sentimental feelings. He wanted to tell her that, but she was just a barmaid.

"How do you want it signed?" the barmaid asked.

"What?"

"She needs to know who it's from."

"She'll know."

"Ya gotta sign a letter," she insisted.

"Fine. Sign it 'Your Uncle.'"

She handed the letter to Lobrano, and he carefully folded it, then pressed it to his chest as he slid it under his suspenders, into his shirt pocket.

He staggered his way to Venus Alley, forgetting he was on the lam. He surveyed Mary's crib from down the block. Seeing that the door was closed, he hurried up, slid the letter under the worn slats, and then quickly stumbled away.

Had Lobrano lingered, he would have seen a john emerge from the crib, the letter sticking to the sole of his muddy boot, unnoticed as he trudged away down the Alley.

Flabacher approached a shabby Baronne Street flat, grimacing as he turned the grimy doorknob. He ascended the staircase to apartment 2E and gave a solid knock. No response. He knocked again. Silence.

"Mister Bellocq?" he called. "The man at the Camera Club told me you were here." He knocked a bit harder. "It's been a number of days now, and I would like very much to see those photographs you've made, friend." Flabacher waited, his ear to the door. "I also need to compensate you for your time and efforts."

At that, the door opened.

Flabacher stepped inside. He was immediately unnerved by the sight: newspaper covered all the windows, and the walls were plastered with photographs. Photographs of tree stumps, doorways, lampposts, and every other mundane object in existence.

As Flabacher scanned what seemed to him like a big mess, Bellocq scurried back to his perch at a desk piled with thick books that he read through a magnifying glass.

"I beg your pardon if I'm interrupting," Flabacher began, but Bellocq cut him off with a sharp point of his finger to a table. There, Flabacher saw a photograph of Lucinda. He squinted at it: she was half-naked and full-out asleep. The image repeated unchanged over several photos laid out in a row.

"Hmpff. Not exactly the yearbook-type pictures I had in mind," Flabacher grunted. He stacked the photos, then placed them in his billfold. He took some dollar bills and looked around for where to set them. His gaze drifted toward a fishing wire strung from the back wall, photographs on clothespins dangling from it. Curious, Flabacher stepped around to see. At this, Bellocq began nervously chirping, waving his arms in the air like a monkey.

"All right, all right," Flabacher said. "Calm down, fellow."

Bellocq tried to catch his breath. "Please take your photographs and leave now," he squeaked.

Flabacher opened the front door and tipped his hat.

Bellocq scurried to lock the door behind him, and, from the hallway, Flabacher could hear the deliberate screech of the door bolt as it slid into place.

"Odd fellow. Very, very odd fellow," Flabacher muttered as he headed down the staircase.

Through a tiny spot not covered by newspaper, Bellocq peeked an eyeball out the window to watch Flabacher leave the building and wobble himself across the street. He watched until the hefty man disappeared from sight. He then stepped toward the fishing line, dipping behind it to face the photographs hung there to dry.

One after another after another, they were of Mary Deubler, draped in a tattered chippie and sitting in a straight-backed chair, her striped silk-stockinged legs crossed daintily. She was a contrast of raggedy, hard edges and gentle, dimpled girly features. From her scuffed buckle shoes to her tousled hair bun to the glass of Raleigh Rye in her hand, she was clearly nothing but an Alley whore. And yet, there was something so earnest about her, something genuine and unashamed in her face. She'd posed for the camera as if she felt beautiful and self-possessed, holding a glass to toast herself. There was a spark in this woman—Bellocq knew that showed through in the photograph.

He moved to a table, from which he lifted a heavy eight-inch by ten-inch glass plate negative and held it under a lamp. On it was the original image of Mary. He stared at it longingly, lovingly. Then he brought the blunt edge of a knife to the glass and grated it across the plate until her face was scratched out.

CHAPTER TWENTY-EIGHT

Actress Sarah Bernhardt

A break in the heavy curtains shot a dagger of early morning sunlight into Lulu's bedroom, rousing her from a fitful sleep. She contemplated rolling over for more beauty rest, but instead found herself compelled to move to the window and pull back the curtain. Squinting in the light, she adjusted her eyes to take in the vacant Victorian.

Throughout the days, she'd watched a parade of workmen, carting out old floorboards and wheelbarrows full of scraps, bringing in rolls of wallpaper and cans of paint. Cracked windowpanes were repaired, roof tiles were patched, doors were removed from their hinges and replaced. She'd found herself stealing to her room several times a day to watch the house, and she became consumed by the details. What pattern was the wallpaper? What color was the paint? Was that marble or granite? Slate or shale? Yesterday she'd balked as she watched men carefully handling long mirrors that were floor-to-ceiling high. *That Miss Arlington, whoever she was, better not be doing a mirrored room like my own!*

None of Lulu's searches on Josie Arlington had turned up fruitful. Even Snitch had responded blankly to the name. From this, Lulu surmised Josie Arlington was a pseudonym—but just where did Tom Anderson pluck up a nobody? And why did he want to turn this particular gal into a somebody?

Mary grew frustrated as she tried to practice Paulina's techniques in front of her own little mirror at home. She sneezed away much of the powder, then blinked out burnt cork from her eye, then blotted up what looked like a bloody lip.

"Oh, Lottie, help," Mary cried. "Mistah Anderson wants to see me, and, after all that, I should show him the new me."

Together, they started over from the beginning as Charlotte squeezed half a lemon into the washbasin, where Mary rinsed with Pears soap. Charlotte blew on the powder puff to rid of the excess before applying while Mary pinched her nose closed. She slicked Vaseline on Mary's lids, then struggled to apply the cork without creating raccoon eyes, but eventually noticed some effects.

"How elegant you are," Charlotte sighed. "Just pinch your cheeks before seeing him."

Mary didn't possess any of the fancy clothes yet, so she had no choice but to put on the same dress she'd worn last time. Still, she felt sweet-smelling and sophisticated as she walked to Anderson's saloon.

Tom Anderson was waiting for Mary at a back table, and when he looked up to see her framed in the sunlight of the doorway, he knew his instincts had been on the money.

Even Sheep-Eye, who usually didn't notice anything unless it smacked him in the face, remarked as she passed him, "You sure clean up nice."

She walked toward the back of the saloon, where Anderson stood to greet her, kissing her hand. "You look fetching, Miss Arlington."

She reddened. "Thank you," she said, bashfully casting her eyes down.

"Come along now, I must introduce you to your new home."

Together, they walked toward the back o' town, with Mary careful to keep a respectable distance between them so their bodies didn't accidentally brush up against each other. She didn't want to worry him that she thought this arrangement was anything other than two people doing business—Josie was a professional sort, just like him. And yet Mary secretly reveled in each step she took with him at her side. She watched for the reactions of those they passed. Surely they must be wondering, Just who was this woman accompanying Tom Anderson?

"I took the liberty of outfitting your new home," Anderson explained. "I've been told I have decent enough taste, so I hope it will be to your liking. It's still in progress, though, so don't let all the construction throw you. It will be a sight when it's all done, I promise."

She could hardly have cared about such things as furnishings; just having walls and doors and more than one room was enough to make her swoon. She did have one suggestion, though, and mustered up the courage to broach it.

"The johns who come to my crib, they like that there's a little bedside table where they can put their billfold and jewelry and keep it in sight. Do you think we could have a bedside table?"

"That's a great idea," Anderson replied. "Wish I'd thought of it myself. Of course, I'll see to it that there are bedside tables."

"And one more thing, if it's not too much trouble. . . . I hung a little mirror near the bed so I could peek at my face before . . . well, sometimes a girl just wants to make sure she looks her best."

Anderson nodded. "I don't believe wall mirrors will be too much trouble at all."

Mary smiled contentedly to herself, wondering if Anderson thought her suggestions made her savvy. But as they turned onto Basin Street, she couldn't help but look questioningly to him.

He didn't return her look, just continued walking straight ahead, an amused smile threatening the corners of his mouth. They passed the Countess's bordello, and both Mary and Anderson quickened their gait, neither aware the other was doing so on purpose.

Mary kept expecting they'd turn onto a side street to find a little cottage she could call her own. Instead, Anderson stopped in front of the Victorian.

He held out his arms. "Welcome home."

Mary looked searchingly. *This* house? There had to be some mistake. How in the world, of all the houses within the blocks of the District, could it be *this* house?

"I thought we could call it The Arlington," Anderson said.

Mary's eyes grew wide as she looked from the cupola to the veranda to the beautiful woman guarding the door. "Yes," she breathed. "It is The Arlington."

Everything was a blur as Anderson led her inside, walking her through one room after another as they stepped around ladders and over paint cans and drop cloths and buckets and brushes. "I thought we'd have some fun, create a little House of Nations," he said. "Here we'll have the Russian parlor. And over here is the Japanese parlor. And then there's the Turkish parlor. And this will be a stunning mirror lounge." Each room ran together in Mary's mind. She was speechless.

They ascended the regal staircase and walked from room to room on the second level, then the third, and good Lord, there were indoor bathrooms—many of them!

"Oh my," she at last exclaimed. "It's so much to keep up!" She immediately regretted opening her mouth. Here he was giving her all this, and these were the words that spilled out?

But Anderson smiled kindly. "Don't worry, you'll have plenty of help."

Mary felt light-headed, but she squeezed her hands into fists. She was *not* going to faint on Anderson again.

"I've been meaning to tell you," he began, "that you remind me of someone, and I hope it's a big compliment. Some years ago, I was fortunate enough to see the famous actress Sarah Bernhardt when she did her American tour. She performed a play here, at the French Opera House. A comedy called *Frou-Frou*, and there was something about Miss Bernhardt . . . the way she was womanly yet strong. Sympathetic yet intense. Her character could've come off as pathetic, but she didn't let her." Anderson rested himself down onto the arm of a chair so that he was suddenly looking up into Mary's face. "This is your play, Josie. You're the famous actress now."

All she could do was nod.

He rose. "I bet you'd like a view of your audience." With that, he led her into the cupola, hanging back while she alone climbed the iron spiral staircase, up and up to the top. She took a deep breath as she peered from the paned window to see the city laid out before her. She could see the railroad just across the street; and beyond that, St. Louis Cemetery Number One, the sunlight eerily glinting off the crumbling whitewashed stucco of the old tombs. She pivoted to look out over Venus Alley, which appeared quiet and peaceful from way up here. She could see farther, to the French Quarter and to church steeples and clock towers that rose above the row houses.

She pivoted again to survey her new street—when she jumped. She pushed herself flat against the wall, out of sight from the window. She pressed her palm against her chest as her rib cage heaved.

From a window in Mahogany Hall, separated from The Arlington by only a razed plot of land, Countess Lulu White stared at Mary.

Slowly, like a child peeking under the bed for monsters, Mary inched back to look out the window. The Countess stood squarely, and her face snapped back to attention as Mary reappeared. Through her glare, the Countess gave a stiff flutter of a wave.

Mary bit her lip. She stood a floor taller than Mahogany Hall. Slowly, she brought her hand to the window to wave down at her number one rival.

Lulu knew she had to take preventative action. She sent for her biggest gun: Miss Eulalie Echo.

Eulalie arrived after sundown, stealing in through the back door. When she entered Lulu's chambers upstairs, the Countess was still staring out the window. "It's that house," Lulu said anxiously. "It's haunting me."

Eulalie looked for herself. She was surprised to see such a lovely Victorian, lit up with flickering gas lamps. She expected to see a dingy aura about it, or to feel a noxious charge, but instead, it just sat there peaceably, as if it were minding its own business.

"There's a new madam," Lulu said, spitting the words like barbs. "I need the sealing curse."

Rarely did anything surprise Eulalie, but this request certainly did. Most of the time, when one woman wanted to outdo another, Eulalie painted red powder on one leg and green powder on the other and cast a spell to lure men. She'd also perform spells for keeping away pregnancy or warding off venereal disease (goat testicles for gonorrhea, wasp blood for syphilis). Occasionally, she'd cast a hex to bring on venereal disease to an enemy. But the worst spell, which wasn't to be taken lightly, was the "sealing power," for it could close up a whore forever. It was a curse reserved only for a woman who'd committed the most heinous of acts.

Eulalie spoke soothingly, "Countess, come, why don't I give you a remedy to ease your worry." She began to unwind a medicine bottle from her hair.

"I said I want the sealing curse," Lulu demanded.

Eulalie had never seen the Countess as vengeful and desperate as this. It was an ugly side to Lulu, and Eulalie knew thoughts like that could harelip you. Besides, she wouldn't perform the sealing curse without significant proof of cause. Otherwise, the whole of the Alley, and now the new district, would be sealing one another up.

It was decided that Eulalie needed to investigate the new house further. She wandered downstairs and across the street and walked the premises, trying to get a feel for the energy. She determined the house's history was long and muddled. More recently, a sad decrepitude had settled in, and she had the urge to do a sage cleanse to rid the house of the cloud of disregard. She peeked in the window. Someone was taking care to make it look nice. But Eulalie couldn't yet gauge a personality. She paused at the relief of the woman over the front door. "Bet ya never thought you'd be housemother of a whorehouse," she said to it.

Back upstairs to Lulu's she went.

"It feels neglected," she reported.

Lulu scoffed. "Let's hope it stays that way. Now, as for that proprietress. All I know is she goes by the name Josie Arlington."

Something resonated with Eulalie. Although she'd never heard the name before, it felt familiar. She was certain she knew, in one way or another, this woman Josie Arlington.

"Ah, dear Countess, can't curse a name, either. Especially not the sealing curse. It ain't like a Voodoo doll that you can call for anybody. This is particular. And *never* do you want to get it wrong, for what unjustly comes to them can come back to you."

"I think I saw her. She looked like a china doll, so young and pink-cheeked." With a snarl, Lulu folded her arms tightly over her chest. "Fine, then, I will just wait until the madam appears for good. Then we'll get to work."

Eulalie shivered with a premonition—it wasn't an image or a voice, rather a heavy feeling, weighted by years yet unlived of jealousy, feuding, fixation, hysteria. A new queen was coming to Basin Street.

CHAPTER TWENTY-NINE

That night, and miles away in the deep thick of the marsh, a cacophony of crickets, frogs, and other swamp creatures joined in the song of an old black man. Dissolving into his wrinkles, he sat on the front porch of a crooked shack balanced atop spindly stilts, itself seeming only inches away from dissolving into the bayou. In a deep, resonant voice he sang.

Go down, Moses
Way down in Egypt la-and . . .

He noticed a raft approaching and tipped his hat. The raft was nothing more than some flat boards that moved as listlessly as everything did around here, including the air that hung so heavy you could practically see it. Lobrano stood on the raft, slogging it along through the bulrush with a branch as a makeshift oar. His eyes darted from bank to bank, searching the weeping treetops.

"Any gum trees here?" he called out.

"Don't know no gum trees," the old man said.

"Forty gum trees is what I'm lookin' for."

The old man's lips flapped together over a toothless jaw. "Can't never look for much here. The swamp don't like no one pokin' round. All them gators and serpents. Guardians o' Hell, if ya asks me."

Lobrano knew what he was up against, and it seemed fitting that he embrace Hell. But what he hadn't expected was that this test was breathing some life into him. The search was his reason to pull his decrepit body awake each morning.

"The awfullest is there ain't no absinthe here," Lobrano called back. He'd been clear of the green fairy for nearly a week now and was at last starting to see the fits and sweats diminish.

The man laughed. "Maybe a little hooch if ya knows the right folk. But ain't no absinthe, that's for sure. That's one for the fancy places. Here you swig from the bottle." He sang out a bluesy tune as Lobrano's shoddy raft floated deeper into the bayou.

Skinny man,
Hunting gum trees,
Under a full moon . . .

It was New Year's Eve day, and malaise hung like a veil of fog over Venus Alley. This would have been one of the busiest days in years past, but now just a smattering of johns came and went, getting in their last cheap tricks before they were forced to pay up in Storyville. Most johns stayed away, though, not wanting to get caught up on the wrong side of the law as the death knell of the Alley tolled.

When Mary arrived, Tater and Sheep-Eye were already there, preempting the police by going crib to crib, warning occupants they must be cleared out by sundown or they'd be sent to jail. The whores wearily nodded, and Mary wondered where they all planned to go; it wasn't as if any of them—or their pimps for that matter—could afford to rent houses in Storyville. She knew some whores thought any shadowy corner in the District would do. But Mary had heard the streets would be patrolled and streetwalkers arrested—no chance they'd let the District turn into another Venus Alley.

A few Alley girls—only the youngest and best-looking ones— had been asked to join houses. Not fancy houses like the Countess's, but small ones situated out of sight in the blocks behind Basin Street, where Mary thought Anderson would've placed her. As far as she'd heard, only one Alley girl had been recruited to a Basin Street house, and it was the raunchy one: Miss Emma Johnson's French Studio, where word was that Emma would hold weekly sex shows that were not for the faint of stomach. Mary couldn't even imagine what these might entail, and she hoped to God that Anderson wouldn't request something atrocious like that from her someday.

Mary hadn't asked any girls yet, although she knew she'd be bringing Beulah with her. With all the recent upheavals, she'd come to regard Beulah as, dare she say, a friend. Or as close to it as she had on the Alley. For years, Beulah had been little more than a nag, and Mary figured she'd probably been regarded as the same. But now, the two had found, if not exactly a fondness, then at least a need for each other. She realized she actually trusted Beulah. She could rely on seeing that face every day, on having someone who'd keep an eye out for her and someone who was wise to the ways of their world. Like Mary, Beulah had kept to her own, minding her business and no one else's, and Mary respected that.

She couldn't wait to see the look on Beulah's face when she told her about The Arlington. But not just yet. She'd hold the secret a little longer, fearing that if she breathed so much as a word, news would travel fast and she'd be bombarded by desperate pleas. It worried her that she wouldn't be able to say no to anyone. How could she? Who was she to say no when she'd shared the same lot day in, day out, year after year? When just a week ago, she was sure she'd be on a street corner begging?

As she surveyed the Alley, she couldn't help but look upon the others with new eyes. After all, it was she, little Mary, who now held the power to change their lives. She caught herself eyeing different whores, wondering if any were refined enough to work in her house. It was strange and awful to stand there and judge the others as if she were better than them all. Silly girl, who would've thought *you* were refined enough?

But she was a madam now, and certainly no one else here could say that.

She looked to a gangly pipsqueak of a whore, hair still in braids, face smudged with dirt. Thumbelina, the Alley called her, and Mary had never bothered to ask her real name. If she were to clean up Thumbelina, send her to the boudoir to cut and style her hair and fit her with the latest fashions, could Thumbelina become a suitable Basin Street girl too? And what if Thumbelina transformed into an even better Basin Street girl than Mary? What if Thumbelina was more the stuff of madam material, whatever that "stuff" may be?

Mary's head suddenly hurt with the burden of her new position. She turned to her crib—for the very last time. She packed her few belongings and set out her kip and little bedside table for anyone who wanted to take them. God willing, she'd never in her life need a kip again.

But she didn't head home just yet. Instead, she turned toward Pete Lala's Café. Please let him be there, she said to herself. Sure enough, as she rounded the corner she could hear the piano from down the block, a somber tune today. She wasn't sure what her new life would bring, but she wanted some happiness where she could get it.

Her gait quickened, and before she could talk herself out of entering, she walked through the door and straight back to the piano.

Ferdinand looked up, and a little smile broke through the tenseness of his face.

Mary said, "I've come to ask an important question."

He stopped playing and swiveled around to face her.

"I've heard your music, and it stays with me," Mary continued. "If I have the choice, and I believe I do, I'd like to hear your music all the time. Will you be the man who plays the piano at my establishment?"

She didn't breathe until the last word had left her mouth.

There, she'd said it—even though she'd felt absurdly pompous blurting out "my establishment." She knew she better get used to it—there was no such thing as a modest madam.

Ferdinand certainly hadn't expected anything of this sort. "A flattering offer," he said. "Where is your establishment?"

At this, Mary paused. She'd assumed he knew what she was. But then again, why would he? Couldn't she have been a girl who walked by sometimes on her way to her parents' home, where she lived a chaste life like most girls her age?

She straightened herself up. "Storyville," she said. "Basin Street."

She studied his face for any hint of his thoughts, but he quickly turned away.

He reached for a sliced roll on a plate atop the piano, then dolloped on some jelly. He offered up the plate. "Please, have some, miss . . . sorry, I don't recall your given name."

"Mar—" She caught herself. "It's Josie Arlington."

"I'm Ferdinand LaMenthe. Please . . ." He offered the plate again. "Miss Hattie makes the best marmalade."

Mary graciously took a small piece of the roll and dipped it in the jam. "That *is* good," she said with a shy smile.

Ferd took in the sight of this young woman, hardly more than a girl, marching in here, speaking to him directly, unabashedly staring him in the face. He knew he'd seen her before, knew they'd made eyes at each other, but at this moment even her prettiness was surpassed by her gumption, and he liked that. In that way, she felt familiar to him.

"Just might be fitting that I become a professor of the piano in the Underworld," he said. "But I'm wondering, would you let me play my own compositions?"

Mary didn't know the difference between his own compositions or anyone else's; all she knew was she liked everything she'd heard him play. "Of course," she said.

A crease of concern shot across Ferdinand's forehead. "I should tell you up front, some folks who frequent those establishments have a problem with the color of my skin."

"Oh, not at my place." Mary vigorously shook her head. "There'll be—" She stopped, remembering that it was her little secret with Tom Anderson. "Let's just say I've been sharing space with a Negra for many years now. No one at my place will mind, I promise you."

Ferd took another bite of his roll, chewing as he mulled it over— not that there was anything to mull except for Grandmère. Oh, Grandmère. Playing at Lala's was bad enough, but if she ever found out he had a gig in the Tenderloin she'd kick him out of the house, that was for certain. But playing on Basin Street meant he'd soon have enough money to leave Grandmère's house anyway, and maybe it was time for him to become a man. At this, Ferdinand thrust his hand forward.

For a moment, Mary wasn't sure what to do, then it occurred to her: I am doing business. She reached out and gave him the heartiest handshake she could muster.

"Mistah LaMenthe, I mean no disrespect, but, if you'd like . . . well, I was asked to take a name of my choosing, and I want to offer that to you. But you don't have to, only if you want."

Giving her a whimsical look, Ferd considered this. "Don't rightly know what I'd choose, never thought about it before. But I agree. I should have a . . . a stage name." He slathered on more marmalade and took another bite. "Now, what suits me?"

"Aw, it'll come to you, Mistah Jelly Roll," Mary said.

He cocked an eyebrow and gave her a knowing smirk.

"What?" Mary asked. Then it hit her. "Oh! I didn't mean *that*!"

They both broke into bashful giggles. "Sure you didn't," Ferd teased. "But, you know, it is my favorite. I'm speaking of the marmalade." He winked.

Ferd played the name over in his head, mouthing it. "Yes, ma'am, I think Mistah Jelly Roll sounds like a right smart ragtime name. Gotta work on the surname, though."

Mary wanted to linger, but she couldn't, not today. "Thank you," she said. "We'll talk again soon."

Ferd watched as she walked out, noticing the way she held herself and the measure of her gait, from the small of her back to her narrow hips. For reasons he couldn't explain, he had the sudden urge to take this young woman to the French Opera House. He decided he would, indeed, do that someday.

CHAPTER THIRTY

The French Market

Sidney Story sent the housemaid to the market with several dollars and instructions to get fine cuts of steak with all the fixings and a fresh-baked pecan pie. At six o'clock sharp, the candles on the dining table were lit and Story and his mother sat down to their New Year's Eve dinner.

"Why all the fuss, Siddie?" Mrs. Story asked as her steak was presented. "The new year is for praying, not flashy celebration."

Story took a sip of his iced tea, then blotted his mouth with an embroidered napkin. "Mother, we're celebrating the achievements of your son," he said. "At the stroke of midnight, your son makes national headlines for putting an end to the depravity that has been threatening our city." His face turned dour. "I just hope they call it by the appropriate name."

Lines feathered across Mrs. Story's thin lips as she pursed them.

Story took a bite of his steak but could hardly enjoy it as he stared at her. He placed his fork back on the plate. "What, Mother?"

She shook off her unpleasantness. "Oh, Siddie, my little lamb. You are indeed leading the flock. But you must be certain as to where."

"I do believe I am quite certain, Mother."

She dropped a sugar cube into her tea and stirred it with a dainty silver spoon. "Such a wide-eyed lamb," she said. She took an audible sip. "But you know how dissolute males are. Men such as your own father, God rest his soul . . ." She stared forlornly into her teacup.

"Yes, Mother, we need not be reminded." They ate silently for some moments.

"Now that you've sequestered vice, Siddie, you must consider how you will . . . manage it? The depraved tastes that many men have, especially for younger females?"

Story looked at her quizzically.

"I just feel for the poor young girls who will no doubt be forced to work in such a place. I really can't bear it, Siddie." She paused for effect, then clapped her hands. "Oh lamb, it's your next calling! To protect underage girls in your district of vice."

He stared at his plate, stifling the urge to blurt out that he'd just fulfilled his calling and no, he did not need another one right now, thank you very much, Mother! But instead, his breath came forced and loud through his nose as he finished his steak.

It wasn't until the maid had served him a modest slice of pie that Story had calmed enough to consider Mother's words. She did have a point.

"As usual," he said wearily, "you are right, Mother. My work is not done. God's work is never done."

Mrs. Story smiled and reached over to cradle her son's face. "My lamb, may Mother Mary guide your righteous work in 1898."

He nuzzled his cheek into her hand.

Flashy celebration was an understatement for Lulu White's New Year's Eve party. Mahogany Hall sparkled with Chinese lanterns hanging from the trees and luminaria lining the walkway and verandas. No matter that Lulu had already thrown several Storyville inauguration parties; she spared no expense on fine Champagne and a buffet of caviar and seafood. The centerpiece: one of her girls, lying on her back naked (but for a strategically placed leaf), her body decorated with dozens of oysters that men could pluck—or slurp—off her.

A brass band played loud and fast while circus performers ate fire, walked on stilts, and contorted themselves. Just before the stroke of midnight the guests rushed outside to wave sparklers, then gaze up to the sky, oohing and aahing as fireworks exploded over Basin Street.

Next door, The Arlington was dark, but for a flickering candle high at the top of the cupola. Mary and Charlotte pressed their noses to the window. Their bellies were the fullest they'd been in years. Sheep-Eye had delivered to Mary a stipend of $15, saying it would be weekly until The Arlington opened. Mary had thought for certain that Anderson meant the $15 to cover the entire month while construction was still in progress. But Sheep-Eye insisted that she'd see him again next week with the same amount.

Mary, Charlotte, and the baby took a trip to the market and bought a chicken and sweet potatoes and eggs, butter, and fresh-baked bread, and a bottle of wine, plus a box of pastries for dessert that Charlotte picked out one by one, as excited as a child. They'd cooked up their meal, packed a basket and blankets, and, after a tour of The Arlington that had Charlotte too overwhelmed to speak, they picnicked in the top of the cupola.

"Here's to a healthy new year," Mary said as the fireworks illuminated her face.

"Oh, Mary. If only Peter—"

"I know," Mary interrupted. "I know."

One Month Later
New Orleans, 1898

❧

CHAPTER THIRTY-ONE

Blue Book

TENDERLOIN
"400."

At the site of New Orleans's Basin Street train depot, a tremendous crowd had gathered. Fathers in top hats took their sons to inspect the timetables and discuss in wonderment the workings of the steam train. Mothers in white gloves held the hands of their daughters as they marveled at drawings of what the glorious atrium of the future train station would look like.

And to all of this, the Basin Street bordellos were the backdrop.

Mayor Flower stood with his wife, a wisp of a woman oddly placed next to her hefty husband. "Petunia," he said, "let me introduce you to the heads of the railroad." He led her to three suited executives in top hats, and they nodded their introductions before moving to the large yellow ribbon wrapped around the depot post and bearing the Basin Street Station placard.

"Ladies and gentlemen," Flower called. "Today, as we stand at the crossroads of New Orleans, we are witness to what will forever change the face of our city. I ask the fine gentlemen from Southern Railway to have this honor." The men snipped the ribbon to great applause.

All heads then turned to watch down the empty track for the Sunset Limited to arrive. Only, not a speck of anything was in sight. One of the Southern Railway men nervously fidgeted with his very expensive gold watch.

Some minutes passed and, still, all eyes were glued down the track—where, still, no train was in sight. After a while, the children became impatient, and the tightly corseted ladies began to fan themselves. At last, came a faint whistle from the distance. The crowd cheered. The railroad executives looked to one another with relief.

"The four o'clock special!" Flower said, not realizing he was only calling more attention to just how tardy the train was.

As the olive green Pullman cars finally chugged into the station, everyone marveled at the wonders of technology. Passengers disembarked, sucking in the Louisiana air. Children ran up and down the train steps, while the adults shook the conductor's hand.

At this point, Tom Anderson strolled confidently through the crowd, a stack of blue booklets under his arm. "Welcome to the finest city in the world!" he boomed. With a broad grin, he held up the freshly printed booklets. On the cover was an illustration of a smartly dressed woman holding a fancy paper fan and the title, *Blue Book*.

"A guide for tourists," Anderson said. "See the best sights New Orleans has to offer."

And as he pressed the booklets into men's hands, he recognized that this was indeed all that he'd expected. The train created in folks an unmatchable enthusiasm—if they could travel the country, they were up for anything and everything! And it was anything and everything that Anderson was offering.

A prim local woman reached for a booklet, and hooking her parasol onto the crook of her elbow, she opened the cover. Her eyes landed on an advertisement for:

SUPER NO. 7
A WELL-KNOWN REMEDY.
YOU WON'T BE AWAY FROM YOUR GIRL LONG!

The woman's placid disposition quickly turned to confusion, and then to disgust. New Orleans natives didn't have to think hard to realize they'd seen the Super No. 7 wagon making its rounds in the vicinity of the Alley.

"Oh!" she gasped. "Vile smut!" Holding the booklet as far from her as possible, she marched up to Tom Anderson. "Take back your putrid, blasphemous drivel!" She dropped the *Blue Book* to the ground and quickly pivoted in the opposite direction.

"It's quite all right if it's not your cup of tea, ma'am," Anderson said jovially. "But you don't have to be so rude about it. I have feelings too!" He broke into his infectious smile.

As the train whistle blew, Anderson turned around to face Basin Street. On cue, Lulu's girls leaned from the windows and balconies of Mahogany Hall, waving and blowing kisses as the locomotive departed.

Then, Anderson turned to look at The Arlington. It was quiet and dark—until a lone bottle rocket launched over the roof of its cupola, exploding in the sky. Then another launched, and another, so that all heads were trained on the mansion just as the French doors flung open and a crowd of girls in ballroom dresses flooded onto the veranda, unfurling a large red, white, and blue banner over the rails that read, JOIN US TONIGHT! THE DAZZLING DEBUT OF THE ARLINGTON!

They loudly began to sing:

Yankee Doodle keep it up,
Yankee Doodle dandy,
Mind the music and the step,
And with the girls be handy.

As the grandfather clock in The Arlington's Turkish parlor struck eight, the house was already bursting with suited men doted upon by pink-cheeked girls. After interviewing and carefully choosing each and every girl, Anderson had assembled what he deemed "a sporting house's dream brigade." Although he had asked Mary to accompany him to the interviews and weigh in on the choices, she had declined, offering up that a man's opinion was far superior in these matters. But the truth was, Mary couldn't stomach the thought of deciding girls' fates. Besides, she'd never had girlfriends and had never placed her trust in a woman other than Charlotte—she didn't know if she'd take pity on each and every girl and say yes to them all or if she'd feel wary and threatened at every turn. So she entrusted Anderson with the task, even though, other than Peter she'd never placed her trust in a man.

Up on the second floor, in the Forbidden Parlor, as Anderson called it, a smaller but no less fancy crew of black girls sashayed about, sharing cordials with suited black men. From under a dashing headdress of feathers and jewels, Beulah held court. The guests would never know that Beulah had hardly recognized herself in the mirror after the beautician had been at her for over an hour. "My, oh my," she'd gasped at her painted lips and cheeks and her tamed, slicked hair. "Lord, oh Lord!"

But one person was conspicuously missing from the festivities. Up on the fourth floor, Mary stood in the cupola, her flushed cheek pressed against the coolness of the window. She didn't know what she'd expected to feel on her inaugural night, but it wasn't this unsettledness that made her stomach churn.

She'd chosen to wear an emerald hue, feeling it was the color of new beginnings, so Paulina had sent to Paris for an emerald dress made to Mary's measurements by the House of Worth. The dress was the loveliest Mary had ever seen, and yet it took two others to hook and cinch her into it, pulling her corset so tight she couldn't take a full breath. The dress's satin was thick and hot, and the crinoline beneath was stiff and scratchy. The neck extended up to Mary's chin, and she felt her skin inflame from the rigid lace. She wouldn't be able to sit, and she'd try not to drink anything, even though she was surrounded by fancy indoor toilet rooms. She even worried over her gorgeous emerald earrings, fearing the heavy jewels would tear right through her newly pierced earlobes. She was fulfilling her long-standing wish of getting all dressed up, complete with velvet gloves—yet in her daydreams, she hadn't been a prisoner in her outfit.

In her hand, she gingerly held the printed photograph that the funny little man had taken, and she pressed it against the window to study it. There she was, back in that dank crib, in her tattered chippie and the torn striped stockings she'd taken from the trash. If only she could go back in time and tell that girl everything would be all right—and plenty more than all right. But then it occurred to her: that girl in the picture, the Mary of the Alley, she had such a look of composure, such a presence as she toasted herself with her splash of Raleigh Rye. Only now, as Mary was able to look back on her Alley life from this perch in what seemed another world, did she realize she'd been all right all along. It made her sad to think she'd so often dreamed of being someone else. This woman in the photo, this was the stuff of who she was. She wasn't these fancy clothes, or this makeup, or these jewels. She wasn't who she was because she was a madam.

Mary moved to the bureau that had been Mama's—the only piece she'd brought with her from her former life. Opening the top drawer, she removed the A-B-C train cigar box. She propped the lid to reveal a roll of cash. She liked the box to feel heavy with her own money. In it, she set the photograph next to the postcard of The Arlington Hotel. She brushed the hair from the back of her neck and burrowed underneath the lace to unfasten Mama's locket. She kissed it before dangling it into the box, next to Peter's broken watch. She cradled the watch for a moment, clicking open its cover then snapping it shut just as he would do. She replaced it and closed the bureau drawer.

From downstairs, she could hear the spirited piano music rising up through the raucous din. She straightened her back, pressed her shoulders down, and lifted her chin.

Mary Deubler left the room and locked the door. Madam Josie Arlington descended the staircase.

EPILOGUE

New Orleans, 1997

As I write this I feel like a schoolgirl again. I had drudged up this dear diary from a box in the attic—dare I say the last entry was from 1945, on V-Day, noting the momentous occasion! And now I am noting another occasion, momentous to only one person, and hardly so: it is the eve of my one hundredth birthday. Who would have ever thought? Certainly not I. It is an unsettling feeling to have outlasted every human being I know. I feel, in a way, like the frozen caveman who, in a rather cruel experiment is thawed and revived, only to realize that the world is unrecognizable.

This part of the world admires age, but not the person; that is to say, other than superficial awe at one's ability to have withstood time, people are, for the most part, cold and unfeeling toward the elderly. At least that has been my experience; then again, perhaps I brought this attitude upon myself. Perhaps the seeds I've sown were not always those of love and devotion, and this is how my final crop will be reaped.

It is true, my past is flawed, and not necessarily by circumstance but by deliberate choice. My choices. It is long past time I make amends, but, alas, I will, in the time I have left, see that things are put right. Dare I say I was blinded by anger at the tender age of seventeen and did the unthinkable: turned against my own blood. Had my mother been able-minded, surely she would have shaken some sense into me, but dear Charlotte Deubler had suffered a stroke and had lost many capacities before passing several years later, may her soul rest in peace.

It was on my aunt Mary's deathbed, her premature deathbed, brought upon by her own will it seemed, that she revealed to me her true identity—for I had been so sheltered as to not know that my dear, kind auntie, who had funded the best education for me in the most revered convents of Europe, made her fortune by sins of the flesh.

I will never forget the moment she told me. I was at her bedside in her lovely home on Esplanade. I held her hand, which was unusually cold, despite her fever.

"I must tell you the truth. All of it," she said, her breath labored. I couldn't believe my ears as she told me that she was known by a different name for reasons that were unsavory. I recall gasping, cursing her for lying. But this was only the beginning of the truths she insisted on revealing, even though I begged her not to. I didn't want to know, I truly didn't. I loved Auntie with all my heart and couldn't bear the thought that she was a sinner.

"My livelihood," she said, her chest heaving, "was made on Basin Street, in Storyville."

I knew very little of Storyville, other than the mutterings I'd hear about debauchery, immorality, the Devil's plot. It took me some moments to even process what she meant by this, that is how sheltered and naive I was.

"I am known as Madam Josie Arlington," she'd said. It all seemed a cruel joke.

"That's impossible. You're Mary Deubler," I insisted, forcing the frail woman to repeat herself again and again: "I am known as Madam Josie Arlington, one of the most notorious, wealthy, and feared madams."

I collapsed into tears and it became she who was trying to console me. But I would have none of it. I cursed her. Yes, cursed her given name. Dare I say I even spat at her bedside. I ran from the room, and *that was the last time I saw my aunt. I can only imagine that I hastened her already untimely death. And I am positive it was I who created the cardinal sin: I disrespected her passage, not showing my face at her funeral, not honoring her memory.*

Please, dear God, please forgive me.

Many years later, I came across a note of Auntie's, which I kept in my own files all these decades. She wrote:

"No woman's innocence was taken on the grounds of my establishment. I was responsible for no woman's entry into the profession; each woman lived and worked within The Arlington house of her own free will."

It is this note, I believe, that reveals her true motives. As I read it now, I feel a sense of pride, at long last, to be her blood.

Despite my years of disgust at her legacy, I have, for reasons I could never explain, preserved what artifacts remained from my aunt after the city set torch to Storyville at the beginning of the Great War (it seems the District had proven too tempting for soldiers at nearby base camps). I will bequeath my aunt Josie Arlington's collection to the University of New Orleans archives. Her history, in the form of her photographs, her jewels, the Blue Book *directories, her license to own a brothel within the District, her record albums signed by Mr. Jelly Roll Morton, and her portraits taken by E. J. Bellocq—the few that remain, even those with her face vandalized—these are all record of a time gone by, a time that should be remembered and taught in classrooms, both the history of New Orleans and the history of feminism. These are relics that should no longer be hidden from view, speech, or thought. My greatest hope is that others may learn from her just as I have, albeit shamefully late.*

I pray that my sweet aunt will open her arms to me when we see each other in Heaven.

May God Rest Her Soul,
Anna Deubler Brady

Historical Note

While *Madam* is based on the true events of Storyville, which existed from 1898 to 1917, we did utilize dramatic license to fill in missing information, to provide detail and context, and to create a linear thread that we felt would best compel the story. All of the major characters are based on real people; although, we used composite characters in limited circumstances, such as: Mary Deubler had two brothers, Peter and Henry. We merged the two since we could find very little about Henry, although he was father to Anna; Peter Deubler was murdered by Philip Lobrano. Mayor Walter Chew Flower held one term during the period when Storyville was inaugurated; however, we merged his character with Mayor Martin Behrman, who was New Orleans's longest-term mayor in history—from 1904 to 1920—and who spoke many of the lines of dialogue throughout the book that we attribute to Flower. Judge Beares was actually a senator who pre-dated Storyville, although he did meet his fate at the hands of New Orleans's first high-class madam. While all other characters based on real people were documented to have been in Storyville, we utilized dramatic license to have them all appear during Storyville's inaugural year; for example, Louis Armstrong did work in the bordellos when he was a boy, but he wasn't yet born during the creation of Storyville (although Armstrong claimed he was born in 1900, records show it was 1901). Lastly, for Lulu White, we borrowed the title of "Countess" from a rival Storyville madam, the Countess Willie V. Piazza.

ACKNOWLEDGMENTS

Throughout our many years of research, we owe a debt of gratitude to scholars, art historians, and Storyville-philes who inspired and guided us along the way. One of our earliest and favorite sources was Al Rose's *Storyville, New Orleans: Being an Authentic, Illustrated Account of the Notorious Red-Light District*. Rose's book is an encyclopedic and photographic romp through the Storyville and jazz era, and much of his collection of photographs and archives can now be found at Tulane University. Al's son, Rex Rose, inherited the torch and is one of the foremost experts on E. J. Bellocq. Rex has been extremely helpful in corresponding over the years, and we are grateful for his time and resources. We benefitted greatly from Alecia P. Long's *The Great Southern Babylon: Sex, Race, and Respectability in New Orleans 1865–1920*. Ken Burns's *JAZZ* PBS series provided some of the feel and context that informed this book, and Alan Lomax's *Mister Jelly Roll* and *Jelly's Blues* by Howard Reich and William Gaines allowed us to hear Jelly Roll Morton's (aka Ferdinand LaMenthe's) voice in our heads and to utilize some of his own words. Likewise, we gleaned details from Danny Barker's *Buddy*

Bolden and the Last Days of Storyville. New Orleans historian Katy Coyle graciously sat down with us and spoke of her years researching Josie Arlington and Storyville. Steven Maklansky, director of the Boca Raton Museum of Art, who previously curated at the Louisiana State Museum and New Orleans Museum of Art, could hardly contain his passion when he talked with us at length about the mysteries of E. J. Bellocq. For help with tracking down the photos used throughout the book, we thank *Mascot* maven Sally Asher, Florence Jumonville at the University of New Orleans, Sean Benjamin of the Louisiana Research Collection at Tulane University, Robert Ticknor at the Historic New Orleans Collection, Donna Ranieri from the Frank Driggs Collection, Irene Wainwright at the New Orleans Public Library, Vintage NOLA, Fred Wilbur, and Corey Jarrell.

But no amount of research and writing could have made this book happen without the support and encouragement of our super smart and delightful editor Julie Miesionczek. Not only did Julie offer invaluable guidance and insight, but she'd keep us chuckling with little notes on edited pages alluding to a lovably quirky side: "Forgive me for any little bite marks on the manuscript, I have a pet bird (a parrotlet) and he's always trying to get involved in what I'm doing." Of course, we would never have found Julie if not for the fantastic team at the Sandra Dijkstra Literary Agency. Jill Marr believed in this project from the get-go, and when she received the very first nervously e-mailed pages, she promptly read them, then e-mailed back, "Proceed with confidence." Jill, the biggest of thank-yous, you are truly a writer's dream! Andrea Cavallaro, you're the ace every writer wants—thank you for your determination and for making the stuff of dreams happen. Also, our gratitude goes to the supportive staff of Plume, especially Phil Budnick, Kathryn Court, Liz Keenan, Jaya Miceli, Lavina Lee, and Eve Kirch.

324

Acknowledgments

We want to give a huge thank-you to all the friends and family who took time to read (and in many cases reread . . . and reread again) various drafts and then give us the real, honest truth (thus, the various drafts!). Also included here are those who offered encouragement and support along the way: Anita Ugent; Keith Christian; Deborah Martin; Kari Ugent; David J. Cohen; Christian A. Jordan; Willie Mercer; Diane Haithman; Jonathan Weinberg; Deborah Vankin; Elena DeCoste Grieco; Alyssa Rapp; Sheryl Kennedy Haydel; Shawn Barber; the Snotty Girls' Book Club, including Lesley Chilcott, Shana Mabari, Heidi Adams, and Christina Ross; and Kathleen Dennehy, Brian Groh, and the Monday Night Writers Group.

IMAGE CREDITS

Chapter 1: "Old Houses, Ursulines St." 1880–1910, George Francis Mugnier. Courtesy of the New Orleans Public Library.

Chapter 2: "Josie, the Railroad Man." *The Nursery: A Monthly Magazine for Youngest Readers*, vol. 16, 1874; p. 118.

Chapter 3: Tom Anderson's Storyville, undated. Courtesy of the Frank Driggs Collection.

Chapter 4: "Brown Mixture." Courtesy of Karen Harris Collection of Printed Ephemera, Earl K. Long Library, University of New Orleans.

Chapter 5: "Vieux Carre #134 Dauphine Street" 1912–15; Contact Print Collection. Courtesy of the New Orleans Public Library

Chapter 6: "Anderson's Exterior," c. 1909. Courtesy of Al Rose papers, Louisiana Research Collection, Tulane University.

Chapter 7: Razzy Dazzy Spasm Band, *The Railroad Trainmen's Journal*, vol. 16, no. 2, February, 1899, p. 497.

Chapter 8: "American Triumph. A. Marschall & Co. American extra dry champagne/National Bureau of Engraving, Philadelphia," ca. 1880; Library of Congress.

Chapter 9: The Mascot cover, "Plague of Prostitutes," June 11, 1832. Courtesy of the Louisiana Research Collection, Tulane University, New Orleans, La.

Chapter 10: *Blue Book*, Mahogany Hall advertisement, c. 1893–1917.

Chapter 11: November 1913, Lewis Wickes Hine; Library of Congress.

Chapter 12: "City Hall, New Orleans," 1880–1910, George Francois Mugnier. Courtesy of the New Orleans Public Library.

Chapter 13: "Pole Peddler" 1880–1910, George Francois Mugnier. Courtesy of the New Orleans Public Library.

Chapter 14: "Queen of the Wheel," 1897, Rose Studio; Library of Congress.

Chapter 15: Buddy Bolden Band, undated. Courtesy of the Frank Driggs Collection.

Chapter 16: "Spanish House, 150 years old," 1880–1910; George Francois Mugnier. Courtesy of the New Orleans Public Library.

Chapter 17: "Jackson Square, New Orleans, La.," 1903, Detroit Publishing Company; Library of Congress.

Chapter 18: "African American children in St. Louis Cemetery #1, 1901," Cornelius Durkee Collection. Courtesy of the New Orleans Public Library.

Chapter 19: "The Clay Monument [Canal Street], New Orleans," William Henry Jackson, c. 1890, Detroit Publishing Company; Library of Congress.

Chapter 20: "Vieux Carre #151 Toulouse Street," 1912–15. Contact Print Collection. Courtesy of the New Orleans Public Library.

Chapter 21: "Mahogany Hall Doorway." Courtesy of Al Rose papers, Louisiana Research Collection, Tulane University.

Chapter 22: "Old Houses, Ursulines Street," 1880–1910, George Francis Mugnier. Courtesy of the New Orleans Public Library.

Chapter 23: "New Orleans Milk Cart, New Orleans, Louisiana," Detroit Publishing Company, no. 033073, 1900–1910. Library of Congress, LC-D4-33073.

Chapter 24: *Blue Book*, interior; c. 1898–1917. Courtesy of the New Orleans Public Library.

Chapter 25: French Balls advertisement, *Blue Book*, 1905. Al Rose. Storyville, New Orleans, University of Alabama Press, 1974; p. 23.

Chapter 26: Corset advertisement, *The Cosmopolitan*, 1895.

Chapter 27: "Old Absinthe House, the bar, New Orleans, La." 1900–06; Detroit Publishing Company, Library of Congress.

Chapter 28: Sarah Bernhardt, promotional postcard, W&D Downey Photographers, London, England, 1918. Harvard Theatre Collection, Houghton Library, Cambridge, Ma.

Chapter 29: "Bayou Scene" 1880–1910, George Francois Mugnier. Courtesy of the New Orleans Public Library.

Chapter 30: "New Orleans, La., a corner of the French Market," 1900–1910, Detroit Publishing Company. Library of Congress.

Chapter 31: *Blue Book* cover, undated. Courtesy of Louisiana Research Collection, Tulane University, New Orleans, La.